EX LIBRIS

Romance Treasury

THE ROMANCE TREASURY ASSOCIATION

NEW YORK · TORONTO · LONDON

ROMANCE TREASURY

These stories were originally published as follows:

TELL ME MY FORTUNE
Copyright © 1975 by Mary Burchell
First published by Mills & Boon Limited in 1975

A SCENT OF LEMONS
Copyright © 1972 by Jill Christian
First published by Mills & Boon Limited in 1972

COUNTRY OF THE VINE
Copyright © 1975 by Mary Wibberley
First published by Mills & Boon Limited in 1975

ROMANCE TREASURY is published by
The Romance Treasury Association, Stratford, Ontario, Canada.

Editorial Board: A. W. Boon, Judith Burgess, Ruth Palmour,
Alice E. Johnson and Ilene Burgess.

Dust Jacket Art by David Craig
Story Illustrations by David Craig
Book Design by Charles Kadin
Printed by The Alger Press Ltd., Oshawa, Ontario
Bound by T. H. Best Co. Ltd., Don Mills, Ontario

ISBN 0-373-04052-0

Printed in Canada

CONTENTS

TELL ME MY FORTUNE

Tell Me
My Fortune

Mary Burchell

CRAIG

Leslie was the only member of the Greeve family who hadn't built her life around the fortune they expected to inherit from Aunt Tabitha.

The future she had in mind centered around a man she'd loved for years.

Then she found that the man was engaged to someone else, on the same day the family learned that Aunt Tabitha had died and left her money to a nephew they hadn't even known. It was a bit much. She felt entitled to a good cry.

When Reid Carthay, the nephew, found her crying, she was willing to be consoled. But his plans for the future shocked her. "I think," he said firmly, "you should become engaged to me."

CHAPTER ONE

"Sometimes," remarked Katherine, regarding herself in the drawing-room mirror with something between satisfaction and regret, "sometimes I can't help reflecting how extraordinarily useless I am, and it depresses me. Then I think how decorative I am, and it seems to even things up a bit, so I suppose it's all right."

"Extraordinarily illogical reasoning," replied her brother, Morley, from the wheelchair to which he had been condemned ever since a car crash some time before. "But, in any case, there is always Great-Aunt Tabitha. Why, after all, should you toil usefully but revoltingly when, by the thoughtful dispensation of Providence, we have a Great-Aunt Tabitha whose large and solid fortune will inevitably come to us around about the time our papa has finished living on his own diminishing capital?"

"But we can't be absolutely sure about Great-Aunt Tabitha's dying at the right moment," put in Alma, with all the cheerful and unmalicious callousness of twelve years. "Someone in the reign of James I lived to be a hundred and twenty."

"This," Morley pointed out unanswerably, "is not the reign of James I." And Alma sucked her underlip and thought again.

"Still . . . ." Leslie, the second daughter, spoke rather soberly. "I know what Kate and Alma mean. It doesn't seem quite decent to plan one's life entirely on the prospect of someone else's dying. Even," she added apologetically, "if one has never seen that person."

Her brother, however, brushed that aside easily.

"Decency, my pet, is a question of geography and history," he reminded her. "Transport someone in the normal beachwear of Honolulu to the drawing room of Queen Victoria, and you have a case of gross indecency. But by the same token—or, probably, a rather different one, now I come to think of it—among certain savage tribes, I don't doubt that to bank on Great-Aunt Tabitha's decease, or even to hasten it, would be considered not only perfectly decent, but even desirable."

"We aren't a savage tribe, though," objected Alma, who liked to bear her part in any family discussion.

"There have been times," Morley replied, "not unconnected with your own activities, when that has been open to doubt."

The others laughed, and Katherine, blinking her goldtipped lashes, and running an absent hand over her fantastically beautiful chestnut hair, said reflectively, "I don't know quite what started me on such an uncomfortable topic."

Morley grinned at her.

"I do. You probably heard father telling mother that the quarterly bills, like all other quarterly bills before them, were larger than ever, and that starvation stared us in the face and we will all have to retire to the two rooms over the stables if we continue to live at our present rate. Or whatever new flights of fancy his immediate annoyance prompted him to."

"What do you mean by flights of fancy?" demanded Alma, regarding her brother severely, though she adored him. "Don't you believe what father says? D'you think he tells *lies* about his money?"

"What have we ever done," inquired Morley resignedly, of no one in particular, "to have this dreadfully literal-minded child thrust into the bosom of our unrealistic family? No, Alma, of course I don't think father tells lies. Or, if I do, I didn't mean to convey that impression. But, like most people who live beyond their incomes, he frequently indulges in financial prophecy—of the most sanguine where his own wishes are concerned, and of the gloomiest when it comes to supplying the wants of someone else."

"I don't know what you're talking about, and I don't believe you do, either," asserted Alma. "And, anyway, I hope Katherine's only speaking for herself when she talks about being useless. I work hard enough at school, goodness knows!"

"But with what result?" inquired her brother unfairly. "With what result?"

"And Leslie isn't useless, either," pursued Alma, refusing to be drawn on the awkward subject of school results.

"No," Morley cast a half-humorous, half-affectionate glance at his second sister, who was sitting in a low chair, sewing, with an industry that certainly lent color to Alma's claim for her. "No, Leslie really isn't a useless person although, according to Katherine's argument, she is sufficiently decorative to warrant her being so. If we were all cast away on a desert island—which Heaven and Great-Aunt Tabitha forbid—Leslie is, of course, the one who would discover edible and nourishing shellfish nestling among the rocks, a spring of fresh water conveniently near at hand, and some method of weaving the surrounding vegetation into shelter for the night."

"All of which simply means," Leslie said, smiling but not looking up, "that a passion for home comforts is stronger in me than in the rest of you, and I should therefore hustle around in search of them, while you were still lying on the beach thinking things over."

Though few might have recognized the fact, probably the most unfortunate thing ever to happen to Richard

Greeve was to be left, on his father's death, with a comfortable fortune over which he had complete control.

He was already married at the time to the pretty, affectionate wife who had passed on her dark eyes and her flawless complexion to each one of her four children, and she had certainly not been the one to provide him with a sensible purpose in life, still less to curb his extravagant tendencies.

Indeed, she belonged to that fast-disappearing race of women—the attractively helpless. And, like the chameleon, she took her "color" and character from her surroundings.

If her husband had happened to be a big, common sense, practical creature, she would probably have clung to him, but been a reasonably practical and common sense partner. As it was, however, her husband was a big, handsome, unpractical creature, with flamboyant ideas and extravagant notions. And she fluttered happily in the bright, ephemeral world that he created for her, adoring him for his often spectacular follies, and encouraging him just when he needed a little tactful restraint.

Whenever Leslie queried their position—which she had done occasionally since she had come to understand the essential insecurity of it—her mother would assume a sweet, vague, but curiously obstinate expression, and say, "It's difficult for women to understand these things, dear. Your father must know best. It stands to reason."

She would also add, like Morley—indeed like all of them in moments of crisis over the years, "And there's always Great-Aunt Tabitha."

For as long as the younger Greeves could remember anything, Great-Aunt Tabitha had been an almost legendary figure in their lives. Incredibly, she had survived to the age of ninety-six, living in a magnificent villa near

Biarritz, from which, it appeared, neither invader nor liberator had been able to eject her.

Indisputably, she was one of the few really wealthy people left in that part of Europe, for her husband—a fabulously shrewd merchant who had died at least fifty years before—had invested his fortune so cleverly and in such various concerns that not famine, pestilence, nor wars appeared to alter Great-Aunt Tabitha's income to any appreciable degree. Or, at least, so the family legend went.

Richard Greeve was her heir, for he and his children were her sole blood relations. And on his own diminishing capital, and the golden prospects of hers, had he existed for the last twenty-five years.

On this particular afternoon, when the young Greeves were all gathered in the long drawing room, lazily pursuing the discussion, which Katherine's remark had prompted, it was hard to imagine that drama could hover anywhere near their lives.

The room in which they were, with its gracious proportions, its mellow tints of brown and soft gold and green, its long, beautiful windows, looking on a flower garden and lawn, at the foot of which a little stream bubbled—this was hardly the setting for drama. And the young things idling there, in their youth and their beauty and their confidence, might have seemed to be the fancifullike beings who inhabited some tranquil world where it was always afternoon, and where one was completely and safely insulated from the shocks and trials of everyday life.

Katherine was, perhaps, the supremely beautiful one of the family, with her chestnut hair, her velvety brown eyes, and her almost apricot-hued complexion. But Morley was extraordinarily handsome in his thin way, and Alma, though given to ruminating in a slightly cowlike manner when any thought possessed her completely, was a good-looking child.

Leslie was the least obviously beautiful. She had the same velvet brown eyes as the others, with the same curious gold-tipped lashes. But her hair, which was soft and fair and cut rather long, lacked the dramatic coloring of the others, and her complexion, though palely beautiful, was almost colorless beside the gorgeous tints of Katherine's.

She had, however, an admirably proportioned forehead and very beautifully set eyes, which combined to give her glance an essential candor and openness that was sweet and endearing, and, at the same time, carried with it a promise of extreme reliability.

They made a charming picture, scattered around the gracious, faintly shabby room. But, as the door opened and their father came in, they immediately became, not a picture in themselves, but merely the background to a portrait.

Richard Greeve, now nearing sixty, was still good-looking in a rather florid, obvious way, but that was not the quality about him that arrested immediate attention. What made him the unquestioned center of the scene—any scene—was his absolute and unshakable conviction that this was his position by right.

He was a big man, with a spendid, organlike speaking voice, on which he played with a shameless, but most effective, virtuosity. In a selfish way, he was extremely fond of his family who, in looks at least, did him great credit. But it is doubtful if he would have been either a kind or an understanding parent to any child who could not add some distinction to his own role as head of the house.

He was being very much head of the house at the moment. Indeed, he addressed them—commandingly, and in a manner that gathered everyone's attention to him instantaneously—as "Children."

It was a term that could hardly be applied with accuracy to any of them except Alma, but it was uttered with such conviction that no one could have dreamed of querying it.

"Children," Richard Greeve said, in the tone of one opening Parliament at a solemn moment in the country's history, "I have news for you."

"Good or bad?" interjected Alma quickly, instinctively sensing a peroration and anxious to settle that point before her father embarked on what he had to say.

She received a quelling glance, which told even her that her intrusion was ill judged.

"In one sense it is sad news," her father conceded, and Morley declared afterward that he bowed his head as he said this, "for death, though splendid, is always sad. But it is news for which we have been prepared a long time, and which will make a great difference in the lives of all of us. It is, I might say, momentous news. Your Great-Aunt Tabitha is dead."

"At last? I mean, oh, dear!" Katherine flushed at her unfortunate choice of exclamation. "We . . . we were just talking about her when you came in," she added, obviously with some faint feeling of guilt.

"Then we're all rich now," said Alma crudely and with no saving expression of regret.

"That, my dear, is not the most suitable comment to make upon your great-aunt's death," her father told her reprovingly.

But Morley said indulgently, "Well, father, we've been expecting this most of our lives, you know, and it isn't as though we've ever seen the old lady. Besides," he added reflectively, "I daresay, come to that, one isn't unwilling to go, at ninety-six."

"Are you going over to France for the funeral, father?" inquired Leslie hastily, hoping to distract his attention from Morley's ill-chosen remarks.

But her choice of distraction was not a happy one, it seemed, for her father frowned.

"Unfortunately, no. Although I would certainly have wished to pay my last respects to Tabitha, the opportunity has been denied me. I learn, to my extreme annoyance, that the funeral has already taken place—before I had even been informed of her death. An extremely disrespectful and high-handed way of doing things, and one for which I hold her legal advisers greatly to blame."

"But she couldn't have advised you about her own funeral," protested Alma, who had been following all this very closely. "It'd be too late, you know."

Richard Greeve looked at his youngest child with a certain lack of favor.

"I am assuming that, in accordance with the usual custom when no immediate relative of the deceased is available, her legal advisers took over the duties—" his voice dropped a couple of notes "—the sad duties—of arranging the funeral and informing the relations. My quarrel with them is that they attended to these matters in the wrong order. *I* should have been informed immediately, and I would then have flown over to make suitable arrangements."

"But don't forget the cousin, dear." Mrs. Greeve, who had slipped into the room almost unnoticed and now stood rather like a beautiful wraith beside her husband, softly entered the discussion. "The cousin probably attended to everything."

"Then he greatly exceeded his rights and position," retorted her husband firmly. "What is he, anyway?" The question was evidently rhetorical as well as contemptuous, because he proceeded to answer it himself immediately. "Merely a third, fourth, or fifth cousin by marriage. Some hanger-on—some remote connection of poor Tabitha's late husband. My Uncle Leopold," he added, in case anyone was getting mixed up about relationships.

"But I didn't know there was any cousin," exclaimed Leslie, with interest. "I didn't know Great-Aunt Tabitha had any relatives except us."

"One would hardly count so remote a connection as a relative, my dear," her father said, smiling faintly and scornfully. "And by marriage, too," he added, as though marriage were a dishonorable state. Though, in point of fact, he had a great and solemn regard for the bond.

"He must be very, very old, if he's a cousin of Great-Aunt Tabitha's," Alma said thoughtfully.

"He seems to feel young enough to undertake the journey to England," Mrs. Greeve said doubtfully.

"In any case, cousinships are such odd things when you begin to get into the third and fourth dimension," Morley pointed out. "I never can remember if second cousins are the children of first cousins, or whether the children of one are second cousins to the original cousin and third cousins to the children."

"Say that again, slowly," Alma begged, concentrating almost audibly.

But her sisters cried, "Oh, no!" in chorus.

Then Leslie added, "What did you say about this cousin coming to England, mother? You said he felt young enough to undertake the journey. Here, do you mean?"

"Yes." Her mother nodded. "He proposes to come here, to Cranley Magna. He wants to make our acquaintance. I thought—" she glanced doubtfully at her husband "—it was rather nice and friendly of him."

"Did you, my dear?" said her husband with deceptive mildness. "Personally, I asked myself if he were not merely following Tabitha's money to England. But perhaps I am of a nasty, suspicious nature." And he gave a beautiful bass-baritone laugh that invited everyone else to join in the mirth over such a preposterous suggestion.

"Perhaps," said Alma, and the moment lost much of its value.

"When is this old man coming?" inquired Katherine.

"Within the next few days, I imagine. I must speak to Mrs. Speers about having a room ready," murmured Mrs. Greeve. And, with a faint, sweet smile around to her family, she drifted out of the room again, in search of her very efficient housekeeper.

Almost immediately her husband followed her, for one of the simple and really endearing things about him was that, although he might pontificate and bluster in her presence, he thought her the loveliest thing in the world, and was never happy long away from her. One could forgive him much for that, Leslie had often thought.

Left to themselves once more, the young Greeves broke into animated discussion. All except Morley, that is to say, who leaned back in his chair once more and listened amusedly to what his sisters had to say.

"This really is going to make a difference to us, as father says," Katherine observed. "Being really rich is quite a different thing from merely having prospects, however good. I wonder if father will let me go to Italy now and study?" For Katherine had singing ambitions, though so far of a rather dilettante quality.

"Curb your notions of our probable worth, my pet," Morley advised her. "The money comes to father, and, by the time he has taken toll of it for what I trust will be a very long life, we shall probably all have to turn to and earn our own living in advanced middle age."

"You do think of the most *disgusting* things," declared Alma, giving her brother a small thump. "And, anyway, I mean to be married long before I'm middle-aged."

"Opportunity is a fine thing, as the offensive old saying has it," Morley reminded her.

At this, however, Alma looked scornful and said, "I would *make* an opportunity, stupid."

"I wonder how long this old cousin of Great-Aunt Tabitha's will stay," exclaimed Katherine, who had been following her own thoughts all this time. "Maybe father is right, and he just wants to park himself here."

"Then, after a suitable interval, during which all the demands of hospitality will have been scrupulously fulfilled, father will hang out an unmistakable No Parking sign, and he will have to go," Morley replied.

"Poor old man," said Alma, with what they all felt to be exaggerated and possibly unnecessary sympathy.

"Anyway, I've already told you, he won't necessarily be an old man," Morley declared. "He may be young and handsome, and fall in love with Kate and marry her."

"Why me?" Katherine wanted to know.

"Because you're the prettiest, I suppose," her brother said. "Anyway, I have an idea it wouldn't be any good his falling in love with Leslie, and Alma is a bit young."

"Why wouldn't it..." began Alma.

But Leslie tossed aside her needlework and interrupted firmly, "I'll leave you to your romantic planning," she said, her color just a little high. "I'm going to the village to get some ribbon and other odds and ends. Anyone else coming?"

No one else was coming, it seemed. And without bothering to fetch either a hat or coat, for it was a beautiful, golden August afternoon, Leslie stepped out of one of the long windows, which served, as did most of the windows in that room, as a garden door, and crossed the lawn to a wicket gate almost hidden in flowering bushes.

She was not at all sorry to be alone. She liked her own company, especially on an afternoon of such absorbing loveliness, and her father's news had provided enough food for thought—inevitably pleasant and speculative thought—without the need for conversation.

She walked slowly, thinking first of the legendary old lady who had just died—with that faintly remorseful, impersonal regret, which is all that any of us can achieve for the death of someone we have never seen—then of the immense and welcome difference that the newly acquired wealth was going to make in their lives.

No more worrying about the essential insecurity of their outwardly comfortable existence. No more dreading the occasional, but violent, outbursts of her father on the subject of any bills other than his own. No more wondering how the family would manage without her when she and Oliver married.

Although to anyone as literal minded as Alma—or even her father—it might seem that nothing absolutely definite had been arranged between Oliver and herself, to Leslie it had been obvious for some while that, as soon as he had a practice, or the reasonable prospect of one, they would be married. The rest of the family might build their future around the name of Great-Aunt Tabitha. To Leslie, the future meant Oliver Bendick, whom she had loved for longer than she could remember.

Even in the days when they were schoolchildren, and Oliver was the doctor's son who knew Morley rather well, while Leslie was merely Morley's sister—even then there had been a degree of understanding and friendship between them that had not existed between any of the other young people of the district. And more than once, after he had got over the inarticulate teens, Oliver had said, "There's no one like you, Leslie. I just couldn't imagine life without you to talk to and plan with."

It was she who had been the recipient of his confidences from the earliest days; she who had sympathized with and encouraged his every ambition. It was to her—even before his parents—he had come with the news that he had passed his final examinations as a doctor. And, now that he was working as a *locum* less than fifty miles away, she saw him most weekends.

She hoped he would be home this weekend, so that she could tell him the news about Great-Aunt Tabitha. To know that the family's future was so clear and satisfactory could not fail to make their own future seem the more secure.

Leslie had several places to visit in the village, and as she entered the little post office, which also served as a general haberdashery store, Miss Meeks popped up from behind the counter to inquire personally after the health of the family.

Having reported satisfactorily, Leslie was about to go on to the purchase of stamps when Miss Meeks, leaning toward her in as confidential a manner as her rather rigid corsets would permit, asked, "Did the telegram arrive safely?" as though all sorts of perils might have beset a telegram on its short journey from the post office to Cranley Magna.

"The telegram?"

"I sent it up only ten minutes ago, and told Bob to go straight to the house without any loitering." A frown began to gather on Miss Meeks's brow and the faint creaking of her corsets indicated that she was beginning to breathe deeply and with displeasure.

"He probably passed me while I was in Farmers', Miss Meeks. I called in for a paper," Leslie explained, anxious to shield Bob who was Miss Meeks's rather downtrodden nephew.

Miss Meeks suspended judgment for the moment.

"I didn't know you were expecting a visitor," she said casually, as she flicked over her supply of stamps.

"Was the telegram about someone arriving to visit us, then?" Leslie spoke with interest, and never questioned Miss Meeks's inalienable village right to digest and discuss the contents of all telegrams that passed through her hands, either outgoing or incoming.

"I think so. I seem to remember something of the sort." Miss Meeks became falsely reticent all at once.

"Who was it from?" Leslie asked.

"Well, I did notice the name, as it was a strange one. It struck me quite forcibly," Miss Meeks explained, giving the expression almost a physical meaning. "It was signed Reid Carthay. And it said, 'Arriving Thursday.' Which, of course, is today," Miss Meeks pointed out. "That's why I told Bob to hurry."

"Then he'll be coming by the 6:20, I suppose." Leslie glanced at her watch.

"A friend of the family?" inquired Miss Meeks delicately, as she counted out change.

"A . . . more sort of a relative," Leslie said. And then thought how much that would have annoyed her father. "I'll have to see about having him met at the station. He won't know that it's a mile and a half from the village, with no chance of a taxi." And she bade Miss Meeks goodbye and went out into the afternoon sunshine once more.

It was still not more than four o'clock, and Leslie reckoned that she had plenty of time to carry out her last commission, which was to collect some honey from a small farm half a mile beyond the village, on the other side from Cranley Magna. And as she walked along the dusty road between the sweet-smelling hedges, she thought about Mr. Reid Carthay and his imminent arrival.

As Morley had said, there was no need to assume that he was an elderly man. But, whatever his age, Leslie hoped he would be sufficiently tolerant in outlook not to mind the various foibles of the Greeves, and not so tender of his dignity that he would resent the slightly hectoring manner her father would undoubtedly adopt toward one he considered to have done him out of the duty and privilege of supervising Great-Aunt Tabitha's funeral.

Leslie collected her honey—two combs of it, dark and of an intoxicating scent—and started homeward. But before she had gone fifty yards, the sound of a high-powered car coming behind her made her move onto the narrow grass verge at the side of the road.

The car swung around a bend in the lane, passed her at speed, and then drew to an abrupt standstill a little way beyond her. It was a long, low, shining black car of un-English design, and as Leslie came nearer, she saw it contained only the driver, a tall, broad-shouldered man, who was obviously waiting for her to come up to him.

Indeed, as she drew abreast of the door, he leaned his arm on the ledge of the open window and said, in a deep voice with a faint accent that she could not quite identify, "Pardon me. Can you tell me if I'm anywhere near Cranleymere?"

"Yes. That's the village straight ahead." She pointed to the small cluster of houses and two or three village shops that made up Cranleymere.

"*That*?" The man half-smiled, with a sort of good-humored contempt for anything so small. "Is that the whole of it?"

"That's the main part of the village," Leslie said, rather resenting this slight on her home village. "There are a few big houses scattered around, as well."

"Including one called Cranley Magna?"

"Why . . . why, yes." Leslie stared at him, surprised doubt crystallizing into not very pleased certainty. "Are you Mr. Carthay?"

"Sure. I'm Reid Carthay." He smiled completely then, showing strong, even teeth. "Don't tell me you're one of my cousins?"

She had no intention of telling him anything of the sort.

"I'm Leslie Greeve," she said, much more distantly than she usually spoke to anyone. "But we're hardly cousins, are we?"

"Near enough," he assured her easily, and opened the door of the car. "Jump in, Leslie, and I'll drive you home."

Leslie was not an unfriendly girl, but she felt herself prickle with resentment at this casual familiarity. However, she could hardly refuse a lift from someone who was going to her own home. So she said, "Thank you," coolly, and got into the car.

"Are you the only girl in the family?" he inquired, as he started the car again, and he spoke as though it were his natural right to ask questions about her.

"No. I have two sisters."

"Both as pretty as you?" He flashed an appreciative smile at her.

Leslie did not take that up. She permitted a slight pause in the conversation, to indicate her opinion of his line of talk, and then added, "And I have one brother."

"A matter of minor interest," he assured her.

"Not to me. I happen to be fond of my brother. He has nice manners, for one thing," she retorted, surprised to find herself speaking like this.

She was no more surprised than her companion, however. He gave her another quick glance—an amused one—and said, "What's the sting in that? Think I'm being fresh?"

"I wasn't really thinking about you at all," replied Leslie, with obvious untruth. "Except to wonder, rather apprehensively, about your impact on my father."

"Put that in plain English, would you? Do I turn left here?"

"No. Straight on. And, in plain English, I mean that my father never heard of you until today, so that your very existence was something of a sho . . . surprise. You would do well to remember that and go rather . . . rather tactfully."

"Implying that I have not exercised tact with you?"

Leslie, who had never before been subjected to the gale of good-humored candor that seemed to be blowing upon her at the moment, was silent.

Whereat Reid Carthay laughed, put out a hand and, to her inexpressible annoyance, patted her as though she were a kitten, and said, "You shouldn't take offense so easily. Is this the driveway?"

"Yes." She quickly withdrew her hand from under the strong, warm, brown one that had touched her so easily, and, as they swept around the curve of the driveway and came to a stop in front of the house, Alma appeared in the open doorway.

An inquisitive and friendly child by nature, she ran down the steps, and addressed the newcomer with all the curiosity and interest that had been lacking in Leslie.

"Hello! Are *you* Reid Carthay?"

"I am." He leaned back, smiling a little, with one hand still resting on the wheel of the car. "Any objections?"

"Oh, no. But I thought you were going to be old."

"There are times when I think I am."

"But I meant *really* old," explained the literal Alma. "You don't look more than forty."

Alma led the way into the drawing room, where the family was present in force.

Most men, Leslie supposed, would have been slightly intimidated by the spectacle of such a united front, and she would have made the introductions in the friendliest manner possible. But Reid Carthay showed no signs of being put out—much less intimidated—and, having greeted Mrs. Greeve pleasantly and taken in the rest in one comprehensive glance, he shook hands with his host, and said, "Fortunately, I stopped to ask Leslie the way, so there wasn't much difficulty in finding the place."

Leslie, as they all knew, was the rather reserved one of the family, and to have this man talking as though he and she were old acquaintances made Morley at least glance at her with interest.

"Mr. Carthay," Leslie explained, with the very slightest emphasis on the name, "overtook me just as I left Jenkins's farm. And, as he asked me the way, of course I guessed who he was."

"Quite, quite," said her father, anxious to monopolize the visitor himself. "Sit down, Carthay, sit down. This is a sad business about poor old Tabitha."

Leslie stole another glance at their visitor.

He didn't *look* a sponger, she reflected. Though of course that cool air of self-confidence might well be part of his stock-in-trade.

A little more critically, Leslie eyed his admirably tailored dark suit, his unobtrusive but expensive wristwatch, and recalled the undoubted luxury of the car in which he had given her a lift.

Great-Aunt Tabitha or no, he did remarkably well out of something. Or someone.

He was talking to her mother now, answering the random, conventional questions that one does ask of a stranger who arrives unexpectedly, and seeing him like that, in profile, Leslie was uncomfortably aware of the firmness, even obstinacy, of his jaw and the hard line of his cheek.

He was not just an ordinary sponger, she decided suddenly. Not anything on a small scale. He might be a great rogue or he might be a force for good. But whatever his line, he was big and forceful and probably not a little ruthless. Cranley Magna seemed suddenly rather a delicate, pastel-colored, unrealistic sort of setting for him, and a vague feeling of apprehension touched Leslie because of it.

However, her mother rose just then to escort their visitor to his room, and the others prepared to scatter, to get ready for tea.

Leslie lingered for a moment to speak to Morley and, seeing this, Katherine came back to join them.

"What did you make of him, Leslie? You seemed to be great friends in a remarkably short time," she said curiously.

"We were nothing of the sort." Leslie spoke with decision. "It was he who made all the advances. I should think he's the kind of man to call you 'honey' the second time he meets you."

"There is a slight American accent," Morley remarked, "I noticed it."

"Oh, that's what it is! I didn't identify it, because there's an overlay of something else."

"Probably a slightly French intonation. He looks like the kind of man who's knocked about a good deal."

"He settled down pretty close to Great-Aunt Tabitha," remarked Leslie.

But Morley said, "Miaow!" and ruffled her fair hair.

"Why did he *come*, though?" Katherine said reflectively.

"Perhaps he heard that father had three beautiful daughters, all now richly endowed," suggested Morley. "And he came to look them over."

"Then Kate and Alma can have him between them," Leslie said, with so much energy that her brother and sister both laughed.

She laughed a little herself then, slightly ashamed of her exaggerated resentment of someone who was, after all, a guest, and had not been guilty of anything more than familiarity.

"No, it couldn't have been that," she said, referring

back to Morley's flippant suggestion. "I remember now.
He asked if I were the only daughter."

"He hoped it all went with you, dear," Morley declared, and laughed again.

"Don't be absurd," Leslie said. Then she remembered
that she had left her various purchases in the car, and
went out to fetch them.

As she came out of the front door, she saw that he
was also there, taking his luggage out of the back of the
car, and at the sound of her footsteps he looked up.

He stopped what he was doing immediately, and
came to the bottom of the steps and said, "Look here, I
must talk to you. Where can we go?"

Leslie's eyebrows rose slightly and her dark eyes widened with surprise and that odd resentment that she
could not control.

"It's almost teatime," she said rather coldly.

"Yes, I know. But there's something I must ask you."

He was so urgent and so authoritative about it that
she found herself leading the way to the small shrubbery
at the side of the house. But they had hardly moved
within the shade of the trees, before she turned to face
him and asked, not very promisingly, because she suspected some new, smiling advance, "Well, what is it?"

He was not smiling, however. He was frowning slightly, and his very keen gray eyes were a little narrowed, as
though he were trying to see something a long way off.

"What makes your father think he was old Aunt Tabitha's heir?" was the extraordinary thing he said.

"What makes him think .... Well, because he is, of
course. He always has been. She made a will soon after
her husband died, when father was still a schoolboy.
We've all known it ... all our lives ...."

Her rapid assurances trailed off suddenly into silence,
and the most horrible, premonitory chill crept down her
spine.

"You don't mean...you can't mean...that she *didn't* leave him her money, after all?"

Reid Carthay thrust his hands into his pockets and regarded her almost moodily for a moment, like a man who very much disliked some task he saw in front of him.

"That's exactly what I do mean," he said at last. "She left her money to me. Every damned cent of it. I didn't even know you people existed until I began to look through her correspondence after she was dead."

CHAPTER TWO

LESLIE HAD NEVER FELT FAINT in her life, but for a moment it seemed to her that the green and gold and blue of that summer afternoon ran together in one blur, and she clutched at Reid Carthay's arm as though she might fall.

"I'm terribly sorry," he began.

Then she recovered herself and stammered, "No ... I'm sorry. I felt ... rather strange ... for a moment."

"I didn't realize that it would be quite such a shock." He was looking down at her with some concern.

"No. How could you?" She looked around helplessly on a world from which the benevolent security of Great-Aunt Tabitha's influence had departed forever.

It was difficult, faced with the bright, slightly puzzled glance of this stranger, to explain how completely they had all left everything to chance and Great-Aunt Tabitha. But she felt bound to try.

"We have always ... depended on her, you see. On the belief that our futures were secure because we would ... would inherit. We built our lives on the expectation—one shouldn't, of course—but we never thought of anything else. We never imagined there could be anyone else. We just knew, quite simply, that we were her only real relatives."

"Yes. I do see. My people come from the other side, of course. Great-Uncle Leopold's side."

"Oh!" she exclaimed. "Where the money really came from."

"All right. I suppose that is literally true," he agreed.

"Though anything there was had belonged to the old lady for nearly half a century."

From the house came the tinkling sound of the tea-bell, and she dragged herself to her feet.

"We shall have to go in. I suppose you . . . want me to explain things?"

He seemed surprised.

"You? Certainly not. You've had enough shock and nerve strain already," he said. "I'll tell your father, and he can break the news to the rest as he pleases."

"It will be a fearful shock for him." Her mouth trembled suddenly. "Please be as . . . gentle as you can about it."

He smiled rather wryly.

"Gentleness isn't much in my line, but I'll do my best."

"Perhaps I'd better do it, after all." Once more she tried to force herself to the task. But he refused to hear of it.

"No, no, you leave that to me. I'll attend to it."

"When?" she asked huskily.

"As soon as tea is over, and I can have a few minutes' private talk with him."

"Very well."

She wondered how she was to get through tea without betraying her agitation, and perhaps he wondered, too, because, as they went back into the house, he said, "You'd better go and fix a bit of color, hadn't you? They'll notice, if you look as white as that, and think that I've been ill-treating you or something."

She gave a ghost of a laugh.

"Do I look as bad as that?"

He gave her that peculiar, flashing glance of appreciation.

"You look swell," he told her, with the faintest suggestion of a drawl in his voice. "But you need the illusion of a little red blood in your cheeks."

She said nothing to that, and went away upstairs to her room, leaving him to find his own way back to the drawing room.

In her bedroom she stood before the mirror and stared at her white reflection while she tried to take in what had really happened. As the realization of the disaster stabbed her afresh, one or two sobbing gasps of sheer fright and distress escaped her.

Then she pulled herself together and told herself not to be a coward. And after touching her cheeks with color and adding a little lipstick to her mouth, she deliberately assumed an air of casual unconcern.

There's always Oliver, she told herself, leaning on that final security with infinite relief. *I'll think of something for the family. Poor darlings, it's going to be fearful for them. But at least I have Oliver. What would I do, if I hadn't him?*

As soon as tea was over, their visitor got up and said to his host, "May I have a word or two with you, sir, in private? It's a matter of business."

"Of course, of course." Richard Greeve, who had never done a stroke of business in his life, always assumed an air of importance and understanding when the word was mentioned. And he led the way to his study rather, Leslie thought with pity, like a very large and inoffensive lamb leading the way, unknowingly, to the slaughter.

The door closed behind the two men, and Alma said, in a tone of enjoyment, "I bet he's going to talk to father about the will, and tell him how much money there is."

Leslie bit her lip at the grimly unconscious truth of that.

But her mother said placidly, "He wouldn't know about that, dear."

"Mother, what makes you think so?" Leslie's voice was a little breathless, but she felt impelled to say something, anything, which might in some small way prepare them for the shock that was coming.

"Why, as your father said, he isn't really *in* the family, Leslie. He wouldn't know anything important. He seems an agreeable sort of man, though inclined to throw his weight around a little. He wouldn't be likely to know anything about Great-Aunt Tabitha's really private affairs. Your father said not."

Leslie wanted to say that father didn't know everything—that it was useless to quote him, in the face of the advancing tide. But she restrained herself, and only said quite quietly, "I think we must accept the fact that Mr. Carthay knew Great-Aunt Tabitha a great deal better than we did. He actually lived in the same place, remember, for something like a year. She . . . may have grown very fond of him, and felt he was the . . . the only member of her family she had near her."

"And he is rather nice, anyway," Alma remarked judicially.

"Old ladies would adore him, I'm sure." Morley rubbed his chin meditatively. "Masterful is, I believe, the word that would describe him in their vocabulary."

"And suppose she did adore him . . . ." Leslie looked straight across at her brother, her eyes wide in her pale face. "What would she be most likely to do?"

"I wouldn't know the answer to that," her brother replied regretfully, "never having been an old lady's darling."

But Alma, with the awful simplicity of the completely literal minded, said, "She might leave him her money, I suppose."

"Exactly," Leslie agreed. And silence fell like a stone among them.

"What . . . do you mean?" Slowly Katherine turned and stared wide-eyed in her turn. "Why do you say 'exactly' in that Greek tragedy tone? You don't mean that you think Great-Aunt Tabitha might have left *him* her money?"

"I mean that I know she did," Leslie said, and expelled her long-held breath in a sigh that almost hurt.

"*What?*" they all chorused, except for Mrs. Greeve.

"What Leslie says is perfectly true," Reid Carthay's voice said dryly from the doorway and turning, with one accord, they found him standing there, surveying the scene with bright, hard eyes and a rather grim expression.

He came slowly forward into the room then, seeming to dominate the situation without any apparent effort.

"I'm sorry. . . . " He looked around on them all, but even when his glance rested on Mrs. Greeve, it did not appreciably soften. "I understand that this must be a great shock for you all. But let us have it quite clear from the beginning—there has been no dirty work on my part. You are perhaps a little more closely related to the old lady than I am. I am perhaps a little more closely related to the money than you are." A faint, sardonic smile just touched his lips. "When all is said and done, however, she was entitled to leave her money exactly as she pleased. I never discussed it with her. For all I knew, she had left the lot to a home for canaries. . . . "

"Was there an awful lot of money?" interrupted Alma, who could not suppress a sort of gloomy curiosity about it, even though it had ceased to concern them personally.

"Not as much as your father seemed to expect."

"Oh, poor Richard!" His wife sprang to her feet. "This will be worse for him than any of us. I must go to him."

With a glance of unmerited reproach at their guest, she brushed past him and out of the room. As she did so, the telephone rang shrilly in the hall.

Leslie supposed it was cowardly of her to seize this chance of escape from a scene that was becoming unbearably tense. But, before anyone else could move to do so, she went to answer the telephone. And, as she lifted the receiver and put it to her ear, to her immeasurable relief it was Oliver's voice that said, "Hello. Is that you, Leslie?"

"Oh, *yes*, Oliver!" She didn't attempt to keep the relief and delight out of her voice. "I wasn't expecting you home yet. I'm so glad you're here. There's some . . . some news, and I want to . . . tell you about it."

"Well, that's a coincidence." Oliver was smiling, she could tell from his tone. "I have some news, too, and I want to tell you about it."

"My news isn't very nice."

But, even as she uttered this piece of understatement, she felt her spirits rise. No news could be quite so terrible if Oliver were home and in such obviously good spirits.

"I *am* sorry. What's happened? May I come over?"

She started to say, "Yes, of course," and then she changed her mind, for there was going to be little chance of a private chat with Oliver, or anyone else, in the house that evening.

"I'll walk over to meet you," she said quickly. "Come by way of the woods, and I'll meet you at the crossroads."

"The old spot?" He laughed and added, "That's rather appropriate somehow," before he rang off. For the "crossroads" in the woods—an open space where two paths met—had been a favorite meeting place of the young Greeves and Oliver Bendick when they were schoolchildren, and a good many confidences had been exchanged there over the years.

Leslie replaced the receiver and cast a glance toward the closed drawing-room door, from behind which came a murmur of voices. There were the characteristic, full overtones of the family, mingling in such a way that it was difficult to distinguish one from another. And then, almost symbolically, there cut across the hum that cool, incisive, alien tone, carrying with it the suggestion of authority that she had noticed before.

Leslie could not distinguish any actual words, but whatever Reid Carthay had said reduced the others to silence. And, fearing for some new development that might interfere with her meeting Oliver, she hastily slipped out of the house, having paused only long enough to leave word with Jessie, their elderly and devoted maid, that she had gone across to the Bendicks' place and might not be in to supper.

Although she had walked rapidly, Leslie saw, as soon as she came in sight of their meeting place, that Oliver was there before her. He was sitting on a fallen tree trunk that had been there and made a rough seat for them all almost since she could remember. But, at the sight of her, he sprang to his feet and came toward her.

In that moment he epitomized for Leslie all that was still secure and familiar and worthwhile. Dark and rather slight, but with an intelligent head and the strong, beautiful hands of a born surgeon, Oliver Bendick had that indefinable something that we call personality. And, as he took both her hands in his light, firm clasp Leslie gave a quick sigh of relief and felt the last of her dark apprehensions slide from her.

Indeed, when Oliver said, "Come and tell me what the trouble is," it seemed absurd to spoil the radiance of the evening and the joy of their meeting by going over the melancholy story again.

Her instinct was to thrust all recollection of Great-Aunt Tabitha and Reid Carthay from her, and she exclaimed, "No. Tell me your news first. I think I've been exaggerating the gloom of mine. Let's talk of something nice."

"Sure?" He looked at her, amused and questioning, but with an air of suppressed excitement, too, which told her how eager he was to talk of his own affairs.

"Quite sure. Let's sit down." And they retraced their steps to the fallen tree trunk and sat down side by side—he still holding one of her hands, she noticed.

"It's all happened so suddenly, Leslie, I can hardly believe in it even now." His dark, lively face was lit up by enthusiasm and pleasure. "You remember the Frentons...?"

She searched her memory and recalled the family of an elderly doctor, with whom Oliver had made friends during his time as a locum.

"Yes." She nodded.

"Well, I was there last weekend, and I had a long talk with old Dr. Frenton. We've had many talks, of course—more than I realized—and he'd drawn me out a good deal on my various theories and intentions. Again more than I had realized. And then he told me, Leslie, that he'd been turning over in his mind for some time the idea of taking me into partnership, and he'd finally decided to do so."

"You mean—just like that?" She was as astonished and delighted as any news bringer could wish.

"Well," he laughed, "there are some conditions and arrangements to discuss, naturally. But it is virtually settled, and I feel I can already look forward to building the exact type of future that my heart was really set on. You see, it's a big and varied practice. So many opportunities for following up the ideas I've been working on for years. Such a chance...."

He broke off and, smiling thoughtfully, looked away from her through the trees, as though already he saw vistas of absorbing work and heart-warming achievement. Until now the choice for him had lain simply between a regulation government appointment or the taking over of his father's diminishing country practice in a sparsely populated neighborhood where another youngish doctor was already the really important figure.

"It would mean living in town, of course—in Pencaster," Leslie said quietly and thoughtfully, because she did not want to disturb his happy reflections. At the same time, she was longing to hear more of something which, she felt, must so closely affect herself.

His eyes—and his attention—came back to her.

"Yes, in Pencaster. And that brings me to the second part of my news."

"Oh, there is some more?" Her lips parted in eager interest, and he laughed aloud.

"Leslie, you're marvelous!" he declared. "The best audience anyone ever had."

She laughed, too, then, pleased and indefinably excited, because she sensed considerable excitement in him.

"You're just like a sister listening to a favorite brother's airy-fairy plans." Oliver looked at her affectionately. "Except, I suppose," he added reflectively, "that most brothers don't appreciate sisterly interest as much as I appreciate yours. Maybe that's because I have no sisters."

She smiled—but a little doubtfully that time, for the brother-sister relationship was not one that she herself had ever thought of in connection with Oliver and herself. It was true, of course, that he had been like one of the family for so long that the expression did describe their degree of intimacy. But she wished he had used some other term, and she said rather quickly, "Well, go on. Tell me the rest."

"I haven't·told anyone else yet except mother," he said earnestly. "But I'd like you to be the first to know, outside my own family, Leslie. I'm going to be married. And one of the nicest things about it all is that Caroline is old Dr. Frenton's niece—it was through her that I met him—so everything has worked in together in the most wonderful way."

Leslie thought there was an odd little silence, then, to her surprise, she heard someone say, "Why, how splendid!" And, to her further surprise, she realized that it was herself.

She didn't really think at all in the next few moments. Not with the surface of her mind, that was to say. Only, deep down in her subconscious, some instinct prompted her to say, "Tell me some more about it. What is she like?" Because those words would force him to further speech, and so put some sort of shield between any perception of his and her own naked, appalled dismay.

His voice went on and, to the best of her belief, she smiled and looked attentive. But nothing that he said really reached her. It was as though some small, vital connection were broken, and she sat there, isolated from the rest of the world by the immensity of what had just happened. Only some obstinate core of pride—some instinct of self-preservation—helped her to play her role so that Oliver would never, never guess what a fool she had been, or what a blow he had dealt her.

But she dragged her mind back from such reflections as that. Unless she kept every scrap of her remaining attention on what Oliver was saying, she would betray herself. And so, while part of her seemed to stand aside in stunned and leaden detachment, the rest of her played—perhaps slightly overplayed—the role of the interested, sisterly confidante.

He was not, however—as she guessed—in a mood to be critical of a good audience. He wanted to talk of his happiness, and if she would listen and smile and put in a word here and there, that was all he needed. Indeed, it was not until she rose, finally, and said that she must be going home, that he recollected affairs other than his own, and exclaimed, "Good lord! I've done all the talking, I'm afraid. What was it that you were going to tell me, Leslie?"

"Tell you?" She looked vague for a moment, for she could not imagine there was anything she could have to tell the stranger that Oliver had become.

"Yes. You said you'd had some bad news at home or something."

"Oh—Great-Aunt Tabitha died."

She made the statement almost indifferently, for Great-Aunt Tabitha and her place in the scheme of things had shrunk all at once to inconsiderable proportions.

But Oliver was impressed. Living so close to the Greeves, and being so much one of them, he naturally knew all the implications that this announcement carried with it.

"It's not exactly bad news, surely? I mean . . . the old lady was a stranger really. And even the most tender-hearted and disinterested person never minded inheriting a fortune."

"We haven't inherited a fortune, after all."

"What!"

"There's a . . . a nephew or cousin or something." Oh, she couldn't go over it all again, she felt. Not now. With every feeling raw and protesting. So she compromised, hastily if a little untruthfully, by saying, "We don't know the exact position yet. But we think it's . . . it's going to be rather disappointing financially."

"Leslie, I am sorry!" He looked grave, and obviously made a valiant attempt to subdue his own radiant spirits to a level more in keeping with the misfortune of his friends.

"Oh, it may not be as bad as we feared at first." She smiled with determined cheerfulness because she longed now to escape, and her uppermost thought was that this conversation must not be allowed to take a new lease on life.

"How did your father take the news?"

"I'm not quite sure."

"You're not sure?" He looked astonished.

"I mean that I . . . came away to meet you without having seen him after the news had been broken to him."

"I say, it was pretty good of you to come here and listen to my vaporings with all that anxiety on your mind," he exclaimed sincerely.

"Oh, no. I thought . . . ." She broke off and smiled vaguely, because that was the only expression with which she could hide the fact that her mouth was suddenly trembling. "I felt sure that whatever you had to say would cheer me, and—" a supreme effort, but she made it "—it certainly has. I'm so . . . glad for you, Oliver. But . . . I must go now to the family," she repeated.

"Yes, of course." He took her hand and wrung it. "Is there anything I could do? Would it be any help if I came along?"

"No, I don't think so." She managed to say that consideringly, instead of on a note of hysterical protest. "I'll . . . let you know how things are."

"Very well." He repeated his assurances of goodwill and, as far as she could remember afterward, she somehow repeated her congratulations. And then, at last, she was free to go—hurrying from him as though her remembered family responsibilities were what drove her on, and not just the terrible, devouring wish to flee from the scene where she had suffered such unutterable humiliation and shock.

Presently, when she knew she was completely out of his sight, she slackened her pace and, with a gesture of weariness and defeat, put up her hand to push back the heavy fair hair from her forehead.

But her hand never reached her hair. Instead, she suddenly found that she was desperately wiping the tears from her face—while she sobbed aloud, and dropped to the ground.

I ought to have seen what had happened, she told herself fiercely. *I would have, but for our fatal family failing of ignoring realities and just waiting complacently for life to deliver the goods we most want. I'll never, never, never be caught like this again! I'll never believe* anything *I want to believe until it's been proved to the hilt.*

The very intensity of her painful resolution forced another sob or two from her. And then to her horrified ears came a sound that drove her to the final depths of humiliation. Someone was coming toward her—she could hear the light crackle of twigs underfoot as he came—and she knew it was a contrite Oliver, coming to reinforce what he doubtless felt had been rather perfunctory expressions of sympathy.

What would he think, finding her here in a passion of tears? What was she to say, caught thus at a complete disadvantage, and stripped of every shred of dignity or defensive pride?

Although she knew he had dropped down on the grass beside her, she resolutely kept her face hidden, as though by doing so she might put off the terrible moment when he must speak, and show in his embarrassed and horrified tone that he had guessed the truth.

To her despairing fancy, the silent moments measured themselves out to incalculable length, punctuated only by a couple of stifled aftersobs from her that betrayed the passion of her previous outburst.

And then he spoke at last, and it was not Oliver's voice. It was Reid Carthay, who said on a note of not unkindly protest, "Oh, come, honey, don't cry like that. No lost fortune was ever worth so many tears." And she was scooped up, a little unceremoniously but with some dexterity, and found herself leaning exhaustedly against the family intruder who was regarding her with a sort of humorous dismay.

CHAPTER THREE

LESLIE'S FIRST IMPULSE was to exclaim that no mere lost fortune would have made her cry so tempestuously. But the next moment she realized that, all unknowing, he had offered her a straw at which her drowning pride might clutch. Neither he nor anyone else need ever know the tragic folly that had prompted these tears.

Mildly embarrassing it might be to be thought capable of weeping unrestrainedly over the loss of a hoped-for fortune. But that was nothing to the agony of humiliation involved in anyone guessing the real truth.

So, instead of pulling away from him with some indignant denial, she continued to lean against his arm for a moment—not altogether averse to having this support in her limp and exhausted condition—and said, "I don't . . . usually cry . . . about such things. But it's a little . . . frightening to realize how different the future is going to be from anything we ever expected."

"Yes, I can understand that."

"Kate and I can manage well enough, I don't doubt. And I suppose Alma will just go on being at school. Though it may have to be a very different school, of course," she murmured in parenthesis. "But . . . Morley. And mother and father. . . ."

"Um-hm," he agreed, rubbing his chin reflectively. "I've gathered that your parents constitute a formidable part of the problem."

"It's easy enough to criticize them," she exclaimed quickly and defensively—and now she did pull away from him, sitting up and trying, with a hasty hand, to smooth her tumbled hair. "It's true that they've lived a comfortable, unrealistic sort of life based on little more than fond hopes. You can say they're silly and outdated and all that sort of thing, but...."

"I wasn't really going to say anything of the kind, you know," he put in mildly.

"But the fact is that they've made a lovely home life for us here—always," she ran on, not heeding his interruption. "Except for what happened to Morley, we've been a completely happy family. I don't think anyone can ever have been happier or more ... more carefree." As she looked back on past contentment, unlikely ever to return, her voice trembled for a moment, and in her effort to steady it once more she achieved a hard, almost resentful tone. "You can't say they've done nothing worthwhile, when they've made their four children happy all these years."

"No one is suggesting they've done nothing worthwhile—least of all myself, my sweet," he returned, and that drawl that tended to broaden his vowels at times was very marked. "I'm not here to comment on the past. I'm here to see what can be done about the future."

"Do you mean—*our* future?" she asked incredulously.

"Your future," he confirmed easily.

"But we aren't—exactly—your business, are we?"

"No?" He smiled at her, so compellingly that she blushed a little and looked away. "You're my only relatives—as far as I know."

"We aren't relatives!" Her father's remembered insistence on that point gave added emphasis to her denial. "At least, it's a relationship of the very remotest kind."

"The best type possible," he assured her, and that lazy smile seemed to travel over her again in a way no man had dared to smile at her before. "Just enough to constitute a claim to notice, and not enough to lapse into conventional dullness."

"I don't know what you mean," she said quickly. But, suddenly, for no special reason, she had a clear recollection of Oliver saying she was like a sister to him, and she thought that in no circumstances whatever would Reid Carthay choose to regard her as a sister.

"I'll explain in more detail, if you like," he offered amusedly.

But she added hastily, "No, thank you." And when he laughed she added, "I don't see what you think you could do about our future."

"No?" He punched little holes in the turf with his thumb and smiled to himself. "The situation isn't all that obscure, you know. You folk have always expected to have the money that has suddenly come to me. It seems you even had very good reason to feel that way. That being so, I can't do less than see you get some of it, surely."

"Nonsense!" She was startled, and a little indignant again. "Father wouldn't hear of such a thing."

Reid Carthay looked skeptical.

"He's in a rather nasty spot if he won't."

"I'm sure he is. But that wouldn't make him take money from a . . . a stranger. He's quite proud in his own way, you know."

"I'm glad you had the grace to hesitate before handing me the word 'stranger.'" He glanced up at her with a grin. "But, apart from that, your father has quite a strong moral right to some of this money, by any standards."

"He wouldn't think so," Leslie insisted. And she hoped rather agitatedly that she was right, for it made her feel oddly uncomfortable to think of their being under a great obligation to this bold, smiling man.

"Then will you tell me what he—indeed all of you—can do as an alternative?"

The question was not offensively put, but it had a sort of good-humored, irresistible logic about it. And she was silent, because, of course, there was no easy answer to that.

"It's too early to say," she declared at last. "We haven't had time to do more than . . . than take in the essential fact."

"Well, at least promise me not to cry about it anymore," he said, getting up and holding out his hand to her.

She longed to tell him, even then, that she had not been crying about that, for she hated to be thought so spineless. But the alternative of even hinting at the truth was so unthinkable that she could only put her hand into his and allow him to help her to her feet, while she said, "I won't cry anymore." And in her heart she added rather bitterly, *not even about Oliver.* For he belonged to someone else now—to Caroline Frenton. And to cry about some other girl's man was the final humiliation.

When they reached home, she could hardly believe that it was only just suppertime. It seemed to her that she had lived through almost a lifetime of experience since she had left the house. And now here was Alma hopping up and down on one foot and chanting, "Cold chicken for supper," just as though the world had not been turned upside down.

Somewhat to the embarrassment of the younger Greeves, neither of their parents appeared at suppertime, and they were left to entertain the stranger as best they could.

And then at last supper was over, and when Katherine suggested they should have coffee in the drawing room, to the profound relief of everyone Reid replied that he didn't want any coffee, but would take his car and drive around and have a look at the district.

After he had gone, they all remained silent for a few minutes. Then Alma said rather defiantly, "I like him."

"*Do* you?" Katherine flicked her gold-tipped lashes effectively. "I can't help feeling what a relief it is to have our home to ourselves again!"

"But I think he means well," Leslie said.

"A confoundedly dull tribute to pay anyone," declared Morley. "I hope he isn't going to thrust his money down our throats. I've always had a sneaking sympathy with the *nouveaux riches* before. But really they mustn't be quite so *nouveaux* or quite so *riches*." And, for a moment, he looked extraordinarily like his father.

"Oh . . . I don't know." Suddenly Leslie felt a most rare irritation with her family, and more particularly with Morley. And because the last thing she wanted was to make Reid a bone of contention in the family circle, she got up and said, "I think I'll take a tray up to mother and see how she's feeling. I do wish she wouldn't behave as though there'd been a death in the house, poor pet."

The others laughed. But with an air of surprise and indulgence. For they were still judging the situation from the family standard of values, while she, Leslie realized with surprise, was beginning to wonder how these things would appear to an outsider.

Puzzled and faintly disturbed by the discovery, she arranged a tempting little meal on a tray, and went upstairs.

"Come in, darling," her mother's voice said plaintively, when she knocked at the door of the pretty, pastel-tinted, Greuzelike room that presented such a perfect setting for its owner. And, as Leslie entered, her mother turned a faintly tear-marked face toward her, and languidly shifted one or two of the frilled pillows of the sofa on which she was reclining.

"How do you feel, dear?" Leslie's voice instinctively softened and took on an indulgent note.

"I'm all right, Leslie. It's your poor father I am thinking about. And Morley." Tears came again into the beautiful dark eyes.

"Yes, I know. It's been a bad shock for us all. But I have a feeling things aren't going to be as bad as we feared," Leslie insisted cheerfully, as she propped up her mother against the cushions and gave her the tray.

"I don't really want anything to eat," Mrs. Greeve said sadly. But she looked with interest at what her daughter had set out, and presently she began to do reasonable justice to the meal, while Leslie sat on a low seat near the sofa and made encouraging comments from time to time.

"I'm glad you feel so hopeful and cheerful about things, darling," she said, looking with an air of melancholic indulgence at her daughter. "But then, of course," she added with a sigh, "all this won't affect you as deeply as the rest of us."

"Oh, mother! Do you think I don't share the family anxieties?"

"Of course, my dear. But you have other plans to make you happy. You haven't actually said anything about it, I know. But you and Oliver...."

"Oh, no!" Leslie cried sharply, and her mother stopped and looked at her in surprise.

Leslie bit her lip and tried to smile quite casually. Deep down in her heart was a sort of relief that she had not been the only one to read the situation wrongly. If her mother, too, had thought Oliver loved her, then perhaps she had not been so foolish and self-deluding to allow herself that belief. But she could not allow her mother, or anyone else, to continue in that fond error.

And so, after a moment, she managed to say lightly, "Don't make any romances between Oliver and any of your daughters, darling. He's just got engaged to some girl in Pencaster and her uncle is going to take him into partnership—and everything in his particular garden is just fine."

"But, my *dear* . . . ." Leslie wished her mother would not look quite so dismayed and astonished. It recalled for an agonizing moment what she herself had felt when Oliver first told her of Caroline Frenton. "I felt certain . . . I thought you did, too . . . ." Mrs. Greeve stopped again, and suddenly her whole manner changed. Her vague and elegant melancholy was gone, and for a moment she became any mother anxious over her hurt child.

"Was it a great shock to you, darling?" she asked, so simply and tenderly that Leslie put her head down against her mother's arm for a long minute and was silent.

"One gets over these things," Leslie said at last, without looking up. "You mustn't think my heart's broken or anything like that." Somehow she must minimize things if she were to save her mother further anxiety. "But . . . I was very fond of him, of course. More like a sister perhaps." She even forced herself to say the hated word. "But I was rather shaken when he told me."

"When did he tell you?"

"This evening."

"Oh, dear. . . . " Mrs. Greeve stroked the bright head against her arm. "Everything seems to be happening at once."

"Maybe it's better that way, so that they can cancel each other out," Leslie suggested, with an unsteady laugh.

"I wish there were something to help cancel out the shock your father has had," Mrs. Greeve said with a sigh.

"Oh . . . I meant to tell you. Reid had a talk with me.

He has an idea that father ought to have at least some of Great-Aunt Tabitha's money. He says he has a moral right to it."

Her mother made no scornful protests about that, as Morley and even Leslie herself had done. She thoughtfully considered what her daughter had reported.

"He is right, of course," she said finally. "But I doubt if your father will see things that way. His pride has been terribly hurt over being omitted from the will, quite apart from the financial disaster involved. I don't think he'd agree to take money from a stranger, even in the present dreadful situation."

"Reid isn't exactly a stranger," Leslie found herself saying.

Her mother regarded her consideringly, as though she were mentally measuring her husband's obstinacy against that of the newcomer's. But when she spoke what she said was, "I wish he'd fall in love with Kate."

"Mother, what an extraordinary thing to say!"

"And she with him, of course. Then he could marry her, and it would keep all the money in the family without hurting your father's pride. Or Morley's," she added as an afterthought. "Morley is going to be very difficult, too."

"Yes, I know. He's shown signs of it already."

"Well . . . it's hard for him," Morley's mother said with a sigh. And they were both silent, thinking what it must be like to be the one young man in the family—and virtually helpless in this crisis.

"Has your father had any supper?" Mrs. Greeve asked at last.

"No, I don't think so."

"Then I'd better go and see what I can do with him." And in one graceful movement Mrs. Greeve rose from the sofa.

And Leslie, picking up the tray and preparing to follow her, wondered if, after all, their mother were quite such a sweet and helpless creature as they all supposed. Or was it that those very soft and feminine women had hidden strength and understanding where their own were concerned?

Leslie returned the tray to the kitchen, noticed that it was past Alma's bedtime, and routed out her younger sister and despatched her, protesting, to bed. Then she went to her own room where, for half an hour at least, she could be alone with her thoughts and take mental stock of all that had happened on this most momentous day of her life.

Someone knocked on the door just then, and she called, "Come in," and then sat up and opened her eyes as Katherine came in.

"Hello." Katherine dropped down gracefully on the end of Leslie's bed. "I just thought I'd like a sisterly exchange of ideas. At the moment, I find it difficult to realize that I'm still myself."

Leslie smiled.

"I'd just come around to thinking the same thing, and trying to decide what the future looked like. By the way—" and she admired the casualness of her own voice as she spoke "—I forgot to tell you all, with so much more going on in the family circle, Oliver has just become engaged."

"Oliver!" Katherine sat up and gave her sister an odd glance. "To whom?"

"A girl in Pencaster of whom I've never heard. She's called Caroline Frenton, and her uncle's taking Oliver into partnership."

"How . . . extraordinary. I always rather thought he might marry you."

"Did you? So did I—when I was about seventeen," Leslie said, and laughed quite naturally.

"Oh, it was like that, was it?" Katherine dismissed the

affair carelessly. "I'm glad it went no deeper." Then she rolled over on her back on the bed and stared at the ceiling. "Now the family fortunes have failed, I suppose you and I are going to have to think seriously about finding rich husbands."

"Or good jobs."

"I'm not the stuff of which career women are made, myself," Katherine said, and laughed. "I shall concentrate on the rich husband."

Leslie was silent. And in the silence they both heard a car coming up the driveway.

"There's one rich possibility approaching the house at the moment," Leslie remarked dryly, thinking of what her mother had said.

"I know. But I don't think I could fall in love with him."

"You're asking rather a lot, aren't you?" Leslie said with a smile. "A rich husband *and* a love match."

When Katherine finally rose to go, and declared that she was suddenly very sleepy, Leslie got up, too, and said, "I think I'll run downstairs for ten minutes. If mother and father haven't been talking to Reid, he'll think it odd and unfriendly that no one bothers even to say good-night to him."

"All right. You go and look after his wounded feelings," Katherine replied with a laugh, and she departed to her own room.

Leslie went rather slowly downstairs. The house was very quiet now, but there was a light still on in the drawing room and the door stood half open. For a moment she thought the room was empty. But when she came in, she saw that he was standing by one of the big windows, looking out into the darkened garden.

He could not have noticed her footsteps, or else he was very deep in thought, because she was halfway across the room before he turned rather sharply to face her.

"I'm sorry. Did I startle you? I'm afraid my steps didn't sound much on this carpet."

"No. I saw your reflection in the windowpane."

She came over to stand beside him, and looked out into the night.

"Did you have a nice drive?"

"Very, thank you."

She felt, rather than saw, that he was looking down at her with amused attention and, though she would not glance up at him, her social conscience stirred a little within her, so that she said, "I hope you haven't been all on your own since you came in."

"No. I had a talk with your parents."

"Oh?" She did glance up then. "With any...result?"

He smiled wryly.

"I discovered you were right when you said your father had his pride—if you call that getting results."

"You mean he wouldn't listen to your proposition about...about the money?"

"No. But I hardly expected him to at first. I suppose I can consider that I won a minor victory, however, in that he pressed me to stay on here some while. As he gets to know me better, he may change his mind a little."

"And you're prepared to stay on here, just in the hope that he will presently agree to accept some of your money? You're an extraordinary man," she said slowly.

"That isn't my only reason for wishing to stay."

"No? I'm afraid you'll find it rather dull here. We're nearly twenty miles from a town of any size."

"I know. Pencaster, isn't it?"

"Yes." She glanced inquiringly at him. "Did you go there this evening?"

"No. But I knew it was near here when I came."

"How odd you should have heard of it. It isn't of any special importance, you know. Just a rather nice market town, with a slightly smarter population than that usually implies."

"Is that so?"

"How did you hear of it?"

He hesitated a moment. Then he said, "I was engaged to a girl who came from there."

"You were .... *Were* you?" Somehow it surprised her profoundly that he should have been engaged, or that, having been so, he had not piloted (or driven) the affair to a successful conclusion. "Is that the other reason why you are interested in staying on here?" she inquired, before she could stop herself.

He smiled, but again he hesitated.

"It could be. I have a certain . . . natural curiosity about her, let us say."

"Was it all a good while ago?"

"About a year."

Something hard in his voice told her that he was recalling a period that had meant a great deal to him, and that even now could not be resigned without pain. With her own unfortunate experience so fresh in her mind, she felt a little throb of sympathy for him, and perhaps that sounded in her voice as she said, "Did she . . . leave you?"

He nodded.

"I'm sorry. It . . . hurt a lot, didn't it?"

"Like hell," he said, but he grinned at her ruefully.

Leslie sighed. "I know. It does."

"Do you mean that you really know?" he inquired. "Or was that just a general comment?"

She withdrew quickly into her shell again.

"Oh, I wasn't thinking of any personal experience, if that's what you mean."

"That's what I meant," he agreed.

She was anxious to shift the talk from her own affairs, and so she asked with more curiosity than she might otherwise have displayed, "Are you hoping to . . . win her back?"

"My dear, I'm taking this admirable opportunity of . . . exploring the position, that's all."

"I see." She looked out of the darkened window again, and then back at him. "If it's any help to . . . bring her here, or . . . use us as a background . . . ."

He interrupted with a slight laugh that sounded friendly.

"That's sweet of you. A family background might certainly give me a little more stability in Caroline's eyes, I suppose. She disapproved of my independent, lone-wolf existence."

Leslie swallowed slightly, and a faint, superstitious chill touched her.

"Did you say her name was . . . Caroline?"

He frowned.

"Did I mention her name? I didn't mean to. But it is Caroline."

"Not . . . Caroline Frenton, by any chance?"

For a long moment he stared at her, his eyes lightly narrowed, as though he suspected some sort of trap. Then he said, "How did you know?"

"I didn't. It just . . . seemed inevitable," Leslie murmured under her breath.

"I don't understand." His voice was cold, and no longer friendly. "Do you know Caroline?"

"No. Only of her. She became engaged today to . . . to someone I know very well."

"I see," he said. And then, almost casually, "Was that why you were crying so bitterly when I found you this evening?"

CHAPTER FOUR

FOR A FEW MOMENTS Leslie said nothing—stunned by the terrible accuracy with which Reid had guessed her feelings for Oliver.

"No one knows," she gasped at last, catching her breath in her anxiety. "Except mother. And even she doesn't know quite how . . . how important he was to me."

"All right. I won't tell anyone, if that's what you mean."

He looked rather moodily away from her into the darkness.

"So Caroline is engaged," he said slowly, as though he were forcing the words into his own consciousness. And then she realized that what she had said must have been a blow for him.

"I'm dreadfully sorry! I was so surprised that I didn't think what I was saying—didn't prepare you for what I was going to say. I'm afraid it was a shock."

"Well, I guess what I said was something of a shock for you, too," he returned, with a slight grimace.

"Not as much as what Oliver said," she murmured. And then she was surprised and dismayed afresh to find that she seemed unable to keep herself from saying just what came into her mind. "Please forget that," she added urgently.

"Honey," he said, and he put his arm around her with an unsentimental good humor impossible to resent, "you and I know a little too much about each other now for either of us to risk telling tales. I'll forget whatever you please about your Oliver if you'll undertake not to remember too much of what I've said about Caroline."

"One doesn't actually forget these things, of course," she said with a sigh. "But I promise not to speak about them, and you've already done the same."

"Fine." He smiled down at her. "Are you feeling a little better for having someone else in the same boat?"

"Oh! That wouldn't be either kind or logical," Leslie declared, avoiding a direct answer, because she was a trifle ashamed to realize that her heart had felt curiously lighter ever since he had told her that he had once been engaged to Caroline Frenton.

"What is he like, Leslie?"

"Oliver?" She looked up, startled. "Why, he's ... dark and good-looking and ... clever."

"The kind most girls would fall for, in fact."

She smiled faintly, but with a sort of obstinate courage.

"I can only say that I fell for him. But then I'd known him most of my life."

"Poor kid! I hadn't realized that."

She frowned, because she didn't think that, even in this new mood of shared confidences, she could bear the pity of a stranger, when her own mother's compassion had hurt.

"Why did you ask about him?" she said curiously.

"I was wondering whether the whole thing could be a temporary infatuation. Something I could get Caroline over."

"Do you mean—*try to take her away* from Oliver?"

She was shocked and showed it. But he laughed without contrition.

"She was mine first," he reminded her.

"But that's over now."

He looked at her humorously and said, "Here, whose side are you on?"

"Neither! At least ... I mean ...."

And then she was silent, because she was realizing, with the clearness given to a scene revealed by a flash of lightning, just what it would mean to her if Reid carried out his threat, and carried it out successfully.

"But Caroline is happily engaged to Oliver now," she protested, with a tenth of the conviction she had shown before.

"How do you know she is?"

"He told me so! It's his happiness, too," she cried, with remorseful fervor, remembering how bemused and enraptured Oliver had looked as he talked of his engagement. "You mustn't interfere now, Reid, between two people who love each other."

"Or think they do," he retorted. "Suppose I tell you that she loved me and that I still love her." He smiled, but in a curiously obstinate way that tightened the line of his jaw and made his eyes seem light and brilliant.

"I'm sure she did once and that you still love her. Just as I . . . I love Oliver," she said with an effort. "But we're outside the present framework, Reid. We're just the . . . unlucky ones. We must accept the fact . . . resign ourselves to . . . ."

"My sweet, I never resigned myself to anything in my life," he broke in dryly. "I am not resigned to the present situation."

"But you can't *do* things like that. There are some decencies that one observes!"

"Good lord! He isn't married to her yet," Reid retorted carelessly. "I'm not setting out to snaffle another man's wife."

"But they are engaged. It's the first step toward their marriage."

"People can retrace first steps."

"Reid, I can't understand your talking like this. I haven't known you long, it's true, but I could have sworn you were not this sort of man."

"What sort?" he wanted to know with genuinely amused curiosity.

"Why, the sort who would try to upset someone else's love story, of course. You've *lost*. Can't you be a better loser than this?"

He frowned thoughtfully and, since she had moved from him a little in her indignation and earnestness, he took his arm away from her.

"Look, Leslie," he said at last, and his tone was as earnest now as hers. "The circumstances of our parting weren't exactly simple, or aboveboard. I found out recently that someone told her lies about me—it doesn't matter now who or why. It was because she thought something quite wrong about me that she manufactured a quarrel and broke the engagement. As soon as I heard the real story, I came after her—it coincided very well with my coming to see your people, too, incidentally—to find out if I could mend things. And, in the circumstances, I'm damned if I'm going to stand aside for a day-old engagement to someone else. Someone you might well comfort if he lost out, I might add."

"No! Don't add that! Leave me out of your calculations," Leslie cried agitatedly, because the leap of her heart frightened her. "Oh, I ... don't know what to say. If what you say is true, it ... it's terribly hard on you, of course. But then there is Oliver and *his* happiness."

"Which is genuinely the most important thing to you in all this?" he said curiously.

"Of course."

He smiled dryly and said, "Oliver seems to have all the luck."

"He won't, if you take Caroline away from him," she retorted a little sullenly.

He smiled at her.

"Don't you feel capable of consoling him?"

"Oh, Reid—please!" She put her hands over her face.

"God, I wish I knew what was right. If it's really rather . . . rather a sudden business between Caroline and Oliver, and if she truly loved you, it makes a difference, of course. And I could make Oliver happy—I know I could—if only she were not there."

"You see?" He took hold of her hands and gently drew them down from her face, so that she had to look at him. "And *I* know that I could make *her* happy, if only your Oliver were not there. It's one of those rare occasions when the values—and the personalities—have got themselves hopelessly mixed. Don't you think we owe it to ourselves, and possibly to them, too, to unmix things?"

"I . . . don't know. It sounds so plausible, of course. But its very plausibility makes me suspect it."

"Darling, you do make heavy weather of your own happiness, don't you?" he said amusedly.

"And you take things much too lightly," she cried accusingly. "You stand there calling me 'darling' and 'my sweet' and things like that, while you're supposed to be dying of love for another girl. It doesn't sound very...."

"Oh, no! Not dying of love," he assured her. "Very, very much alive and determined to fight for it. And as for calling you 'darling'—I think you *are* a darling, and I see no reason why I shouldn't put the thought into words occasionally."

She laughed vexedly, defeated by his unshakable good humor.

"You have an answer for everything—like Satan," she declared.

"I hope you think the likeness ends there."

"I don't know." Leslie looked at him reflectively. "I've always thought Satan sounded attractive and full of vitality."

He laughed a good deal at that, and said it was no wonder he called her "darling" when she said such charming things. Whereupon Leslie suddenly realized just what she had said, and frowned and colored a little.

"Well, let's leave this soul-searching for tonight," he suggested. "Tomorrow you may see things more as I do...."

"Or vice versa," she countered quickly.

He shook his head.

"No, my dear, I have my mind made up about this. But it's too late for us to pursue the discussion further. I'm sure you have a lot of courage and staying power, but today must have been a whale of a day for you, and if you're not feeling exhausted by now, you ought to be."

When he said that, Leslie became aware that she was indeed dead tired, in an excited, agitated way, and that, try as she would to look at the new problem in a fair and objective way, she simply could not do so. He was right. In all fairness they must break off the discussion now.

"You'd better go on ahead," she told him. "I know where the light switches are."

But he smiled and said that if he was going to live there, the sooner he found out these things, the better.

So she went on ahead. And as he put out the lights, and came up the stairs behind her, she had the odd feeling that, in little or big things, one would very easily get into the habit of leaving responsibilities to Reid Carthay.

In the rather dim light of the upstairs landing, she looked at him with a flash of mischievous humor in her eyes and, because the rest of the household were probably asleep by now, it was in a whisper that she said to him, "Do you do things for people because you're kind, or because you're arrogant?"

" 'Bossy' was the word you meant," he returned, also in a whisper. "And the answer is—neither. I do things only when I like people. Good night, my sweet." And he patted her cheek rather sharply and left her.

Leslie went into her own room, shut the door and leaned against it. For almost a minute she made no attempt to put on the light; only gazed almost absently around the palely moonlit room, while her mind drifted idly from point to point of her conversation with Reid Carthay.

Next day, when she was in the kitchen garden gathering peas, she saw Reid coming toward her with an air of purpose that suggested a deliberate seeking of her society, rather than any chance encounter. She went on rather deliberately with her task, but she experienced a little flutter of excited anticipation—not, she assured herself, because of anything in Reid's personality, but because one instinctively expected things to happen when he was around.

"Leslie . . . ." He gathered a handful of pods and tossed them into her basket as a sort of token contribution. "There's something I want to ask you. I take it that . . . Oliver is more or less a friend of the family?"

"Oh, yes. Certainly."

"So that it would be quite in keeping with the general situation if you were to ring him up and suggest he bring his fiancée over here to meet the others?"

There was a moment's pause. Then she said, "It would be quite a . . . likely proceeding, yes. But why should I? Do you think it would serve any useful purpose?"

"It would give the protagonists a chance to meet each other."

"Oh, Reid!"

"Well, we've got to meet sometime, you know. Don't you want to see what your rival—what Caroline—is like?"

She winced.

"Not . . . much. I'm a little afraid to see her."

"Hell! Why?" He evidently simply could not accept the idea of fearing to measure oneself against an adversary.

"Oh, Reid, I wish I had half your confidence," Leslie exclaimed, without actually answering his query.

"Nonsense. You're sweet as you are," he told her. "But take a grip on your courage and arrange for Oliver to bring her over here. It's probably your best and most painless way of meeting her, you know."

She knew reluctantly that he was right.

"Very well. But...when?"

"The first moment possible, of course!"

"This evening?"

"This evening would be fine."

"All right. I'll go and do it now." And she set down her basket and ran into the house before her courage and resolution could fail her.

It was Oliver himself who answered her call, and he was obviously pleased at the idea of bringing Caroline to meet his old friends.

"She's staying here overnight," he explained. "I'll bring her to your place after dinner. Thanks, Leslie. It's a splendid idea. You think of everything."

She forbore to say that someone else had thought of this. Merely remarked, "That's all right, Oliver," in what she grimly hoped was a sisterly tone, and replaced the receiver.

As she did so, Morley wheeled himself out into the hall. He must have heard her last few words, because he said, "That was Oliver, was it?"

"Yes."

"He's engaged, mother tells me."

"Yes. He is bringing her—bringing Caroline—over this evening, to meet us."

"Does he have to do that?" growled Morley.

"Oh, Morley! We're his oldest friends. I suggested he should bring her over."

"You did?" Morley looked at his sister, and his thin, rather haggard face softened. "No one can say you don't take your fences well, Leslie."

She wondered if she should say that Reid had urged her to take this particular fence. But it would involve too much explaining of what was best left alone, and would lead into the very debatable subject of her own exact motives in asking Oliver and his new fiancée to Cranley Magna. She contented herself with patting Morley's shoulder, smiling and saying, "I'm not the most courageous member of this family. But I hope I'm not a bad loser."

He looked at her with anxious curiosity.

"Was it a bad shock, Leslie?"

"Say rather—a nasty jar," she retorted almost lightly. And she went back into the garden, marveling to herself that she could conceal her inmost feelings from her brother, and yet reveal them to a comparative stranger.

"It's settled," she told Reid in a matter-of-fact voice.

"And don't pick any more peas, *please*. We have enough for a siege as it is."

He laughed.

"Sorry. I thought I'd better finish your job while you busied yourself about my affairs."

She looked at him reflectively.

"Would you say that telephone call was a question of your affairs or mine?"

He grinned.

"It's all in the way you look at it, I guess. What do you say?"

"I don't know. I wish I did," Leslie said, and took her peas into the kitchen.

Outwardly she might appear extremely calm and matter-of-fact, but inwardly she felt frightened and agitated. Not only was there the direct ordeal of meeting Oliver's fiancée, and somehow making herself calmly

accept the display of affection that he would presumably show for another girl, there was also the dreadful
uncertainty in her own mind of what she meant to do.

Did she intend to stand by and watch Reid try to take
Caroline away from Oliver? Or, rather—since there was
nothing, it seemed, that she could do to influence Reid
one way or the other—did she intend to keep a close
watch on the situation and profit by it if she could?

Mentally she rejected the word "profit" as sounding
too unscrupulous, and substituted the word "benefit."
But she still felt uneasily that she was adopting the role
of schemer, rather than good loser.

Only, if Caroline did turn to her first love, what sense
would there be in Leslie not trying to console Oliver?

It's all in the way one looks at it, she assured herself,
unconsciously using Reid's own words. Suppose she
had been a good friend of Reid's and had never seen
Oliver, she would feel quite differently. If she knew Reid
had lost his girl through no fault of his own, she would
be only too eager for him to win her back. And even if,
in the intervening months, the girl had got herself entan-
gled with someone else, she, Leslie, would still hope that
Reid would regain her. She would be sorry for the other
man, but she wouldn't rate his claim as high as Reid's.

It sounded wonderful, put that way. If only she had
had no stake in the game herself!

Am I being quite objective? she asked herself anxiously. *And if I am, and if I really think Reid has the better
claim to Caroline, am I prepared even to help him get her
back?*

But it was useless to pretend that she was still being
objective when she reached that point in her reflections.

I'm not being honest now! she told herself ruthlessly.
*But I have agreed to set the stage as Reid wants it this eve-
ning. Was that quite honest?*

Her common sense argued then that she had done

nothing but arrange a perfectly harmless and ordinary family gathering. But her conscience would not let her entirely alone, and by the time the evening came she was sure that her conduct had not been entirely disinterested.

"It's funny we've never seen this Caroline Frenton before," remarked Alma. "You'd think Oliver would want to marry someone he *knew,* not a stranger."

"He probably feels he knows this girl now," Morley pointed out patiently.

"Oh, now—yes," Alma agreed. "But I mean you'd expect him to have married someone he'd known for ages, like Leslie or Kate."

"Much obliged," Katherine said. "I'm fond of Oliver, in a general, family way, but his Caroline may have him, for me."

Leslie smiled faintly, and even a little indulgently. But by no effort of will could she bring herself to second Katherine's sentiments.

"Oliver is our best friend, you know," Alma was busily explaining to Reid. "He lived quite near, and we've always known him. He's a doctor, but he's living in Pencaster now, and I suppose that's where he met this Caroline."

"She is not, as you might suppose from my young sister's remarks, a 'groupie,' " Morley added. "She is apparently the niece of a perfectly reputable doctor in our nearest town."

"What did you say her name was?" Reid asked, so casually that Leslie could hardly suppress a smile of admiration.

"Caroline Frenton."

"Oh, then I know her already."

"You *do?*" Alma registered inordinate astonishment. "But what an extraordinary thing! Do you hear that, everyone? Reid knows this girl Oliver's going to marry."

There was a chorus of mild surprise, in which Leslie contrived to join convincingly. And Katherine added curiously, "What is she like?"

"Dark, desirable, graceful, and with lots of oomph," replied Reid, with unexpected comprehensiveness.

There was a funny little silence, while they all registered this curiously vivid portrait of Caroline Frenton. Then Morley said reflectively, "She doesn't sound like Oliver's cup of tea, somehow."

"She may not be," Reid remarked amiably.

"But he's going to marry her," Alma protested in a shocked tone.

And Leslie found herself saying severely, "He sounded devoted to her when he told me about her."

But Reid merely smiled lazily and said, "Maybe, maybe."

And before Alma could voice any of the half-dozen questions that were obviously trembling on her lips, there were sounds of arrival in the hall, and a moment later Oliver came into the room in company with a girl whom they all recognized immediately under Reid's description of "dark, desirable, graceful and with lots of oomph."

In the first flurry of introductions, Leslie found, to her unutterable relief, that she was able to display complete self-control and a nice, impersonal pleasantness. But after a few moments, she found that her desire to sink into the background had been gratified beyond anything she had intended. In some curious way, she was overwhelmed by the personality of Caroline Frenton, and she had the peculiar, and most unwelcome, impression that her own coloring faded to something neutral and subdued beside the vivid drama of the other girl's looks.

Caroline was one of those people who naturally, and without either insistence or conceit, took the center of the stage. No wonder Oliver had fallen for her! No wonder Reid hoped to win her back!

Leslie, in a fascinated, helpless way, found herself irresistibly assuming the identity of the sisterly, rather uninteresting friend who wished Oliver well without being of any particular importance in the scheme of things. She struggled against it. In that moment, she would have been gay and fast and a little outrageous, if she had known how to be. But Caroline held everyone's attention. And not until she stopped before Reid, with a startled exclamation, did the spell of her enchanting invulnerability seem, momentarily, broken.

"Why, *Reid!* Where did you spring from?"

"France, darling. On a visit to my charming relatives."

Immediately there was an outburst of explanations, in which Alma firmly took a leading part. Caroline contented herself with giving Reid a slow, pulse-disturbing smile, while she said to Oliver, "He is one of my old flames, darling. But there's no need to call for pistols for two."

"I don't intend to." Oliver gave her an answering smile, which Katherine afterward described as "besotted," and then turned on Reid an absent, indulgent glance of compassion that said as plainly as words that he was sorry for the poor fellow who was a back number, but had no intention of losing any sleep over him.

Oliver was talking energetically to Morley. But Caroline, who seemed able, in spite of her slightly lazy manner, to keep track of most of what was going on around her, smilingly terminated her conversation with her host and drifted over to a seat nearer Leslie.

"Oliver has told me so much about you," she said, in a perfectly friendly tone. "I feel I know you better than the others, somehow."

"She's the easiest one to know. Aren't you, my

sweet?" Reid said. And Leslie knew from his tone that he was looking down at her with an air that must be bordering on affectionate.

"Well, I wouldn't know about that." Leslie's voice was beautifully controlled, but her pulse leaped excitedly, for into the other girl's lazy, smiling eyes had come an entirely different expression. She was looking above Leslie's head at Reid now, and there was deliberate challenge in her face.

"And how do you spend *your* time, in this rural retreat?" she asked him, in an easy, mocking tone employed only between people who know each other very, very well.

"In the pleasantest way possible. Getting to know my cousins better," Reid assured her. "Especially this one." And to Leslie's amazement, amusement—and a little bit to her indignation, too—she felt him drop a light, but unmistakable kiss on the top of her head.

For the life of her, she could not keep herself from glancing at the other girl, to see the effect on her, and she was a good deal startled to see Caroline's fine nostrils flare with some sudden emotion, and the line of her white teeth show for an instant on her lower lip.

Faintly embarrassed, Leslie looked quickly away again, and as she did so she encountered Oliver's astonished and angry gaze.

She gave a slight, audible gasp as, with a sort of breathless, icy exhilaration, she recognized something of the feelings that had prompted that expression. For the first time for days, Oliver had emerged from his happy bewilderment. And the shock that had accomplished that miracle was the disagreeable discovery that someone else apparently considered he had a right to be affectionately possessive toward a girl he had taken happily for granted all his life.

CHAPTER FIVE

LIKE ALL FAMILY PARTIES where most of the people know each other well, this one kept on forming into little groups, disintegrating and regrouping, in a very informal way. And it was not long before Oliver detached himself quite naturally from his conversation with Morley and drifted casually into the group comprising Caroline, Leslie and Reid.

At first, Leslie thought he was seeking to rejoin his beloved, from whom he doubtless felt he had been separated long enough. But, after a minute or two, it dawned upon her that it was to her he wished to talk.

Caroline and Reid were getting on splendidly, in an exchange of gay and rapid cross talk that kept things balanced on that curious knife edge between intimacy and remoteness, only to be maintained when the protagonists are both amusing and quick-witted.

"Come and tell me how your parents are reacting to the new position, now they are getting used to it," Oliver said to Leslie, and skillfully extricating her from the position of conversational buffer state in which she had found herself, he drew her over to one of the deep window seats, and sat down there with her.

As soon as they were established, however, in a reasonable degree of privacy, he seemed to forget his kind interest in her parents' welfare, because, without pressing the inquiry further, he looked across the room at Reid and said, "So that's the fellow who has cut you all out with Great-Aunt Tabitha."

"Oh, that isn't quite how we feel about him, you

know," Leslie protested, forgetting that this was exactly how they had felt about him twenty-four hours ago. "He is really very nice, and seems anxious to act in a most generous way."

Oliver was unimpressed.

"And what form does his generosity take?" he inquired, with a slight note of irony in his voice.

"He thinks father should regard himself as morally entitled to some of the money at any rate, and he appears ready to go to a great deal of trouble to convince him of the fact."

"All of which entails his staying on at Cranley Magna for some time, I suppose."

"Naturally."

There was a rather pregnant silence. Then, without any finesse at all, Oliver said, "I can't say I like his manner toward you."

"Why, Oliver ...." Leslie was divided between amusement and a certain tenderness for him in his newfound concern on her behalf. "He is very nice to me, I assure you."

Oliver frowned.

"Leslie, you mustn't take it amiss if I say that you girls are almost too sweet and naïve too keep certain types in their place. I mean, it's all very well for Morley and me to treat you with brotherly intimacy and ... well, affection. But, hang it! That bounder's only known you since yesterday. What did he think he was doing, kissing your hair?"

Leslie bit her lip very hard. Mostly to keep herself from saying exactly what Reid *had* thought he was doing, kissing her hair. And a very successful maneuver it appeared to have been, too.

"He doesn't mean anything serious, Oliver. He's very free and easy in his manner, I know, because ...."

"Much too free and easy."

"He regards himself as more or less of a relative."

"Nonsense." Oliver seemed more annoyed than soothed by this view. "Does he regard himself as more or less of a relative of Caroline's, too?"

A little startled by the change of attack, Leslie glanced quickly across to where Caroline and Reid were still sparring enjoyably.

"Well . . ." she began, seeking for words to reassure Oliver, without actually descending to an untruth.

But she had no need to worry, for he went on immediately, "Not that Caroline isn't well able to look after herself." He smiled reminiscently, and something of his natural good humor returned. "I don't worry about her. She can take the measure of anyone, and she has evidently handled him well before."

"Ye-es," murmured Leslie, overwhelmed with astonishment that Caroline should awake no protective feelings in Oliver, while she herself, for the first time in their joint existence, seemed to strike him as someone in need of support and advice.

"It's you I'm worried about," Oliver went on, with a degree of earnestness that might, perhaps, have been called brotherly but certainly transcended anything Morley would have presumed to display on her behalf.

"You really don't need to worry, Oliver!" Leslie was beginning to grow restive in her role of foolish, unprotected innocent. "Believe me, I am perfectly capable of managing Reid Carthay—or anyone else, come to that."

As she said the words, she knew they were not strictly true. Managing Reid Carthay—though in a sense other than that in Oliver's mind—had proved beyond her once or twice already.

"Well, my dear, of course I don't want to interfere," said Oliver, who quite obviously did. "But, as you know, I've a good deal of brotherly . . . ." He stopped, as though suddenly discovering something that surprised him. "Well, no, 'brotherly' isn't quite the word, I sup-

pose. But, anyway, I've always regarded you girls as
very much my concern, and particularly you, Leslie.
You must forgive me if I was taking a bit too much on
myself. But what I wanted to say was that you'd better
keep this so-called cousin at a distance, and if you have
any sort of trouble with him, just let me know."

"Thank you, Oliver. I will," Leslie promised rather
meekly. "But I really don't expect any trouble."

"Then don't encourage him," Oliver retorted, with an
unusual spurt of irritation. And he seemed a good deal
surprised when Leslie laughed.

Oliver and Caroline stayed for about an hour. And
when they had taken their leave, the Greeves, in the
manner of families, immediately embarked on a delightful, though not unkindly, inquest on the newcomer.

Aware as she was of Reid's particular place in things,
Leslie felt rather uncomfortable for the first few minutes. But she very soon realized that she was worrying
herself unduly. It would have taken much more than a
gaggle of Greeves to disconcert Reid Carthay.

"She's very good-looking," remarked Alma—always
quickest off the mark when it came to personalities.

"She's exactly as Reid described her," replied Morley.

"You must have known her very well, Reid." Katherine glanced at him in idle curiosity.

"Reasonably well," Reid agreed, but seemed otherwise disinclined to join in the discussion.

"I mean . . . it was clever of you to describe her right
away so accurately and in so few words."

"A very beautiful and attractive girl," remarked Richard Greeve at that moment, in a tone that silenced all
other comment. "I am just a little surprised that she
took anyone so . . . ordinary as our good Oliver."

And, with this final and rather depressing dictum on
Oliver, Richard Greeve made his exit.

Leslie looked after him with a vexed laugh. But Morley said, "For once, I'm rather in agreement with papa, I think. I also am a little surprised that she took Oliver. And as I said before, I don't think she sounds—and I don't think she is—Oliver's cup of tea, either."

"Then perhaps this will be one of those cases when there is a slip between cup and lip," Reid suggested lightly. "Coming into the garden for a breath of air, Leslie?"

Part of her—the responsible, conscientious part of her—very much wanted to refuse. But although she despised herself for wanting to talk things over with him, Leslie could not, for anything, have resisted the urge to hear what Reid had to say when none of the others were nearby.

She nodded in a casual, friendly way, and they went out together into the warm dusk.

For the first few minutes they strolled in silence, each perhaps intending that the other should start the conversation. Then he said reflectively—almost softly, "I'd forgotten how beautiful she is."

"Forgotten!"

"Oh, only in the final, sharpest sense. I had a clear picture of her in my mind, of course. But no mental recollection ever really supplies that final glow of color or clarity of outline. It's like having a beautiful lamp, without the light inside."

"Yes. I know what you mean. You're still . . . very much in love with her, aren't you, Reid?"

"Lord, yes! Sometimes I wish I weren't. But there'll never be any other girl for me."

"Even . . . if you don't get her?"

"I shall get her, Leslie."

She held her breath for a moment and tried to steady the beating of her heart.

"Was it something that happened this evening that makes you so sure of that, Reid?"

He didn't answer her at first, but seemed to follow his own thoughts on some rather dark path. Then his attention came back to her with a start and he said, "What did you say? Yes, of course. Everything that happened this evening. She isn't for him, my sweet." He was in his characteristic, half-mocking mood of self-confidence again. "And she knows it as well as I do. It won't take so very much to make her think again."

"And what about Oliver?" Leslie inquired rather flatly.

"Oliver?" Reid laughed suddenly and rather shamelessly. "Oh, he's restive and possessive about you already. Did you see the way he looked when I kissed you?"

"Yes. I did. And you ought to have been ashamed of yourself, Reid. It was taking things too far."

"Nonsense! Did he say so?"

"He did, as a matter of fact."

Reid gave a shout of laughter. Triumphant laughter.

"What did I tell you? Fate unkindly mixed up the characters in this little drama, and all we have to do is unmix them. Oliver is already wishing irritably that he had the right to protect you from my attentions."

"Reid!" She was half-vexed, half-amused. "That doesn't alter the fact that he is, at this moment, very much in love with Caroline."

"Every man is in love with Caroline when he first knows her," Reid declared carelessly. "Even your father felt romantic stirrings when she smiled at him."

Leslie's reluctant laugh admitted the probable truth of that. But aloud she only said, "That would make her rather an uncomfortable person to be married to, I should have thought."

"Divine discomfort," Reid countered easily. "But, allow me to say, a discomfort that I could tackle very much better than your Oliver."

"I suppose you are right." She glanced at Reid in the faint evening light and, seeing the brilliant, wicked smile he gave, she thought she could well imagine that he could manage even Caroline.

"Reid," she said almost timidly. "How . . . I mean, what...."

"You mean—what is the next move?" he prompted her airily. "Though you are rather too nice a girl to choose your wording to sound as though you're scheming."

She pressed her lips together.

"Well," she said at last, "let's be honest before everything. What *is* the next move?" And she paused to pick a withered flower head from one of the rose bushes.

"I think," he said, pausing beside her, "that the next move is for you to become engaged to me."

She straightened up and looked at him.

"What did you say?"

"Just exactly what you thought I said, sweetheart. And don't tell me that you don't know what on earth I am talking about, because of course you do."

She was completely silent, all her protests and indignant denials dying on her lips.

"You mean," she said slowly at last, "that the shock of seeing you apparently belonging to someone else is all that is needed to make her realize it's you she wants?"

"I was thinking a little of Oliver, too," he replied modestly. "How do you think he will take the news of your engagement to me?"

"Oh!" For a moment she saw again Oliver's disturbed, dissatisfied face as he warned her against allowing Reid too many liberties. "He'll . . . I mean, he would just hate it."

"A healthy bit of hate," remarked Reid in an amused tone.

"Reid, sometimes you terrify me, with your ruthlessness about what you want and your confidence that you're right!"

"And you," he said, laughing a little and putting his arm around her, "are much too timid for this job. Don't endow other people with your own delicacies and scruples. You're sweet, and I wouldn't change you for the world. But can't you see that Caroline and I are much more violent, ruthless, earthy creatures than you are?"

"I wasn't thinking of you and Caroline so much," she said rather faintly. "I was thinking of Oliver."

"Well, then, Oliver, I suppose, is much more your own kind. Don't you think you ought to rescue him from Caroline?" And he laughed softly and kissed the tip of her ear.

She was completely still. So still that he drew her back lightly against him without any resistance on her part. For a few moments they were silent. Then he realized suddenly that she was crying. Not stormily, as she had wept the previous day, but quietly, with the tears slipping rather helplessly down her cheeks.

"Leslie, don't!" He was surprised, and a good deal dismayed, and on a sudden impulse he gathered her in his arms as though she were a child. "What's the matter, sweetheart? I didn't mean to tease you as far as that. What's wrong?"

She hid her face against his shoulder for a moment, and was understood to say that she hated herself.

"Yourself? Oh, no!" he exclaimed in amused protest. "Really, that's terribly illogical of you. You can hate me, if you like, or Caroline, or even Oliver. But not yourself. You're much the nicest person in this setup."

"Oh, I'm *not*!" She dried her eyes on the handkerchief he offered her, and gave a faint smile of protest. "I . . . I hardly know myself, ever since I learned that Oliver didn't love me after all. I don't seem to have any . . . any

dignity or decency or proper standards at all. I couldn't
have believed that I'd even entertain the idea of faking
an engagement with one man, to make myself more desirable to another. And yet, when you talk to me about
it...."

"I know—I'm a plausible scoundrel," he said regretfully, and smiled at her.

"No, you're not." To her own great astonishment, she
put up her hand and just touched his cheek. "You're
bold and perhaps a bit ruthless and cruelly realistic. But
I don't think you're a scoundrel. You honestly think
you have the greater claim on Caroline, don't you?"

"Sure." He was watching her rather closely.

"I *think* I think so, too."

"Come, that's something."

"And I do honestly believe that, in the long run, I
could probably make Oliver happier than she could.
Though of course it's terribly easy to deceive oneself
over anything that matters so much."

"Terribly. But I'm sure you're right there," he said,
smiling.

She paused, as though unwilling to follow the line of
argument further. But, characteristically, he cleared the
next fence for her.

"In fact," he said, "you agree about the probability of
its being generally desirable that I should marry Caroline, and Oliver should marry you, even if we argue
from the highest motives. What really worries you is the
idea of our achieving that by a bit of lighthearted deception."

"Lighthearted?" She looked at him with rather shadowed eyes, and queried the word a little reproachfully.

"Certainly. Don't you think you could rather enjoy
being engaged to me on a purely temporary basis? If we
do this thing at all, we may as well enjoy it."

"I haven't said I will do it," she whispered hastily.

"No."

He did not elaborate on that, as though willing to let her make up her own mind in the final analysis. And then he was so still that she had the curious impression that he was like a bird-watcher, who feared to make the slightest movement lest he should frighten away something he thought almost within his grasp.

"Reid...how long would we have to...keep it up?"

"What, darling?"

He bent his head down to hers, because her question had been so low that it was almost impossible to catch.

She repeated the words, curiously aware of a nearness that was not only physical.

"The engagement? Not very long, I imagine."

"And then, when it had served its purpose, it could be...dissolved quite easily."

"Of course."

"I wish I didn't feel so ... mean about it. As though my one thought were to take away the girl Oliver wants."

"Dear heart, you won't take her away, if she truly loves him. Remember, if Oliver is the man she wants, your being engaged to me won't make me any the more desirable to her."

"No, that's true." Leslie glanced up with a relieved smile. "It's only a sort of...of test."

"If you like to put it that way."

She thought she did like to put it that way and, though she drew a long sigh, a much more satisfied and contented look came into her face.

He watched her, with a sort of indulgent amusement.

"Well, when do we announce the engagement?"

"Oh ...." Her glance came quickly to his face again then. "We shall have to do *some* leading up to it, Reid. After all, I only met you yesterday."

"Don't you think I might have swept you off your feet?"

She smiled and said, "No." But in her heart she thought he probably was the sort who swept one off one's feet.

"Perhaps the real argument is that I'm not the kind to *be* swept off my feet," she said. "Give me a few days, Reid."

"Whatever you say. But don't make it too long."

"I promise," she said rather soberly. And they went back into the house together.

Only Morley and Katherine were still in the drawing room and, glancing around, Leslie asked absently, "Where's Alma?"

"Why, gone to bed, of course. Long ago." Katherine looked at her curiously. And only then did it dawn on Leslie that she and Reid had been out in the garden a very long time, and that both her brother and sister looked a little oddly at her because of it.

"I didn't realize it was so late," she said, and felt a certain embarrassed annoyance that she should have put herself in that position. Then she realized that, quite unwittingly, she had planted the first interested sense of query in their minds, and she supposed she ought to be glad of it.

She went and sat by Morley, and asked him in a low voice how he was feeling, because once or twice during that harassing evening she had thought he looked more than ordinarily pale and drawn, and her anxiety returned in full force now that she saw him directly under the light.

He put down his book and smiled at her.

"Not too good. But not too awful, either."

"What about having Dr. Bendick look in tomorrow?"

"He's going to. There's a specialist coming down from London, too."

"Morley!" She was overwhelmed by remorseful anxiety, and her own affairs were completely forgotten. "Is there something wrong?"

"Not more so than usual. Don't get excited."

"But I didn't know anything about this."

"It was necessary. Oliver arranged it all. He told me this evening that it was all fixed."

"You mean that you've been feeling lately that you're in need of more ... of different treatment? Haven't you been as well as usual, Morley?"

"No. There's been a slow deterioration and—"

"Oh, why didn't you tell me, dear?" she exclaimed in a tone of loving concern.

Morley smiled at her.

"Because you girls get in a fearful flap over nothing," he countered with brotherly candor. "Besides, we've none of us exactly needed something extra to worry over lately. There was nothing you could have done, Leslie, even if you'd known. Except worry—and I'd rather you didn't do that. I only told you now because you're bound to know about the specialist tomorrow, and it might be a bit of a shock if I'd said nothing in advance. But he's supposed to be a splendid man—Sir James Trevant—and old Bendick seems to think he might not only be able to deal with the present trouble, but even perhaps do more for me than anyone's managed to do before. So, for heaven's sake, look on the bright side, and don't think that the mere arrival of a specialist means something disastrous."

Leslie paused when she reached the top of the stairs, because she saw that the light was still on in her mother's room, and the idea came to her that perhaps her mother most of all would need convincing whenever she declared her newfound passion for Reid. After all, to her mother she had been frankest about her feelings for Oliver. It was going to be rather difficult to reverse all that in so short a time.

Leslie knocked on the door and, in answer to the rather subdued "Come in," she entered.

Her mother was not in bed. She was standing by her dressing table and, as Leslie came in, she turned upon her daughter a face that bore faint but unmistakable traces of tears.

"Why, mother, what is it? What are you doing?"

Leslie came quickly across the room. But she stopped short before the dressing table and, silent in her turn, she stared down at what was spread out there.

A pretty, old-fashioned jewel case stood open, and half its contents were spilled out, as though an eager hand had turned them over and rejected them. There was nothing there of genuine value. Only—in that most pathetic of phrases—of sentimental value. And even as Leslie gazed down at the pretty little oddments with a suddenly tightened throat, her mother said, "They aren't worth much, I'm afraid—not any of them. Except to me. There's my engagement ring, of course. . . . " She turned it nervously on her delicate hand.

But Leslie broke in almost sharply because she was so moved, "Don't be silly, mother dear. We haven't reached the point of having to sell your jewelry yet. Whatever made you think of it?"

"Morley."

"You don't mean he said something. . . ."

"No, of course not! But he's very ill, you know, Leslie. Much more ill than any of us realized. I spoke to Dr. Bendick half an hour ago on the telephone, when you were out in the garden. He thinks almost certainly that Morley will need immediate and expensive treatment . . . possibly even an operation."

"I . . . didn't know." Nervously and absently, Leslie fingered the trinkets in her turn. "But didn't Reid tell father that he wanted to help? That he thought . . . ."

"Morley wouldn't have it."

"But of course he would! How ridiculous!"

"He's very proud, Leslie. In the way injured people

are sometimes proud. It's as though they can't help making more difficulties for themselves. He regards Reid as a stranger. He wouldn't take money from a stranger."

"But Reid isn't that! He's a relative—well, almost a relative."

"Oh, no, dear." Her mother shook her head sadly. "We all repudiated that relationship when it didn't mean any advantage to us. Morley isn't the one to accept it now, just because we need money. Your father will be much easier to convince than Morley."

"It's absurd to call Reid a stranger, mother," Leslie reiterated almost angrily. "He doesn't even *feel* like one. He...he seems like one of the family."

Her mother smiled faintly but protestingly.

"I only wish he did, Leslie. I only wish he *were* one of us. I know I shocked you yesterday when I said I wished Katherine would fall in love with him and marry him. But when I think what it would mean to have him for a son-in-law, I can hardly keep myself from asking Kate if she doesn't rather like him, after all."

"Oh . . . . " Leslie said. Then she looked at the coral brooch she had absently picked up, and she felt her color rise as she forced a protesting smile to her lips. "Please don't say anything like that to Kate...."

"Oh, I wouldn't really!"

"It makes me feel a little...jealous."

"Jealous, Leslie! Of whom, my dear? I don't understand."

Leslie laughed nervously. And the nervousness was genuine, if the laughter was not.

"Why does Kate have to be the only one cast for the role? Why shouldn't I be considered, too?"

"You, my dear? But I thought.... You told me...."

"Oh, mother, I don't know really what's come over me," Leslie cried, with enough genuine fervor to make that ring true. "But . . . aren't people sometimes swept off their feet?" Reid's useful phrase. "Can't you imagine that Reid might seem . . . seem overwhelmingly attractive to some girls? I mean . . . crazily attractive. To the exclusion of everyone else."

"Yes," her mother said slowly. "I can imagine exactly that. Only I wouldn't have expected it to happen with you."

"Nor would I," Leslie said breathlessly. "But he asked me to marry him just now, mother. And I . . . said I would."

"Leslie! Because you felt you should, or because you wanted to?"

"Because I wanted to. Because I love him," Leslie said with complete recklessness.

And then her mother sat down and cried tears of such aching relief that Leslie could only stand and stare at her in unutterable dismay.

CHAPTER SIX

"DON'T, MOTHER," Leslie said at last. "Don't cry like that. It isn't necessary. I . . . I thought you would consider my news good news."

"But I do, darling!" Her mother dried her eyes and managed a pale smile. "You mustn't think I'm unhappy. I was crying with relief, I think. Relief and . . . and a sort of dismay that it can mean so much to me that my daughter should marry a rich man. Oh, Leslie, are you sure?"

"Sure that he's going to marry me?" Leslie smiled faintly in her turn.

"No, no! Sure that you love him. But how can you be, in so short a time? It's absurd even to talk of it. But do you feel truly that you will love him? It's not just that marrying him would be such a wonderful, wonderful solution to our troubles?"

"I'm not marrying him for his money, mother, if you want my categorical assurance of that."

"I can hardly believe it." Her mother clasped her thin hands together and smiled less uncertainly this time. "Even Morley couldn't resent help from his brother-in-law."

"No," Leslie said, and suddenly her lips went dry. For, in her eagerness to convince her mother, she had overplayed her part—laid the emphasis where no emphasis was due.

The term "brother-in-law" had roused her to a realization of the hollowness of the comfort she was urging upon her mother. Engaged to Reid she might be, for so long or short a time as was necessary to bring Caroline to her senses. But there was no question of a marriage.

Impossible to draw that delicate distinction for her mother. But Leslie could already see the complications ahead, already visualize the cruel disappointment that must follow on the false hopes she was raising.

Well, I can't help it, she thought desperately. *Let mother take what comfort she can from it while it lasts. I suppose I can come to some sort of arrangement with Reid. I have no pride where Morley's good is concerned. If anyone could make Morley well, I'd be satisfied to have Reid pay, in any identity—my fiancé, my husband-to-be—anything.*

Aloud, she said, "Go to bed, mother dear. You don't need to worry anymore. Everything is going to be all right . . . you'll see."

Her mother kissed her lovingly.

"Leslie darling, you know I wouldn't have you sacrifice your own happiness, even to give Morley the best chance in the world, don't you? But if, in a little while, when you've given yourself some time to think things over, you are sure you love Reid, then nothing would make me happier. It isn't only because of what it will mean to all of us, I think he'd make any woman he loved very happy."

"Do you, mother?" Leslie smiled as she returned her mother's kiss, but she spoke a little too absently, too impersonally for a girl who had just fallen in love. "I wonder what makes you sure of that?"

"Reid himself, I suppose." Her mother looked reflective. "He could make one *un*happy, too, I am sure, because of his obstinacy and his ruthlessness. But there's an underlying generosity of spirit to which one could always appeal. If he truly loves you, you would be . . . safe with him, Leslie. I know that."

"I'm . . . sure of it," Leslie said, but again there was that slight nervous laugh.

"But all the same, dear, think a little longer before you become actually engaged."

"Oh, no . . . ." Leslie, who was at the door, turned quickly for a last word. "No, mother. He is set on our announcing our engagement as quickly as possible. I . . . I want that, too."

And then she went away, before her mother could say more, aware that she had burnt her boats with a speed and thoroughness beyond anything she had intended.

She thought of seeking out Reid, late though it now was, and telling him that they were already completely committed to their faked engagement. But she suddenly felt so limp and so emotionally weary that she knew she could handle no more scenes of this sort. Certainly no scenes with anyone of Reid's vitality and exuberance.

Tomorrow would be soon enough to tell him. Tomorrow would be soon enough to enter on the dangerous piece of make-believe they had undertaken.

In spite of a restless night, Leslie was up early and, having already seen from her window that Reid was out in the garden, she went downstairs and out into the bright morning air.

"Reid. . . . " She came up to him, where he was standing watching, with a good deal of amusement, the indefatigable labors of a large striped spider.

"Hello, there." He threw a casual, friendly glance at her. "Come and look at this fellow. If we carry out our intentions with half his persistence we won't do badly."

"Aren't spiders usually supposed to be 'she'?" Leslie said. But she came up and stood beside him.

"You're probably right at that." He grinned, though he did not take his eyes off the spider. "That probably accounts for the persistence. I'm going to rely a lot on you in the coming weeks."

"You may," she said quietly, and he glanced at her quickly.

"You haven't changed your mind, eh?" He smiled and drew her arm through his.

"On the contrary, I've already made a good beginning with the job, by telling my mother."

"Good God!" His admiration was unmistakable that time. "And did she believe you?"

"Certainly she believed me."

"I'm a little surprised she would."

"Oh, no . . . ." She stopped, and then her voice dropped a little as she said, "Mother so terribly *wanted* to believe, poor darling!"

"Because of your father?"

"No. Because of Morley," Leslie said. And then told him what her mother had told her the previous evening.

He listened in silence. Then he said, "You know I will do everything he will let me do, don't you?"

It was almost matter-of-fact in its simplicity and its completeness, this undertaking of his. And suddenly she found herself remembering what her mother had said about his having an underlying generosity of spirit.

She pressed Reid's arm with more intimacy and gratitude than she knew.

"It isn't incumbent on you, you know. Mother said that Morley probably would accept help from his brother-in-law. But you and I know that you'll never really be in that position."

"Hell! What does that matter?" Reid retorted with careless impatience. "I've been trying to hand back some of this damned money to your family ever since I acquired it. Don't spoil a good opportunity by saying it doesn't really exist."

Leslie laughed softly. She was beginning to know by now that even when he swore it usually meant either that he was moved or in high good humor. She could not imagine that he ever swore in temper.

"Mother says you have an underlying generosity of

spirit," she said thoughtfully. "I think I see what she means."

"Nonsense." He spoke a little roughly. "I usually get a good return for anything I do."

She looked skeptical and, for some reason, a trifle amused.

"Is that so? What return are you expecting for helping Morley?"

"Well, you're obliging me pretty handsomely, aren't you?"

"By becoming engaged to you? I thought that was for our mutual pleasure and advantage."

He laughed reluctantly, gave her an odd glance and said, "I don't know you in this mood."

"No," Leslie said with a slight sigh. "I don't know myself very well, either. Perhaps I'm demonstrating that Oliver was wrong when he declared I was too nice and naïve to keep a man like you in his place."

"He said that? The man's a fool," Reid declared contemptuously.

Leslie flushed and pulled her arm away, indescribably annoyed by this insult to Oliver.

"He is nothing of the sort! And he knows me a great deal better than you ever will," she cried angrily.

"Then he should know that you could manage most men with one hand tied behind you," was the astonishing thing Reid said.

"You . . . think that?" Her anger was quenched in her surprise, and, to tell the truth, in a peculiar feeling of gratification, too.

"Of course," he said, but a little disagreeably for him. "Shall we go in and receive the family's congratulations?"

"If you like." They turned and strolled toward the house together. "But mother may not have told them yet."

"Then we will tell them."

The family were already gathered at the breakfast table when they came in, only Morley's place being empty. And when Leslie saw the ceremonious air with which her father rose to address her, she realized that he at least needed no telling.

"My dear, this is wonderful news," he began.

But his wife caught his arm and said urgently, "Richard, I told you Leslie may not want it to be public property yet."

"We don't mind," Reid said, with a smile at her.

"What isn't to be public property?" demanded Alma, who had preternaturally acute hearing where semisecrets were concerned.

"Dear Leslie and Reid...."

"If I may be allowed to make my voice heard," boomed Richard Greeve in rich, but slightly sulky, tones, because he was annoyed at having his speech of congratulations mangled like this, "I would like to congratulate my dear daughter—" he put a paternal hand on Leslie's shoulder "—and my good friend Reid—" by reaching rather uncomfortably far he was able to clap his other hand on Reid's shoulder "—on their engagement. I can only say that it is a marriage that will give me the very greatest happiness and satisfaction."

The news of Leslie's engagement, viewed through the rosy spectacles of Alma and her father, proved something of an antidote to the news about Morley—broken now for the first time to Alma and Katherine. But afterward Leslie's elder sister caught her by the arm and drew her into one of the window alcoves, and demanded with some urgency, "You aren't marrying Reid in order to repair the family fortunes, are you?"

"No, of course not, Kate. Why should you think so?"

"Well, you know we did talk over the idea of acquiring rich husbands a night or two ago."

Leslie laughed.

"And you didn't show any signs of being shocked by the prospect then," Leslie reminded her. "In fact, you were rather frank about your plans for yourself."

"Oh, for *myself* . . . yes," Katherine agreed almost naïvely. "But you're made for something different. I don't think you'd be happy, Leslie, if you married for anything but love."

"Well, I'm marrying for love," Leslie retorted. And she spoke with a sudden fierceness, so that Katherine fell back, almost literally, in surprise, and somehow found herself unable to continue the discussion.

It was an anxious, uncertain day, until Dr. Bendick and the specialist had come and given their verdict on Morley. Leslie particularly, consumed with loving care for her brother, found it increasingly difficult to remember that she was also supposed to be the happy, newly engaged girl, with sweet distractions to temper her sisterly anxiety.

Only Reid's watchfulness and, to tell the truth, his tact kept her from giving herself away on more than one occasion. He did also offer her some very real comfort when he heard who the specialist was whom Dr. Bendick had summoned.

"Oh, Trevant is reckoned to be almost a miracle man at his job," he assured Leslie confidently. "Do you mean to say you've never heard or read about him?"

"Only to remember the name. Is he *really* so good, Reid?"

"He has a tremendous reputation—both as a personality and as a surgeon. A very handsome man, you know—rather like an elderly film star from all accounts—and something of a show-off. But a genius. Even his most jealous rivals concede him that."

When Sir James Trevant arrived, Leslie caught a glimpse of him before he was taken into Morley's room, and the little she saw confirmed much of what Reid had

said. The famous surgeon was a tall, handsome, picturesque figure. But there was about him also that indefinable aura of success and calm confidence that belongs
only to the man who *knows* he cannot fail.

Even so, Leslie remained in a state of nervous sus-
pense, and she passionately wished it were she, rather
than her parents, who would have a chance of speaking
to him afterward. Would her mother, in her anxious
diffidence, or her father in his pompous attitudinizing,
make it perfectly clear that no expense was to be spared
in the effort to make Morley better?

"The ideal would be, of course, to have Morley re-
moved to Trevant's own nursing home for a few
months," Dr. Bendick said after Sir James had left.
"But . . . I don't know. . . ." He fondled his chin meditatively and looked round sympathetically on his old
friends with an expression that showed plainly that Oliver had told him of their recent reverse.

"Then please make the arrangements as soon as possible."

It was Reid who spoke, and Dr. Bendick swung
around in his chair to regard him.

Mrs. Greeve murmured a belated introduction, and
her husband, in the tone of one who endorsed what his
personal representative had said, remarked, "To be
sure. Let the arrangements be made as soon as possible."

Leslie saw the faintest grim smile lift the corners of
Reid's mouth. But he emphasized his own words with
an authoritative little nod to Dr. Bendick, and the doctor, rising with an extremely satisfied look, prepared to
take his leave.

Mrs. Greeve then remembered social and friendly ob-
ligations, and charmingly expressed their pleasure and
congratulations on Oliver's engagement.

"Well, I don't know, I don't know. I suppose young

people always think they know their own minds best,"
Dr. Bendick said a little obscurely.

Whereupon Richard Greeve, unable to resist the
temptations of family competition even in the matter of
engagements, smiled indulgently and remarked, "We,
too, have had our share of surprises in this line. Our
dear Leslie—" she had never been more dear to him
"—presented us this morning with a *fait accompli*. She is
engaged to our young friend here."

Dr. Bendick, like most elderly experienced practition-
ers, was a shrewd man and a close observer of human
nature. If his son's engagement had surprised—and a
little disappointed—him, Leslie's engagement quite obviously astounded and troubled him.

Instead of offering the congratulations that Richard
Greeve evidently expected, he frowned at Leslie and
said bluntly, "Very sudden, isn't it, Leslie? What's the
idea?"

"These things *are* sudden, my good friend," declared
his host genially, clapping him on the shoulder, because
that was one of his favorite ways of displaying congrat-
ulation and pleasure. "We mustn't let ourselves grow
too old to remember that, you know."

Dr. Bendick glanced at his neighbor as though he
thought him a likable ass, which he did. But to the girl
he had hoped to have as his daughter-in-law he repeated, "Isn't this rather too sudden—too impulsive?"

"I don't think so." Leslie managed to smile at him,
though she knew he was much more difficult to deceive
than her parents. "I know it seems like that. But as ... as
father says, it sometimes does happen that way."

A little shaken by this encounter, Leslie found she
very much disliked the prospect of having to give her
news to Morley and submit to what she guessed would
be the most searching cross-examination of all. This, at
least, she told herself suddenly, she would delegate to

someone else, and as the door closed behind Dr. Bendick she turned impulsively to her mother.

"Mother, will you tell Morley about Reid and me? I don't expect he ought to have many visitors or much excitement today. You'll be able to judge the best time and the...the best way of telling him."

Her mother, knowing how close Leslie and Morley were, looked surprised.

"Don't you think he'd rather hear from you yourself, darling?"

"No." She was emphatic in her sudden nervousness. "I don't want to explain and ... and argue anymore. I want just to...enjoy my engagement."

"She wants to come with me and buy her ring, Mrs. Greeve," Reid remarked carelessly, for he, probably more than her mother, had sensed the note of nervous strain in Leslie's voice. "I'm going to run her over to Pencaster in my car this afternoon, so that she can choose what she likes."

"Oh...." began Leslie, rather startled.

But the small exclamation was lost in the smiling, indulgent emphasis with which her mother said, "Why, of course! Enjoy yourself, darling, and don't worry about Morley. I'll tell him. You go and have every bit of pleasure you can. I don't want you to remember this as a day of anxiety. It's a day of great rejoicing, too."

"Thank you," Leslie said softly. And for a moment the difference between reality and romantic deception weighed on her so heavily that she felt the tears come into her eyes.

The moment she and Reid were alone together, she exclaimed, "I don't know that I meant to force things as far as this!"

"As far as what?" He looked surprised.

"Oh, a ring and...and everything."

He laughed in good-humored derision.

"There's woman's logic for you! You haven't winced over the boldest measures, and now you shy at a little thing like a ring."

"It's not a little thing, Reid. It's a ... a symbol."

"Well, come along and let's find you the handsomest symbol we can," he returned, unmoved.

And presently Leslie found herself beside him in his car—with a fleeting thought for how much had happened since she last sat there—driving through the alternating showers and sunlight to Pencaster.

Reid, as she had expected, proved well able to find exactly what he sought with the minimum of fuss.

Leslie thought she remembered hearing once that "diamonds always command their value." And so, with the vague idea of ensuring Reid against too heavy a loss when the ring had to be returned, she chose a diamond ring, with a light but curiously beautiful setting.

"Like it?" he asked with a smile, when it was safely on her finger.

"Very much," Leslie assured him.

But a few minutes later she saw him glance at it restlessly and a little moodily, and she supposed he was thinking, not unnaturally, how much he would rather have put it on another girl's hand. To be confident of the success of one's little escapade was one thing. To enjoy the counterfeit of what should have been a cherished reality was very much something else.

On the whole, she felt sorry for Reid in that moment.

He took her out to tea, and she realized, rather to her amusement, that they found each other good company. Not that they had a great deal in common, she supposed. At least, not in their special interests, or their way of looking at life.

But perhaps having so few secrets from each other made a difference. They had been so ruthlessly frank with each other, stripping every bit of romantic or even social pretense from their relationship, that what was left was a good-humored, half-cynical understanding of each other that made conversation remarkably refreshing and simple.

When she came to think of it, each probably knew more of the other than anyone else of their acquaintance.

It was a sobering thought, that. To imagine that this smiling, confident half-stranger sitting opposite her knew more of her inmost thoughts and feelings than her own mother did—or her brother or sisters, or the man she really loved.

"It's an odd relationship," she said aloud.

He raised his eyebrows and smiled at her, but made no pretense of not understanding her.

"Rather satisfying though," he countered consideringly. To which she agreed, with a half-reluctant laugh.

And then Caroline came into the restaurant, and right up to their table and almost past them before she realized that they were there.

"Hello, you two!" She paused, her slow beautiful smile in evidence, but her big dark eyes widening, as Reid rose to his feet to greet her with careless friendliness. "What brought you here?"

"We . . . drove into Pencaster to have tea," Leslie said a little quickly, because she flinched suddenly before the final dramatic disclosure.

"We drove into Pencaster to buy an engagement ring," amended Reid good-humoredly. "Leslie and I have just got engaged."

Leslie watched, fascinated, as the lazy calm of Caroline's usual expression splintered before her eyes. Just for a moment she saw the dark, strong currents of emotion that ran below the usually unruffled surface, and she was not quite sure if she were frightened or elated or apprehensive.

Then Caroline, with a tremendous effort, regained her normal expression, and in a voice that hardly even trembled she said, "Engaged? But you can't be. Oh, no, really that's quite impossible."

CHAPTER SEVEN

THE COOL REASONABLENESS of the tone in which Caroline uttered her objection to their engagement shook Leslie. It seemed to imply that she was about to produce some overriding argument that would reduce to absurdity the very idea of such an engagement—real or fictitious.

But if Leslie's sense of security crumbled, Reid's showed itself cheerfully impervious to this form of attack. On the contrary, it was he who reduced Caroline's objection to absurdity by saying, "My dear, incredulous Caroline, it is not only possible, but an accomplished fact. There is no known cause or just impediment, you know," and for a moment his eyes glittered dangerously. "Why should you think an engagement between Leslie and me so impossible?"

Caroline was shaken in her turn.

"It's so sudden . . . such short notice." She was still standing by the table, having brushed aside Reid's invitation to join them, and her glance drifted puzzledly over Leslie, as though seeking to find in her some explanation of the inexplicable.

Leslie withstood the glance admirably, and said quite gently, "*I* feel as though it's very sudden and almost unbelievable, too. But that doesn't make it any less . . . less wonderful."

She thought for a moment that she had overplayed her part. The breathless way she had said "wonderful," for instance, sounded almost touching, even to her own ears.

But Reid seemed well satisfied.

"You see, my dear," he said pleasantly to Caroline. "I think you are answered."

It was not in Caroline to be completely routed. She remained for a minute or two, offering cool congratulations now, and asking perfunctory questions, such as when were they going to be married?

"Soon," declared Reid, before Leslie could commit herself. "Leslie has had too much worry lately. I want to give her a little happiness and gaiety."

"In Paris?" Caroline's glance slid over him with a degree of significance that Leslie curiously resented.

"We might spend part of our honeymoon in Paris," Reid agreed. "What do you say?" And he smiled an indulgent query at Leslie.

"That would be ... lovely. I've never been to Paris."

"You'll enjoy showing Paris to someone who's never seen it, won't you?" Caroline said.

Then she apparently saw an acquaintance at the other side of the room, and she nodded carelessly to Reid and Leslie and moved away.

For almost a minute after she had gone there was silence between them. Then Reid said softly and amusedly, "The value of shock tactics."

"Do you think they worked?"

"At least we arrested her attention."

"Oh, certainly."

Reid glanced at her sharply.

"Weren't you satisfied with our degree of success?"

"I don't know. . . ." Leslie moved uneasily. "You know her better than I do. But I thought it was more a question of . . . of pique, than horrified realization of a mistake on her own part."

He frowned impatiently.

"One doesn't expect to reverse the whole position at one blow."

"No, of course not. Only...."

"Yes?"

"Oh, sometimes it seems to me that we just plunge deeper and deeper into a very doubtful situation, without achieving much of what we hope to do."

He grinned, however, at that.

"You're not a natural gambler, darling," he said, patting her hand as it lay on the table. "I know what shook you. The talk of a Paris honeymoon, wasn't it?"

She flushed and laughed reluctantly.

"No . . . not really. Except that it seemed to make everything alarmingly real and detailed, all at once. But it's all right. I was just being silly, I expect." Then she glanced at him curiously and said, "You both know Paris very well, don't you?"

"As far as two people in love ever know a place that is simply a background to their happiness."

She gave him a smile of warm sympathy and exclaimed impulsively, "Oh, I hope you get her, if you really want her so much!"

"Definitely withdrawn your backing from Oliver, eh?" he asked teasingly.

"Oh . . . Oliver . . . ." She had forgotten about him for the last half hour. "I wasn't backing Oliver anyway, as you most vulgarly put it. Surely I've done enough to show I don't want him to marry Caroline!"

"Yes, yes. I was really thinking of how eagerly you canvassed dear Oliver's happiness, as being the most important thing in all this."

"I still think his happiness most important," she countered a littler resentfully.

"Fine," he said rather dryly. And then they rose to go.

She thought how amazing his self-control was, that he even managed to leave the place without so much as a backward glance at where Caroline was sitting. If it had been Oliver who was sitting there, could she have done as much? She thought not.

At home once more, she received the fresh congratulations and comments of her family on her beautiful engagement ring, and contrived to look happy and carefree, even when Alma put her own thoughts into words
with a reflective, "It seems to make it much more *real*,
when you wear a ring."

Leslie turned away quickly and said, "Did you tell
Morley, mother?"

"Oh, yes, dear. He said he thought he'd seen something like that coming."

She laughed incredulously and with a good deal of relief.

"He said *that?* In what tone exactly?"

"How do you mean?"

"Well, was he pleased, dissatisfied, skeptical,
shocked...what?"

Her mother laughed in her turn.

"I couldn't say, my dear. You'll have to find that out
yourself."

"Can I go and see him now?"

"No. I think I'd leave him to rest, if I were you. He
was a good deal exhausted by the examination and is
probably sleeping now."

"Of course."

"But if you want to do something, I wish you'd pop
over to Dr. Bendick's surgery, Leslie, and get his medicine."

"Why, yes. I'll go at once."

Not at all displeased to escape on her own and have a
respite from playing her rather exacting role, Leslie
slipped on a coat and went out by the side gate. It was a
pleasant walk to the Bendicks' house, and if she only
knocked at the office entrance she could probably escape seeing either the doctor or his wife, and avoid any
further comment or question. Oliver, she was sure,
would have returned to his job by now.

But in this she had miscalculated. Leslie had only just received the medicine at the hands of the assistant and turned away to take the path home through the woods, when Oliver's voice hailed her, urgently—even a little peremptorily—and he came quickly along the garden path to overtake her.

"Hello. I thought you'd gone back."

"No. I've some extra time. But what's this extraordinary story father's got hold of?"

"About Morley?"

"No. About you." He fell into step beside her, with a purposeful air that said that he was accompanying her until he had found out all he wanted to.

She felt her heart flutter dangerously and her breath come a little unevenly, but she managed to say quite calmly, "Oh, you mean my engagement. I know it's very sudden, but it's quite true. I'm engaged to Reid."

"But you can't be! I never heard of such nonsense. You've not known the fellow a week. And, anyway, he's simply not your sort."

"Oliver dear, are you so sure you know what 'my sort' is?"

"Of course I do. I've known you all your life, haven't I?"

And never guessed the most important thing about me, thought Leslie, with faintly bitter amusement.

Aloud she said, "I don't know that that helps much. I was just a bit surprised that Caroline appealed to you quite so powerfully. I don't think even the best of friends are very good at guessing things about each other when it comes to falling in love."

"But, Leslie . . . ." He was evidently deeply disturbed, and she thought how much she loved him for it. "I don't think you even know this Reid well enough to have made up your mind properly. You're usually so well balanced, so . . . so sane and unhurried. This whole business isn't a bit like you."

She laughed—without much effort, because it made her feel lighthearted, and just a little light-headed, too, to have Oliver worrying about her in this way.

"But, Oliver, you can't expect anyone to be well balanced and sane over falling in love. It's a contradiction in terms, surely?"

He looked at her gloomily and said, "You really are in love with him, then?"

"Why, of course. You don't think I would ... would marry for any other reason, do you?"

"Yes. That was the very thing I was afraid of," he assured her with some grimness. "I thought you were marrying him because he'd inherited all your great-aunt's money, and you didn't see how the hell the family was going to manage if you didn't do something about it."

"I suppose it's bound to look a bit like that," she conceded, with a judicial air that she privately thought rather good. "But that isn't what made me decide, Oliver. Really and truly it isn't."

"You're asking me to believe that you've fallen so hopelessly and romantically in love with this comparative stranger that, in the course of a couple of days, you're quite sure you want to spend the rest of your life with him? Leslie, do think again. I'm sure you're making the most dreadful mistake."

"What you mean is that you don't like him," Leslie retorted, and because she did like Reid, the faint hostility in her voice was genuine.

"I can't stand him," agreed Oliver with great heartiness. "I think he's self-confident to a degree, and cynical and arrogant, too. And I think you're being silly and willfully blind, just because he's good-looking and rich and excessively male."

"Oliver!"

There was an astonished silence. Then he said, in a slightly shamed tone, "I'm sorry I called you silly."

"Oh, it's not *that*." She brushed the mild insult aside. "Do you really see Reid like that?" she asked curiously.

"More or less."

"You're quite wrong, you know." Suddenly she found herself most anxious to justify Reid to Oliver. "He isn't a bit like that."

"Not self-confident?" he queried dryly.

"Well...." She laughed.

"Or arrogant, or cynical? My dear Leslie, use your excellent judgment!"

"It's a very good-natured cynicism, Oliver. I rather like it."

"You *rather like it?* Good God, girl!" exclaimed Oliver, who had never addressed her like that in her life before. "Do you realize you're talking about the qualities of the man you say you love? One doesn't 'rather like' things about the person one proposes to marry."

"Do you more than rather like the way Caroline looks at other men?" she asked suddenly, and then was astonished that she could speak so coolly and ironically to Oliver.

"Caroline doesn't enter into this," he said stiffly, after another astonished little silence.

"Oh, yes, she does! Believe me, I'm quite as much surprised at your choice as you are at mine," exclaimed Leslie, suddenly feeling some wise precaution in her collapse, so that she had a horrid feeling that she was going to say things for which she would be sorry, while being powerless to stop herself. "If anyone had told me beforehand that Caroline was the kind of girl to attract you, I'd have said 'Nonsense' in my turn. But it's your own business. I'm not trying to dissuade you from marrying her, am I? I've given you my congratulations and decided to mind my own business. Even if you decide afterward that you made a mistake and don't want her after all, I'm not going to say 'I could have told you.' It's for you—"

"I should hope not, indeed!" He was nearly as indignant as she by now. "And what on earth should give you the idea that I might change my mind about Caroline? I never heard of anything so ridiculous, and I very much resent it."

Aloud she said, making a great effort to speak calmly, "I'm sorry, Oliver. It wasn't very tasteful of me to use your own circumstances to reinforce my argument. But we're both being rather angry and ill balanced about this. Don't you think we ought to agree not to interfere with each other?"

"Leslie . . . ." He took her arm, and he, too, had lost his anger now. "I don't mean to interfere, my dear. But you mean a great deal to me . . . you're like my own family. . . ."

"I know. Like a sister," she said, and somehow she kept the irony out of her voice that time.

"Well . . . something like that. I can't help knowing that neither of your parents would give you much good advice over this. Your father will see only the material advantages, particularly to himself, and your mother, bless her, will be swayed this way and that by her sentiment and her desire to think the best of everything. Morley's in no condition to take a hand. I *can't* let you do this thing without protesting. There was a time when you'd have conceded my right to do so. I seem to have lost touch with you, Leslie, and I don't know whether I am to blame myself or not."

"You're not to blame in any way," she assured him quickly. "And I don't really mind your talking to me, Oliver dear. Only I can't have you speaking against Reid. You must see I can't."

He was silent for a moment. Then he said in a more reasonable tone, "Well, you won't rush into a hasty marriage, will you?"

She thought of what Reid had said to Caroline that very afternoon.

"We haven't made any definite decision yet." That much she had to concede him. "But no one has a very long engagement nowadays. I don't expect you mean to yourself, do you?"

He looked faintly restive once more at being side-tracked onto his own affairs.

"We haven't decided, either," he said rather curtly.

"Well, then, couldn't we both agree to leave our affairs in a pleasant state of uncertainty for the moment?" They had reached the side gate of Cranley Magna by now and she turned, smiling, to face him. "Are you coming in?"

"Not tonight. I expect you're right about leaving our affairs uncertain for the moment. At any rate, your affairs."

"Oh, no, Oliver!" She laughed. "I didn't mean it in that sense. What I meant was that neither of us seems likely to rush into an irrevocable decision in the next twenty-four hours, so let's agree not to question each other closely." She held out her hand in a friendly way, but with an air of decision.

He took her hand a little doubtfully, as though he still hardly knew what to make of her in this new mood.

"No hard feelings about my interference?" he said, with a wry smile.

"None at all, Oliver. I'm a good deal . . . touched that you should care enough about me to feel so anxious."

"Good Lord, Leslie! You know how much I . . . well, anyway, I wouldn't have any unhappiness come to any one of you girls if I could prevent it."

"I know you wouldn't." Her tone was still friendly, but a shade colder that time. And she withdrew her hand with a definite "Good night."

But as she turned away he detained her a moment longer.

"Leslie . . . ."

"Yes?" She turned back, a little surprised.

"What did you mean, exactly, when you spoke of the... the way Caroline looks at other men?"

She experienced a disagreeable little shock. Perhaps at being pinned down to her own unwise wording. Perhaps at the discovery that his final thoughts ran, after all, on Caroline.

"I... nothing very much. I spoke hastily."

"But you must have been thinking of something definite when you said that." He looked obstinate and, she thought, vaguely disturbed.

"I'm sorry. I suppose it was a rather... catty remark. It would be nicer—and just as true—to say that she has very beautiful eyes and knows how to use them to advantage. I didn't want to imply any more than that."

He smiled, not entirely satisfied, she saw. Then he said, "She can't help attracting people, of course." And with a friendly wave of his hand, he left her.

As she crossed the lawn, Reid came out of one of the French windows to meet her.

"Was that Oliver who escorted you home?"

"It was."

He glanced at her, evidently speculating on the reason for her curtness.

"Had he anything to say about your engagement?"

"Good gracious, yes! A lecture under three headings. His anxiety, my foolishness and your undesirability."

Reid laughed and began to look as though he were enjoying himself.

"Do tell me what he said about me?"

"No. Your ego is quite sufficiently developed as it is."

"Don't tell me he praised me?"

"Of course not. But to a man of your type, some censure is better than praise.'.

"That's true," he agreed equably. "I won't question you about the particular, then. I'll just ask, in general terms, did he react as you hoped he would?"

"Oh, Reid...." She pushed back her hair with sudden weariness. "I don't know. Sometimes I ask myself what I'm really trying to do. If it weren't too late to turn back, I'd say it's wrong and ridiculous to interfere so arrogantly with the natural course of events."

"There is no natural course of events, my sweet," he told her, smiling, but rather kindly. "There are those who direct events and those who submit to them. You are in the habit of submitting, and it worries you to find yourself moving the pieces on the board, instead of being moved around. But you're tired...." He put his arm around her lightly and, somehow, rather comfortingly. "Don't torment yourself with any more self-analysis. Be satisfied if your Oliver showed signs of being concerned about your welfare and anxious about your future. Stop planning, and let events take their course during the next few days. We have done all the interfering that's necessary for the moment."

"Thank heaven for that," Leslie retorted grimly.

But he laughed, and lightly kissed the side of her cheek. And for no reason that she could possibly define, she felt her spirits rise once more.

During the next few days, to her immeasurable relief, it really did seem that events might be permitted to take their own course. Reid and she had established the idea of their engagement, not only in the minds of the family, but also with Caroline and Oliver. It remained now to be seen what gradual reaction this would provoke.

Twice Caroline telephoned, and each time she unashamedly asked for Reid. He didn't offer to give Leslie his version of the conversations. But she heard snatches of the first one, and again she had the impression of two people who knew each other remarkably well sparring gaily and feeling out each other's defenses.

One afternoon Leslie had the opportunity of a long, quiet talk with her brother. He had kept to his own room since the specialist's visit and now was only waiting for a vacancy in Sir James Trevant's nursing home. Leslie found him in a curiously tranquil, indulgent sort of mood, luxuriating in freedom from the secret anxiety about his health, which, she realized now, must have weighed terribly on his spirits in recent months.

"You feel every confidence in Sir James, don't you, Morley?" she said to him, noticing with delight the brightness of his eyes and the hopeful lift to the corners of his mouth.

"Yes. I have no doubt at all that he can make me better. And if I believed that any man could make me walk again, I should believe it of Trevant."

"Do you mean," Leslie said almost fearfully, "that you think there *might* be a chance of his doing that?"

"I don't know." Morley idly curled the tassel of his dressing gown around his hand. "I only know that *he* thinks there's a chance."

"Did he say so?"

"No. But he has the most expressive face I've ever seen. And I know he thinks there's a faint chance. So faint that he couldn't possibly mention it to me. But that's one reason why he's so anxious to have me in his nursing home, under his own eye."

"Morley! I . . . I hardly dare even think of such a thing."

"Nor I. But the thought of it made the taking of Reid's money more justified, somehow."

"Oh, Morley, you don't have to think of that! Reid told me, with all sincerity, that he would give every penny of Great-Aunt Tabitha's money if it would make you well."

"Because he's in love with you?"

"Oh, n . . . . Well, yes. I suppose so."

"And you took him on those terms?"

"No, Morley. That isn't true."

"Are you telling me that you love him?"

She hesitated only a second before she said, "Certainly."

"Swear it?" He was smiling at her, but his eyes were bright and exceedingly watchful.

She passed the tip of her tongue over her lips.

"I swear that I'm not marrying Reid for his money."

Morley gave her a long, thoughtful look.

"You changed that wording, didn't you?" he said musingly. "I wonder why. You wouldn't swear that you love him."

"Please, Morley, don't go imagining things. Believe me, I had agreed to become engaged to Reid *before* I knew about your needing this expensive treatment."

"Because of the family?"

"No. Because of myself."

He laughed, not altogether satisfied, she saw. But he was too happy and hopeful about his own prospects to question her more closely. Besides, Morley being Morley, he would undoubtedly concede that she had a right to reticence about her own affairs. Having satisfied himself that no specific sacrifice had been made on his behalf, he obviously considered that anything further was, broadly speaking, her own business.

To Leslie's delight and relief, when the summons finally came for Morley to go to the nursing home, she was the one who was chosen to accompany him and see him safely installed. Reid offered to accompany them, too. But Morley was not enthusiastic and, since Dr. Bendick insisted on being of the party, Reid's presence was not really necessary.

For two or three days, Leslie stayed on in London, although Dr. Bendick, having seen his patient safely installed, returned to Cranleymere the same day. She rather enjoyed the curiously detached existence of one stranger among many other strangers in a quiet hotel, and it was wonderful not to have to pretend about herself to anyone. Each day she went to see Morley, so that in those first difficult days he should not feel bereft of everything and everyone familiar. But toward the end of the week he said to her, "If you want to get back to the family—and Reid—you don't need to hang around here any longer on my behalf, you know."

"I'm rather enjoying it, as a matter of fact." Leslie smiled.

"You are? Curious point of view for a newly engaged girl," Morley remarked, with his characteristically quizzical glance.

"Well . . . ." She colored a little. "I meant, really, that anyone can enjoy herself in London for a few days, and I don't want to go until you feel perfectly settled here."

"I am perfectly settled, my dear. And though I enjoy seeing you every afternoon, that can hardly go on indefinitely and may as well stop now as any other time. Besides—" he smiled with that touch of real sweetness that could sometimes irradiate his thin, sardonic young face "—I owe Reid enough. It's not exactly fair to keep you away from him, too."

"Oh . . . ." She looked faintly surprised, because she never could quite get used to the idea that Reid was supposed to be consumed with passion for her. "I dare say. . . . Well, perhaps you're right, Morley."

"I think I probably am," he agreed. And they arranged then that Leslie should return within the next two days, though probably she, or another of the family, would visit him again in a few weeks' time.

As she made her preparations for returning home, Leslie found her thoughts running on ahead of her. To everyone expecting a letter—some news—an event, it always seems that a short absence from home works some sort of miracle. Because one has not been there to watch every post and every change of event, it seems that limitless opportunities must have occurred for the thing one hoped or dreaded to have happened.

As the train drew slowly and reluctantly into the station, she caught a glimpse of Reid's car standing outside.

Well . . . it had been rather fantastic to imagine that Oliver might somehow be there. Reid was perhaps the one best suited to give her the news. And as she came out of the station and he got out of the car to open the door for her, she greeted him with a brilliant smile.

"Everything satisfactory so far as Morley is concerned, I see," he observed. And she laughed and agreed that this was so.

While they drove down the slope from the station and along the first half mile of the road home, she gave him further details about her brother, and the one or two items of personal news about her stay in London. But when they turned into the long, familiar, winding lane that eventually led to Cranley Magna, he slowed the car and, as though sensing that something was coming, she said, "You didn't write to me, Reid."

"No. Did you expect me to?"

"Only if there were . . . something special to tell me."

"There was nothing special to tell you, during the first five days."

She was indescribably chilled and disappointed.

"You mean . . . nothing at all happened?"

"Nothing."

"No . . . news of either Oliver or Caroline?"

"Not until yesterday."

"And then there was some news?"

"Yes."

"Of which of them?"

"Of both."

"Well, then, tell me," she cried, half-frightened suddenly by his manner, though she hardly knew why. "What happened?"

"They were married, Leslie, by special license, yesterday morning."

CHAPTER EIGHT

THERE WAS COMPLETE and stunned silence for perhaps twenty seconds, except for the sound of the motor. Then Leslie cried, "I don't believe it! It can't possibly be true. I simply don't believe it. Is this some ridiculous sort of joke or something?"

"It is not a joke," Reid said flatly. "It's the simple, damnable, inescapable truth. Oliver and Caroline are now man and wife, and as far as we and our schemes are concerned, we can call it a day."

Even in that moment she resented the word "schemes," but these silly details had no significance anymore. She stared at him helplessly, wondering why she had not noticed before that he looked grim and strained.

At last she said, "How did it happen?" Heavily, like one inquiring for details of a fatal accident.

"I don't know."

"Well then, how did you hear about it?"

"Mrs. Bendick telephoned your mother and told her. I gather she and the doctor were a bit upset. But why they did it, or why they decided to act so suddenly, I don't know. And I've been such a complete fool in all my calculations up to now that I'd rather someone else made the next guess."

She was silent again, delving reluctantly into the recesses of her memory. Had there been anything—anything at all—in her conversation with Oliver that could have given her the slightest hint of what was coming?

"He said—" she was speaking her thoughts aloud "—that they hadn't come to any decision about the length of their engagement. Oliver *said* that to me, not two weeks ago."

"Well, they came to a decision," retorted Reid dryly. "A pretty thorough one, it seems."

"But there was nothing...."

She stopped suddenly, and passed her hand over her eyes."

"Oh...wait a minute! I said something stupid...."

"*You* did?"

"Yes. About ... about the way Caroline looked at other men. She...has a special way, you know."

"You're telling me," he said dryly.

Leslie muttered, "Oh, I'm sorry."

"Never mind. Go on. What did he say then?"

"At the time he was just angry, and I more or less took the words back. Then we got off the subject. But, just as we were separating—when we'd been talking of quite other things, I mean, and come to a more or less agreeable understanding—he said, as a sort of after-thought, 'What did you mean exactly, when you spoke of the way Caroline looks at other men?' "

"I thought I got out of it fairly neatly, Reid. I thought I satisfied him. But I think I know now why he was so angry with me. It was not that he felt I did her an injustice. It was that what I said made him really jealous."

"So what?" He stared ahead gloomily at an awkward corner.

"Why, don't you see? Sooner or later that induced him to have some sort of showdown with her about her...her attracting other men. I suppose she protested that it all meant nothing. And to prove it—or perhaps just to seal their reconciliation after they had had a row about it—she suggested they should get married right away. It was the perfect answer to the suspicions that *I* had been fool enough to put into his mind. And Oliver would be swept off his feet by such a gesture, you know. He would fall for it unhesitatingly. In fact, I probably had quite a lot to do with hurrying on the one thing we hoped to delay," she finished bitterly.

He considered that in silence. Then he took his hand from the wheel and patted hers, rather as he had the first time they met. A familiarity which, she remembered, had annoyed her greatly at that time.

"I don't think I'd torment myself with that one, if I were you," he said. And the touch, as well as the words, oddly comforted her.

"I shall always feel I muffed my part, though," she said with a sigh. "And after you had shown such skill in managing her, too."

"Like hell I did!" He laughed rather bitterly in his turn. "I flattered myself I was such a smart fellow, rousing healthy doubt and jealousy in her. Don't you remember, you told me at the time that you thought she wasn't suffering from anything more than pique? Quite right, my dear! And what I was suffering from was willful blindness and egregious conceit."

"Oh, no, Reid!" She thought he was being a little too hard on himself.

"Um-hm. I just couldn't, or wouldn't, accept the fact that she might prefer someone else to me."

"It is rather difficult to accept these things," Leslie said sadly. "Poor Reid! I'm so sorry. In a way, it's much worse for you."

"Hell! Why?" he wanted to know.

"Because you hadn't ever really imagined losing. I'd already had my major shock. *I* could never quite imagine our hopes succeeding."

He laughed reluctantly.

"Sweetheart, I'm most dreadfully sorry, too," he said ruefully. "I'm entirely responsible for waking all sorts of hopes in you which your courage and determination were trying to put to sleep. I wonder if I haven't let you down even worse than Oliver."

"Oh, no, Reid!" Again she felt she could not have him blame himself so completely. "I was just as anxious as you to try what we could do. Well, nearly," she amended.

At which he laughed again and said, "The proportion of blame doesn't much matter now, I guess. Look—we're in sight of Cranley Magna. Do you feel able to face them? Or do you want me to drive around a bit?"

"Oh, no! I'll face them," she exclaimed, with a touch of obstinate pride. "I've learned a little about self-control in the past few weeks and, anyway, I'd be ashamed not to be able to . . . to hide anything like that from the family. Besides, they will be longing to hear every detail about Morley, you know. It wouldn't be fair to keep them waiting."

"Good girl," he said approvingly, and turned in at the gates of Cranley Magna.

It was not so difficult, really, Leslie thought, when they all crowded around her in the drawing room later, eager for the latest news of Morley. They wanted to know how he had looked, if she had left him cheerful, what she thought of the nursing home, and any possible information she might have gleaned about Sir James Trevant himself and his hopes of success.

They were so affectionate to her and, through her, to Morley that, if she concentrated hard on what they were saying and on what they wanted to know, she could almost ignore that great aching blank that had replaced all her hopes and fears and expectations as far as Oliver was concerned.

Until halfway through tea they continued their questions, and she her account of her stay in London. Then at last Alma, who had obviously been bursting with ill-suppressed news on her side for the last few minutes, said, "You'll never guess what *we* have to tell *you*."

"Sorry, Alma. I'm afraid I told Leslie," Reid put in contritely. "Did I steal your scoop?"

"Well—" Alma looked a little dashed "—I didn't think of your being interested enough to tell her. After all, you hardly knew Oliver, did you?"

"True," Reid agreed. "But I did," he added dryly, "know Caroline."

"Yes, of course. I'd forgotten that. But it wasn't as though she *meant* anything much to you," Alma explained comfortably. "Oliver was about our oldest friend."

"Yes, since you put it that way, I do see it must have been a shock to you."

Alma looked surprised.

"Well, I don't know about a shock," she said protestingly. "After all, a marriage is something nice, isn't it?"

"That," Reid assured her, "depends entirely on the parties concerned—and the circumstances."

Richard Greeve gave his mellow, understanding man-to-man laugh.

"All right, my dear boy. No one expects you to take much interest in any marriage but your own at this point. And indeed all of us—now that we have such excellent reports of our dear Morley—can prepare with confidence and pleasure for what I might call that next event in the family's affairs."

For a moment Leslie looked so blank that Reid gave her a warning glance. And, with reluctance, her mind accepted the idea that, to the outside observer, nothing in their affairs had changed. Though Oliver and Caroline might have rendered their engagement a tragic farce from the point of view of Reid and herself, in the eyes of the family she and Reid were as firmly and hap-

pily linked as ever. Not only that. The family's comfortable enjoyment in the good news about Morley depended for what one might call its financial support on
that engagement continuing.

All at once she felt indescribably trapped. She wanted
to cry out against the forces that were being gently and
smilingly arrayed around her. But, even as the idea
came to her, she heard Reid, calmly and pleasantly, answering some specific inquiry that her father had added
to his genial, if heavy, generalization.

"We didn't think of making any very definite arrangements until Morley was home again, sir," he was
saying, aware—as Leslie knew—that an occasional "sir"
tended to put Richard Greeve in an excellent humor.

On this occasion, however, Richard Greeve was more
intent on seeing that no one departed from a line of
conduct that would have the desirable result of providing financial stability without imposing any slight on his
personal pride.

"We don't need to let the affairs of one member of
the family wait so exactly on those of another," he
stated agreeably but firmly. "There is no reason whatever, my dear Reid, for you and Leslie to wait for your
happiness. Indeed, though I deprecate any such un-
seemly haste as Oliver has shown, nothing would please
me ... or my family," he added as an inconsiderable afterthought, "more than to have you and Leslie fix an
early date for your wedding. For my part, I was going to
suggest—"

"Oh, father, do leave us to settle these things for ourselves!" exclaimed Leslie, her nerves drawn taut, so that
she spoke with unusual irritation.

All she had done by her impatient objection, she saw
now, was to fix her father's attention, with offended determination, on the whole question of an early marriage.

"I keep on making mistakes in technique, it seems,"

she said ruefully to Reid later, when they snatched a few moments alone together. "It makes me feel afraid to open my mouth."

He laughed and patted her shoulder consolingly.

"Your father will forget about wedding arrangements in some new interest quite soon."

"Oh, no." Leslie shook her head. "You don't know him, Reid, if you can say that. He's got his teeth into this business now, and just won't let go. Besides . . . ." She stopped, colored a little and looked distressed.

"All right. Don't distress yourself about it. I know quite well that there's the money aspect. The poor old boy feels—not unjustifiably—that he'll be a lot more comfortable when he has a rich daughter than when he merely has a rich prospective son-in-law."

Leslie thought how greatly her father would have resented being referred to as a poor old boy. But the statement, as such, represented the situation exactly.

"I know it must seem hypocritical and inconsistent of him," she said apologetically, "to strike such an attitude of pride and integrity about refusing to take money from a stranger, and then to try, with almost indecent haste, to hustle that stranger into becoming a relative, so that he can profit from the arrangement with almost ingenuous openness. But, Reid, he honestly believes in the essential rightness of both attitudes. Both the pride, I mean, and the genial plundering of a close relative."

"Yes. I've worked that out some time ago," Reid assured her good-humoredly. "And as, in my heart, I consider the money largely his by right, I don't very much mind by what specious argument he can convince himself that he may take it. What does worry me is that, so far, he seems only willing to accept it if it's offered, so to speak, on our marriage certificate."

"Reid, I don't know how you can joke about it! It's terribly serious, you know."

"Terribly," agreed Reid, with a grin. "I feel the bands of matrimony tighten around me every time he calls me 'my dear boy.'"

She laughed reluctantly. And then, because she had been through enough to test the strongest nerves, she suddenly felt the tears come.

"I wish . . . I knew . . . what to do." She had turned away from him, but the unevenness of her voice betrayed her.

"Sweetheart, don't cry." He came up behind her.

"I'm not crying."

"Well, don't sound so exactly as though you are, then," he said, and took her in his arms.

"Oh, *Reid!*" She turned against him, and found the strangest comfort in being held very tightly while she sobbed once or twice.

"Now look, honey, nothing's ever so bad that one can't make something of it." He ruffled her hair, with a half-amused, half-tender gesture. "You've had altogether too much to handle lately. But, although I made such a howling fiasco of the Caroline-Oliver business, I promise you I'll get you out of this somehow."

"Oh, it isn't really that. At least, of course, it is partly. Only everything seems so . . . so out of hand and I can't see my way ahead one little bit, and . . . . Well, anyway, that's how it is."

"I know. And, most of all, the thing you didn't mention. It must be the very devil losing your confounded Oliver all over again."

She was silent. Then she nodded her head slightly, because he seemed to expect her to. But to her immense surprise she realized that, until he mentioned Oliver, she hadn't really been thinking of him.

"We can't do anything for the moment but go on with this engagement. You do see that, don't you?"

"Yes, of course." She wasn't really paying much attention to him. She was turning over in her mind the incredible fact that "losing Oliver all over again," as Reid put it, was not the agonizing central point of her distress, as it should have been.

He has really *gone this time. He's Caroline's husband,* she told herself, like someone pressing on a doubtful tooth to see if it really ached.

But there was a sort of dull acceptance, rather than anguished protest, and she told herself that she was probably past feeling very acutely about anything that day.

"Feeling better?" inquired Reid at that moment. And she laughed, because she knew there was no reason why she should be feeling better, except for his comforting presence. Only she did.

"Much better," she said, and flung her arms around him, as she had that time in the hall when she had first known that she could call on every penny he had to make Morley well. "Much, much better, Reid. Because one can't help feeling better and more hopeful when you're around. There's something about you. It's your...your special gift to mankind."

"Make it womankind," he said, and kissed her. Not just a light, teasing kiss. But the kiss of someone who had shared some varied experiences with her and valued her after the test. She felt the rather hard line of his cheek against hers, and knew the most real and primitive consolation of all—the sheer physical contact of someone in whom there was the answering spark of understanding.

It became clear during the next few days, however, that no one else in the family was thinking of her engagement in terms of prolonging it. Only from the point of view of shortening it.

Even Alma said importantly, "I'll have to know fairly soon about the wedding, because I suppose I'll be a bridesmaid, and it'll mean getting a day's holiday from school."

"Maybe we won't have the wedding until your next holidays," Leslie said, with seeming carelessness.

"Oh, Leslie! You *couldn't* delay it as long as that! Besides, I think it's mean of you to talk about having it in the holidays. What a *waste* of a perfectly good reason for having a day off."

Alma looked so reproachful that Leslie had to laugh and say that at least she would keep that important point in mind.

"Anyway, what's the need for delay?" Alma threw at her as a parting shot, as she flounced off into the garden on some affairs of her own.

"Yes, Leslie dear. What need *is* there for delay?" asked her mother, the only other person who had been in the room when this conversation took place.

"There isn't any, mother!" Leslie tried to look perfectly natural and mildly surprised at the question. "Some people like a longer engagement than others."

"But I thought . . . . The whole impression in the beginning was that you were both swept off your feet, and the sooner you were married the happier you would both be."

"Well, of . . . of course. But there's no *frantic* hurry. It's just that father has this bee in his bonnet about it."

"No, darling, it isn't. No one wants to hurry you. Not even your father really." This was said without complete conviction. "Only, there's no denying that if you are both sure of your own minds, in the . . . the peculiar circumstances, an early marriage would certainly solve a lot of difficulties. As it is . . . ." She broke off and sighed.

"You mean that the day-to-day financial position is pretty grim?"

"I'm afraid so. I hate to sound as though we're only waiting to sponge on Reid, but . . . ."

"It isn't sponging! Reid told me himself that he regards Great-Aunt Tabitha's money as largely father's own due."

"I know, Leslie dear. He told us that, too, and I'm quite sure he means it. But you know what your father is. He keeps on saying that he wants the position regularized."

"Well!" cried Leslie in amused indignation. "I can think of better ways of describing my wedding."

Her mother smiled, too. But passingly, like someone whose worries were too near for her to indulge in real laughter.

"He means, you know, that once the family is one, so to speak, there is a perfectly just basis for discussing how the money should be divided. Until then, he says he feels he can't accept any of the money without putting himself in the undignified position of a man who 'touches' his prospective son-in-law for a loan, on the strength of doubtful expectations."

Leslie inwardly cursed her father's preposterous hairsplitting, which dictated stubborn pride in one set of circumstances and almost ingenuous exploitation in another.

"I know, darling. I do understand." She glanced affectionately at her mother, and wished anxiously that she looked less harassed. It made one feel so horribly guilty.

"I wouldn't have spoken like this, Leslie . . . it's so entirely your own business, dear, I do know that . . . only—" for a moment her mother smiled almost brilliantly "—I feel so reassured by the way you look at Reid sometimes."

Leslie was astounded.

"The way I look at Reid?" she repeated. "How do I look at him?"

"Oh, I was thinking of the way your face lights up

when he comes into the room, as though you feel that, the moment he appears, any worries are over."

"Oh . . . oh, yes. Of course."

"And then sometimes you have such a sweet look of . . . discovery, darling." Her mother's smile became very affectionate. "As though you hardly know yourself how fond you are of him. Lots of engaged girls become very gay and confident in their attitude, you know. You aren't a bit like that. It's as though you feel you're trembling on the verge of a still greater discovery any moment."

"Mother, you . . . you're fanciful." Leslie had gone very pale suddenly.

"Oh, Leslie dear, you mustn't mind my noticing these things. Mothers do like to flatter themselves that they have a very special understanding about their daughters. At least, sentimental mothers do. And I suppose I'm sentimental," Mrs. Greeve said, without regret.

"You certainly are." Leslie laughed, trying to make the laugh sound indulgent and understanding.

But it came out rather shaky and uncertain.

"Do I . . . really . . . look at Reid like that?"

"Occasionally, in the past few days. You needn't be so taken aback, dear." Her mother was genuinely amused. "It's quite a proper way for an engaged girl to look."

"Yes . . . I know. I only thought . . . ."

Her voice trailed off into dismayed silence. But as her father's voice was heard in the hall just then demanding to know where his wife was, Leslie's silence passed unremarked. In fact, Mrs. Greeve got up and hurried out to her husband, and Leslie was left alone in the room.

Slowly she went to the mirror over the fireplace and studied her own pale reflection.

Stupid of her to have lost her color like that. She hoped her mother had not noticed. But even now her eyes widened and darkened again as she thought of the words that had given her such a shock. A shock of half-acknowledged realization.

"It's as though you feel you're trembling on the verge of a still greater discovery any moment," was what her mother had said. And her mother was a singularly acute woman where people were concerned.

"It couldn't be true! Oh, Reid, it couldn't possibly be true!"

Leslie dropped her head on her arms on the mantelpiece, and tried to recall her horror and heartbreak when she had first known that Oliver was lost to her. In that moment, she would almost have welcomed a return of the first anguish she had suffered that evening in the wood. But she felt—she admitted it ruthlessly—a sort of nostalgic regret. Nothing more.

But perhaps I am just getting over him . . . quite naturally. It doesn't have to be a case of one passion driving out another. Mother is just being fanciful. And so am I. She raised her head and looked at herself for a long time again. "Or am I?" she said aloud at last.

"Are you what, my sweet?"

He had come into the room without her noticing, but at the sound of his voice she swung around to face him, coloring, so that no one could have guessed how pale she had been only a few minutes ago.

"Oh, I . . . ." She laughed embarrassingly. "It's a bad habit, talking to one's own reflection. I think I was just asking myself if I . . . if I were really managing the present situation well," she finished hastily.

"So far as a masterly inactivity can be described as doing things well, we are managing splendidly," he assured her. "But it's no good concealing the fact from ourselves . . . we are merely marking time. There *will* be a moment when we simply have to make a decision. And, as far as I can see, we're neither of us one whit nearer knowing what that decision will be."

"If we could only make father see things in a more sensible light. . . . " Leslie sighed. But, even as she said the words, she knew they were a waste of time and breath. Her father had taken up a particularly obstinate line on the question of the inheritance, and—as an extension of the same question—her marriage. Nothing would move him now.

And as though echoing her thoughts, Reid said regretfully, "It's damned difficult to unstrike an attitude. Your father couldn't do it without a considerable sacrifice of pride. Can you see him climbing down? Because I can't."

"No, no. Of course he wouldn't do that. I know once or twice in the past he's made things dreadfully difficult by taking up a stand that he couldn't abandon without looking silly. Nothing would change him now. I do believe he would literally rather starve, or . . . or even sacrifice Morley's best interests. But then . . . what can we *do?*"

Reid gave her a rather quizzical glance. Then, with his hands in his pockets, he strolled slowly up the room and back again.

"There are two courses open to us, my pet. There always have been. We can either tell the exact truth and have your father order me from the house, refuse all financial help and generally plunge you into disaster while I return to France or . . . . "

"Oh, Reid!"

At the thought of his going she was assailed by such cold despair that she felt literally sick.

"Or," he said reflectively, "we could, quite simply, go on with this marriage."

"You . . . you mean in actual fact?"

"I mean in actual fact."

"But . . . . " She turned away from him, in case he should see from her face that, for her, the heavens had suddenly opened and the angels sung. "But . . . you said . . . there would never be any girl but Caroline for you."

"Sure." The angels stopped singing, and the world went gray again. "Sure. And you said there would never be any man but Oliver for you. We were both right, of course. But the question is—what does any sensible person do when he can't have the thing he has set his heart on?"

"He . . . he makes do with the second best," she stammered, fascinated into saying what she supposed he wanted her to say.

"It sounds a bit ungracious, put into words," he said with a laugh. "But it applies to both of us equally. We know an awful lot about each other, honey, so that we don't have to pretend the least little bit. Look here. . . ." He turned again and came toward her.

Don't take me in your arms! she thought wildly. *Don't take me in your arms, or I shall give myself away.*

But he didn't put his arms around her. He took both her hands lightly in his.

"It's like this. We've both lost out on the thing that means most in the world to us, but we have a good deal in common, Leslie, besides that experience. After a rather bad start, I think we've always liked—possibly admired—each other. I know I admire most things about you. I can give you a pretty good married life, and I can make your family happy and free from anxiety. It's not a bad basis, my dear."

She stared at him wordlessly. And after a moment he said, "There's no need to hurry. Think it over. But, if you marry me, I promise that most of your problems will be over. If you don't . . . God knows when or how they can be solved."

"I know," she said almost in a whisper. "I know . . . that's true."

But she was not really thinking about that. At least, not much.

She was thinking of her mother saying that she sometimes looked as though she were trembling on the verge of a great discovery. She had made that discovery now.

It was Reid she loved. The long pretense had become a reality. But only with her. Not with him.

CHAPTER NINE

LESLIE WONDERED AFTERWARD how long she stood there, with her hands slack in Reid's, while she tried to make up her mind on the most momentous question of her life.

If she married him, she knew now, she would be marrying the man she really loved. But he had, as far as a man can say such a thing, said that he did not love her. He liked her.

Did one ever find happiness in a marriage where one loved without return? Was there not, on the contrary, a very special and poignant suffering implicit in the very meaning of the phrase?

But if she did not marry him, he would go away.

Quite simply, that was the alternative. And she knew that she could not face it.

There would be problems and anxieties to face, if he went away. There would be explanations and possibly reproaches. But none of these really weighed with Leslie. She got no further than the fact that if he went away from her, she simply could not bear it. That was what mattered. If he went away from her, she did not want to face life anymore.

"Do you want to think it over until tomorrow?" he asked at last, and the sound of his voice made her start.

"No," she said a little hoarsely. "Oh, no." For at the suggestion of delay she was suddenly overwhelmed by panic in case *he* should change his mind, or say that, after all, they must not act without more thought. "I have made up my mind, Reid."

"Sure?"

"Quite sure." Her voice cleared, and she looked up and smiled at him. "I'll marry you."

"Darling, will you really?" He gave a half-incredulous little laugh, and kissed her upturned face. "I thought all that grave consideration couldn't end in anything but a refusal."

"I...I had to weigh up everything carefully."

"Of course."

She wished she had not said that then. It made her decision sound such a poor and passionless thing. In that moment she longed, from the bottom of her soul, for a breathless, reckless, glorious romance with Reid.

She felt her heart beat more quickly and her blood race in her veins at the thought of what it must be like to be the real object of his bold, generous, almost arrogant love.

But that was not for her. Only Caroline had been able to command that. She must be satisfied to be liked and admired.

In one last surge of panic, she almost drew back even then. But she steadied herself, and heard him say, "When is it to be, my sweet? Alma has already lectured me on the grave responsibilities of a bridesmaid."

"What, you too?" Leslie laughed, and she was pleased to hear that it sounded a perfectly natural and self-possessed laugh. "She was here not an hour ago, telling me that I should upset all her plans for the term if I didn't make up my mind soon."

"Well, we can put her out of her misery now. And your father, too," he added, as a good-humored afterthought.

"Yes." Leslie thought of her mother's pathetically controlled anxiety, and her not very successful efforts to hide her longing for happier, safer times, when she didn't have to think of money—or the lack of it—every hour of the day.

"I suppose we may as well make it soon, then." She tried so hard to make her tone cool and judicial that she succeeded in making it flat and indifferent.

So much so that she must have piqued him, for he laughed a little angrily and, catching her in his arms, exclaimed, "'May as well' is no term to use to your bridegroom, you cold little fish! This *is* going to be a marriage, you know. Not a business arrangement."

"Yes. I . . . I know."

"And I'll stake my male pride on your finding it a bit more interesting than you seem to think," he added almost threateningly, although he was laughing. "When do you marry me, eh?" And, bending her back lightly against his arm, he gave her a long, hard kiss on her mouth.

"Reid!" She struggled free.

"Don't you like it?"

"I . . . ." She liked it so desperately that she was afraid she could not hide how much. "Of course, but . . . I can't very well answer your question if you go on kissing me like that."

"It has been done." He was suddenly in a remarkably good humor. "But we'll take one thing at a time, if you like. When are you going to marry me?"

"Next . . . next month."

She had nearly said "next week," because when he held her and kissed her as he had just now, it was almost impossible not to say exactly what was in her mind. But she retained enough self-control to produce a reasonable answer. An answer that would show that she was ready to play her part, and yet not betray the wild eagerness and rapture that shook her at the very thought of being married to him.

"Next month. . . ." He repeated her answer thoughtfully. "Fine. Early next month?"

"If you like." But she smiled at him, to show that she "liked" also.

It was perfectly safe to like. Only one must not love.

They told the rest of the family later that evening, and received approving congratulations all around. Indeed, to Leslie, in her secret, frightened joy, it seemed that these were the only congratulations that mattered. The earlier ones, when she had first become engaged, had not meant anything. This was the real thing now. More real than even Reid guessed.

"It wasn't anything I said, was it, darling?" her mother asked anxiously when she got Leslie alone. "I mean . . . you aren't hurrying things on more than you want just because I poured out my worries to you?"

"No, mother. It's all right." Leslie was very calm and tranquil about that. "The idea of an early wedding was . . . was Reid's. And I found I liked it very much indeed."

"I'm so glad! I'm so terribly glad for you . . . and so relieved for your father," she added naïvely.

Leslie smiled.

"Yes. He looked as though it were his own wedding, when we started to tell him of our decision."

"Well, I can tell you why now, dear. Why he and I are so specially relieved and delighted. We heard from the nursing home today—from Sir James. He does think there is a very reasonable chance that Morley may even walk again, if we can afford to let him go in for a long and expensive course of almost experimental treatment."

"Mother! How marvelous! Why didn't you tell me before?"

"Because—I'm ashamed to say it—our acceptance did depend on Reid giving his full financial support."

"But he'd promised that anyway!" Leslie cried impatiently.

"Yes, I know. But I don't need to explain your father's attitude all over again."

"No, indeed!" Leslie laughed protestingly.

"Well, since you know his rather unreasonable views so well, you can see that what the situation amounted to was that the beginning of Morley's treatment more or less depended on the date of your wedding. I didn't want you to know that, Leslie, until you had decided your own future on personal considerations. We owed that to you, my dear. But I can't tell you how glad I am that you have finally decided for an early marriage."

"I'm glad, too," Leslie said soberly. "For Morley's sake as well as my own."

"There'll be a lot to arrange in a very short time, of course." But her mother sounded pleased rather than harassed by the prospect, Leslie noticed, and she guessed that wedding preparations were very dear to her mother's ingenuous and rather extravagant heart.

"We want things rather quiet, you know," she said, but she smiled indulgently at her mother.

"Of course, dear, of course."

But a look of enjoyable vagueness was beginning to come into Mrs. Greeve's beautiful dark eyes, and Leslie thought, *She's beginning to think in dozens! I'll have to keep a curb on her. If Reid is going to pay out all that money for Morley, I'm not going to have him saddled with the expense of an extravagant trousseau for me.*

Reid, however, had different views. Or so it turned out when she broached the subject to him and warned him to be firm on the question.

"Why shouldn't you have a swell trousseau?" he wanted to know. "Don't you like pretty clothes just as much as the next girl?"

"Of course. But that isn't the point."

"It's quite a good point, so far as I am concerned."

"But, Reid, in the circumstances, it's faintly dishonest. They will try to spend a lot of *your* money on what is, after all, *our* obligation. I don't mind exploiting you, or anyone else, for the sake of Morley's health. But I don't want an extravagant outfit at your expense."

He grinned at her.

"Don't you? I rather like the idea, personally."

"It's . . . it's not strictly necessary." She looked faintly put out.

"It doesn't have to be," he assured her. "I hope you don't regard me as the sort of man who sees his bride only in terms of strict necessity."

She laughed reluctantly.

"Sweetheart," he said, "you haven't had much fun out of your marriage affairs up to now. Relax and enjoy yourself for the next month. Regard your parents as the inheritors of at least half of the Tabitha fortune, and shop accordingly. The bills will be paid, I promise you, and it doesn't much matter through whose banking account they pass. It's the same money. And if we stop to work out each time whose money it really is, we're none of us going to enjoy any of it."

There was a good deal of common sense in this—as in most of Reid's flippant utterances—and in the end Leslie accepted his advice.

Her mother—completely reassured by this new mood—accompanied her to London on a whirlwind shopping tour, and there, of course, they took every opportunity to see Morley.

To both of them it was obvious that he was already a different person. Hopeful, even confident, he greeted them like a man who *expected* everything to go well. Except for an occasional characteristically dry remark, there was no trace of that good-humoured but cynical melancholy that had distinguished him for so many years, and Leslie and her mother could hardly hide their joy at the change.

Afraid even then to raise too many hopes, they both at first avoided speaking much of the future. But Morley, to their surprise, showed no such reserve.

"I'm sorry I can't be at your wedding, Leslie dear,"

he said. "But I promise to be in circulation before the first christening, and if you'll make me godfather to the Reid heir, I'll undertake to carry out my duties as actively as the rest."

She laughed rather tenderly at that, and the tenderness was not all for Morley.

"It's a bargain," she promised.

"How does father get on with his prospective son-in-law now?" Morley asked with candor.

"Very well," Leslie assured him.

"Even to the extent of agreeing to accept half his fortune?"

That was the old Morley, and his mother murmured a not very convincing protest.

"Oh, yes. I think they are thrashing that out with father's lawyers while we are away. And you needn't be deprecating about it, mother," Leslie said. "Reid's perfectly right in saying that father had a moral claim on part of the fortune. The only difficulty was in devising the exact circumstances in which father would agree to see it in that way."

It was Morley who laughed indulgently that time.

"Well, I hope someone has managed to convey to Reid how grateful I am," he said more soberly. "Whatever moral rights there may be about the division of this inheritance, Reid would have been perfectly within his rights to hold on to the lot. And I'm well aware that, actually or figuratively, he has financed the miracle that's going to put me on my feet again."

His sister glanced at him affectionately.

"It's all right, Morley. I conveyed all that to him."

"Ye-es." Her brother looked at her with a certain amount of amused indulgence. "I suppose you certainly chose the best way possible of expressing the family gratitude. Happy, Leslie?"

"Divinely happy."

"It's odd . . . I thought I knew you so well. I was certain you were very much in love with Oliver."

"So was I. Certain, I mean."

"And it was a mistake?"

"Not in the sense that I misread my feelings at the time. I *was* very romantic about him. Particularly when I was a good deal younger." Both her mother and brother smiled indulgently at that. "But I suppose it was the old story of being in love with love—and the most attractive man I knew well at that time. After Reid came, there . . . wasn't anyone else."

"A good thing it was Oliver that Caroline fancied, then, and not Reid," observed Morley with candor.

"Thanks a lot! You mean you wouldn't back me in any competition?"

"Not against Caroline, my love," her brother insisted teasingly. "She's a natural winner in any feminine competition. In the slightly *démodé* expression—which has not, however, been successfully replaced—she's got what it takes."

"And I haven't?"

He was surprised as well as amused, she saw, by the sharpness with which she said that.

"We-ell, it isn't a quality that brothers usually detect in their own sisters, you know. Only in other people's sisters."

"He's teasing you, Leslie dear," her mother put in peaceably. "You know perfectly well that Morley thinks the world of you."

"Say, rather, that Reid thinks the world of her, mamma," Morley corrected, with a smile. "At the moment, his is the only opinion that interests Leslie—and quite rightly so."

"Well, he does think the world of her. Otherwise, why would he do all he has done?"

"You see, Leslie?" Morley smiled at her, still teasing,

but with a great deal of affection, too. "And remember that he had known the fatal Caroline once—and still he chose you."

"But suppose . . . ." began Leslie. Then she stopped. Not only because of the amused lift of her brother's eyebrows, but because she realized with dismay that she had almost stumbled into the fatal mistake of demanding reassurance.

She changed the subject—laughed off the conversation as though she found it no more than the light-hearted teasing Morley had meant it to be. But she was disturbed, and took herself to task afterward.

That's the danger in any marriage where one feels insecure, she thought remorsefully. *I must accept, and be thankful for, what I have. Not try to find reassurance of what doesn't really exist in any careless word that someone likes to utter.*

She was glad she had identified this danger so early, and she imagined she was safely armed against it now that she recognized it. Just as she was pretty sure, while she was in London and regarding Reid from a distance, that she could learn to achieve a nice balance in her relationship with him.

There was no reason why she should not show an easy, pleasant affection to him. That he would expect. All she must guard against was any display of the inner, breathless rapture that alternately enchanted and tormented her.

It should not be too difficult, she told herself.

But when she saw him again for the first time, after nearly a week's absence, it was all she could do not to throw herself into his arms and cling to him.

In her effort to appear self-contained, she threatened to turn their reunion into a very tame affair. But, fortunately, Reid had a natural talent for lovemaking—whether flirtatious or serious—and he greeted her in a manner that must not only have satisfied any member of the family who was nearby, but that reminded her of his cheerful boast that she should find their marriage rather more interesting than she seemed to expect.

Alma, who was a weekly boarder at a school in Pencaster, was at home on this occasion as it was a Saturday, and when she said to Leslie, "Only two more weekends until your wedding," it seemed to give an exciting reality to the whole thing, which until now, it had lacked.

"Yes. I . . . find it hard to believe," Leslie confessed.

"Why?" the literal-minded Alma wanted to know.

"Well, I suppose any big and wonderful change is always rather difficult to accept in advance."

"I can always believe in anything I *want* to believe in," Alma asserted argumentatively. "Have you settled where you're going for your honeymoon yet?" For she resented that there had been a certain amount of reticence over the discussion of this.

"I don't know about the first part." Leslie smiled. "But later we are going to Laintenon."

"Where Great-Aunt Tabitha lived?"

"Yes."

"I say! She had a fabulous sort of villa there, didn't she? Will you stay there?"

"I doubt it. The place must be very big, and most of it would have been out of use for many years. It would be rather melancholy."

To Reid, Leslie said, "Alma's just been asking where we are going to spend the first part of our honeymoon. I told her, quite truly, that I don't know. We can go to Laintenon after the first week or ten days, of course, but we still haven't settled on the first part."

"What about Paris?"

"Oh, no!" she cried sharply, remembering what Caroline had said about Paris, and how she had looked as she said it.

Reid regarded her thoughtfully, and she found herself blushing, and hoping wildly that he did not remember the occasion, too.

There were few things that Reid forgot, however.

He made no attempt to ask her why she objected so strongly to Paris. He merely said, "Have you ever been to Italy?"

"No."

"Would you like that?"

"Very much," she said eagerly. Caroline had no associations with Italy, as far as she knew.

"Not one of the obvious places, like Rome or Florence. We might go to Verona, and we could rent a car and I'd take you around Lake Garda." He was speaking thoughtfully, as though he already visualized the scene and liked it.

"That sounds lovely," she said softly, anxious to make up for her slip over Paris. Besides, it did sound lovely.

"We could go to Venice for a day or two, if you liked."

"Yes. I would...love that."

"All right. I'll look after the arrangements. We'll fly to Milan and go on from there."

"Reid...."

"Yes?" He had been turning away, but he looked back at her now, over his shoulder.

"You didn't specially want to go to Paris, did you?"

"No, my sweet." He smiled full at her, and she found it very reassuring. "I want to go some place that you would like equally well. It's your honeymoon, too, you know."

"Oh...thank you. I've always wanted to go to Italy."

That was true, and she hoped he would take it as sufficient reason for her almost violent refusal of Paris.

"Well, you're going now," he told her. "And I hope you'll have every reason to enjoy it."

She hoped so, too—passionately. Hoped there would be no unforeseen crisis. Hoped that when people said a honeymoon could be more of an ordeal than an enjoyment, they were just being cynical. Hoped that somehow—somehow—when she took this terrible glorious risk, she would find that she had gambled on her happiness and won.

During the last days before her wedding, Leslie achieved a sort of detachment. She was the one in the household who usually shouldered most of the real work in any arrangements made, and her own wedding was no exception.

"You're so cool about everything . . . one would think it was someone else's wedding," Katherine said.

To which Leslie replied that she liked things done well, even at her own wedding.

"Leave her alone. She's just so sure of her happiness that she doesn't need to bother about anything else," her mother declared indulgently.

"But she *is* bothering about everything else," protested Katherine amusedly. "That's just it. She attends to every detail, so calmly and efficiently."

"Because she hasn't any inner worries," her mother explained. "That's it, isn't it, darling?"

Leslie said that was exactly what it was. And her mother looked peculiarly satisfied.

When her dress was sent home, the day before the wedding, she spread it out on the bed, and all the family—even her father—came to inspect it.

To be sure, he only said, 'Very handsome, very handsome," in a modest tone, as though he were personally responsible for it, and then walked off. But her mother and her two sisters hung over it, exclaiming and admiring.

Leslie stood a little way back in the room, answering their remarks at random, gazing fascinatedly at the dress and thinking, *When I put that dress on tomorrow, I shall be going to the church to marry Reid. I couldn't turn back now if I wanted to. I'm absolutely committed. If I've made a terrible mistake, I can't do anything about it now.*

"You do like it, don't you?" Katherine looked up and across the room at her.

"I adore it!"

"Oh . . . you were so quiet, I wondered if you were disappointed. Though I couldn't imagine how anyone could be."

"I think it's the loveliest wedding dress anyone ever had," Leslie said deliberately.

Her mother gave a pleased laugh.

"You'd better tell Reid that, darling. He told me I was to spare no expense whatever in finding you the dress of your dreams."

"He said that?" She flushed delightedly.

"He certainly did."

"Oh . . . ." She laughed suddenly and felt indescribably happy. For surely no man thought or spoke on those lines, if his heart were completely set on another girl.

Why should she not hope and believe in her future happiness? Why should not Reid recover from his infatuation for Caroline, just as she herself had grown out of her youthful passion for Oliver?

Looking back afterward, she was always glad to remember that nothing spoilt the tranquil joy of her own wedding.

Worries there might have been beforehand. Problems there might be afterward. But, during the service, and the small, intimate family reception that followed, she was quietly and completely happy.

"I don't think I ever saw anyone look as happy as you did," Katherine said to her, as she helped her sister change into her going-away suit of gray, edged with squirrel. "Once or twice, in the beginning, you know, I felt anxious about you. I thought maybe you were taking Reid for family reasons, in spite of all your protests. But when I saw the way you looked as you came down the aisle after the ceremony, I knew it was all right."

"Oh, Kate! Was it so obvious?"

"You bet it was! And quite right, too," Katherine said, giving her a hug. "Have a wonderful time in Italy. But I'm sure you will, Reid's the kind to give any girl a wonderful time. What a good thing Caroline What's-her-name went and snaffled old Oliver, or you might have got yourself tied up with him."

"I don't think I would have. It simply *had* to be Reid," Leslie insisted. And in that moment she was actually grateful to Caroline for having taken Oliver off her hands.

Such are the beautiful, arrogant heights to which happiness can lift us.

It was over at last. They had run the gauntlet of parental blessing (her father), a few sentimental but happy tears (her mother), and an ill-directed shower of confetti (Alma). And they were in the car on the way to London, where they were to spend the night, and take the early-morning plane to Milan the next day.

They drove through the bright, early autumn afternoon, past orchards where apples and pears hung heavy on the tress, and fields where the dark golden corn was being stacked. And Leslie thought the world had never been more beautiful, and that it was not humanly possible to be more happy than she.

"How did you enjoy your wedding, my sweet?" Reid asked at last, and she was aware that they must have been silent for a long time.

"I loved it."

He laughed.

"Girls always like weddings, I understand. Even other people's."

"Maybe. But one's own is always something special."

"Why, yes, I suppose it is. Even ...." He stopped, because a big car was racing toward them, and he had to take the bend carefully.

"Rash idiot," he remarked to Leslie, when they were past.

"Yes. But ... what were you saying, Reid?"

"Something in general praise of weddings, wasn't I? Good heavens, just look at that orchard. Heaviest crop we've seen so far."

She stared at the orchard, and hated its mellow beauty. But she managed to say something appropriate. And—much harder—she managed not to yield to the temptation of forcing him back onto the subject they had so abruptly left.

What was the qualification he had been going to make, with such careless matter-of-factness, about their own wedding? Until they reached London, and the hotel where they were to stay, the question tormented her.

In the luxury hotel where Reid had assumed she would like to stay, a very beautiful suite had been reserved. And so obviously pleased was he to be providing her with the very best of everything on her honeymoon that she had to conceal from him, at all costs, her dismay at discovering how very palatial and unintimate the suite was.

There were two bedrooms and a sitting room, which seemed excessive for one night, Leslie could not help thinking. And, for the first time, the dreadful idea came to her that perhaps he still regarded their marriage as a friendly compromise rather than an actual fact.

Was this his tactful way of indicating that the wedding need not radically change the relationship between them for the time being?

She told herself that she was being fanciful. And then that—even if she had guessed right—she must be patient. The family necessity had forced them into a seeming intimacy for which he might think neither of them was ready.

But, if he thinks that, how am I to make him see otherwise, she thought desperately. *And, if I can't make him see it, how am I to bear it?*

They had arrived too late for dinner. But they had supper together in a brilliant, beautiful restaurant, and danced for a while afterward to a superb band. But, all the while, this new and terrible problem hovered in the back of her consciousness and, try as she would, she could not be at ease with him.

"Well, we're due at the air office at a fiendishly early hour in the morning," he said at last. "It's about time we turned in, isn't it, and got what sleep we can?"

"I expect so."

"Would you like a drink before you go up?"

"No, thank you."

She wondered if she sounded as cold and casual to him as she did to herself. She thought perhaps she must have, because he gave her an amused, rather quizzical glance as he patted her shoulder, and said, "All right. I think I will. Good night, my sweet. Sleep well. I'll see you tomorrow morning about six."

"Good night," she said, and went calmly toward the elevator. And no one—least of all Reid—could have guessed that her heart was dead within her.

CHAPTER TEN

No Smoking! Fasten Safety Belts! ordered the electric sign at the front of the airplane cabin. And Leslie, occupied though she was with her own private problem, could not suppress an instinctive thrill of excitement at this indication that her first flight was about to begin.

"All right?" Reid, in the seat beside her, smiled at her as the plane bowled forward over the field, bumping over the unevenness of the ground with a slow clumsiness that completely concealed the grace and speed that would distinguish it as soon as it was in the air.

"Yes, of course." She smiled back at him. For was not their relationship one of pleasant friendliness? "I'm terribly excited, that's all."

He laughed indulgently and patted her hand, reminding her yet again of the time he had done that when they first met.

How angry she had been with him, that afternoon when he first asked her the way to Cranley Magna. She remembered exactly the feel of his long, strong brown hand on hers then, and how she had resented the familiarity.

Now she loved to have him touch her. She loved everything about him, if only....

"We're off," he said. And she realized that they had left the ground without her even noticing the fact.

It was a perfectly smooth flight, almost monotonous in its early uneventfulness, until they began to cross the Alps.

Leslie thought that never in her life had she seen anything as beautiful as the scene spread below her. The blues and purples of the mountain shadows, with the jewellike gleam of a lake here and there. The great snowy peaks, gilded by the midday sunshine, rising on every hand. The green of thick vegetation in the valleys, when they came low enough to pick that out. And even an occasional stream and waterfall.

It was like some immense and beautiful toy, viewed from this height, and to look down upon it gave one an almost godlike sense of detachment and wonder.

"Oh, Reid! I'm so glad we came!" she exclaimed.

And he laughed and said, "I'm glad, too. It's wonderful, isn't it?"

She wanted to ask if he had ever looked down on this scene, or any similar one, with Caroline. But she knew that even so prosaic a honeymoon as he evidently intended theirs to be could be ruined by a few foolish questions or comments. Caroline was definitely a subject to be left alone.

They arrived in Milan in time for lunch. But, as they had decided to go on to Verona the same day, there was time for little more than a stroll through the Galleria, a glance at the Scala and a breathless few minutes before the beauty of the cathedral.

Then they were on their way again, this time by train.

It was Leslie's first journey abroad, and she was fascinated by every detail. Just to have people around her talking a beautiful and unfamiliar language was exciting. And, since Reid appeared to know enough Italian to deal with most emergencies, she was able to enjoy the novelty of it all without any of the minor anxieties that usually beset an inexperienced traveler.

It was early evening by the time they reached Verona, but there was still enough light for Reid to point out the main features as they drove to their hotel.

Sharply etched against the evening sky, and dominating the town, rose the great broken arches of the Roman amphitheatre, and Reid promised her that they would explore this on the following day.

"We're too late for the season of open-air opera that they do here in the summer," he said. "But you'll still have plenty of more informal music in the open-air cafés around the center of the town."

"It's fascinating!" She was glancing eagerly from side to side at the curious, almost medieval streets through which they were passing. And when they drew up at their hotel, she thought the place looked more like a rather broken-down palace than any hotel she had ever been in.

There was nothing in the nature of palatial suites in this hotel. No private sitting room. But they were shown into a couple of pleasant rooms, with a communicating door. And when the porter pulled up the green Venetian blinds, Leslie looked out into a romantic-looking court-yard, where vines were growing, and a beautiful, brown-skinned youth was twanging some stringed instrument and singing "O Sole Mio."

It was all very picturesque and intriguing.

"How do you like it?"

They had been left alone now, and Reid had come in from his room to look around hers and see that she had everything she wanted.

"It's enchanting. Do you think the boy out there is a special stage effect? Or did he just happen to be there?"

"Oh, just happened, I expect." Reid went to the window and leaned out to exchange a few laughing words with the boy, who almost immediately broke into the poignantly gay strains of "Marechiare."

"It's delightful at first," Reid said. "They're a bit inclined to keep it up to all hours, but that's all part of the life here. Nearly everyone goes to sleep in the middle of the day because it's so hot, and that means that they stay up late into the night. Even the children. You'll see, when we go out to get something to eat."

"Aren't we dining at the hotel, then?"

"No, no. It's more fun out-of-doors."

She agreed that it would be.

"Give me twenty minutes to wash and change, and I'll be ready for anything," she promised. "I must get into something cooler."

"But take a coat," he warned, as he went back into his own room. "It gets cold very suddenly."

As she changed, she hummed a soft accompaniment to the song outside and felt her spirits lighten. The faintly fantastic atmosphere here, so unlike anything she had ever known before, seemed to whisper to her that anything could happen, after all.

The warm night air, the music and something else quite indefinable seemed to combine to create a sense of drama and romance, and like everyone else who has ever known the beauty of Romeo and Juliet's city, Leslie fell a victim then and there to the purple twilight of Verona and the spell that it casts.

"There's something about this place, Reid!" she declared, when she joined him later, cool and enchanting in a flowered silk dress, patterned in vivid blues and greens against a white background, which seemed to accentuate her fairness and make her look very young.

"Sure. That's what Romeo thought, I guess," Reid agreed, smiling his approval as he took her coat from her and tossed it over his arm.

"Do we take a taxi?"

"No. We walk. Everyone walks here, in the center of the town. Lots of the streets haven't even got a separate sidewalk and road."

So they strolled through the chattering, laughing, flirting crowds who thronged the streets, until they came to the great Piazza Bra, where, sure enough, a band was playing, and under the artificial lights the trees and plants in the gardens looked like something on a stage.

Couples strolled arm in arm in the darker paths of the gardens; plump, motherly-looking peasant women sat on the benches and knitted and gossiped as though it were early afternoon. And everywhere the dark-eyed, golden-skinned *bambini* tumbled and played and laughed and cried and got in everyone's way.

"They ought to be in bed, surely!" Leslie exclaimed. "They're just babies."

"They've done a good deal of sleeping during the heat of the day, I expect," Reid said. "They enjoy the cool as much as anyone else now. And if it seems an odd way to bring up children, by our standards, they none of them seem any the worse for it."

That was true enough. Leslie thought she had never seen prettier, happier children. And presently, when she and Reid sat down at a table on the sidewalk and proceeded to have their supper, she divided her attention almost equally between her excellent meal and the charming, amusing children, who appeared to be kissed or slapped with equal impartiality by their fond parents.

Gradually any sense of time slipped away. One had the absurd and pleasant feeling that one could go on like this all night. And when, after a while, they rose to go, Reid said, "You don't want to go in yet, do you?"

"Oh, no. I feel I would be missing something."

He laughed.

"We'll stroll some more." No one seemed to think in terms of anything more hurried here. "And I'll show you one or two places that we can glance at now and explore better by daylight."

As they walked along, he slipped his arm around her, partly to keep her near him when they came to crowded places, and partly because it seemed the natural way for couples to walk if they were young and happy.

She looked up at him and laughed a little, responding to the pressure of his arm with an eagerness she would not probably have shown if they had been at home in England.

"Decided you aren't frightened of me, after all?" he inquired, with an air of not unkindly teasing.

"Frightened of you! I've never been frightened of you," declared Leslie with truth.

"Oh, yes. You were frightened of me yesterday evening. Kept on giving me nervous, wide-eyed looks, until I began to feel like the villain of the piece who'd threatened to ruin the old homestead if the heroine didn't come to heel."

"Reid! I've never looked like that in my life."

"Then what was the trouble yesterday?"

"Why, I...I.... There wasn't any."

He didn't dispute that. He let them walk in silence for a few moments longer. Then he said, quite gently, "Do you feel this marriage is a little too much for you in some ways, honey?"

"No, Reid." She spoke softly, but without hesitation. "Not in any way at all."

"Not even if I tell you that no man would bring his wife to Verona, of all places, and not expect to make love to her?"

"Not even then." She was smiling, and some of the sweet confidence that had come to her during her wedding returned to her now.

He laughed softly, and bent his head to kiss the side of her cheek—a proceeding that was watched with approval and no surprise whatever by a plump, elderly Italian who was passing.

"Aren't you going to tell me what was wrong yesterday?"

"Just that I thought...when I saw that great suite... and you were rather matter-of-fact about everything... and I remembered about...Caroline—"

"Why the hell do you want to quote Caroline at this moment?" he demanded, but not angrily.

"I don't! It was just that .... Oh, I didn't *know* how you regarded me, Reid. I got nervous, if you like. But only in case you had some idea that the marriage was truly just one of convenience, and...and...."

"You've been reading too many modern novels, my sweet, all about people who behave any way but the normal one," Reid assured her good-humoredly. "You don't really think any man would marry anything as pretty and sweet as you are, and then decide to be brotherly, do you?"

She laughed, even a little more than the occasion demanded. For, out of the past, there had risen the ridiculous memory of Oliver saying she was like a sister to him. It had hurt so unbearably at the time, and now it hurt no longer.

And with that memory went the further recollection that she had drawn some sort of comparison even then, and told herself that in no circumstances whatever would Reid regard her as a sister.

"It's all right," she said happily. "I expect I was silly and fanciful. It isn't always easy to . . . to understand someone else's reactions, even when you know them very well."

"And you consider that you know me very well?"

"Pretty well."

"But you're satisfied with the idea that you should know me better." It was almost a statement, rather than a question.

"Yes, Reid," she said, and for a moment he tightened his arm around her.

Then he paused to point out to her the beauties of some twelfth-century church they were passing, and they didn't talk anymore about their inmost feelings or reactions. They might have been any couple of interested tourists taking their first enchanted look at one of the old Italian cities.

Except that there was a glow of happiness in her face not achieved by all tourists.

THEY STAYED IN VERONA for about ten days, visiting Venice and Padua, and hiring a car sometimes and driving out to Lake Garda when it became too hot to be comfortable on the plains.

If the scene had been dull and humdrum and the weather disastrous, Leslie would still have thought it the most wonderful place in the world, and this the most wonderful holiday. For in her newfound happy intimacy with Reid she had discovered, it seemed to her, an entirely new meaning to life.

She had always been of a reasonably happy nature, and her home background had been—in spite of Morley's tragedy and her father's weaknesses—a very contented one. But it seemed to her now that all the years before she had known Reid had a pleasantly negative quality. She had been happy, of course. As happy as she knew how to be then.

But as Reid's wife she had discovered a source and spring of such radiant, positive happiness that she sometimes wondered how she had been able to bear life before she knew him.

She made no attempt to discuss it with him. To do so would have been to betray more to him than she felt she safely could as yet. But she could not know him as well as she did now without realizing that he too was happy.

How far it went with him, she could not tell. His relationship with her might well supply no more than the "negative content" she had known herself before she met him. It was possible that for him the heights could only be touched with Caroline.

As far as Leslie was concerned, they could have stayed there for weeks. But one morning, when they were idling happily over their breakfast of coffee and rolls, creamy butter and cherry jam, their mail was brought to them, and Reid's included a letter that had been forwarded on from France.

"I think we'll have to push on to Laintenon soon, my sweet," he said, frowning a little over the letter. "There are quite a number of things to settle still. This letter is from Aunt Tabitha's lawyers, to remind me that, when I dashed off to England, I left a good deal undone."

"Well . . . ." She looked up, smiling, from an originally spelled bulletin of Alma's. "Whenever you say. However long I stay, I won't really want to leave here. But no honeymoon can go on forever."

"The honeymoon doesn't have to stop, just because we shift the scene," he reminded her.

"No? Maybe not."

But she privately thought that neither Laintenon, nor any other place, would ever hold for her the charm and magic of this city where she had come to know Reid as her husband.

"I'll go and inquire about train times." Reid got up. "Don't hurry. Stay and finish your breakfast . . . and your mail."

"There's an incredible epistle from Alma, which you'll enjoy later. I never knew anyone more naturally resistant to education. Her spelling's a disgrace," Leslie remarked indulgently. "But I see there's a letter from Kate, too. That should have all the local gossip."

When Reid had gone, she poured herself out another cup of coffee, and prepared to enjoy Katherine's letter at her leisure.

Katherine, for all her slightly languid beauty, was a clearheaded young woman, and always gave her news crisply and in what Leslie mentally called the right order of importance. Her letters were almost invariably a pleasure, because she told one exactly what one most wanted to know.

This one was no exception. In two pages, she had given Leslie a satisfactory account of the family's affairs, and left her with the pleasant impression that life at Cranley Magna was easier and less problematical than it had been for many a long day.

In addition, she was able to report that Morley made continuously satisfactory progress, and that, within a week or so, the great effort was to be made to put him literally on his feet again.

Even to read about it brought such a lump into Leslie's throat that, for a moment, she laid down the page and looked away across the sunny piazza with tears in her eyes.

Dear Morley, who had been so patient and so uncomplaining! If he really regained the use of his legs, she thought she would never be able to ask more of heaven again. That . . . and to have Reid, too! It was almost too much.

She picked up the last sheet of the letter, and in this Katherine had arrived at the general local gossip, as distinct from family news. She wrote:

I met Mrs. Bendick the other day. Our Mrs. B., I mean . . . not Oliver's glamorous lady. She told me that they didn't have more than about four days' honeymoon (I was glad to be able to report that you did much better) because Oliver hadn't any more holiday due to him at that time.

However, he has had his release now, and they're off somewhere else, to make up for the short time they had in the beginning. Mrs. B. wagged her head and tut-tutted a bit about her new daughter-in-law. I think she considers C. rather a bird of paradise for any man to keep happily cooped up in an ordinary domestic pen. And I must say I agree with her.

Still, we won't look for trouble. Oliver's very steadiness may appeal to her, though personally I would have thought Reid was more her type. Not that I wish to suggest your Reid lacks steadiness. But he's what the Victorians used to call "dashing," as well. And, unless I'm much mistaken, Caroline likes a little dash about her men.

Again Leslie put down the letter. But not with sympathetic tears in her eyes this time. She looked away across the piazza again, it was true, but now there was a thoughtful look in her eyes and they were a little narrowed. Like the eyes of someone who strives to see something just out of range.

Kate was smart, of course. She would see unerringly that Reid was more Caroline's type of man than Oliver was.

And yet...Caroline had chosen Oliver.

If only one could be sure that she had chosen him coolly and with judgment. If one could be certain that there had been no element of pique, or disappointment, in her choice.

But I shall never know that now, thought Leslie. *And I would be a fool if I let my thoughts dwell on it.*

She wondered if Reid sometimes went over and over the past in his own mind. He must, she supposed. And if he wondered uneasily whether Caroline had made her choice out of little more than pique, the reflection must cause him even more disquiet than it did her.

It was at that moment that Leslie took a very firm decision for the future.

When she and Reid finally settled in England they would not, she determined, make their home anywhere near Cranley Magna or, still less, Pencaster.

She would be terribly sorry not to be near the family, of course, and she knew that they probably expected that her future home would be at any rate within easy reach of them. She hated to have to admit so much fear of any woman—Caroline or anyone else—but there were risks one should not take. Better to face the fact, and act accordingly, than ignore a known danger and pretend that bravado and pride could take one past it.

Reid—and Oliver, too—were, she was sure, the stuff of which faithful husbands are made. And, little though she wished to pay tributes to Caroline, she had no reason to think the girl was a willful troublemaker.

But the whole situation was alive with danger. And when emotional gunpowder was lying around, only a fool struck matches.

By the time Reid came back, with the news that they could set off on their journey to Laintenon on the morrow, she had finished her coffee, read Katherine's letter and put it away in her handbag, and was ready to divert Reid with Alma's illiterate epistle.

"Had Kate any news?" he asked, looking up once, with a laugh, from Alma's letter.

"Just general family gossip, and a cautiously expressed hope that Morley might try to walk sometime next week."

"Good work! Don't get excited in advance, sweetheart, in case there's a disappointment. But, if it's a success, we'll have a long-distance call from Laintenon, and you can talk to Kate and hear all about it."

She smiled at him. He thought of everything.

But she hoped he would not think of ensuring that they settled near her family in case she became homesick.

The next day they left Italy, and it was not until the early afternoon of the following day that they arrived at Laintenon. Laintenon was about ten miles in from the coast, and so exactly like what Leslie had always supposed a French country town would be that she could have laughed aloud with amusement and delight.

It was a little bigger than she expected and, because of some rather famous health springs in the district, there were still a good many tourists, even though it was strictly out of the season.

For them, however, there was no question of difficulties of accommodation, even apart from Great-Aunt Tabitha's deserted villa. Reid drove straight to the tall, narrow house where he had lodged during the months he had lived in Laintenon, and was welcomed as a long-lost son by his voluble and sentimental landlady.

Leaving her to unpack, Reid went off immediately to see the lawyers and, with the aid of a good many gestures and a certain amount of schoolgirl French, Leslie managed to have a nice informative chat with Madame Blanchard.

Reid, she gathered, was all that was good, noble and generous, a reputation he appeared to have established for himself during the year or so he lived there.

No one, it seemed, was better pleased than Madame Blanchard when *"ce cher Monsieur Carté"*—which was her version of Reid's name—had inherited a great fortune from the mysterious old lady who lived in the Villa Rossignol.

No . . . she didn't know why it was called that. There had never been any nightingales there in her time. But perhaps when the old lady first came there as a bride there might have been. That would be seventy years ago or more.

The old lady had not been seen in the town for at least fifteen years before her death, but everyone said the villa was very handsome inside, and the grounds were beautiful, though out of condition now.

No doubt Monsieur Carté would be taking his bride to see the place. He had been very good to the old lady. Everyone agreed about that, and no one—if Madame Blanchard were to be believed—grudged him what she called his splendid inheritance.

Being naturally curious, she tried very hard, though with great politeness, to find out from Leslie how much the splendid inheritance had amounted to. But as Leslie really did not know, she was able to withhold this piece of information.

By the time Reid returned, Leslie and Madame Blanchard were firm friends.

"After we've had something to eat, we'll go up and have a look at the villa, if you like," Reid offered. "A good deal of the stuff won't be much good to us, and will hardly have even a sentimental value for anyone in your family. But you had better have a look at everything. A few of the things are very beautiful, as well as valuable."

Leslie was only too eager to accept the suggestion and, after an early dinner, they walked out in the cool of the evening to the Villa Rossignol, which stood about half a mile outside the town, almost hidden in a beautiful grove of cypress trees.

To Leslie, there was something melancholy, as well as intensely interesting, in this visit to the home of the legendary figure who had stood for so much in their family life.

The place must have been magnificent once, with the heavy magnificence of a past age. But now it was all so silent and dusty and lifeless. No one lived there any longer, except the elderly caretaker and his wife, and for years and years before that only an old lady, who had long outlived all her contemporaries, and a couple of ancient servants.

"It's hard to believe that *she* came here once as a happy, youthful bride, isn't it?" Leslie said, when they had seen all they wanted to see of the house itself, and were strolling through the vast, tangled gardens.

"I suppose it is." Reid held aside a great bunch of some sweet-smelling shrub so that Leslie could pass. "But she was quite happy, you know, even toward the end when she was getting tired and very old."

"Was she, Reid? You made her happy, didn't you?"

He smiled.

"I had something to do with it. She was a lively old lady, and used to say that she could still enjoy active life at secondhand. She used to like me to come up to the villa and talk to her—tell her stories of what I had done in the years before I came to Laintenon. I knocked about the world a good bit, you know, and she enjoyed a good story better than almost anyone I ever knew. I wish she could have seen you," he added suddenly. "She'd have liked you."

"Would she?" Leslie was indescribably gratified. "How do you know?"

"She used to say she knew the sort of girl I ought to marry. And she used to describe something very like you."

She didn't like Caroline, thought Leslie, with inner conviction. *I suppose he brought her here once or twice, during their engaged days.*

Ridiculously, she felt a sudden kinship with old Great-Aunt Tabitha, which had nothing whatever to do with their very flimsy relationship in fact. And she was very glad she had come to the villa and seen it for herself.

When they finally left the place, she was smiling a little, so that Reid put his arm around her as they walked down the hill to the town again. It reminded her of the first magical evening in Verona, and she thought, *I am going to be just as happy here.*

She even wondered why she had been so foolish and so cowardly as to have doubted her happiness at any time, because everything seemed simple and secure now.

And then she looked up, and coming along the road toward them was Caroline, dressed in white and swinging a beach hat by the strings, for all the world as though she had walked out specially to meet them.

CHAPTER ELEVEN

FOR A FEW SECONDS, Leslie stared at the advancing figure. Then she said in an odd, matter-of-fact little voice, "Why, there's . . . Caroline," almost as though she had been expecting her. As perhaps, in a way, she had.

"Caroline!" exclaimed Reid. Then he said, "Hell!" And for the first time since she had known him, Leslie detected a note of something like alarm in his voice.

By that time, Caroline had come right up to them, and she took off her sunglasses and exclaimed, "Well, for heaven's sake! Look who's here. Where did you two spring from?"

And then she laughed. But she could afford to laugh, thought Leslie. It was not her life that was in ruins.

Then Leslie heard herself laugh, too, and say something about ridiculous coincidences. So apparently she was doing quite well, too. And Reid was joking and speaking in his usual half-flippant manner. Only his arm round Leslie's waist was uncomfortably tight.

"You're staying at your old place, I suppose?" Caroline looked at and spoke to Reid as someone who knew all his usual haunts and habits.

"Yes, of course. Madame Blanchard has gathered us both under her wing by this time. Where are you staying?"

"Oliver and I are renting the smallest villa ever. We were lucky to get it at a few days' notice, of course. It's not fifty yards along the road. You must come back with me for a drink."

Leslie would have given anything to say that unfortu-

nately they were going on somewhere else. But they
were not going anywhere else, and if she said they were,
Reid—and perhaps Caroline, too—would know that she
was running away.

So they turned back and fell into step beside Caroline, who was busy explaining what Leslie already knew
from Katherine's letter—that, as soon as Oliver's re-
placement arrived, they had decided to have the second
instalment of their honeymoon.

"But why Laintenon?" Reid asked dryly.

"I had a fancy for it," Caroline retorted, and for a
moment her strange, significant glance drifted over him,
expressing something Leslie felt she herself could not
understand. "I knew how attractive it could be at this
time of year, you see."

"Yes, of course."

Usually Reid's voice was full and expressive. Now it
sounded flat and without any overtones.

They turned in at the gate of a small, white villa set in
a pretty formal garden, and Caroline led the way
around to the back of the house. Here, sprawling comfortably in a deck chair on the veranda, was Oliver,
looking exactly as though he were at home in Cranleymere.

To see his familiar figure in these utterly unfamiliar
surroundings seemed so much the last touch of fantasy
that Leslie began to think she must be in some dreadful
sort of dream.

But there was nothing dreamlike about the way Oliver sprang to his feet at the sight of them, and came forward exclaiming with obvious pleasure.

There were the same incredulous questions and the
same half-joking answers as there had been with Caroline, and everyone made at least a very good appearance of being delighted to see everyone else. And then
Caroline said that she would bring drinks out onto the

veranda, and suggested Leslie might like to come into the house and help her collect things.

They went indoors and, for the first time in their short acquaintance, Leslie realized, she and Caroline were alone together. Somehow the situation embarrassed her, though she hardly knew why. But evidently there was nothing in it to disturb Caroline.

She opened cupboards—still obviously unfamiliar to her—and searched for what she wanted, and all the time she kept up a desultory stream of conversation.

It was natural for her to refer to Leslie's wedding, of course, but Leslie felt herself almost wince when Caroline remarked casually, "In the end, Reid and you made nearly as much of a rush job of it as we did, didn't you?"

"Not quite. We did fix our wedding date about a month ahead, which gave me a little time for preparation. Here's the corkscrew, if that's what you're looking for."

"Oh, thanks." Caroline was arranging her tray with apparent carelessness but completely efficient result. "We settled things in a matter of days, in the end, you know."

"Yes, I know," Leslie said. "Why?"

The question—curt and almost rude though it might be—was out before Leslie could stop it.

But Caroline did not seem to mind. She laughed, with a sort of reminiscent amusement, and said, "We had a row, as a matter of fact. And then a making up. And—you know how these things are—suddenly we found ourselves arranging to get married the first moment we could. It's funny . . . quarrels sometimes clear the air, don't they?"

"Sometimes," Leslie agreed. "This isn't your . . . first visit to Laintenon, is it?"

"Oh, no. I was here in the days when I was engaged

to Reid," explained Caroline, who had no inhibitions about past loves apparently.

"I see," said Leslie, who had. And then they went out into the garden again.

Both men sprang to their feet. But it was Reid who came to take the tray from Caroline. And Leslie called herself mean and petty because she could not help noticing that his hands almost closed over Caroline's as he did so.

Oliver, meanwhile, was setting a chair for her and asking her how she liked her first glimpse of France.

Again there was something completely unreal about the scene. By every association of childhood and girlhood, she was much nearer to Oliver than she was to Reid. And, knowing, as she did, the link between Reid and Caroline, she could not help finding it horribly natural that they should be laughing over the same tray of drinks, while she paired off with Oliver.

It was like some stage comedy in which two couples had got mixed, but would probably sort themselves out in the last act.

But what will the sorting out amount to in our case, she thought unhappily. And she looked at Oliver, very charmingly playing host to her, and wondered what she had ever seen in him.

Naturally, he was intensely interested in everything she had to tell him about Morley, and usually Leslie would have asked nothing better than to talk of her beloved brother. But all the time she was dreadfully aware of Reid and Caroline, sitting side by side, laughing and talking, recalling shared experiences and exchanging common allusions.

She knew she was being absurd. They were not saying a word that could not easily be heard by herself and Oliver, if they cared to suspend their own conversation and listen. It was impossible to suppose that they were indulging in any more than lively social chat. And yet, she could hardly keep her attention on her own talk with Oliver, and it was all she could do to look interested and natural.

Oliver did drop his voice once, but only to say, in the amused, teasing kind of way that is permissible between lifelong friends, "You solved the Aunt Tabitha problem very satisfactorily in the end, didn't you?"

"The . . . . Oh . . . oh, yes. Reid has been wonderfully generous."

"Someone taking my name in vain?" Reid looked up at that moment, and Leslie managed to smile at him quite naturally.

"I was only telling Oliver how generous you were over Great-Aunt Tabitha's fortune."

"What was that?" Caroline pricked up her ears. "I like to hear about fortunes. The trouble is . . . they never come my way."

There was an odd little silence. Then Leslie said, with a composure that surprised herself, "Didn't Oliver ever tell you about my Great-Aunt Tabitha . . . and how we always expected her to leave her fortune to us, as a family?"

"No. Don't tell me there was nothing in the end. I couldn't bear it." Caroline smiled her lazy smile.

"She left it to Reid instead."

"*Reid!*" Caroline, who had been lounging in her chair, sat up suddenly. "Do you mean to say you had a fortune left to you, Reid, and never told me about it?"

"It was after your time, my sweet," Reid said composedly.

I wish he wouldn't call her that, thought Leslie angrily. She *isn't his* "sweet" now.

"But tell me now." Caroline seemed extraordinarily interested. "Leslie's relative went and left you her money?"

"Well, she was . . . very remotely . . . related to both of us, you see. She was the old lady at the Villa Rossignol."

"*No!*" Caroline seemed really impressed. "Oh, oh! and I never bothered to make her like me when I was here. She might have left *me* something, if I had."

"Don't be such a shameless hussy," Oliver put in affectionately.

And Leslie thought, *They're both playing up to her now!*

Aloud, however, she only said, "I'm surprised you never happened to tell Caroline our family story, Oliver."

"I thought she might set her cap at Reid and his fortune, if I did," Oliver replied promptly. "And see how right I was. She's displaying a dreadfully mercenary streak at the moment, aren't you, darling?"

"Well, no one likes to think they've let a fortune slip," Caroline objected. "Leslie will sympathize with me, won't you, Leslie? She knows what it feels like to see a fortune vanish."

"She doesn't need to worry. She brought it back into the family again, by marrying my charming self," Reid pointed out.

"So *that* was it!"

Leslie dug her nails into the palms of her hands to keep herself calm and smiling. She *knew* they were all chaffing each other, and that there wasn't a word of serious meaning in the whole conversation. But oh, it was too near the hurtful truth! She felt she could hardly bear it.

And even as she told herself it was all just flippant nonsense, something deep down inside her protested that perhaps there was a grain of truth in it all.

Perhaps Caroline *would* have chosen differently if she had known Reid was a very rich man.

But, in that case, why had Reid not told her? He had

had opportunity enough. Or, if not, he could have made an opportunity. *His* silence was less understandable than Oliver's, now she came to think of it. And perhaps he was bitterly regretting his silence by now.

She told herself that she must leave the subject alone. That all these delvings into the recent past were dangerous. She thought she had convinced herself of the wisdom of this. And yet, when at last they were on the way home, almost the first thing she said to Reid was, "Don't you think it was odd that Oliver hadn't told her . . . told Caroline, I mean . . . all about Great-Aunt Tabitha's leaving her fortune to you?"

"Not particularly." He grinned and switched lightly at the tall grass by the roadside with a stick he was carrying. "No man actually advertises the attractions of his rivals."

"He didn't know you were a rival of his," she said almost coldly.

"That's true. But he might have thought that news of the inheritance would turn me into one," countered Reid, still smiling.

She longed to be able to smile and joke about it with him. Or else she longed for him to be serious about it with her. She was not quite sure which.

What she did know was that, however unwise it might be, she had to ask that other question . . . about his own reactions.

"Reid," she said, and she was glad that she kept her voice light and steady, "why didn't you tell her yourself? It . . . it might have made a difference."

"I didn't want to be married for my money, my love. We all like to preserve the fond illusion that we are loved for ourselves alone," he pointed out, still in the same half-laughing tone.

She didn't laugh, however. She said, slowly and almost somberly, "And you were very anxious for Caroline to love you for yourself alone, weren't you?"

He looked at her then, with a sharpened attention of which she was immediately aware. And when he spoke his voice was just a little dry.

"Look here, honey," he said, "do you really think there's any good purpose in raking up the past like this?"

"I didn't rake it up," she exclaimed bitterly. "It came to meet us, of its own accord. Oh, why did they have to choose here, of all the places in Europe? Why couldn't they have gone anywhere else?"

"Yes, I guess it was a nasty backhander of fate," he agreed. "But it might not be a bad thing, in the end, you know. There's something to be said for facing out a situation and taking stock of it, instead of perpetually running away from it."

"Oh, that's taking things too far! I didn't mind the thought of . . . of meeting them later on, in my own home circle. But here . . . on our honeymoon . . . the only other people in the place whom we know! It's . . . it's too much."

"Darling, I didn't realize it was so unpleasant for you." He put out his hand toward her but, for the first time since she had said she would marry him, she flinched away angrily from the contact.

"No, don't touch me, or . . . or pet me! I couldn't bear it just now."

"All right," he said, in the most matter-of-fact tone possible, and they walked on in silence. A silence during which she was able to review her disastrous behavior of the past ten minutes.

How could she have betrayed herself like that? How could she have lost her self-control so hopelessly? She had behaved like a jealous, overfond creature, instead of the cool, intelligent companion she had tried to be to him.

What was he thinking now? Was he appalled at the revelation that she minded enough to be jealous?

He was sauntering along beside her, a little serious, but otherwise much as he usually was. But what was he thinking, what was he thinking?

"Reid," she said at last, "I'm awfully sorry. I don't know why I spoke the way I did. I—"

"That's all right, honey. There are no apologies called for," he interrupted. 'This is one of the times when the less one says, the better one feels about it afterward. I know it isn't easy for you, the way things have turned out."

For a terrible moment, she thought he meant that he had guessed how she felt about him.

And then, with a relief that almost made her laugh hysterically, she realized what was in his mind. He thought she was upset at seeing *Oliver* again.

It was perfectly natural that he should, of course. He was not to know that neither Oliver nor any man other than himself meant anything to her now. He was sorry she had had to watch what he believed to be the love of her life enjoying his honeymoon with someone else.

"Oh, Reid . . ." she began. And then she saw that he was indeed right when he said that the less they talked about it, the better. "Th-thank you for being so understanding," was all she ventured in the end. And he gave her a friendly smile and spoke of other things.

It was not until quite a long time afterward that she wondered whether Oliver accepted as the reason for her distress was not almost worse than to have Reid suspect the truth.

She was saved, it was true, from the humiliation of having him know her real feelings. But, instead, Reid was confirmed in the belief that Oliver still remained as the man she loved.

And I wanted so desperately for us to move gradually and naturally away from that! she thought wretchedly. *I wanted him to feel that our marriage already meant enough to me for the situation to work out happily one day. Now—just as he is unsettled by his meeting Caroline again—I have given him the impression that the links between ourselves are very thin and unimportant after all.*

She had even, in that final moment of nervous revulsion, implied that she quite hated any advance of his when Oliver was very much in her mind.

All the beauty and the happy confidence of their days in Verona seemed gone suddenly. They were very pleasant and friendly to each other—they even joked a little—but the inner sympathy and understanding were gone.

If it ever existed, thought Leslie. *If it ever existed. Perhaps I just imagined that, too, and the only real thing is the way he looks at Caroline, and the memories he has of her here.*

During the next few days, she tried in every way she could to keep their relationship on an easy, almost conventional, basis. In this she was unexpectedly helped by the sentimental and chatty Madame Blanchard, who was so determined that she and Reid *were* a happy honeymoon couple that they were almost hypnotized into playing the part in detail.

Laintenon was too small a place for one not to run into anyone one knew from time to time. And it was only a few days before Leslie, out shopping one morning with Madame Blanchard, found herself face to face with Caroline in the small marketplace.

They stopped, of course, and exchanged a few friendly words, though an atmosphere of mild hostility immediately wrapped Madame Blanchard around like a protective cloud. And when they had moved on again, she said to Leslie, in a hissing undertone, "She is what you say 'no good,' that one."

"Oh, I wouldn't say that!" Leslie felt bound to protest . . . with some sincerity, as a matter of fact, because she was almost sure there was no real vice in Caroline. Only she could not help naturally attracting men. "She is here on her honeymoon, too, you know."

Madame Blanchard seemed unnaturally surprised. But transparently relieved, too.

"She is married now? So much the better. Though with some it makes no difference," she added rather darkly.

Leslie laughed. She could take Madame Blanchard's suspicions so much more easily than Reid's teasing.

"You're a little prejudiced, *madame*, because she was engaged to your favorite, and then threw him over," she declared.

"You knew this, then?" Again Madame Blanchard was greatly surprised.

"Oh, certainly."

Leslie's companion muttered something to herself, but in such rapid and idiomatic French that Leslie found it impossible to follow. The general gist, however, seemed to be that the English were an extraordinary race, and quite unpredictable when it came to a question of the emotions.

This so genuinely amused Leslie that she could not resist adding teasingly, "She married an old sweetheart of mine, as a matter of fact."

But this seemed to Madame Blanchard to border on the indecent. So, after a few protesting exclamations from her, they returned to the more normal topic of menus and supplies.

Well, at least I've seen Caroline again, and managed to face the encounter calmly, Leslie told herself. *Being without Reid helped, of course. Perhaps if we don't all have to meet together again.... If Reid and I can leave here fairly soon.... If....*

That evening she broached the subject to him, casually, and as though she had not thought much about it.

"How long do you think we shall be staying here, Reid?"

"Well . . . ." he began, then he stopped and looked at her. "Do you want to go soon?"

"Not particularly. I just wondered."

"It's all taking longer than I expected," he confessed. "But I do feel that now we're here I'd better get the whole thing settled."

"Yes. Of course. There isn't anything I can do, is there? I don't mean with the lawyers. But perhaps in connection with the house. Sorting out things, and so on."

"Why, of course, if you like to. I thought you found the place melancholy."

"Oh . . . only in a rather sentimental way. It wouldn't depress me to be there alone, if that's what you mean. Anyway, the old caretaking couple are still there, aren't they?"

"Oh, certainly. Though they wouldn't be much company, I imagine. I would be in and out, of course. Or, if you like, you could get Caroline to go along with you. She's unexpectedly efficient, when it comes to the point."

"I'm sure she is." Leslie hoped he didn't notice that her voice chilled a little. "But I'll try first on my own. She and Oliver will have their own affairs to attend to."

"No doubt," Reid agreed equably. And so it was arranged.

During the next few days, Leslie went each morning to the deserted villa outside the town and methodically dealt with each room in turn, deciding what should be kept, what should be sold and what might be given away.

She made lists for Reid to run through and approve or query at a later stage. And because she had plenty to do and less time to think, she was, on the whole, happier.

Each morning, as she approached the small white house where Oliver and Caroline were staying, she would feel her heart beat anxiously, in case she might have to stop and speak to one or the other of them in the garden. But each morning she was spared this ordeal, and her heartbeats would subside again once she had passed the house and was safely on the stretch of road leading on to the Villa Rossignol.

So well and energetically did she work that, by the end of a week, she was able to tell Reid that she had dealt with all the principal rooms.

"Tomorrow I'll do what must have been a boudoir or personal sitting room or something. It's quite small, but there's a great desk there, with all sorts of odds and ends, and one drawer at least full of correspondence," she told Reid.

"Is that so?" He looked both surprised and interested. "What sort of correspondence?"

"All mixed, I think—bills, receipts, personal letters and one or two books that look something like account books."

"I wonder...." began Reid, and then stopped.

"What do you wonder?" She smiled at him.

"Nothing. Something just came to my mind, but it's not important." He pushed back his chair and got up from the dinner table. "Look here, sweetheart, I'm sorry, but I'll have to leave you for this evening. There are still one or two things to attend to."

"Not the lawyers again, surely, at this time of night?" She looked surprised in her turn. "You certainly have them working overtime on Great-Aunt Tabitha's affairs. I should have thought the old lady could have left things a little straighter after ninety-odd years' experience of this wicked world."

"That's the trouble. She had time to make a lot of confusion in her ninety-odd years," Reid retorted lightly.

But he kissed her goodbye before he went—a thing he had not done since the evening she had told him to leave her alone—and she felt happier.

If he were returning to his habit of casually natural endearments that must mean that he felt they were more at ease with each other again.

When he had gone, she wrote a long letter home. Ever since they had come to Laintenon she had felt unable to write freely and happily as she had in Verona. Instead, she had contented herself with postcards and the reiterated plea that she was very busy.

Now, with a sudden lightening of her heart, she felt that she could very well write to her mother, telling her all sorts of details about their life in Laintenon, her work at the villa and so on.

Once she had started, there seemed to be so much to say, that for over an hour Leslie wrote steadily.

Even when she had finished, there was still enough of the evening left to tempt her out-of-doors, and she decided to mail her letter, and perhaps stroll up to the villa. She had meant to bring Madame Blanchard some flowers from the lovely, overgrown garden that afternoon, but had forgotten them. This would be a good occasion to rectify the omission.

Slipping on a coat, for the evening air could be very chilly, but not bothering about a hat, she went out and, having mailed her letter, started along the road to the Villa.

This time there was someone in the garden of the little house. As she came abreast of the gate, Oliver straightened up from some desultory weeding and came to lean his arms on the gate and greet her.

She stopped, to tell him where she was going and give him the latest news from home. And he volunteered, in his turn, the information that he and Caroline had just bought a car.

"Not a new one, or a particularly elegant one," he confessed. "But it will get us up and down to the coast. You and Reid must come along with us one day."

"It would be lovely," Leslie said, as sincerely as she could. "How is Caroline?"

"Blooming, as usual. She isn't in just now, otherwise she'd have come out to speak to you. She went off on some affairs of her own," Oliver explained, smiling indulgently. "Wouldn't tell me where she was going. She likes her little mysteries."

Leslie managed a creditable smile, also.

"She'll probably arrive home with some special local dish for supper or something of the kind. Caroline is great on discovering things of that sort."

"Well, I hope it will be good," Leslie said politely. And went on her way.

When she reached the villa, she went in by a side gate. She knew the grounds very well by now, and was quite clear about where to find the best flowers for Madame Blanchard.

They took some finding, because so much of the garden was overgrown now, but Leslie liked the half-wild appearance of the place, and she liked the atmosphere of deep solitude the high stone walls induced.

She picked her flowers slowly and with enjoyment, arranging them with some care. And then, just as she selected the last few, the silence of the garden was broken by the sound of voices. Not the thin, rather wavering voices of the old people in charge of the house. But strong, laughing familiar voices.

Prompted by some instinct she could not have explained, Leslie drew behind a thick, overgrown hedge, which hid her completely from sight. As she did so, Reid and Caroline came into view, walking along one of the more distant paths.

They were too far away for Leslie to hear what they

were saying, but they were both obviously in an excellent humor and laughing.

Then, even as she watched them with widened, angry eyes, they paused, evidently to say goodbye to each other.

Caroline put her hands on Reid's arms and said something that made him smile. Then she reached up and kissed him.

It was not a prolonged or passionate kiss. But it was a kiss. She went off toward the gate after that, and he turned and walked toward the house.

And even from where she was, Leslie could see that he was smiling in a very well satisfied way.

CHAPTER TWELVE

LESLIE MOVED AT LAST, because she realized that she was getting cold, but still she walked up and down some of the paths most distant from the house and tried to decide what she was going to do.

In the end, it was Reid who settled the question for her. He came out into the garden, having evidently seen her from one of the windows, and waved his hand and called to her.

"Hello! What brought you here?"

She came toward him until she was within easy speaking range. And then, because he seemed so unabashed, she knew she could not speak of what she had seen. *She* would be so ashamed for him. "I just looked in to get some flowers for Madame Blanchard. I meant to bring some home this afternoon. Have you been here long?"

"Yes. Most of the evening. I thought I'd like to have a look through those papers you mentioned."

Well, perhaps that was true!

"Did you find anything interesting?"

"Not what I was looking for."

"Were you looking for something special, then?"

"Not really." He was suddenly evasive. "I thought there might be something . . . . It doesn't matter. Have *you* been here long?"

There was nothing suspicious or anxious about his tone.

"No," she said coolly.

"Well, I'm ready to go home now, if you are."

"Yes, I'm ready," she said. And they left the place together.

As they approached Oliver and Caroline's place, Leslie saw that the discussed car was standing outside in the road, and both of them were hanging over it, presumably in ecstatic admiration.

"Hello," they all said, more or less together. And Reid and Caroline, she noticed, showed no signs of having seen each other before during that evening.

"Come and look at the latest addition to our family," Caroline invited them.

And they, too, examined the finer points of the middle-aged car, and agreed that it was certainly capable of conveying one to the sea and back.

"Why don't we make a day of it tomorrow?" Caroline looked up, flushed a little from having been bent over the hood examining the car's interior. "The four of us, I mean. You don't *have* to shut yourself up in that stuffy lawyer's office every day, Reid, do you?"

"No. I don't have to."

"But it's as well to get things finished," Leslie cut in quickly.

"It's much better to seize on any good weather one can," countered Caroline promptly. "After all, you two are on your honeymoon, too. It's going to be a wonderful day tomorrow. Look at that sky! Let's make a beach party, take our food and go down for the day."

"Sounds all right to me," said Oliver.

"To me, too," Reid agreed.

They waited for Leslie's added agreement, as a foregone conclusion.

There was no objection she could raise—no argument she could oppose to this generally accepted idea of a party of pleasure. She made a virtue of necessity, smiled and said it was a wonderful idea. And everyone looked very well satisfied.

It was a matter of minutes to arrange the details. Oliver and Caroline undertook to call for the other two about ten the next morning, and each couple promised to bring a sufficient supply of food and drink.

"And swimsuits," Caroline added. "Down here the water will still be beautifully warm, and they say it's a wonderful shore."

"Not an entirely safe one, though," Reid said. "There are some tricky undercurrents. But we'll keep an eye on you girls."

"I like that! I'm a better swimmer than you are," boasted Caroline.

"Well, don't show off," her husband said, patting her dark head. "It isn't nice before company."

"Don't worry! I'll make her eat her words tomorrow," Reid declared gaily. And then he and Leslie went on their way.

She was very silent on the way home, and if Reid found that disturbing, she told herself, she could not help it.

If she had started to say anything beyond the merest conventional remarks, she would have found herself breaking into angry, frightened protests about the expedition on the morrow.

And I must not have another of those outbursts, she told herself. *I must not. I would find myself upbraiding him for his meeting with Caroline tonight. I must be calm, and pleasant and unknowing. Oh, how I wish tomorrow were over!*

But tomorrow, like every other day since the world began, had to be lived through somehow, hour by hour.

She woke to a sense of indescribable foreboding, which the brightness of the day did nothing to dispel. And she thought, if it took so much effort to be reasonably bright at breakfast, what was it going to be like to pretend and pretend and pretend all day?

I can't do it! Leslie thought at one point.

And then, as though to give her a little strength and happiness to help her carry the burden of the day, the long-awaited miracle, which she had almost forgotten in her personal misery, actually happened.

Madame Blanchard came in carrying a telegram, and set it down before Leslie with an air of suppressed drama very suitable to the occasion.

"For me?" Leslie looked rather startled, and tore the envelope open.

The next moment she was crying aloud, "Reid! Reid, come and look at this!"

And Reid, coming in from the next room, leant over her chair to read the message that trembled in her hand.

"Triumphant greetings," the telegram ran. "I salute you both—standing. Love and more thanks than I can say. Morley."

"Oh, Morley! Darling, darling Morley!"

She began to cry excitedly—something of her pent-up feelings of the past few days going into those tears. And when Reid took her into his arms and stroked her hair, she clung to him, just as though he had never made secret assignations with Caroline or kissed her.

"There, honey, there!" He laughed very tenderly and kissed her. "There's nothing to cry about. It's wonderful news."

"That's why I'm crying," she sobbed, half laughing, too. "Just because it *is* so wonderful and unbelievable."

"Well, I guess that's as good a reason as any for a few tears," Reid conceded with a laugh. And then, still holding Leslie, he turned to explain to Madame Blanchard, who had stood in the doorway during all this scene, divided between delight and dismay, and very much inclined to contribute a few tears herself.

Their landlady added her warm and most heartfelt congratulations, and advised them to waste no time in going off to celebrate the glad news with a day's pleasure.

As Caroline and Oliver arrived more or less at this moment, this seemed admirable advice. And, in the end, Leslie started off on the expedition with happier feelings and higher spirits than she would ever have thought possible an hour before.

Oliver drove, of course, with Caroline sitting beside him, and contributing a little lazy advice from time to time. The other two sat behind and, because it seemed natural in their mood of shared excitement and relief, he held her hand rather tightly part of the time.

Once Caroline threw an amused, indulgent glance at them, and after that Leslie gently drew her hand away. But she had a warm little feeling at her heart because Reid's impulse had been to share her happiness, and what Caroline might think about it she really did not care.

Oliver was unfeignedly delighted at the news about Morley, and Caroline showed a pleasant degree of sympathy, considering that she knew so little of the background of the struggle that had preceded this triumphant achievement.

"I suppose you had been worrying a lot about your brother, although you didn't say much," she said to Leslie.

"Well, from time to time I did worry," Leslie admitted, remembering guiltily that sometimes, in the worry of her own affairs, she had momentarily almost forgotten Morley's. "Not that there was any likelihood of his being worse, you know. It was just that I knew what tremendously high hopes he had set on this experiment of Trevant's. It would have been so fearful for him if it had all been a failure."

"And you had been expecting the result almost any day?"

"I .... Yes, I knew it must be soon."

"I thought you seemed very depressed last night," Caroline said. "I suppose that was the trouble."

"No," Leslie replied levelly. "It was something else last night."

She felt Reid turn and glance at her. But Oliver said at that moment, "Does anyone know this road? I think we went wrong about half a mile back."

The usual discussion followed, everyone holding a different opinion. And by the time they had discovered that they were on the right road, after all, Leslie guessed that no one would remember her remark.

She was wrong, however. Reid bent his head down to hers and said in an undertone, "Was something wrong last night? What was the trouble?"

"Nothing I can talk about just now, Reid. Don't ask me now."

"All right. Will you tell me later?"

"Maybe."

She was not quite sure what had induced her to say that. Only, after the news about Morley, she had gathered a sort of inner courage. And, on the strength of that, she felt that perhaps it would be better to have the whole thing out with Reid. Quietly, of course, and without too much emotion. But so that at least everything was truthful and dignified between them.

The coast at this point was a beautiful one. Wild and rather rocky, but with a splendid stretch of golden sand when the tide was out, and it was not difficult to find the ideal place for a day-long picnic.

After they had taken all the things they needed out of the car, Oliver drove it a quarter of a mile into the tiny nearby village to park it safely, so that they need not worry about it while they swam or lounged on the shore all day.

It was a superb day, as Caroline had predicted, and as they were all more than reasonably good swimmers they spent a good deal of time in the water, only coming out to enjoy their excellent lunch.

Afterward they lay on the sand, tossing an occasional remark to each other, but growing a little sleepy, if the truth be told.

Leslie, in fact, was just beginning to see the whole scene as a dim mist of blue and green and gold, when they were aroused by an urgent shout from a short, stout French official, who was climbing over the rocks with a purposeful air toward them.

"He can't be warning us off, surely? Isn't the seashore public property?" said Caroline, sitting up and rubbing her eyes.

"He's saying something about a car," replied Reid, whose French was, naturally, a good deal more service-able than that of the others.

Indeed, when the Frenchman, panting a little, had come right up to them, it was Reid who conducted the conversation from their side. Oliver, however, evidently caught enough to follow the general line, because at one point he shouted, "What's that he says? Our car's been stolen?"

"No." Reid shook his head. "He says you stole it."

"Good lord! I like that. I've got the receipt for the damned thing. At least, I suppose I have."

He reached for his coat and began going through his pockets with some urgency.

"I don't think a receipt's going to help you much." Reid was attending still to the flow of talk from the pur-poseful official, but managed to slip in a word or two of explanation to the others from time to time. "He seems quite sure that it was stolen property—the thief didn't even bother to change the number plates—and if his story's true, you've been sold someone else's pup, old boy."

"But, look here—" Oliver had, to his own surprise, actually produced the receipt by now "—this means something, for the Lord's sake! Tell him to get on to the fellow in Laintenon who sold me the thing."

"I think," Reid said, getting to his feet, "that you and I had better put a few clothes on and go along with this chap to the garage where the car is. We don't want the police collaring our only means of returning home."

"Need we both go?"

"Well, you're the owner, and perhaps I can do the explaining better."

"Yes, that's true. Will you girls be all right?" Oliver glanced at Caroline and Leslie.

"Yes, of course." They spoke simultaneously, and Leslie added, "We'll stay and look after everything here. You go along."

The two men threw on their coats and prepared to accompany the Frenchman.

"We won't be long," Oliver promised optimistically.

But Reid, who had more experience of French small-town officialdom, said, "Back tonight, I hope."

Leslie looked after them for a few minutes, and then dropped back on the sand.

She felt she did not want a long afternoon alone with Caroline, that the strain of making agreeable conversation would be more than she could stand, and, for a while at least, she was going to pretend to be sleepy.

Caroline fished a book out of their varied luggage, and seemed quite prepared to follow her own devices. Possibly, of course, she was no more anxious than Leslie for this prolonged *tête-à-tête*.

Overhead seabirds wheeled and called, and there was the ceaseless murmur of waves breaking on the shore. Otherwise there was silence and, after a while, Leslie's pretense at sleep gradually merged into the real thing.

When she woke up some time later, she was, to her surprise, alone. But, raising herself on her elbow and looking around, she saw that Caroline was swimming about leisurely quite close inshore.

Seeing Leslie sit up, she waved a hand and called, "Come on in. It's wonderful now."

Certainly the sea looked inviting, with the afternoon sun sparkling on the water. And unbuttoning the skirt of her beachdress, to reveal her slim green suit, Leslie ran down to the water's edge and waded out into the cream-edged, curling waves.

She swam near enough to Caroline to address a sociable word to her from time to time, but not near enough to feel that she was definitely in her company.

Presently she turned on her back and floated lazily, and reveled in the sensation of sun and sea.

"Race me to the tip of the promontory over there?" suggested Caroline amiably, swimming up alongside of her. "It's just about far enough for a warm afternoon."

Leslie didn't really want to bestir herself to that extent. But somehow a challenge from Caroline—even a challenge of this sort—was not to be refused. Besides... she was pretty sure she was the stronger swimmer.

"Right," she agreed, abandoning her pleasantly indolent floating. And a moment later they were traveling, neck and neck, toward the rather distant promontory.

It's farther than she thought, reflected Leslie. And something sensible and reasonable in her warned her to suggest that they abandon the attempt.

But Caroline was looking very fresh and going strongly. She was not, Leslie thought, in a mood to abandon any sort of competitive effort at this moment.

It was a perfectly friendly piece of rivalry, of course, proposed in genuine good nature on Caroline's part. But, as the test lengthened and began to make real demands upon her, Leslie felt grimly that, in this as in the much more important matter, she and Caroline were real adversaries.

She must win. There was something symbolic about it. To fail would be to suffer a quite disproportionate loss of self-confidence. The failure in itself would not matter. It would be the fact that she had lost to *Caroline* that would rankle unbearably.

The distance really was much greater than she had imagined. And glancing over her shoulder at Caroline, who was a short length behind her, Leslie thought that she, too, had been disagreeably surprised by the amount of effort required to cover the distance.

Well, it was much too late to turn back now. They would have to go on, and allow themselves a considerable rest on that promontory before they attempted the journey back.

At the thought of having to cover this distance all over again, Leslie experienced a most unpleasant sinking of the heart. But she firmly reassured herself. They would feel better after a rest. And, anyway, the thing to concentrate upon at the moment was the journey out there.

As though in response to her common-sense determination, the difficulties seemed to ease slightly. She was traveling with less effort, and the rocky bulk of the promontory loomed very near now. With very little difficulty, she increased her speed, and shot ahead to victory in the last two minutes.

As she hauled herself out of the water, dripping and trembling rather with exertion, Caroline came up only a yard or two behind her. She, too, seemed to have found the last stretch less trying.

But she looked none the less anxious for that.

"You certainly made that in good time," she said, as she pulled herself up onto the rock beside Leslie. "But I don't like the implication of that last easy bit."

"You mean there was a strong undercurrent running with us?"

"Yes. And it will be against us going back."

Leslie turned her head suddenly and looked full at Caroline.

"I know. I'm thinking we're a couple of fools, too. But we're strong swimmers, both of us. After a rest...."

"We can't afford a long rest," Caroline cut in shortly. "Look at that." She pointed to the stretch of water they had so recently covered.

Leslie stared at it for a long moment. At first, she thought it was her imagination that seemed to make it wider. Then she realized, with an uncomfortable thump of her heart, that there was no imagination about it. The tide was rising rapidly, and the distance between them and a safe shore was increasing every minute.

"At any rate the tide will be with us," she said steadily.

"Yes. But what about the pull of this darned underswell?" Caroline retorted. "We're in a nasty spot, Leslie. And I think, although we're tired, the sooner we try to get out of it, the better."

Leslie did not answer for a moment. She knew what Caroline was saying was horribly true. It was just a question of balancing between the length of time it would take to regain their strength, and the length of time it would take for the incoming tide to broaden that stretch of water beyond their fullest capacity.

"I think we'd better go," she agreed quietly.

And at that moment, to her inexpressible thankfulness, there appeared on the distant—terribly distant—shore where they had spent the morning, a figure. Only one figure. But, even at that distance, she knew it was Reid.

If they were to get into insuperable difficulties, he would be able to help them. No ... one of them.

He was waving now, having evidently seen their bright, distinctive caps as they still clung to the rock, and his urgent gestures undoubtedly meant, "Hurry! Hurry!"

They probably meant, thought Leslie, with a wry gleam of humor as she struck out into the water again, "Hurry, you unmitigated little idiots! Are you crazy, ever to have got yourselves into such a place?"

And then she didn't think any more humorous thoughts. Or, to tell the truth, of anything else at all but the terrible, overriding necessity of pitting her strength and skill against the remorseless pull of the water.

They kept close together this time, a little perhaps to encourage each other, but they wasted no effort on words.

Mentally, Leslie was counting to herself, very much as she had when she first learned swimming, because a rhythmical count seemed to help. But, beyond that, she tried not to think at all, because she had to concentrate, she told herself. She *had* to concentrate.

Once she raised herself slightly in the water and took a look at the distant shore. But she was so discouraged to find how comparatively little distance they had covered with such terrible effort that she decided not to look again.

Then she realized that her glimpse of the shore had shown it to be empty, and she knew, with a hopeful beat of her overtaxed heart, that Reid was on his way to help one of them.

Glancing to one side, she saw that Caroline, too, was still going strongly, but the effort was evidently telling on her equally. She was in quite as pressing need of help as Leslie herself.

In spite of her desire to concentrate on nothing but her swimming. Leslie's tired and harassed mind presented her suddenly with a completely clear picture.

There they were, the two of them, still struggling but with the odds most powerfully against them. Without assistance, it was doubtful if either of them would ever reach the shore and safety. Yet Reid could not hope to take on more than one of them.

It's as simple as that, she thought, a great sob rising in her throat. *He can rescue only one of us. The one who matters more to him. And that is Caroline.*

At that moment, Leslie very nearly gave up the struggle. But because the sheer will to live is probably the most powerful impulse in any human being, somehow she drove her exhausted body on through the water.

But she was going much more slowly now, and the effort seemed superhuman. Once a wave went over her head. She came up again, gasping and shuddering, and very, very frightened. And for the first time in all her life she really looked death in the face, and thought, *It could really happen. If I get too tired to go on anymore, it's over. I'll never see mother's face again, nor lie in Reid's arms, nor feel the sun and the wind. The world will go on, but I won't be there.*

If only she could have been sure that she was safely on the incoming tide, she would have dared to float for a few minutes and rest. But she knew that, if she were not clear of that treacherous outgoing current, she might in a few moments lose half the distance she had gained, and she could never find the strength to recover it now.

"I can't...go on," she gasped once.

But no one heard her. And she went on. Endlessly, as it seemed.

All her life she must have been doing this. There had never been a time when she had not been struggling, in this fearful, heavy mechanical way.

She did not think of Caroline anymore, nor even of Reid. She just went on and on and on and on.

CHAPTER THIRTEEN

AND THEN, AT LAST, Leslie knew that she was finished. She would stop. It would be so much easier. She wondered why she had not given in before, instead....

"All right, darling," Reid's voice said, not a couple of yards away from her. "Let yourself float. I can manage you."

Incredibly, the sound of his voice tore away the veils of illusion. There was still a life to be lived and a struggle to be made.

And there were other considerations, too. Recollections which forced themselves back on her with remorseless clarity.

"Caroline," she gasped. "She's ... in danger ... too."

"I can't manage more than one." His tone was grim and uncompromising.

"I know ... understand." Mechanically, she was doing what he told her to do, but something in her urged her to protest. "That's why ... you must ... take her."

"Stop talking. My wife comes first."

She knew it was idiotic to waste words and breath now. But, though the effort brought the tears to her eyes, something greater than herself forced the final protest from her.

"No. She's ... your love. She ... comes first."

"You are my love and my wife," he said. "Now be quiet, for God's sake. We need our breath for something else."

She was quiet. Incredulously, rapturously, obediently quiet. She did exactly what he told her. She was even able to help herself a little, once his supporting arm had given her a tiny respite. In any case, the most difficult part of the journey was over.

But what gave her strength, far beyond any material consideration, was the fact that he had said she was his love.

The next few minutes were just a little vague. She was dimly aware that Reid was rubbing her vigorously with towels, wrapping her in a coat and making her drink brandy.

There were two or three other people there, she realized presently, and someone was sobbing breathlessly quite near her. With a dreadful feeling of guilt, she thought, *Caroline!* And though the effort hurt she rolled over on the sand to gaze in the direction of the sound.

It was a moment before she realized that the sobbing was not for Caroline, but from her. She was lying there, as exhausted as Leslie herself, and beside her knelt a dripping Oliver, his face a whitish gray with anxiety and fear.

"She's safe, too!" Leslie gasped, in a cracked little voice, and she felt the tears of hysteria rising in her also. "Reid...."

"Stop it!" Reid told her peremptorily. "Caroline will be as right as rain in an hour or two, and twice as dry. Don't you start crying, or probably Oliver and I will do the same. Come on, I'm taking you home now."

And he rolled her in a blanket and lifted her in his arms.

One or two eager bystanders offered to carry her for him, seeing that he was a good deal exhausted already. But he would not let anyone else touch her.

Rather slowly, he carried her to the car that some kind passerby had offered to put at their disposal. And still half-dazed she was driven back to Laintenon, lying in Reid's arms, indescribably warmed by his tenderness

and nearness, and possibly a little by the liberal amount
of brandy he had poured down her throat.

She thought, *There are so many things to ask him and
to tell him.* But she could not think of the words in
which to express any of them. And, since he seemed
very well satisfied just to hold her and be silent, she felt
that perhaps that was what she wanted, too.

When they arrived at Madame Blanchard's, that
good lady rushed out, with a natural premonition of
disaster—or at least sensation—little short of miracu-
lous. But though she exclaimed in a variety of keys and
three different languages, she was intensely practical
and helpful, too. And in a remarkably short time Leslie
had been undressed and put to bed with hot-water bottles.

The warmth and ease and quiet were so delicious
after the ordeal through which she had gone that Leslie
could not restrain one or two little groans of sheer relief.

Then, because it seemed the loveliest and the most
natural thing in the world to do, she went to sleep, and
bothered no more about anything or anyone for several
hours.

When Leslie woke, the last of the golden evening light
was filtering into the room, and she lay there loving it
with the grateful tenderness we attach only to a beautiful, familiar thing we have very nearly lost. She was
alive when she might have been dead, and the world
was a wonderful place.

Then a very slight movement beside her made her
turn her head, and she saw, with a fresh rush of grateful
tenderness, that Reid was lying back in the chair by her
bed, quieter and more thoughtful than she usually saw
him.

"Hello," she said softly. And he turned his head then
and smiled at her.

"Hello, sweet. Feeling better?"

"I feel wonderful."

He leaned forward, with his arm on the bed, so that he was very close to her.

"Promise me that you'll never take a risk like that again. I wouldn't relive this afternoon for all Great-Aunt Tabitha's fortune."

"I promise. I'm awfully sorry, Reid. It was very wrong and silly of us, I know. We started to race and... I felt I had to win. It seemed otherwise as though...."

"Yes?" he said, because she had stopped.

Her lashes came down, making shadows on her cheeks, and a very faint color showed under her pale skin.

"Come on. Tell me," he coaxed, and kissed the side of her cheek softly.

"Reid... I thought you loved her."

"So I did," he retorted with cheerful candor. "Once."

"Oh, darling, I thought... as late as last night."

"Last night?" He looked mystified. "Why did you think I loved her last night, for heaven's sake?"

"Please don't think I was... was prying or suspicious or anything. But I came up to the villa last night earlier than I told you, *really* just to get flowers for Madame Blanchard. And while I was there I saw you and Caroline laughing and talking together and she... she kissed you goodbye."

"Yes, that's true. She did," he agreed reflectively, as though recalling that with surprise.

"You had told me, Reid, that you had to go out and attend to some business affairs. I thought you meant you had to see the lawyers. And then... when I saw you with her in the garden...."

She broke off again, almost apologetically.

"Yes, I see. I'm sorry, my sweet. I wish I'd known. It was really a perfectly innocent meeting, you know. And quite unpremeditated on my part."

"Not on hers," she countered quickly.

"What makes you think that?" He twined his fingers loosely in hers and then raised her hand and kissed it lightly.

"I stopped to speak to Oliver on the way up—he was in their garden—and he remarked quite casually that she had gone out and refused to say where she was going. He thought it quite amusing, and was sure she was planning some small domestic surprise for him."

"Whereas you thought he was just being the blind husband?" Reid suggested, smiling.

"I didn't think anything about it until I saw her with you in the garden. Then I felt sure she had gone out on purpose to meet you."

"So far as it goes, that was true," Reid said slowly. "She saw me go past, up to the villa, and she followed me because there was something she wanted to say to me."

"And what was that?" Leslie asked softly and quickly. "I mean...if it's not private and you can tell me."

"I can tell you, honey. Caroline has a passion for getting things straight, you know. Emotional situations, I mean. Probably it's because she has few inhibitions, and is naively interested in her own feelings. She wanted me to know—I believe for my own good as well as hers," he interjected with a dry smile, "that she was completely happy with Oliver and that she knew now that she had made a wise choice."

"She...said that?" gasped Leslie rather incredulously. "But why? I mean...why go out of her way to come and tell you that?"

"Because this visit of theirs to Laintenon had been in the nature of a test. On her part, I mean. I don't imagine Oliver knew anything of what was in her mind," Reid said, again with that smile. "She married him in a good deal of a hurry, remember. I guess she had her moments of doubt. It was not unlike her, you know, deliberately to come to this place that was full of . . . well, shall we say romantic memories of someone else? That was the final proof to her. If, in this place, she could still find Oliver the supreme attraction, then she'd know she had laid all the romantic ghosts of the past.''

"She hadn't," Leslie said slowly, "reckoned on our being here, too."

"Candidly, I think it added a zest to her own proof," Reid remarked with an air of reflective amusement. "When she found that, even in the flesh, I no longer attracted her, although the scene was identical with the days when I had . . . .''

"*Didn't* you any longer attract her?"

"Not to any degree that counted beside her Oliver," he confessed with a grin.

"I can't understand it," Leslie said with naive simplicity. At which Reid laughed immoderately, but kissed her with great tenderness.

"Darling, is that how you see Oliver and me now? You never told me, you know."

"How could I?" She rubbed her cheek affectionately against his. "I thought you were still in love with Caroline."

"Yes, I see. You know, there's something to be said for Caroline's direct method. Having found that she loved only Oliver, she took quite a pleasure in letting me know that was the exact state of affairs. I'm not quite sure—" he rubbed his chin thoughtfully "—whether she thought I needed a final warning, or whether she just wanted to share her glorious discovery with someone else who knew a lot about her reactions."

"Reid . . . .''

"Yes."

"What did you say, when she told you that?"

"If I remember exactly, I said, 'Thank God! Then there's no harm in telling you that I adore my wife and am supremely happy with her.' ''

"You *really*...said that?"

"I did."

"Because, you know, I'd rather you told me the exact truth than...invented something to please me."

"There's no invention, my darling, about either the words or the sentiment. I do adore you and I am supremely happy with you," he said quietly. "Do you think you are such a difficult person to adore?"

"I don't know about that. I only know that I have always thought of you as being obsessed by a passion for Caroline."

He was silent for a few minutes. Then he said, "When did you know you were no longer in love with Oliver?"

"Oh...after you and I decided to go on with the marriage in actual fact."

"And yet you had been very much in love with him for a long time before that, hadn't you?"

"Yes, I suppose—" rather reluctantly "—I had."

"You see, these changes can take place. I fell in love with you in Verona, and after that there could be no other woman for me. Neither Caroline nor anyone else. It isn't any stranger than your falling out of love with Oliver. Or, I suppose," he added reflectively, "Caroline falling out of love with me."

"That's the strangest of all," Leslie said, and was swept up in his arms and kissed several times.

"I shall hardly be able to let you out of my sight, after so nearly losing you," he declared.

"It wasn't such a bad thing, really, Reid." She was smiling brilliantly now. "It was the only thing that would have made me really convinced that you loved me better."

"Hell, why? I must say you girls think up some pretty grueling tests."

She laughed outright then.

"Why, you see, I knew you could save only one of us. You *had* to make it the one you really loved."

He held her away from him and gave her a long, quizzical glance. Then he said, "Darling, I just hate to undeceive you, and I hope this won't undermine your faith in my love for you. But I did know that Oliver was coming along a few yards behind me, and I would have reckoned in any case that his wife was his affair and my wife was mine."

"Oh," Leslie said very soberly. And then there was a long silence between them.

"Does it matter very much?" he asked at last, watching her serious face with loving and amused eyes.

"I think it does, rather."

He took her right into his arms then and kissed her cheek and then her mouth.

"Do you really fell any doubt about my love for you?" he said. "Any doubts that could possibly be resolved by some swimming contest or artificial proof, I mean?"

She smiled slowly and pressed close against him.

"You think I'm very silly, don't you?" she said softly.

"Darling, I think everything about you is dear and lovely," he replied, with a gravity unusual in him. "But—" and his characteristic smile flashed out "—don't ask me to prove it with any trial by water. There are so many more interesting ways of doing it."

She laughed at that. A sweet, happy, relieved laugh.

"You don't have to prove it. I *know*," she said, and she felt her cares fall from her.

She lay there for a long while in the circle of his arm, both of them so happy and so much at one that there was hardly the need for words between them. Then she said lazily, "Why did you go to the villa yesterday evening?"

"What?" He roused himself. "Oh . . . I forgot. I went to look at those letters and account books you mentioned. You see, the old lady's lawyers were almost sure that she made all sorts of notes and tentative bequests before she actually settled on that final will, leaving everything to me. I thought if we could find some recent indication that she meant your father to have a good deal, he would accept what I'm making over to him with a better heart."

"Couldn't you have told me that," she said a little reproachfully, "and have let me help to look?"

"Oh . . . I guess it was silly of me. I wanted to find it for myself, and then bring it to you as a surprise."

"Reid! Who's the childish one now?" She put up her hand and touched his cheek lovingly. "And didn't you find anything, poor darling?"

"No. But there are still one or two things to look through. I hadn't time to finish."

She smiled at him indulgently, not knowing it was the first time she had ever felt sufficiently sure of him to do that.

"Do you want to go and complete the search now?"

"Not particularly."

"You can if you like." She gave a luxurious little yawn. "I'm getting sleepy again, anyway."

"All right." He held her for a moment longer, almost painfully tight. Then he kissed her and put her down.

At the door, he turned and smiled at her, so that she remembered the magic of those days in Verona and sensed all the magic of the days to come.

When he had gone, she lay there watching the last streak of the evening sun moving slowly across the opposite wall. She thought what a strange and wonderful day it had been. First the glorious news about Morley. Then the terrible struggle in the water. And finally the discovery that Reid loved her.

It would be quite in keeping now for him to find that Great-Aunt Tabitha left father half her money after all, she thought.

But that was a fanciful idea, and one that made her smile sleepily.

Anyway, it didn't really matter. For herself, she hardly cared at all who had the money. The only important thing about that inheritance was that in leaving the money to Reid, Great-Aunt Tabitha had brought them together.

Bless her, wherever she is! thought Leslie. And, thinking that, she fell asleep again.

A SCENT OF LEMONS

A Scent
of Lemons
Jill Christian

"You mean to turn our lives upside down, don't you?" Evie accused Rory McDermot. She'd had a premonition the first time she'd seen him on the quay of the small Greek island. She was not surprised he was prepared to take the roof from over their heads.

Admittedly, it was her mother's fault. Her dream to educate her young son, Georgi, in England had become an obsession. Selling their home was the only way to make it possible.

Evie sought ways to thwart the sale, but falling in love with the gentle Irishman Rory complicated her plans. There was a solution—but could a young Greek girl ask a man to marry her?

CHAPTER ONE

RORY MCDERMOT, having nothing to hurry for, stood
on the small quay watching the high-prowed caïque un-
load. He had shared the three-hour voyage from Kyrenia, Cyprus, with an oddly assorted cargo that included
two flop-eared goats and a bright scarlet bicycle, and
felt some interest in identifying the consignees. His human fellow passengers had been met noisily and affectionately by friends and families, and had repaired with
them to the wooden chairs under the vine-shaded veranda of the *taverna* on the quayside.

Later, Rory promised himself, he, too, would retire to
the shade of the *taverna* and trickle a measure of fiery
ouzo down his throat. But there was no hurry. The
Mediterranean sun, warm on his back, was not yet too
hot.

The island smelled sweet. The water was turquoise
clear and he could see small fish darting in the shadow
of the gaily painted caïque. The paint was sun bleached
into soft hues, though the staring open eye on either side
of the prow had been renewed lately.

He let his glance travel slowly along the quayside
houses, and beyond to the rest of the village, which
straggled a short way up the hillside and ended in olive
groves. All the houses were white, with red pantiled
roofs and outside stairs. There was a shop with neither
window nor door, just a three-sided room where the
proprietor sat on a wooden chair in the midst of his
wares.

A small excitement twisted in his breast. This might

be the place he was looking for. If that Greek waiter was
right and the house by the monastery could be bought,
this might be his home for the forseeable future. He
drew in a deep breath, relishing the herby scent, the
sharp lemon blossom in it, and wood smoke. A man
might live on the island well enough and have no need
of what they called civilization, which had grown so
uncivil of late; and if he behaved himself and walked se-
dately, in time he might come to be accepted by the in-
habitants.

He was not unaware of eyes watching him. Of course
they watched a stranger. In his boyhood in Connemara,
the arrival of a stranger had meant two days' excitement
and chatter. Slowly, he lowered his backpack to the
warm white stones and turned a little to let them see
him, as was friendly. Later they would want to know his
name and business, and maybe they'd ask or maybe
not; but he knew what was due to a village and would
let them know, obliquely or directly as they preferred it.

Out of the corner of his eye he saw two girls. One
dark and plump, a typical Mediterranean young woman
you could see anywhere from Crete to Anatolia. Dark,
plump, inviting, a quick-ripening beauty already with a
hint of the fatness to come. The other?

He held his breath and turned carefully to see her
better without seeming to stare. Where on earth did *she*
come from? She was a beauty—slim, fair, delicate
boned, holding herself proudly aloof. A goddess, risen
like Aphrodite from the foam of the sea? Yet she wore
the usual drab black garment of no particular style,
which he'd seen on women of all ages and sizes lately.
In it, she looked as graceful, as elegant, as a young
queen. Her hair shone pale gold and her skin was like
pearl. *B'golly*, he thought with a sudden grin at the fancy, *I'll be writing poetry before I'm much older. And it
wasn't for women I came to this place, or any place. Anyway, she's a child, no more.*

Suddenly there was a good-natured cheer, which brought his attention back to the caïque. A big square-built man held a red bicycle high above his head, and a small fair boy danced on the quay with excitement.

"Hi, Georgi! Here it comes! Watch out, I'll throw it."

The boy squealed, "No, don't. Don't throw it! It'll get broken."

The men laughed. The fair girl appeared by his side as if by magic, and her voice rang out. "He's teasing you, Georgi! Wait now, I'll help you."

The island patois was Greek basically, but with a twist of its own that made it hard to follow. So far he had only understood the boy and the girl clearly, but coming across, the boatman had understood his own careful, bookish Greek sufficiently. He would manage, and he had a quick ear and tongue for picking up words.

It was Georgi's birthday. The girl's name was Evie, and she was his sister. The pair of them were not out of the island basket, that was plain to see. Yet not strangers or visitors. They were accepted by everyone.

A touch on his arm took his attention from the brother and sister. It was the dark girl, who introduced herself as Sofia.

"You're welcome to the island, sir. Is there anything you want to see particularly? That's the monastery up there through the pepper trees. You can go up by the river if you like. Or there's the church. Maybe you'd like to take a photograph, or drink some coffee?"

He experienced a sudden sense of delight, a feeling of homecoming. A conviction that he had not met the Greek waiter by chance, and that the house would be for sale, as the Greek had hinted. His dream would come true here. It had started already.

"Coffee," he told the girl. "My name is Rory. I come from Ireland."

She frowned, not quite understanding his painstaking Greek. "Today? Is that in Cyprus?"

"No, no. I was born in Ireland. Today from Cyprus. Last week from Athens. The week before from . . . ."

The dark head nodded firmly. Now she understood.

"You are a tourist," Sofia told him.

He bent his head, not daring to contradict. Some day he might know the words to explain to her that a tourist had some place to go home to; that he had none.

Instead he told her he was hungry. The golden girl had disappeared with the boy and the shining bicycle, and he was sorry for it. He wanted to look at her again, having a feeling that a man might look at that lovely, withdrawn face a long time and not tire of looking. But she had gone and it was a long time since breakfast, and the sea always made him hungry; even the gentle summer tideless Mediterranean, so far and so different from the cold sea that crashed forever below the black cliffs of Moher on the far west coast of Ireland.

Sofia took his hand and led him to the *taverna* as if he were a blind man, though it wasn't twenty paces from where they'd been standing. She shouted in a shrill, fast dialect into the back of the inn, and a man's voice answered. And presently the man himself came out of the shadows through a shabby flowered cotton curtain carrying two plates, one laden with bread and green olives, the other with dates and goat cheese. Not what Rory would have chosen if asked, but he accepted the assortment with a murmured thank you. He had learned to enjoy fish and chips in England and hamburgers and corn on the cob in the States. He stood no nonsense from his taste buds. They took what he gave them and had to be thankful.

EVIE AND GEORGI MARSDEN were obliged to push the bicycle when they came to the end of the village road and started to climb up to their home. There was no proper road up to the monastery and the Villa Julia, only a hard-trodden path up a slope of rock and scrub open to the sun. Beside the path a stream tumbled, bordered with ferns and blooms of white anemones and poppies. Most days Georgi could stable his new mount in the village or, boylike, leave it lying on the rocks at the foot of the track. Unless goats ate the tires it would be safe. The machine was Georgi's. No one on the island would touch it without invitation.

But today it must be taken home to show to mama.

Julia Marsden rarely went down to the village except on Sundays when, mounted on the high wooden saddle of her donkey and wearing a stiff black silk gown, she attended the Greek Orthodox church with her children. Afterwards she would drink a glass or two of wine under the awning of the *taverna* with her women friends and relatives and listen to the family news. Twenty years ago Julia had been a village girl like the others, but even then, Evie sometimes thought, she must have had some special quality that set her apart. For it had been Julia whom the Englishman, George Marsden, wooed and married. For Julia he had built the white villa up on the fertile little plateau, bought and cultivated the land that now supported his family.

And ever since the wedding day, Julia had set herself apart. Never failing to take an interest in island affairs, in the children and grandchildren, the weddings and funerals, but aloof, like a great lady, like a queen.

Even when George Marsden left her, tiring perhaps of seven years of village life and the cultivation of his lemons, and longing for the company of educated men of his own kind, Julia never relaxed her dignity. George was merely taking a holiday, as he deserved. He would be back, in his own time.

The pair had to carry the bike up the last stretch and emerged onto an open plateau like a ledge on the hillside. Here were fields carefully cultivated to grow fruit and vegetables. Julia's olive trees, and those belonging to the four old brothers of the monastery, were separated by a wide ditch.

"There's mama," said Georgi, "working in the field. She said I needn't, because of my birthday, but I didn't want her to do my work. I'm a man now. I'm eleven and I can manage fine. When I'm bigger we'll be able to cultivate right up to the edge of the brothers' land, and we'll be rich and you'll be able to get married."

Evie hugged his narrow shoulders. "I don't want to get married. I want to stay here with you and mama, forever and ever. If I were a man, I think I'd go into a monastery and be a brother, and live with God, and grow things."

"And paint icons? I shan't. I shall plant grapefruit and oranges, and stop growing all these tiresome vegetables. I'll plant the whole island with my fruit trees, and sit and watch them grow money for me."

"You won't. If mama sells the house, you'll go to England to school, and get educated and be a businessman in an office. That's what she wants."

"It's *my* land. She can't sell it."

"If it's for your own good, she can. Father wanted a proper English education for you. Everybody knows that. So they'll tell her she's right to carry out her husband's wishes."

"If they force me to go, I shall run away."

Evie was torn between her respect for her mother's authority and sympathy with the boy. Lying awake on hot nights, she had formulated a dozen plans for circumventing her mother's determination, and comforted herself with the knowledge that there would never be enough money to send Georgi away unless the house

and land were sold. And who would buy? If any man on
Exos had the price of it, he would have bought already,
for the land was fertile and well cultivated, sheltered
from winds and watered by the stream, which rarely
dried up even at the height of summer. The real danger
lay in the homecomers: islanders returning with a fat
bank balance after a few years' work in Greece, Malta,
Rome, or even England, ready to invest it in land and
olives to support them in old age.

Georgi, crimson with effort, pointed down to the village and the shimmering sea. "There was a man in the
caïque, a foreigner. Perhaps he'll buy the house."

The dazzling white houses were like toys now. The
boats lay still, painted toys on painted water. The quay,
the street, were deserted. For hours, the men would sit
in the shade on those ubiquitous wooden chairs, playing
cards, playing chess, talking, staring into nowhere. Even
the stranger had gone.

Evie weighed the possibilities, then shook her head.
"Too poor. He had no luggage, only a pack on his back.
He hadn't a camera, or a gold wristwatch. He'll stay for
a few days at the *taverna*, walk in the hills a bit, then
he'll go away. Don't worry about him."

Their mother had seen them and waved. Georgi rode
toward her, wobbling a little on the narrow trodden
path toward the house.

"Mama," Evie reproved, "it's too hot to work outside.
Come indoors and let me make coffee for you. Everyone
is resting in the shade but my foolish mother."

The rooms of the villa had high blue ceilings and
arched windows, which were now shuttered for cool-
ness. On the seaward side of the house, George Marsden had built a wide balcony with a trellised roof, which
over the years had become smothered with vines and
jasmine. To this cool terrace Evie brought the coffee.

Georgi lay on his stomach, entranced by the shining

splendor of his present. He reached out an inattentive hand for the chilled bottle of his favourite fizzy drink and applied the straw to his lips absentmindedly.

"He is happy," Julia murmured. She was tired and despised herself for being so, after so little work today. It seemed no time at all since she had been a girl able to work long hours in the fields, or shake down ripe olives all day, or help with the lemon harvest and dance on the quay till midnight afterward.

"Do you think Georgi's father will be pleased with him?" she asked now, not for the first time. "He's a fine boy for his age, isn't he? And clever, the brothers tell me. Were there any letters for us by the boat?"

"Nothing, mama. Do you think ... I mean, have you ever wondered if our father is still alive? All these years, and you still wait for a letter. Wouldn't we be happier if we accepted the idea that he will never come back?"

"*Never come back*? Of course your father will come back! He has a wandering nature, that's all. He loves us all, and he will want to see us soon. He'll be pleased with you, Evie. You take after him with your fair hair and blue eyes. You look English."

Evie bit her lip and kept silent. That she resembled her absent father annoyed her unspeakably. As the years stretched out, as she saw hope fade in her mother's eyes, as even small Georgi had to work to grow and harvest the lemons that supported them, the childish affection for her father had changed to implacable hatred. But her mother must never know it, so she merely nodded.

"But his son! I've failed him there. He wanted a proper education for his boy, an English education. He will be grieved with me about that."

"It wasn't your fault, mama. Father should have come back, or sent you the money. Where would we get the fare to England, or clothes for the boy? And who would arrange it all for us? We don't know anybody over there."

"When I sell the house...."

"Mama, give up this idea. Georgi is old enough to know what he wants, and we should respect his wishes. He has a good inheritance here, land and a fine house. What need is there to send him away from everything he knows, and everybody he loves, to that horrible country where it rains every day and is so cold? Will he thank you for it, when he becomes a man without roots, without the house and land his father bought? Do be careful what you're doing."

Julia shot her daughter a look half-defiant, half-ashamed. Two passions fought in her, two deep-rooted traditions: the passion of the peasant for land, and the ingrained belief that her husband was lord and master, to be obeyed even in his absence. To obey her husband's wishes would rob her son of his patch of fertile soil, but to disregard them was unthinkable. Already she had dillydallied so long. She sighed heavily.

"If only George would come, I should not have to decide. Evie, I think you must go and find him, tell him the boy is growing up."

Evie sat back on her naked heels and stared at her mother. She felt cold with shock. How long had that idea been simmering in mama's devious mind?

"But where should I find him, mama? It could take years. He could be anywhere in the whole world. Where could I begin?"

"In England. There must be people there who know him."

Evie sighed impatiently. "Mama, I've told you again and again, England is enormous, many times bigger than Cyprus. Nicosia is a village compared with London. There are millions of people there, packed as close together as pebbles on a beach."

"They must have some way of knowing whether a man is alive or dead, if they're so clever."

"He might be in America, or Africa."

Georgi had fallen asleep on the floor beside the bike. Now he woke up suddenly and asked if he might ride across to the monastery to show the brothers his bike. "They'll be interested, mama. Truly they will. And I can tell them about the boat, and who's home. And about the Englishman."

Julia darted a look at Evie. "What Englishman?"

"A stranger. He came on the boat. He hadn't any luggage, only a canvas bag. He looked English . . . well, not American."

"Where is he now?"

Evie shrugged. "How should I know? In the *taverna*, perhaps, or asleep under an olive tree. He's one of those holidayers who come with nothing and expect everything on the cheap. No one down there will make a fortune out of him, I'll be bound."

"I have a fool for a daughter! Why didn't you invite him here? He might know something about your father. He might even have a message for us. Or—or he might have come to buy a house on Exos."

"Mama, I tell you, he isn't rich. And a man doesn't buy a house without his wife. And if father sent him with a message, he'd tell him where we lived. Dear, sweet little mama, please stop hoping so much. I can't bear it when you're disappointed. The world's so big, so many people in it. Yet you expect every stranger who lands here will know about George Marsden."

Georgi jigged from one foot to the other. "May I go, mama?"

"Yes, yes, boy. But don't be a trouble to the brothers. If they are busy, come home. And don't forget to say a prayer in the chapel before you leave."

Georgi ran off happily.

"One day," said his mother, folding her hands on her lap again, "the Englishman will pass this way to visit the monastery. Visitors always do. I shall invite him in to taste our honey and sheep cheese, and I shall ask him if he wants to buy the house."

"A house? A tent, more like. He'll laugh at you."

Julia drew herself up. "Nobody laughs at *me*, Evie, least of all, a guest in my house. Where is this man staying? At the *taverna*? When I was a girl it was famous for fleas. Your father stayed there two nights when he arrived, and took his bed into the fields, until my mother offered him our hospitality."

"Funny, to think my existence depends upon a flea. If they'd bitten harder, he might have left the island after one night. If they hadn't bitten at all, he'd have remained at the *taverna* and you'd never have married him."

"Yes, I would. He fell in love with me the moment he landed. We girls were watching the boat arriving at the quay, and laughing, the way girls do. He looked up and saw us, five of us. There and then he fell in love with the girl in the middle. I had a sky-blue silk dress, and white lace round the neck of my dress. It looked so pretty, he said, against my brown skin. You never make lace, Evie. We all used to be so proud to wear the lace we'd made ourselves."

"I'm not a lace person. I wish I'd been a boy. Anyway, I can wear your lace when I have to. You made enough for a whole family, and it's far more beautiful than anything I could manage."

"You're like your father, you have no patience to sit still. Bring me my embroidery. You are right, it's too hot now to work outside."

Like most of the Exos women, Julia earned a little by her exquisite embroidery on linen, which was collected once a year and sent over to Cyprus to be sold in the luxury hotels of Nicosia. She was now working on a circular white tablecloth, covered so closely with open-work that hardly an inch of the original material remained visible. Already she had worked on it for almost two years, and this summer she hoped to finish it. It would find a buyer among the rich Americans, but the high price paid for it would scarcely repay Julia for the hundreds of hours she had spent on it.

Evie settled her mother to work in a spot where the sun would not reach too soon, with all her materials around her; then she changed into a sleek black bathing suit and ran to swim. There was a short cut to the best beach down the side of the seaward-facing cliff, down which she scrambled, dropping from one herb-scented ledge to another till she reached the level patch of ground where flowers grew in profusion: anemones, marigolds, daisies, cyclamen, wild gladioli, and lilies. The air was awash with scent and loud with honeybees.

Only a small cypress grove stood now between Evie and the water, which shimmered in the sun in bars of emerald and azure. Eager for the pleasure of the salt water, she ran, head thrown back and fair hair streaming.

Till she fell headlong and landed heavily across the chest and arms of a stranger sleeping under a pepper tree.

His voice spoke in her ear. Very loud and startled it was, and with an accent the like of which she had never heard. The grip of his arms was like iron.

"Glory be! I'm sleeping under a pepper tree dreaming of angels when the goddess Aphrodite herself falls spang out of the sky into me arms. And she screaming blue murder! For the love of holy Michael, woman, will you shut up yelling!"

Evie, the breath knocked out of her, stopped struggling and sat up, first removing herself from the man's bare chest.

"Why don't you keep your legs to yourself?" she demanded crossly when she could speak. "I didn't see you stretched out flat among the tree shadows. Lucky I didn't break a limb falling like that."

"I did my best to catch you," he said, not humbly. "Why don't you look where you're going so fast?"

"There's never anyone here. You're the Englishman who landed this morning, aren't you? Do you have fleas?"

"Good lord, no. Why? It's not a question I'd ask my best friend, never mind a total stranger."

"I mean, at the *taverna*, if you're staying there. I didn't mean to ask out loud, but we were talking of it, my mother and I, and the question of fleas turned out to be quite important to my existence. Sorry, it sort of popped out. I don't suppose you have."

"If I find one in the *taverna*'s bed, I'll let you know at once," he promised gravely. "My name, since you didn't ask, is Rory McDermot, and I'm not English."

"Good. I dislike the English intensely."

"So do I. Let us sit down here where it's cool, and explain to each other why we have no use for the English."

"My father is one. But it's not on account of him, exactly. What about you?"

"It's because I come from Ireland."

"Ireland? Where's that? What is it famous for?"

"For princesses, ma'am. We export them. Have you never heard of the Princess Etain?"

"Never. What do you mean, 'export them'?"

"In men's hearts, ma'am. Not an Irishman the width of the world but has a princess, maybe two, in his heart."

She saw at once that this was no Englishman, but a man who could tell a stranger a legend at the drop of a hat. She fell in with his mood at once.

"So the world must be full of your princesses. Do they never get home again?"

"Oh, yes, now and again. Sometimes a princess will fall right out of the sky into a man's arms, same like now. You were going swimming?"

She was sufficiently collected to see now that he, too, was wearing swimming things, and was a great deal browner and leaner than the average vacationer who landed on Exos. His straight fair hair was sun bleached, his jaw and nose aggressive, his eyes blue and as bright as washed pebbles. For the first time in her life, masculinity—the simple fact that here was a young, personable man—intrigued her.

He smelled good. She wrinkled her nose, so recently squashed against his bare chest, thinking that he smelled more like the young freshness of her brother than like any man of the village. They smelled mostly of goat and sweat, fish, garlic and cheese.

Out of nowhere, fear dropped a shadow across her mind. This was how it had been with her mother. A blond god out of the blue, and love blossoming suddenly; and a lifetime of waiting and watching for that wandering god to come again. How it had always been, perhaps, for the girls of the islands, right back to the time when, they say, gods walked the earth like men.

She retreated from the situation. "Yes, I . . . I always swim alone. And I don't like to be watched."

"Point taken." He unwound himself, coming to his feet in one smooth movement. "I'll go. I'm sorry, I never asked if you were hurt. You did go a purler."

She frowned. "Purler? I don't know that word."

"A bump. That's one your father didn't teach you. I suppose you speak fluent Greek, too?"

"My mother is Greek—Exos-Greek."

"I see. And you live here? Up on the cliff? Isn't that where the monastery is? I must walk up there and have a look at it. They say the brothers paint magnificent icons."

If he went to the monastery, he would pass the Villa Julia and mama would invite him in and sell him the house, whether he wanted it or not. "No," she said quickly. "I mean, they do paint, but it's rubbish, really. Nothing up there is worth the climb. The best part of the island is to the north and west. Go there. You'll like it."

She turned and ran across the white sand, fear giving her feet wings.

I'm not afraid of him, she thought. *He's kind and gentle, and tells fairy stories. What I'm afraid of is myself.*

She met the warm, silky water with a quiver of pure pleasure, rested upon it, and swam strongly and steadily. After a time she turned on her back and floated, looking back toward the land. From here one could see the white monastery with its little bell tower; and the pink-washed walls of the Villa Julia.

Also the cypress grove, which would be empty now.

The water had washed away her foolish panic and quieted her beating heart. She trod water, regretfully. It would have been pleasant, after all, to have company for her swim. He could swim well, she fancied, with those strong brown arms cleaving the blue and emerald.

"We export princesses—and sometimes one falls out of the sky."

She laughed and dived, swimming underwater with eyes open, seeing small, bright fish flash and turn as one, shells on the sea floor, and coralline weed.

Well, he would soon tire of the island north and west. There was nothing there to see but a small copper mine, and a flat gray salt bed. The stranger would be back.

CHAPTER TWO

FOR TWO DAYS Evie kept a careful watch for the Irishman, worked in the field close to home, in the house, or even, desperately, at her somewhat lumpy embroidery on the shaded balcony. But Rory McDermot did not approach, either from the seaward side of the cliff, or from the village up the track by the tumbling little river.

She had no idea what she intended to do if he did appear. Head him off, if possible, or steer him wide of the house in the direction of the monastery so that her mother would not see him.

For three years now, Julia Marsden had been talking vaguely of selling the house that was too big for three, and settling down in the village among her cronies in a small cottage belonging to her own family. It had stood empty because too many cousins and second cousins were leaving the island these days to make their fortunes in a bigger sphere. Some actually did, but showed no inclination to return to Exos to a tiny, cramped house with an outside stair and no sanitation. But now, startled by the impact of Georgi's eleventh birthday, she meant business. Evie could feel the change in her bones.

It was, the girl reflected, as she hoed along the neat rows of vegetables, a thousand pities that the Villa Julia was Julia's. By one of those extraordinary quirks of the English character so incomprehensible to the islanders, George Marsden had bought the place, not for himself, but for his wife. There was nothing to stop her selling it, if she wished. And Julia could be so gently determined to get her own way that she was capable of selling it to the Irishman, even if all he wanted was a melon or a ripe pomegranate. The only safe way was to keep the two apart.

But on the third day Evie became bored with keeping so close to home, and longed for a chat with Sofia, who was sure to know what the man was up to. Sofia was very reliable with news, for she was related to the Stratos family who kept the *taverna*, and when it suited her she put an hour or two in as a waitress. Small as the tourist trade was for Exos, Sofia liked to be at the centre of it. Besides, she said, it was good practice. One day she'd be off to see the world of Cyprus or even farther afield, and it is good to have a trade in one's hands then.

Sofia laughed, throwing her head back and showing her strong, creamy throat. She had a new black dress on, and a strip of lace, and a scarlet silk apron, which last year she had worn only for feast days.

"He's mad, that Irishman. This morning at dawn he hired a donkey and rode off to the copper mines. Would you believe it? He says everyone in his country rides a donkey, but they don't have wooden saddles like ours. He took some food in a bag. What, for goodness' sake, is there to see in a copper mine?"

"Perhaps he's a miner? Perhaps he wants to buy copper."

"Not he. He has no money. You should see his bedroom. Only two shirts, Evie! He's twenty-six and not married, and his eyes are gray."

Evie opened her mouth to say "blue," but asked instead how Sofia knew.

"From his passport, of course. He left it on the wooden chest."

"You can't read English. If it *is* in English?"

"Your young brother can. I brought it down in my pocket and asked him yesterday."

"Sofia! You know it was wrong. You shouldn't spy on a guest. Nor should Georgi."

The plump shoulders shrugged. "He isn't my guest. Why are you so interested? You haven't asked about Marcus."

Evie frowned, puzzled. "Marcus?"

"He came home the day the stranger came. I told you."

"Why should I ask about him? He was always a horrid creature. We agreed we didn't like him, even before he went away."

Sofia slapped her arm and giggled. "Do grow up, Evie! Marcus has changed. He's charming now. Such beautiful manners, and he's grown really handsome. You'd hardly know him, if you're still thinking of that tiresome, spotty youth we used to know. He's a man of the world, no less. He has money, too, and a very good job in Athens. You should have been here last night. Nothing would please him but dancing on the quay, with the lanterns out and everything. We're going to do it again tonight. Will your mother let you come?"

"She might. I'd have to bring Georgi. He wouldn't want to miss anything. Does the Irishman dance?"

Sofia nodded vigorously. "And plays the accordion, too. And once he sang. It was a terribly sad song, I think. Everybody went quiet while he sang it. Music over the water can be sad, don't you think?"

Evie made up her mind. "I'll come."

"That's right. And wear your white dress. Don't come in that old black one, though you're perfectly capable of such a trick. Put your hair up in a loop on top of your head, and wear shoes and stockings. Honestly, Evie, anyone would think you're about fifteen, not a lady turned eighteen. You're so skinny, too."

"I know. I wish I were as plump as you, and with your coloring." Evie sighed regretfully, aware that in the white dress she looked even paler and more insignificant than Sofia. But she had no other, and had never bothered to take the boat as far as Kyrenia to fit herself out with something more fashionable.

"Princesses," he'd said. Girls with bouncing black hair and bright brown eyes, and lips like the inside of a ripe pomegranate bursting on the tree.

She finished her shopping and began to walk home with a loaded basket on each arm. Her feet felt light as air, and even going up the steepest part of the climb, she seemed to be skimming over the ground, uplifted by excited anticipation. In some book, she remembered, there had been flaxen-haired princesses, and it may be the Irishman thought as much of long, straight fair hair as of short, bouncy curls that shone like black olives.

In the white dress, with shoes and stockings, and her hair piled high and tied with a broad blue ribbon that matched her eyes, she might find an evening of dancing under the lanterns on the waterfront exciting. Music, and the colored lights dancing in long bars across the water, and maybe the Irishman would sing his sad song again.

She thought a little about Marcus. Could that rough, detestable boy really have become a good-looking man with beautiful manners, as Sofia said? The warm dark hours after sunset promised to be interesting, and she hugged her heavy baskets to her, hardly able to contain her delight. Such a perfect day! Such a wonderful place to live! How could anyone bear to leave it?

IN THE LATE AFTERNOON Rory McDermot trudged along a hot, dusty road, leading a reluctant donkey. He was angry. He enlivened his walk by rehearsing what he meant to say to that lying little creature who had sent him off on a wild-goose chase to the other side of the island, to find nothing for his trouble but the ugly waste tips of an old copper mine and the gray concrete huts of the mine offices and workers' dwellings.

It was longer than he had thought since his donkey-riding days in Connemara. In those days he had been able to kick the hairy ribs of his mount with his bare heels, but now his feet almost reached the ground. Then, he had ridden bareback; today he was lumbered with a high wooden saddle directly descended, it seemed, from some medieval instrument of torture. If some horny-handed man—such as her father—put her across his knee and walloped her till she couldn't sit down, it would be no more than she deserved. Too late for him to do it, more's the pity. The child was almost a woman, very nearly a beauty.

Suddenly he remembered his talk of princesses and laughed aloud, startling the delicate legged, chocolate-colored donkey. Much talk of their beauty, pale faces, golden hair and such. Nothing to say the same princesses of old time mightn't be the great fibbers.

The sea and the row of date palms along the water-front of the village came into view around the bend in the road. He jerked the halter, and mounted the donkey again, groaning at his protesting muscles.

"Come on, Beelzebub, get moving! Let us ride in like a pair of conquerors. At least you'll tell no one I've walked as far as you have today, for the sake of your thin legs as much as for my creaking bones. I've gone soft, boyo. I've seen the time when I thought nothing to see a grown man riding a donkey carrying two loaded panniers of peat besides."

The donkey, smelling home, put on a show of willingness and Rory had to watch out for his dangling feet on the rough road. He had no wish to break an ankle, dashing it against a boulder.

If there was dancing again tonight, he would cut a poor figure, stiff as he was. Last night he had had plenty of choice of partners, and the plump little Sofia had used him to tease the handsome Greek boy, Marcus.

Well, he didn't mind helping in a good cause, and twice he remembered snatching the girl almost out of the Greek's grasp. Between whiles he'd looked around once or twice hoping to see his companion of the afternoon, young Aphrodite fallen out of the sky, knocking the breath out of him; but she wasn't there. Too young, perhaps, and kept close to home by strict parents.

One day soon, he thought aloud, flicking the donkey with a cut stick, we shall meet again, my girl, and I shall give you the rough edge of my tongue, for liars I cannot abide.

A lizard, startled by his rumbling voice, flicked off a gray boulder and vanished. The donkey pricked his ears and broke into a trot. It could not understand the English words but knew from experience how a man's voice sounded when he was angry.

EVIE WASHED HER WHITE DRESS and while waiting for it to dry for ironing, corrected Georgi's arithmetic.

"Look, little one, if you get your sums wrong now, it doesn't matter so much. But you must try to get them right, because when you're a man, a grower, with big groves of lemons, grapefruit, olives, it will matter then. If you get your sums wrong, a whole year's work could be wasted. You'll have to buy and sell, pay wages and know how many trees to plant in an acre of land. You'll have to ship your crops to the mainland and pay freight at so much a load."

"When I'm the boss, I'll make somebody else do the sums."

"Then you'll be cheated."

His mouth firmed. He looked up scowling, his strong brows drawn together. "No one will cheat *me*."

"Not if you're cleverer than they are. That's why I make you have extra lessons, little one. I know it comes

hard, in the heat and when there are so many better
things to do." She sat cross-legged on the floor beside
him. "Look now. Let's start again. Pretend you're the
owner of a simply enormous plantation and I've come
to buy half your crop."

His serious eyes met hers. "Evie, mama will send me
away if she sells the house. Don't let her. I just want to
stay here on my island and grow things. If I have to go
away to the cold and dark, I'll die. I *know* I'll die."

She swept him into her arms. "I'll try. I swear I'll try
my best to keep you here. But you'll have to help yourself, too. You'll have to work at getting an education
here, or the priest will tell mama you're to go away to
learn more. We all want the best for you, Georgi. Only
mama's idea of what is best is to do what father would
have wanted for you, and she might be right."

The boy twisted out of her arms and flung himself on
the floor sobbing. "Don't let her make me go! I want to
stay here, at home. I don't want her to sell the house to
get the money. It's mine. The land is mine. If she sells it,
I'll never get it back. It isn't fair, Evie!"

That was the rub. What *was* fair, for the child? Was it
right to keep an intelligent boy here on the island,
taught only by the priest and a girl? Would he later be
as full of reproaches as he was now full of pleading? He
had an English father, alive or dead. Ought he not to see
something of England then?

But could it be right to sell the boy's inheritance of
good land and a good house? To send him, protesting,
away to a future he might not care for?

She crouched down beside him, stroked his hair. "I
won't let her sell this land, Georgi, that I swear. Even if
you do have to go away to be taught, you'll have the
land to come back to, if you choose. I'll do
anything—absolutely anything at all—to keep your
land for you. The house I may not be able to save, if

mama is set on it; but we shall have a house down in the village, the one that belonged to mama's family, and it's not a bad house, is it?"

"It's not *my* house."

"No. I'll fight any idea of selling this house, too, but I may not win. We might have to compromise, Georgi, but there are two of us, and only one of mama, so we shan't lose all the battles."

Georgi dried his eyes, but he was too upset for further arithmetic, so Evie sent him off to play while she ironed her dress. "Then we'll go swimming, I promise."

The white dress had been new for Easter Sunday last year. Evie pressed the lace around the neck carefully. She would wear the Maltese cross on a gold chain, which her father had given her all those years ago. She remembered so little of him, but she did recall the day he had come home with the little trinket in his pocket, and mama had made her put it away till she was older.

I'm older now, she decided firmly. *I shall wear the necklet now, every day if I want to.*

The ironing finished, she experimented with her hair. Easy enough to plait it into a single heavy rope, but not so easy to twist it into a coil and pin it high on her head. But the result pleased her. She touched her neck wonderingly. Now, it did seem to matter that it was longer and thinner than Sofia's. Under the coronet of hair, her small head was poised gracefully, reminding her of the old Greek statues in the museum she had visited once as a schoolgirl. Like the head on a coin!

Shaking with excitement, she tugged off the old black dress and carefully dropped the white one over her head without damaging the coronet. If the piled-up hair could work a tiny miracle for her head and neck, perhaps it would work for the dress, too.

Looking at herself in the long glass, she fell from joy to depression. The dress would not do. It was a schoolgirl's Sunday dress, neat but shapeless. And she had grown out of it. It wouldn't even fasten properly. Dismay shook her, a lump rose in her throat. After the long hours of happy anticipation, she would not consider running down to the village in her black dress, with her hair swinging over her shoulders. Yesterday, she could have done it. But yesterday existed in time past. Today was different because she was different.

She ran out onto the terrace, where Julia was embroidering in the cool shade.

"Mama! My dress!"

Julia looked up, and kept on looking in silence for a long drawn-out minute. Then she stabbed her needle into her work and stood up.

"No, Evie, it won't do. You can't go in that. We must do something about it."

"Moving the buttons again won't do. It's a child's dress."

Julia, surprisingly, kissed her daughter lightly. She was a reserved woman, not demonstrative ever. "And you are not a child anymore! How time races away. Your father should see you now, Evie. You are going to be beautiful very soon. He always said you had a perfect nose and the rest of your face would live up to it eventually. Come along. I'll find something for you to wear. And I think I must come, too. I can't let you run wild anymore."

The idea of having a chaperone did not disconcert Evie in the least. All the mothers would be there, sitting in rows behind little tables, each with her glass of wine, her gossip, her son or daughter to be proud of; to be the only dancer who had no mama or papa watching would be odd and uncomfortable. What did worry her was the fear of what mama might produce as suitable for her to wear.

In mama's bedroom there was a great carved chest

built of oak bleached and stained with seawater. Her father insisted that it was British and had come with the
crusaders, perhaps floated ashore from some shipwreck
all those centuries ago. This Julia now unlocked, though
it took both of them to lift back the lid.

The first layer was burial clothes for all the members
of the family, handwoven, bleached, and ironed ready.
Next came several suits belonging to George Marsden,
smelling strongly of cloves and put by for his son if
George himself never came back. Then there was the
family wedding dress, the lace a trifle yellowed now, the
tiny crown wrapped in white linen.

"Time we were thinking about a husband for you,
Evie. Your father wouldn't want you to marry an island
man. He'll come and take you to England, you'll see.
You'll live in London and have a proper house with taps
indoors and a chain to pull, and what your father called
a proper lavatory seat. Some of them even have taps in
the bedroom."

"I know. But they don't have the sun, or the sea.
When I open my shutters in the morning, the sun comes
in like a sword, a long, bright sword lying across the
floor."

"And a washing machine."

"I'll need it," the girl said glumly. "Everything covered in black soot, and raining every single day so you
can't dry anything."

Julia sat back on her heels and looked up at her
daughter quizzically. "Sometimes I think you exagger-
ate when you talk about England, child. I'm sure your
father wouldn't stay there so long if it rained every single day. He loved—loves—the sun, too. As you do."

"Then why doesn't he come home? Isn't there anything else in the chest? I can't wear the wedding dress
tonight."

"Be patient." Carefully, with some grunting and

groaning, Julia leaned far into the deep oak and brought up a wrapped package. "It's what I wore for feast days. There can't be many about now. Open it, child."

A cornflower-blue satin skirt over layers of white starched petticoats. A yellow bibbed apron embroidered in purple and black, green and blue and crimson. A white blouse with full sleeves tight at the wrist, a pretty lace cap. To wear with it, long white stockings and scarlet shoes.

"Oh, mama!" Evie breathed. "Is it really for me?"

"I don't see why not. I had it from my mother. Will it fit? I had a better figure than you—round as a cherry, I was. It's the English in you that makes you so skinny."

NEWS OF THE PREVIOUS NIGHT'S DANCING having spread on the wind, the village of Peleas was full when Julia arrived, stately in black satin and sitting very erect on her donkey. Georgi led the animal, and Evie, self-conscious and shy, but trying hard not to show it, followed in the blue swinging skirt over a dozen freshly pressed petticoats.

Straw mats had been thrown over the wooden stands, which had been empty all winter, and tables set up under their shade. Colored electric lights swung from end to end of the quay, bright painted chairs were set out, and the mixed band of musicians was already in place in one of the fishing boats. Families from the small Turkish village on the other side of the island had walked over and were greeted as friends, the cruel passions of the Cyprus feud of no concern to neighbors who had lived cheek by jowl for generations. The men came in their black baggy trousers, the women with black shawls over their heads, out of which their oval faces peered, smiling. The proprietor of the *taverna* dusted off the communal hubble-bubble pipe and set it on the table outside to be smoked by three men at once.

Julia found a seat and held court. Half the people present were related to her, more or less distantly, and came to pay their respects. Soon she had a handful of flowers, and a bloom tucked into her hair.

Sofia was spellbound by Evie's dress. "I can't wait to show Marcus! He'll be so surprised. He used to pull your hair."

Evie grinned. "I pulled his. If he tries it again, so will I. Is—er—anybody else here?"

Sofia's laugh made heads turn in their direction. "You silly! Everybody's here! There are to be fireworks. Marcus brought them, great boxes! If you mean the Irishman, I think he's gone to bed. Not that he'll sleep in this uproar."

Evie knew a stab of disappointment. Her own appearance in Julia's long looking glass had startled her into the realization that she possessed a special quality of looks that might well compete with the other girls of the island; even with Sofia, who, up till now had been Evie's ideal. Clad in her heavenly-blue dress, the lace cap on her silver blonde hair, cheeks flushed a little with excitement, she had stared and stared, unable to believe her eyes.

With her hands she had explored the soft curves of her figure, understanding that there might be a more subtle beauty than the emphasized plumpness of her friends. Skinny, they called her teasingly. But out of the shapeless old black frock she wasn't skinny at all. She was....

"Beautiful?" she whispered. "Am I? Could someone think me beautiful, I wonder?"

She was trembling with the sudden discovery of herself. All the way down to the village she had hugged the knowledge. No one would notice, of course. She would still be the pale, skinny one among the dark plump beauties. But perhaps Rory, the Irishman, might see—he with his talk of princesses. She held her head high, as if it bore an imaginary crown.

And now the wretched man had gone to bed. As if the dancing didn't matter, as if he despised them all, the laughing girls, the friendly hospitality, the music, the fireworks to come.

"We're not good enough for him, then?" she said to Sofia. "Well, we don't want strangers here. Once tourists come, all the fun will be for them, and we'll only exist for cooking and serving meals. Come on, let's find Marcus."

Marcus had found them. He came toward them smiling, a bunch of spring flowers in his hands. He had filled out in his two years' absence. He was, Evie thought, two inches taller. As Sofia had said, he was a man, and good to look at.

His dark eyes were shining with the happiness of being home, being king of the castle tonight as provider of the fireworks to come. The girl he chose would be queen tonight. Of old unwritten custom, he would make his choice with the flowers he had picked and tied into a bunch with ribbon. If it was not exactly a proposal of marriage, the presentation of the flowers was certainly an indication of a strong interest in the recipient—the opening gambit in a courtship to come.

And Marcus was making straight for Sofia. Evie glanced quickly at her friend, feeling a faint chill of sadness. She would miss Sofia, for with instinctive prescience she knew that the long island courtship and marriage would put an end to the closeness. Friends they would always be, but after tonight, perhaps, never so warm and near to each other.

Sofia's face was easy to read, for one who knew her—proud, happy, shy. Not yet in love, but standing tiptoe on the edge of it.

Marcus walked straight past her and put the flowers into Evie's hands. Then kissed her firmly on both cheeks.

"No, Marcus. No!" She pushed away, trying to make him take back the bouquet. The heady scent of it choked her.

"Come on, Evie!" He laughed happily. "Don't pretend you've never been kissed before." He took a pace back and looked her up and down. "You've grown up in two years. Where's that tomboy scarecrow gone? You're the prettiest girl here, and I'm claiming the right to the first dance."

Sick at heart, she asked, "Don't you want to dance with Sofia?"

"Sure I do. With every girl there is. But you first, because you're the prettiest."

No one, as far as she knew, had ever refused a young man's flowers. It would be an insult to him and his family. It might start a feud that lasted for a century. She cast a helpless glance at Sofia, whose smile was stuck to her mouth like a leftover flower on a winter tree. Then Marcus whirled her off into the dancing.

"What a surprise for a man to come home and find all the girls so pretty!"

"What a surprise," she returned, "to find you so tall and handsome." *And so stupid*, she added to herself. "Aren't they much prettier in Athens?"

"Some are. But they don't smell of honey and flowers, and most of them judge a man by the depth of his pocket. I like kissing them, but I'd never feel like marrying one."

"Cheers for the island, then. Are you staying long?"

"That depends." He smiled down at her, and increased the pressure of his arm around her.

"You don't want to come home and settle down?"

"Not yet. In time I might. I'd like my own restaurant, but on one of the bigger islands."

"That takes money, Marcus."

He shrugged. "It can be earned. With the right wife, it wouldn't take so long. Two can earn and save quicker than one."

"Two of the same mind. You'd have to pick the right one."

He laughed. "I know what I want, Evie. There's time enough, and we're young yet."

"*We*?"

With relief she saw a way to withdraw without offense. "There's Melanie. She's brought her baby. I *must* see it. It's her first. Doesn't she look proud?"

With a quick wriggle she was out of his grasp and among the baby-worshippers gathered around the young mother. She prayed hard to St. Polystemon to make Marcus go back to Sofia. It didn't seem the sort of prayer to bother the greater saints with, but St. Poly had been a boy of the island himself, so they said; and not more than twenty years old when he died for his faith. So perhaps he would understand how it was to be young and in love, and hoping too much.

Father Bernard, the island priest, smiled and patted the chair beside him. His squat, black-clad figure was never far away from the centre of any activity—except swimming. Every child firmly believed that Father Bernard had been born into his long black gown, with his tall veiled headdress stuck on his head, though each was prepared to believe there might have been a time when his beard was not so long, so curly, or so gray.

"Marcus has become a fine man," the priest commented, his eyes everywhere and smiling on his beloved flock. "I hope to see him married to one of our own, an island girl."

"You will, Father. I'm sure of it."

"Yes, I've noticed a man comes back to his own, if he has good sense. I like to think of our dear St. Poly as a lad like Marcus, a big handsome boy."

"Do you think he pulled the girls' hair and tormented them?"

The priest shook with quiet laughter. "I'm sure he did. I know I did when I was his age. But it didn't come to me to become a martyr, you see. Bless me, I remember your mother in that dress, Evie. It is the same one? It was the day your father arrived, so he probably set eyes on her for the first time in that very outfit. No wonder he loved her. And now it's your turn, eh?"

"Not yet. I have things to do. What's to become of Georgi, Father? My mother wants to sell the property to buy him a good education, but I don't think she should. It's his inheritance. A man with land, that's something."

"An education is also something, child."

"You teach him. I teach him. What can he learn that will be better for him? Where would it take him, all this education?"

"No one can say what a boy will become, Evie. I know this problem. Your mother has talked of it many times. It is your father's wish. I think she should do it."

"Against the boy's wish? Surely he has some rights? The right not to have his land sold over his head? Father, I think my father must be dead. If only I could be sure, one way or the other. How can one find out?"

"From official records, maybe. But where? There are British officials in Kyrenia, I believe. Certainly in Nicosia. Why don't you ask them?"

"I will. We must know soon, or it will be too late for Georgi. My mother is so determined. Sometimes I wonder if . . . " she hesitated, half-afraid of seeming to criticize, "if she is too lonely up there, and wants to come down to the house in the village among her friends. There'd be enough for her to live on, she says. She works on our land and I think she finds it hard going now."

"You mean she is not altogether thinking of Georgi, but just a little of herself?"

Evie placed an impulsive hand on the priest's sleeve. "Not consciously. If she's doing that, she's not aware of it. But you do understand I have to do what's best for Georgi? And I don't know what *is* best."

The old man nodded two or three times. "I, too, child. I have asked myself this question. Is your father dead or alive? If alive, his wishes must prevail. But if he is dead? Yes, I think you must try to find out."

They were interrupted. An Irish voice said, "Excuse me, Father. I would like a minute's private talk with this young lady."

Evie turned quickly. Her head thudded. It was Rory, and he had sought her out after all. She was suddenly self-conscious, aware of herself, her hands, her feet, the coiled hair on top of her head. The blood pounded in her long throat. In all the world there was only herself and Rory the Irishman. The priest, Melanie and the baby, even Marcus and Sofia, did not exist.

"Come on," he said roughly. "I want you."

She rose and followed him. He led her to a corner of the harbor wall, which was away from the crowd and deserted.

"Well," he said in a cold, furious voice. "Aren't you the splendid liar! A deceitful woman I cannot abide and never could. But I'll thank you to explain what was in the back of your mind, to be sending me and a harmless poor donkey on a wild-goose chase that led nowhere but to a nasty, old copper mine? Come on, you must have some reason."

She swallowed. "I thought you were interested in old things. The copper mine was started by the Romans."

"Come off it, you little fool! I'm not swallowing that." He gripped her arm above the elbow. "I thought we were so friendly, but maybe I was wrong." He spoke to her lightly. "Copper mines, I said. I'm waiting?"

She could find no words and kept silent.

"Look," he said more gently, "I was angry. In fact, I spent several walking miles thinking how I'd like to spank you till you yelled. But I'm over that now, and just darned curious. You haven't the look of a liar, and I've met a few that had. What made you do it? What is there up by the monastery you don't want me to see?"

"Our house. It's for sale. I don't want anybody to buy it."

"You flatter me. Do I have a moneyed appearance or something?"

"No. But mother could sell you the moon, if she had a mind."

His head went back as he laughed. "I must meet her. She sounds as plausible as her daughter. But listen to me . . . ." He shook a long finger close to her nose. "If you ever tell me a whopping great fib again, or deceive me, so help me I'll—I'll tan the hide off you. Understand?"

"Don't try. The island men would kill you if you touched me."

He nodded. "They'd be right at that. But I'll give you the rough edge of my tongue, that I do promise. Now . . . about this house. How did you know I wanted to buy one? I didn't tell anybody."

"I didn't know. It's just that ours could be for sale."

"And you don't approve? But your parents must have a good reason. Have you considered they might need the money?"

"I have. The money is needed."

"Then isn't your attitude extremely selfish? I don't think I can allow unreasonable prejudice to stand between me and a house I'd like to own. I give you fair warning, I intend to see your father about it tomorrow."

"You can't. He's away."

"Another of your lies?"

"No."

He eyed her. "That has a ring of truth. So your da is away. When is he expected home?"

She said firmly, "My mother expects him home any day now."

Their eyes met. She held his in a long stare. She was telling the truth—the precise truth, and had no reason for looking away.

"Any day?"

She nodded.

"Very well, then. I'll wait."

Her mouth curved in a soft smile. "Do just that, Irishman. Wait for my father."

The first firework went up with a swoosh and exploded red and green and gold.

CHAPTER THREE

THERE IS NOTHING one can do about fireworks except stand there and stare into the sky. Blue and silver, white and gold, scarlet and orange, there they go like pieces of magic, to the accompaniment of "ahs and "ohs" from the throats of the enchanted.

Rory watched Evie's upturned face and his conscience smote him. Glory be, what had he done! This was no child, but a woman as lovely as any of his dreams. How could he have thought otherwise? A firm little chin, a tender mouth, the curve of a cheek so enchanting that—he went suddenly hot, his shirt stuck clammily to his back. What had he suggested? That he should spank her, no less. Called her a liar to her face.

Well, she *was* a liar, his aching bones reminded him sharply. As dishonest a deceiver as ever he'd met. And selfish, for if her mam and da needed the money from selling the house and she was going around telling lies to stop it being sold, she deserved all he'd said and more.

"Look here . . . ." he began, half meaning to apologize in spite of himself.

She turned on him a look of cool disdain more snubbing than any words. Then, without a word, she ran to join the crowd watching the fireworks and melted into it. Not before he had observed her scarlet shoes, and ankles as delicate as a racing filly's that a man might hold between finger and thumb. Too many girls, he reflected out of long experience, failed at the ankles.

He sat on the wall, shoulders hunched, and kicked

himself in his mind for a clumsy, ham-handed lout. Women! Yesterday a child, a tomboy aping the dignity of a grown-up sister. Today, this.

Rory, my son, he reminded himself, you are finished with the female sex forever. After Clodagh—no more. You will not put yourself in the power of a woman again. Be damned to the creatures—there are other things in this world to hold a man's interest and engage his soul.

Such as the house by the monastery. Tomorrow, if the blister on his heel permitted, he would take a walk up there and look at it. Again he felt the itch of excitement he had known on first seeing the island. This might be the place.

He had dreamed his dream ever since the day Clodagh rode away on the great bay horse paid for by the Englishman out of Somerset and was lost to him forever. Young Clodagh he had grown up with and never thought but to marry. All that was water under the bridge now, and only the dream remained.

A white house on a cliff over a warm blue sea. A terrace shaded by vines. A high cool room of his own, in which to write and think, with only the bell of a monastery to mark the hours.

He did not find it odd that there was a monastery close to this house, which might or might not be for sale. Wasn't there a monastery—or two, or three—on every island in the Mediterranean?

He would not be lonely in his house, for he planned to fill it with people with a need for solitude, silence and simplicity. A sort of monastic guest house, where the guests paid for necessities but no luxuries, if you didn't count simplicity as a luxury. He would employ a woman or two to clean and cook, though the guests must do their share.

There would be fruit sun-warm from the tree, milk

from one's own goats, newlaid eggs, and bread fresh baked in a beehive-shaped adobe oven in the yard.

Women? He had not decided. They could be a disturbing influence and he did not want his dream spoiled by emotions and strife. On the other hand, if there came one who genuinely needed his peace, for work or to mend her soul, the doors would not be closed, ever.

"*Kyrie*," murmured Sofia at his side. "You are not dancing?"

"Two blisters on my heels, and my bones aching from that terrible saddle?"

Sofia pouted, her lips soft and warm. "Please, *kyrie*, dance with me. Just a few minutes. It's important to me." She flicked a glance across the square to where Marcus was laughing with a group of boys. Her eyes were moist. Rory thought she had been crying and took pity on her.

"Very well, but be merciful. You're pretty enough to make dead bones jingle, and I'm not dead yet."

He had observed the byplay with the flowers, and half blamed Evie for it. Sofia had been helpful from the moment he landed on Exos. She knew how to please a man in small ways and see to his comfort, and was also well aware of her own charming femininity. So if it would please this jolly little creature to be whirled under that Greek oaf's nose in the arms of a stranger, whirled she would be, if it killed him.

As they moved out under the flickering lanterns, he caught sight of Evie sitting demurely in the circle of mothers. She looked somehow woebegone in spite of her magnificent dress—a child dressed up and nowhere to go. He reproached himself for not having asked her to dance and chuckled suddenly, enjoying the trick she had played on him to keep him away from her part of the island.

Sofia looked up under her long dark lashes. "The *kyrios* is amused?"

"Small donkey, large saddle—neither being my size. It must have looked funny, Sofia. You were kind enough not to laugh."

She giggled. "Your l-legs are so long, and the donkey's so short...."

Evie, watching covertly, saw them laughing heartily together. *Are they laughing at me*, she wondered miserably.

She felt small and guilty. Never before had anyone accused her of lying, and she had imagined herself to be a truthful person.

She wasn't. The guilt she felt spread over her like a stain, till she felt everyone must see her for what she was. The reason she did not normally tell lies was, she realized, because she had had no reason to do so. And the first time real temptation had come her way, she had fallen into it so dreadfully easily.

The enjoyment had gone out of the evening for her. The flowers Marcus had given her already seemed to droop. The new Evie she had met for the first time today was the old Evie after all. The man she had hoped to surprise and enthrall despised her. The man she *had* attracted almost belonged to her best friend, and Sofia might never speak to her again.

If only she could go home now and never see Rory McDermot again. If only she had worn her old dress and Marcus hadn't noticed her.

If only Rory the Irishman wasn't so attractive, even when angry! His voice had music in it, and he seemed to be laughing somewhere inside himself, even when his face was grim and angry, his eyes as hard as stones.

She shivered in the warm evening, remembering the other lie she had told. Not exactly a lie, for it was nothing but the truth. Her mother was expecting her father to arrive any day, but she had been expecting that for the past eleven years or so. Sooner or later that terrible man would find out.

Cautiously, she turned her head to look at him again. He had gone from the seawall where she had left him. Gone where, and with whom?

"Oh, there you are!" said Marcus over her shoulder. "Where did you get to? I wanted you to sit in my boat to watch the fireworks. Did you enjoy them?"

"They were fine, Marcus. Where's Sofia? Don't you think she looks pretty tonight?"

He grinned. His hair was black as carob pods, and curled crisply, close to his head. His dark eyes traveled over her face, as if searching. "Sofia's making eyes at the Irishman. He thinks she's pretty, judging by the way he was holding her when they danced just now. Didn't you see? Last night, too."

"He has good taste. He'd charm any girl, Marcus. You island men will have to watch out, or he'll whisk her away to his own country before you can stone an olive."

Marcus sat up, and a small frown appeared between his strongly marked black brows. "Will he? There are a few men here who'll see about that."

So Marcus could be jealous, could he? Good. She added a little more fuel to the small fire by saying, "He has a silver tongue, and she tells me he sings like an angel. Can you sing Marcus?"

He scowled again. "Certainly I can. Wait. Listen." He strode off and presently snatched a guitar from one of the players on the boat.

The fireworks being over, everyone was ready for more entertainment. Marcus sang well and was rewarded with applause and shouts. Someone thrust a glass of wine into his hand.

"Now the visitors," Stratos shouted. "Sing again, *kyrie*—the song you gave us last night."

Evie clenched her hands tightly. *Oh, no! Let Marcus have his triumph. This is his night.*

But an expectant silence fell and into the scented darkness came a clear, trained tenor. A sad, homesick song floating over the water: "She is far from the land where her young hero sleeps."

What land? What young hero? Evie pressed her palms together, and tears trickled behind her eyes. The sadness in the voice chimed with her own unhappiness. *He must*, she thought, *he must tell me the story of this song, I must know about the young hero and the lady who had to leave her own land.* But how could she ask him? He had branded her a liar, and he couldn't abide liars. And tomorrow or the next day, he would find out about her father. Everyone was happy here tonight. Her mother was chatting. Georgi and his friends were swimming in the warm, dark water. Marcus was surrounded with friends, having apparently forgotten he had given his bouquet to Evie Marsden. *And look at Sofia and Rory McDermot, laughing and sharing secrets as they danced the old-fashioned island dances!*

She was the odd one out.

An older man asked her to dance, then one and another of the younger ones, and soon she was whirling as fast as anyone, more lightly than most, to the insistent beat of the local instruments. And then Marcus caught her again and danced with her until she was out of breath and obliged to sit down to recover.

"I hate you," whispered Sofia close to her ear. "I thought we were friends. I thought you knew I'd always wanted Marcus. If you don't want a man of your own, or can't get one, don't steal mine!"

Evie swung round to face a Sofia she hardly recognized. The girl's face was distorted with hatred. "I didn't steal him. He offered me the flowers. It's an insult to refuse a man's flowers offered like that."

"He can't look at anyone but you. You could discourage him if you were my true friend, as I thought you were."

"Sofia," Evie said firmly, "if Marcus doesn't find you as attractive as you find him, that isn't my fault. Stop crying—you look terrible. And why cry anyway? You were getting on well enough with the Kyrios McDermot."

"Only to make Marcus jealous. I wanted to hurt him."

"Trying to make someone unhappy seems a funny way of loving him."

"Don't you know, you can't show a man you love him? Not at first. You have to keep him guessing, and then choose the right moment for letting him know how you really feel. When you're certain you know how he really feels."

"Wouldn't it be simpler to tell the truth, both of you? It would save a lot of worry and unhappiness."

Sofia sighed. "You're such a child, Evie. Don't you know anything? How will you ever get yourself a husband, if you go about it so stupidly?"

"I shall wait for a man who falls in love with me to come and ask me to marry him."

"You'll be an old maid, then. Men don't want to get married. They have to be caught, like wild birds."

Evie stood up. "Catch yours, then, and tame him. I won't hinder. We're friends. Let's stay friends. Run home and tidy up your face, and I'll persuade my mother she's tired and wants to leave now. I'll get out of your way."

"Well . . . ." Sofia hesitated only a moment. "It isn't as if you were dancing, is it? I mean, tonight isn't terribly important to you, as it is for me. You're sure you don't mind?"

Evie did mind. Very much. Only now, with the prospect of going home and leaving everybody enjoying themselves on the quay, did she understand how much she wanted to stay; and to ask the Irishman to explain his song to her.

Sofia, eager to go, still hesitated. "You wouldn't lend me your red shoes, I suppose? I've never had red shoes."

Without a word, Evie took off her shoes and handed them over.

"Thanks. Wait here and I'll bring you my sandals. You can't walk home in your best stockings."

Sofia had no sooner disappeared than Rory McDermot stood before her.

"Will you dance with me, princess?"

"I can't."

"Because you are annoyed with me? Won't you take my olive branch? It's offered by way of apology. Only my aching bones spoke, I assure you."

"You said nothing but the truth. I did lie to you. I meant to."

He shrugged. "Can't we both forget it? It's a heavenly night for dancing."

"I'm sorry, I can't dance with you."

He bowed stiffly. "Very well. You prefer to swim alone. No doubt you prefer to dance alone, though it seems a pity when everyone else is dancing with a partner. Or is there another partner who likes to keep you to himself?"

She shook her head dumbly. It really was not possible to explain how she came to be without shoes suddenly. Disappointment brought tears to her eyes. Why had she not understood earlier that what she wanted most in the world was to dance with the Irishman, wearing her scarlet shoes?

He stalked away stiff legged and she knew in her bones, from the tilt of his head and the set of his shoulders, that he was hurt and angry with her stupid refusal to dance when everyone else was dancing.

I don't understand myself anymore, she thought. *Why couldn't I say simply that I had no shoes? We could have laughed about it, and waited for Sofia to come back with*

*her sandals. What kept me silent, what made me hurt him
like that? I really don't know what got into me.*

When Sofia came tripping back, smiling and happy
wearing the red shoes, Evie thrust her feet into borrowed sandals and went to saddle her mother's donkey.
Even at the top of the path to the Villa Julia the sound
of music could still be heard, the lights still twinkled,
reflected in the sea.

"Why did we have to come home so soon?" Georgi
grumbled. "I hadn't eaten nearly as many kebabs as I
could have."

Why indeed? Evie stared at the winking colored lights
below. What had gone wrong—and why?

EVIE WAS MILKING THE GOATS when she saw Rory
McDermot come striding through the lemon trees. *He
knows,* she thought with a sinking heart. She kept still
and quiet, hoping he wouldn't see her in the dappled
shadows of the wooden shelter, dazzled as he must be
by the bright morning sun. But he came straight toward
her, and leaned on the crooked doorpost looking in.

"No wonder you ran away, with another whopping
falsehood on your conscience! And living next to the
monastery, too, and those saintly old brothers. What
would they say if they knew?"

She kept on milking, not looking up. His shadow lay
long and thin across the beaten earth floor.

"So your mother expects your father home any day?"

"It's the truth. She does."

"Aye," he said slowly, "maybe it is. Maybe there was
no need to add that she'd been doing just that for the
past dozen years. When do *you* expect him?"

"Never. I think he's dead. He must be."

He folded his long legs and sat beside her on a handful of clean straw. "So?"

"I would like to be sure, for my brother's sake. It would make all the difference to him."

"Why?"

"He'd be the head of the family, and my mother would respect his wishes."

"Which are?"

"To keep his farm and his home. He has land of his own, which he wants to cultivate. He and I can do it together. We don't want to go elsewhere."

"Isn't that rather limiting? A man should see the world."

"You've seen the world. Why do you want to buy our house?"

"Primarily, to live in it."

"There you are! You've seen the world and you'd live here if you could choose. So why can't you let Georgi alone? He's got what you want, and you are eager to push him out of it for your own benefit."

"A barbed point, my lady, and thrust deep. Can't you see it's different? I've made a choice. Georgi has had no choice. He gets his notions of England from you, I think?"

"I don't tell lies to him. He believes what I say. He's happy here, he has a future. Please go away and leave us in peace."

He was silent a long minute. A goat bleated restlessly.

"What do you do with all this milk?"

"I make cheese. Oh, I'm sorry, I should invite you to breakfast—dates, our own cheese, and milk to drink. My mother makes good bread."

"Thank you. I accept."

"I wish you wouldn't. You mean to turn our lives upside down, don't you? I think I had a premonition, that first day when you landed on the quay. We don't want strangers on this island. We've had too many in our history. Mostly they haven't been good for the islanders."

"Strangers bring trade. Ask the men if they'll refuse that. If everybody thought as you do, you'd be living in caves up the mountain. You can't turn your back on civilization, child. Don't be so narrow-minded."

"Some people," she said crossly, "are so narrow-minded that they can't see anything but money, or hear anything but the rustle of money. Have you seen the tourist islands? Do they belong to the people anymore? Leave us alone!"

His eyes having accustomed themselves to the deep shade, he could see her small, passionate face, the tenseness of her slim body. He was moved with pity and regret. She could never win her single-handed fight against progress, and she was terribly wrong about her little brother. When would she understand that the handsome, sturdy boy would be a man sooner than she thought, and might then accuse her of having kept him ignorant and inexperienced, a farmer with a few acres, a few trees, a few goats? The mother was right about that.

Regret—that he was not five years younger, five years less experienced and world-weary. He saw himself as he had once been, riding his father's fine Connemara ponies along the Atlantic shore, young and free in the years before Clodagh, free as the gulls over the sea, and the piping oyster catchers among the tangy wrack of the beach.

"You invited me to breakfast," he reminded her gently.

Without a word, she put her milk-bucket by the wall and untied the goat. "That's the last. I expect you find it a bit smelly in here. Most people do. We eat on the terrace. Come along."

He took the bucket from her. "Let me carry that."

She followed him into the sun. "You mean to buy our house, don't you?"

"I mean to try. It's what I had in mind and I can't let

one girl with a lot of prejudices come between me and what I need. I've planned my future and somehow, somewhere, I shall carry my plans out. Besides...."

She took the bucket from him. "In here. If you want to wash, there's water and soap on the table by the door. Besides what?"

"You're wrong about Georgi. Your mother is right. He must get away from here before he's too old to learn. And there's another thing you ought to know about me—"

"Evie? Is that you? Did you have trouble with the goats?" Julia came out into the yard. She had changed into her best black dress, put on an embroidered apron and a lace cap. Evie saw at once. So she had seen Rory come through the lemon trees and knew exactly what had detained her daughter.

In the harsh morning sun her face looked seamed and yellow. *She's aging,* Evie thought with a stab of fear. *But she can't be old? Not twenty years since she was a bride. Twenty years, so many of them lonely and hardworking. Poor mama, she needs rest and security, not a peasant's life on the land. Am I cruel to her, my little mama?*

Julia advanced towards Rory, giving him a gracious welcome and inviting him to share the morning meal. Evie, she said, would make him an omelette. She brushed aside his protest.

"A man needs a good breakfast, my husband used to tell me. Evie will be happy to do it, and you and I will sit and talk while we wait. You are a traveler, like my husband. Who knows, you may have met him on your journeys."

With gentle dignity, Julia led her guest away, and Evie heard their voices murmuring on the terrace; her mother's silvery tones, Rory McDermot's masculine voice striking a deeper chord. There was a lilt in his speech that fascinated Evie, a music she had heard in no English or American voice.

She whisked eggs angrily, aware that her mother had meant to get rid of her for a time to have the visitor to herself. What were they talking about? It was unlikely that Julia would come at once to the question of selling the house. That wasn't the island way. There would be much delicate maneuvering around the subject, long discussions into which others would be drawn—the priest, without question, and Julia's male kin. Even with a willing seller and a willing buyer, such an important transaction as buying a house might last a month. Once in a lifetime, perhaps, a man might have such important business, so it was not to be hurried. The utmost enjoyment must be squeezed out of every step of the slow progress.

Maybe, she thought as the golden eggs foamed in the bowl, Rory would lose patience and go away. An Englishman certainly would. Name a price, say yes or no, and close the bargain—that was the English way.

She felt in her bones that the Irishman might be different. He gave the impression of living by God's time, as the islanders did. Time which could wait for a tree to blossom, fruit, and ripen its fruit; time which did not try to hurry the sun in the sky.

When she hurried on to the terrace with the perfectly-made omelette, the pair was sitting close together, Rory's head bent to listen to her mama.

He rose courteously and pulled out a chair for her. "Am I to eat this enormous omelette alone? You've brought only one plate."

"We ate an hour ago. We are always up by sunrise, and try to finish the work before the sun gets hot. We are not as lazy as we appear to northern visitors who lie in bed till seven or eight in the morning. How long are you staying on the island, Mr. McDermot?"

Rory's eyebrows rose in surprise, finding her so dignified and distant suddenly. Milking the goat, she had

seemed to him like a child. Now, straight-backed at the
table, her golden hair smooth and a lace shawl—which
had not been there before, he felt sure—thrown over her
shoulders, she was no child, but a gracious, lovely lady.
Suddenly it seemed important that he know her age, but
a man could hardly ask.

Julia answered for him. "Mr. McDermot would like
to stay a long time, if he could find a house for sale here.
We were discussing the matter."

"You have a house," Evie said bluntly. "The one by
the harbor. That's just big enough for two people. He
can buy that."

"Two?" Rory asked.

"Well, I suppose you have a wife? Or perhaps you
have a family and want something bigger?"

"I have no wife and no family."

She cried, astonished, "Then why do you want a
house? You are free. You can live at the *taverna* as long
as you wish, and leave any day you feel like leaving."

"Evie," her mother reproved, "that is not our affair. It
is not polite to question Mr. McDermot. It is enough to
know that he wants a house. Why, is his concern."

Embarrassed, Evie rose to pour fresh coffee. "I'm sorry," she murmured. "It was just that I was surprised.
You see, mama, it is not a small house Mr. McDermot
is looking for. He wants this house. *Our* house."

Now it was his turn to look embarrassed. Evie smiled
secretly to see his discomfiture, thinking it served him
right for being so selfish. One man had no business trying to take away the home of a family.

One man? So he had no wife, and apparently no intention of bringing one to the island. The thought set
her humming softly, and to hide her quick surge of
pleasure she ran to the edge of the terrace and pre-
tended to look for Georgi. "That boy! He's with the
brothers again, I'll be bound. They'll be busy, this hour

in the morning, and he likes to help, Mr. McDermot. He'd be with them all day if he could." She spoke challengingly, knowing he was against her in the matter of Georgi.

"Is that good for an eleven-year-old? A boy needs the company of younger men. Old brothers in religion, worthy as they are, cannot teach him everything."

Evie waved a hand in the direction of the village. "Georgi is a friend of every man on the island, and every man is his father. They take him out in the fishing boats and teach him about growing fruit and selling. This whole place is a school for all the boys. We don't need a stranger to teach us how to bring up the children."

Julia interrupted gently. She had been smiling from one to the other, as if unaware of the tension between her daughter and the visitor. "All the same, child, your brother has an English father and he needs an English education. But that needs money and I have only enough to keep us here. When my husband comes home, of course, he will pay. But, Kyrie McDermot, he is a little forgetful. A woman can wait twenty years; a man can wait five; but a child cannot wait at all. We must have the money *now*, to send the boy away. I have nothing to sell but the house and the land."

"You have a hard choice to make, *kyria*. I am half a peasant myself, from the west of Ireland, which is in some ways like your island. What will you live on, if you sell the land?"

"I have enough for myself, and a small place to live. Evie will get married, naturally. There is only Georgi's future to consider, and if my husband comes home and finds his son an ignorant islander, he will be angry with me. He set great store by the boy's education."

"He should come back," Evie muttered rebelliously. "He has forgotten us. I don't mind it for myself, but he

hurts my mother every day he stays away, and he is rob-
bing his son."

Rory tilted his chair on its back legs and stretched out
his feet to the terrace edge. "If you ask me, that boy
should go to England or the States soon, before he set-
tles into the mold of a small farmer knowing nothing
beyond the brim of his hat."

Evie beat her fist on the table. "No, no, *no*! Those
boys would laugh at him and call him ignorant because
he wouldn't understand their stupid games. He swims
like a fish, he speaks three languages fluently, he knows
a lot of history. Mr. McDermot, history was *born* here,
all around the Mediterranean. Greece and Rome, the
Ottoman Empire, the crusaders, the Venetians—we live
with it. But Georgi has never played cricket or baseball,
so he wouldn't be accepted by the boys of his own age.
Can't you understand how miserable he would be?"

Rory studied the angry girl gravely. "Almost thou
persuadest me. But just now I have business to talk over
with your mother. Later, perhaps, you may be able to
endure my company long enough to show me the
monastery? Or don't they allow young females over
their doorstep?"

He had the air of one humoring a child, buying its absence with the promise of a future treat. For a searing
moment she was cruelly hurt and wanted to hurt him. It
was years since she had thrown one of her wild tantrums, but now that old, almost uncontrollable rage rose
up in her once more and she had to fight for self-
control, knowing that to lose her temper would be to
lower herself still further in his eyes.

"The brothers have a fine sense of hospitality, Mr.
McDermot, and we are neighbors besides. My mama
and I are always welcome under that roof, though at the
moment I don't seem to be wanted under this."

Head high, she marched angrily away. Only when she

was safe in the wide, dark kitchen did she let her fury have its way. She pressed her clenched fists to her temples, stamping her feet on the cool marble floor.

I hate him, I hate him! I won't endure being treated like a child. I'll never speak to him again. Never!

She ran out and through the lemon grove, making for the mountain above the house.

She climbed high and fast, till the exertion exhausted her anger, leaving her only with a strange, disturbed feeling she could not analyze. A feeling in which her fear of losing the Villa Julia had a part—and the memory of Marcus's dark eyes smiling into hers, and the brief warm touch of their hands' encounter when he gave her the flowers. And the humiliation of being treated and spoken to like a child by the Irishman, who seemed to be laughing at her all the time, even when he spoke sharply, vexed by her childish lies.

In times of stress she had one refuge, the peak of the highest cliff on the island, where the land fell sheer into the sea, as if a giant had sliced it off. A red cliff, which glowed at sunset like a jewel. There she would lie flat and inch forward to the very edge, and peep over the terrifying drop into the satin sea a dizzying distance below. The height made every nerve in her body crawl with fear, and her bare toes press hard into the barren rocks. Legend had it that long ago the islanders had punished wrongdoers by throwing them over to their death on the rocks below. Even now, though no one admitted it for fear of the kind old priest's disapproval, men and women would steal to the top and drop some valued possession into the sea with a prayer to the ancient gods for some much-desired favor; to the old gods whose time-fretted, headless statues still stood everywhere in the islands; so many still remaining after all these centuries, the Old Ones whose special care had been the silken Mediterranean, the dark wine, the olives, the jeweled islands blessed by the warm and lambent air. Was it possible, whispered some, that the Old Ones had forgotten their magic lands and their people?

Breathless at the top of her climb, she sat and hugged her knees, gazing down into the sea, which was now quilted by a whisp of wind. When she heard footsteps on the bare pink rocks she turned quickly, half expecting Rory.

It was Marcus, mahogany brown and deep chested, wearing only a pair of old faded shorts and canvas shoes.

"Evie! What are you doing there! Come back. Girls shouldn't sit so near the edge. You might get dizzy and fall over."

"I always sit here. I'm not in the least dizzy. When we were younger you threatened to push me over, do you remember?"

He grinned cheerfully. "I remember. You'd bitten me. You had sharp little teeth." He eased himself to the ground beside her, avoiding a gray thistle with long thorns as fine as needles. "You're a mystery, Evie. How is it Sofia is a woman grown, ready for marriage and children, and you . . . ." His eyes traveled over her appraisingly. "You are a child still. At least, you are today. The other night, in your blue dress and red shoes, I thought you were grown-up, too. Then suddenly you changed back into the old Evie and ran away."

"Like Cinderella."

He looked blank. "Who's she?"

"A girl in a story. She changed back into her ordinary self and ran away from a prince—a young man who thought she was grown-up."

"What did he do?" An islander loved a story. Marcus bit a long thorn with his broad white teeth and looked at her expectantly.

"Went to look for her. But didn't find her till the

grown-up shoe she'd kicked off fitted her. He didn't want anybody else, so he had to wait and search."

The young man nodded. "No one else would do. What if another man found her first?"

"He probably worried about that, too, but it isn't mentioned in the story. Where is Sofia today?"

He scowled. "Working at home. Her father beat her black and blue last night."

"Poor Sofia!"

"She deserved it. She's been making a fool of herself with that Kyrios McDermot, going everywhere with him and not attending to her duties. They went off on a picnic together yesterday, took the boat and went swimming, when her mother needed her for whitewashing the house."

"With Kyrios McDermot? So why beat poor Sofia? Why not beat him?"

"A man does what he wants to do. McDermot is on holiday and a guest at the *taverna*. It was Sofia's duty to tell him she was needed for whitewashing." He was sulking, looking so like Georgi when deprived of a treat that Evie felt elder-sisterly and teased him.

Staring out to sea, she said lightly, "Such an outing would be worth a beating or two."

"You'd go with him?"

"I wasn't invited."

He pressed the point. "But if he did invite you?"

"I'd tell him I had work to do."

"You wouldn't. You'd do as Sofia did. What's so wonderful about a stranger? Island girls should go with island boys."

Evie felt sick with jealousy. It was a sensation new to her and she found it disagreeable. Rory was hers. He had held her in his arms for a fleeting moment, though by accident. He had called her a goddess and a princess. In spite of his tiresome urge to buy the Villa Julia, he was the first man who had ever interested her as a man and it was for him she had gone down to the waterfront in the blue dress and red slippers. So why couldn't Sofia content herself with Marcus and keep her little brown paws off Rory? Island girls should go with island boys.

"I agree entirely. So why don't you cut him out, Marcus? You're better-looking and probably richer, and Sofia likes you very much. You upset her by giving me the flowers. Why didn't you give them to her?"

"I meant to," he admitted, grinning. "Then—there you were! You took my breath away."

She stared up at an eagle wheeling like a speck in the wide blue expanse of sky. "Would you marry me, Marcus?"

"Have you a dowry?"

"Certainly I have. Did you think I wouldn't have? Well? Would you marry me?"

He tilted his handsome head back and looked up at her under lowered lids. "You're not strong enough."

She stretched out her hands and stared at them. "What do you mean? I work as hard as anybody else."

"I plan to have my own restaurant soon. That's killing work for both husband and wife. I want a lot of children, too, sons to keep me in my old age. No, I'm sorry, you won't do, Evie."

She laughed. "Sofia could do it. And she's prettier than I am."

He said glumly. "I know. She's one of us—hard as nails for working, and more—" he shrugged, "more to hug. She'd be a more comfortable wife. You'll always be skinny, Evie."

"I'm not skinny, I'm slender—that's different. You really want Sofia, don't you? Well then, go and get her."

The boy hesitated. "I'm not sure. You're so beautiful, Evie. I could work twice as hard. I could—"

She sprang up. Far below the monastery lay like a

white cube of sugar glistening in the sun. Four toy figures crossed the courtyard, their shadows like black pins. Three were monks, the other was Rory McDermot.

"No, Marcus, I won't work myself into the ground helping you to run a restaurant. One day soon you'll be fat and lazy, and Sofia will do all the work for you and give you lovely children with eyes like yours. It's not for me. When I marry, I'll need to find another kind of husband altogether."

He eyed her frankly. "Not in that dress, Evie. You're a wild thing, aren't you? A dreaming girl with her ears full of the sea and her eyes full of the sky. Why don't you grow up?"

She watched the four black shadows cross the white yard. Nothing had been the same with her since the Irishman came to the island. Even if he now went back to his own country without saying goodbye to her, she would never be quite the same again. He had called her a princess and stirred her out of her dream.

It was a long time before she answered Marcus, and by then he was striding off down the hill, leaping from stone to stone in a hurry.

"Grown up? I rather think I have, Marcus. And I don't think I'm going to like it at all."

But the words fell between the soaring eagle and the sea.

Realizing she was alone, Evie laughed. Marcus would comfort poor bruised Sofia before nightfall unless he sprained an ankle in his hurry to get down to her.

Then she lay flat and crept to the rim of the great red cliff.

Peering over, she let the terror of the height and the crawling water below take possession of her. This must be how eagles saw the land and sea below them.

What was Rory saying to the monks?

Had her mother agreed to sell the house? If so—if so....

She had promised Georgi to do anything in her power to save his house, but she had no power. None at all. The Villa Julia was not hers and if her mother chose to sell she could not prevent it happening.

She still wore the tiny Maltese cross around her neck, true to her resolve to wear it always now. Reluctantly, she took it off and held it out over the water.

"Goddess of wisdom, please tell me what to do and I'll do it. I promise you I will. Just give me an idea, or bring my father back in time if you can." She had an idea that the bit about her father ought to be addressed to another god, but she had only one sacrifice.

With a tiny flash of light, the necklace diappeared. She lost sight of it long before it reached the sea.

CHAPTER FOUR

RORY AND BROTHER BARNABAS paced the shaded cloister. Barnabas was younger than Rory expected, aged in appearance by a long beard and black robe, tall black headdress, and fluttering veil. To have such a man of great wisdom and cultured mind as a neighbor increased Rory's longing to own the Villa Julia.

"You and the mother are right." The monk's English was fair, though now and again he used Greek. "The boy should see something of the world. Evie, too. Exos is not one of the famous islands. We do not attract tourists, but it has its own charm. For your purpose, it is perfect." He paused to examine a pomegranate tree carefully. "We have nothing on Exos to draw pilgrims, but we pray that one day St. Polystemon will come home—a local boy, martyred here on his own island a thousand years ago. If we had his skull, which now rests in a Cyprus monastery, he might work miracles for us. Then the pilgrims would flock, and with them would come more prosperity. Not that we, the brothers, want prosperity. We are vowed to poverty. But the people are poor, and our young men have to leave us to get work and good wages."

"I'm a God-fearing man, but I don't believe miracles happen anywhere, these days."

"They don't, for the people who don't believe in them. The miracle-working relics never work for tourists. They think the power lies in the belt, the skull, the hole in the pillar. It lies in the mind, sir."

"In the minds of ignorant peasants?"

Brother Barnabas smiled remotely. "Never underrate the poor and the ignorant, *kyrie*. You may teach them much about book-learning, no doubt. But they could teach you much about faith. The relic of a saint merely serves as an aid to concentration. Any small object would do. So the skull of our St. Poly would work miracles here, because we all love him and trust him."

"Wouldn't the other monastery give him to you?"

"Alas, even monks need money, if only to keep the roof on. We should have to pay them for St. Poly. Where is such a poor island as this to raise the price?"

Rory brought the conversation firmly back to the subject nearest his thoughts. "Evie is determined the house should not be sold. I am equally determined to buy it. But if the mother spends the proceeds on the boy, what will they live on? That bothers me."

"It's no problem. The son will support his mother. The girl will marry. She has a dowry."

But marry whom? Rory paced beside the monk, turning that over in his mind. The life of a married woman in this part of the world could be hard. Too much work in the house and the field. Too many babies. Often a lazy husband to be waited on hand and foot. In early middle age, many became worn-out drudges. Evie deserved better. But if few strangers came to Exos, or if she didn't get away soon, there might be no other choice for her. The thought hit him like a blow over the heart.

"Will the father ever return?" he wondered aloud.

Barnabas considered the question in his slow way. "We talked much, the Kyrios Marsden and I. He had some property in England, but I alway felt he went only to settle his affairs and come back. That he failed to do so suggests to me he is dead."

"Why have no inquiries been made all these years?"

"Julia is a daughter of the Middle East. She accepts her husband's decrees without question. The ways of a man and his wife are unknown to me, but I do remember my mother never asked my father whether he would be gone a day, a week, or an hour. Nor did he ever think of telling her."

"Evie is asking."

"She is half English. She won't be content to wait now she is eighteen. She will make it her business to find out."

Rory stared at the monk. "Eighteen? But surely she can be no more than sixteen? She's a woman masquerading as a child, and I thought her a child masquerading as a woman! They will do it, Brother. One day, one thing. Another day, quite another. At least a man knows where he is with a good horse or a good dog. Most of the beauty and none of the mystery. That girl reminds me of my young sister in many ways."

He meant, *she reminds me of Clodagh in our golden days, when she was sixteen and I just turned twenty. All that long summer spent together, sailing, fishing, swimming. The smell of the horses, the smell of the seaweed tangle, the smell of Clodagh's hair blowing across my face.*

Brother Barnabas smoothed his beard with a thin hand. "You seem disturbed?"

"I've been talking to her as if she were my kid sister. Only this morning I sent her packing because I had business to discuss with her mother. I half saw it, and still let myself be fooled. I should have known better. I remember . . . ."

What did it matter to a monk, that he remembered the first day Clodagh seemed to him grown-up? Almost overnight, she had done something mysterious to herself . . . or perhaps it was the soft look in her eyes and about her mouth that changed her. That was the day he first understood he loved her as a man loves the woman he will marry. He discovered later it was the first day she met the Englishman who was now her husband.

The monk chuckled. "Julia is a kindly hen with a pair of cygnets. The children have the mind and blood of their father in them. He was a fine man—big, handsome, generous of nature. I do what I can for his son, but it is not enough. If there is anything you can do ...."

"I offered to rent the house. But to carry out Julia's plans, she needs a substantial lump sum. Education in England is expensive if you pay for it. Or it is free. Either he would have to go to a boarding school, or one of them would have to make a home for him over there. There's the matter of examinations, too, she seems not to understand. The English are great on their examinations. The whole project is more difficult than she imagines. There are fares. And clothes."

Barnabas stopped his pacing. "Georgi is intelligent and has been well grounded. If his father is dead, he is also a landowner. He needs nothing England can give him, except a wider experience of life. If that is to be, God will attend to it. Now it is time I went to my prayers. Our hours are not our own, but God's. If you care to join us in our chapel, you're welcome."

"Thank you. Will you answer one more question? Kyria Julia has invited me to move in to the villa. The *taverna* is noisy and I can't work there. The offer of a big, quiet room over the sea is tempting. Would the island sanction such a move?"

"Wise man! You feel your way carefully, eh? Yes, you could do that without causing gossip. Julia is above reproach, well respected. She is, you understand, related to almost every family on Exos."

Rory nodded. He knew about small communities and had guessed as much.

"And as to buying the house? It is what I dreamed of, and if I scoured the whole Mediterranean I could not find anything nearer my mind. But I don't want to rush the family into doing something they will later regret."

"There will be no rush, *kyrie*. There will be a go-between appointed, and the talking will go on for weeks. Julia will have advice from every man and woman in the place, and in the end will make up her own mind. Make her an offer for it if you really want it, and leave the outcome in the hands of God."

BETWEEN NOON AND THREE at this time of year, the island slept. A soft mist blurred the sharp shadows; the tiny wavelets died to nothing; and the boats lay motionless over their reflections in still water. The birds slept, the trees slept, and it seemed as if even the air slept. On the whole of Exos, no one moved except under dire compulsion.

Evie left the top of the huge cliff and sought out her private retreat, a small deserted temple heavily overgrown, where four headless statues of Greek gods had stood for more than two thousand years. This had been her playroom as a child, the four vast draped figures her friends and companions. She had never minded that they had no heads, for her imagination provided them with friendly faces and voices to match their sturdy bodies and firmly-planted bare feet. They had always been more real and everyday than the bodiless saints, big-eyed and hungry looking, which she saw on the icons in the church and monastery. Here she curled up and went to sleep in the shade. The still air was heavy with the scent of wild flowers.

She woke suddenly, realizing she had slept longer than usual and her mother might be wondering where she was, and would be wanting her afternoon coffee. The peace of the empty temple had soothed away the burning anger, and she was prepared to accept some blame herself. She rested her chin on her knees, and conducted a conversation with the four gods as she had done as a child.

"Your fault," said the armless woman who had such splendid stone feet. "Go to Kyrenia tomorrow and buy yourself some proper clothes. It's time you behaved like a young lady. Look at *me*."

"Your fault," said the deep-chested man whose left leg was cut off below the knee. "You should do something about your father. Find out if he's still alive, and tell him to come home."

"But where, and how shall I find him?" She must have spoken aloud, for an echo came back. It brought no answer.

Yet when she reached the house, the answer was in her head. It was so simple. Tomorrow she would take the daily caïque to Kyrenia, buy some dress material for herself, and a pattern; and then consult a lawyer. If he didn't know how to trace a lost father, he would at least know how to contact someone who would tell her.

Her hand on the latch of the door, she threw a glance over her shoulder at the summit of the mountain, where a knowledgeable eye could just detect the ruin. "Thank you," she said in a whisper. "I'll take your advice."

Her mother was talking in her visitor-English. When Evie entered the big blue-painted room she saw Rory McDermot. He stood up when she entered. The small courtesy made her vividly conscious of her dusty bare feet.

They were drinking coffee, eating the tiny almond and honey cakes her mother made for special occasions.

"The *kyrios* has accepted my invitation to stay here, Evie," Julia said, half nervously. "He is a writer, did you know? The *taverna* is noisy and there is no table in his room. We have your father's room vacant, so why should he not move in? There is a desk by the window and a view over the sea. Of course, he understands that he must move out at once, if your father comes home."

"Of course," Rory murmured. "And if you would call

me Rory I should feel myself at home. You don't mind, Miss Marsden?"

Evie's eyes widened. In her whole life, no one had ever addressed her as Miss. "You are welcome," she murmured formally. "May your stay be a happy one."

"Thank you."

The conversation flagged. Julia put in a few stitches at the embroidery in her frame.

"You visited the brothers?" Evie said at last, in her best English.

Rory nodded. "And had a long talk with Barnabas."

"About us?"

"About everything under the sun, which includes you, naturally. He is fond of young Georgi and thinks him a clever boy. We also spoke of the lemon trade and he gave me a good recipe for dumplings for soup."

Evie searched her mind for new topics of conversation. She had never suffered from shyness, having had nobody of whom she need be shy. So she did not recognize the condition immediately, and blamed herself for lack of hospitality.

"I'll show you my private temple if you like." As soon as the words were out, she regretted them. Her temple was her own.

"I'd like that very much. Unless it is near the copper mines."

She looked up sharply and caught a smile in his eyes. Then suddenly he laughed and she laughed with him, till Julia stared at the pair of them in bewilderment.

"What is funny about the copper mines?" she asked plaintively.

A clatter from the outside answered her. "That's Georgi. Why can't that boy arrive without making such a noise? I sent him down to the village with a note to the priest and my cousin Stephanos, and told him to wait for an answer."

Evie drew a long breath. Her mother's cousin was famous for his skill as a go-between. So was the priest, for holding the scales fairly between buyer and seller. Two such formidable persons approached by Julia at one and the same time could only mean one thing. Quick anger mounted in the girl. Had her mother decided to sell the house, Georgi's land, without consulting her? Without making any real attempt to find George Marsden, whose home, after all, the Villa Julia was?

"What answer?" she asked in a low tense voice. "What do you want of Cousin Stephanos?"

Julia was tart. "That's my business."

"Is it, mama? Are you sure? Isn't it perhaps Rory's business also? What were you and he talking about, this morning?"

She knew her mother's mood, a curious mixture of outward meekness and inward stubbornness, which meant she intended to do, or already had done, something of which her family would probably not approve.

Before Julia answered, Georgi came in with a note. "This is from the priest. Cousin Stephanos didn't write, but he says he'll do it if you are sure you know your own mind, and if the foreigner can pay a good price."

"I can pay a fair price," Rory put in quietly, and Julia crimsoned.

"So I'm right?" Evie looked from one to the other, "You mean to buy our house and turn us out, Mr. McDermot? You've crept in here and talked my mother into selling, having first got rid of me because you knew neither my brother nor I want to lose our home and land. Now I find you've even got yourself into the house as a lodger. Couldn't you wait till the whole place was yours? Do you have to come lording it before the sale has been properly discussed?"

"I *have* discussed it," Rory told her sharply, the laughter gone from his eyes. "With the owner. I offered your mother a price this morning, but she quite properly prefers me to discuss terms with her representatives. She won't be talked into selling, nor would I dream of doing so unless she is advised by her family. The grown-up members of it," he added pointedly.

"What do my uncles care? It's Georgi I'm worried about. Because he is only a child, must he lose his land? Mama, I demand that Georgi has a representative, too. Someone to speak for him in his interests."

Julia's mouth was set stubbornly. "It's my house, my land. I make the decisions in your father's absence. And I say my husband's wishes must be carried out; he always talked of an English education for his son."

"I won't go," said Georgi, as stubborn as his mother, looking, Evie noticed suddenly, very like her, with the same thrust-out jaw and set of the head. "You can't make me learn anything, even if you can force me to go to an English school. Your money will be wasted, every *mil* of it."

"Don't dare to speak to me—your *mother*—like that! You're a baby yet. You'll do exactly as I say or I shall beat you."

"Beat me, then! I don't care, I don't care!" The boy was sobbing hysterically. He swung around suddenly and flew at Rory, pounding the man with his clenched fists. "Go away! It's your fault. Why did you come here? Get away from us, do you hear? We don't want you!"

Rory caught the flailing wrists, held the boy away from him till he ceased struggling and stood still, crimson faced and gasping.

"That's better," Rory said quietly. "Now I suggest you apologize to your mother for that outburst. Then you and I will go outside and have a talk about it, man to man. We might stroll up to the monastery and discuss it with your friends there, eh?"

"No. I won't speak to you again, ever. And I won't have you living in my house!"

"Mama's house," Evie reminded him. "Losing your temper won't help, darling. If it would, I'd lose mine. Come with me. Let's go up the mountain and think. But first apologize to mama."

Rory massaged his chin thoughtfully. "Who started it, mavourneen? You are a bit of a rebel yourself. You set the example."

Evie put an arm around Georgi's shoulder and met Rory's gaze firmly. "Very well. We both apologize for being rude to mama. But not to you. Georgi is right, all this trouble is your fault. I'd be obliged if you would go away and leave us in peace, as we were before you came. We don't want you."

Rory reached for a dilapidated straw hat, which he clapped on his head at an angle. "Very well, ma'am, I'll go. Kyria Julia my offer is withdrawn. I am defeated by your children. I can't bring myself to take the roof from over their heads. I'll leave the island by tomorrow's boat."

He bowed to Julia, and ignoring the brother and sister, marched out of the house into the white sun. His brisk feet set up little spurts of dry red soil as he went. He whistled a lilting tune.

"Look what you've done, you ungrateful children!" Julia began to cry.

"Good riddance," said Evie severely.

She watched her enemy out of sight. There was something about the hunch of a shoulder, the tilt of a head, the sound of that gay little whistle, that gripped her heart. A man defeated, and not showing it. Hurt, and trying not to care. A man whose dream had fallen about his ears, and he making the best of things.

She almost opened her mouth to call him back. Then catching sight of Georgi's distressed face, the soft mouth quivering but pressed shut, she hugged the boy again and dropped a light kiss on his tousled hair.

"Maybe we were hard on him, little brother. The war isn't won yet. I fancy he'll be back some day."

She knelt by her mother's chair and took the work-worn hands in her own. "Mama, I'm sorry. Did it mean so much to you? If only my father were here! How could he—how could he leave us like this? Dear mama, don't you see, we can't go on forever, waiting for him to come back. We must make some effort to find out what happened to him. Let me try."

Julia covered her face and sobbed silently with quiet despair. Evie motioned to the boy to go away. Then she waited patiently till grief had exhausted itself.

"What is it, mama? Do you know something you haven't told us? I've never seen you cry like this before. You are always so hopeful and so confident. You will let me try to find him?"

"But that would be to admit I doubted him. My belief in George is all I have. Don't you understand that? To admit doubt—what would that do to my pride? Every-body would be saying, 'Julia's afraid he's left her!' And from that, it's only a step to everybody saying, 'He has left her.' I couldn't bear that. He was such a good man, and so happy to be here with us. He really loved us."

"In that case, I think he must be dead. I'm sorry, mama, but we must face it and not pretend anymore. Let me go to a lawyer in Kyrenia and ask him to make inquiries in England. There must be ways of finding out, which we don't know."

"You'd take my hope away from me."

"I know, love. But isn't it better to know the truth?"

"Young people are for knowing the truth, however cruel. All right, go and ask, if the truth is what you want. You're not old enough to be glad of a veil over the face of reality. When you've faced the truth often

enough and long enough, you won't be so eager to see it
naked. Go with my blessing. You'll need some money,
won't you?"

"Yes, please. And also—" Evie pulled at her shabby
skirt "—I need something to wear, mama. I'll make myself some dresses if you'll help me. We could get out the
old sewing machine, couldn't we?"

"Yes, of course. I've neglected my daughter. We must
think about a husband for you, and that means pretty
dresses. One of the brothers will oil the machine and get
it working again. Your father bought it for a wedding
present, you know."

Julia cheered up with the thought of dresses to make,
and began to talk of likely young men on the island.
"But you're not the sort to marry an island man, Evie.
Too much like your father. We must have something
better for you. Perhaps we should wait till George
comes home?"

Her eyes filled with tears again as she remembered
that old excuse for postponing action would no longer
be acceptable to her children.

"Well, all the same, I think you should meet more
nice families. If only you'd let me sell the house, you
could use the money to take Georgi to England, and
maybe get work there for a while. You're a good cook,
and awfully clever with the goats and with growing
things. Or you could teach Greek, couldn't you? In a
school? George used to say English schools always
taught Latin and Greek, though what they wanted to
speak Latin for, I can't imagine."

"Not modern Greek, I believe, mama. The old Greek
that nobody knows anymore."

"Really? How stupid! Two languages nobody wants
to know? Perhaps English schools are not so good after
all."

"Perhaps they have different ideas now."

"Or you could go to Athens and teach English. Your father was very particular about your having a good accent."

Evie left her mother preparing *moussaka* for the evening meal, attended the goats, then walked slowly down to the sea. A broad stripe of gold lay across the blue, the last of the day's sun—a path, she used to think, to adventure somewhere beyond the horizon.

And now, when she was old enough to take the path, and her mother willing to let her go, she no longer wanted it. Life felt flat, dull, and lacking in all excitement. *Why can't I be like Sofia*, she thought crossly, *and be excited at the thought of going to Kyrenia tomorrow to buy material for new dresses? It isn't as if I wanted to stay here any more. Even my beloved Exos suddenly seems empty. I feel hollow, as if my heart had gone out of my body.*

She kicked off her sandals and walked along the beach, letting the tiny edge of foam roll up over her ankles. She wondered about her father. What had taken him away so suddenly? Why had he not come back? What could there be, anywhere in the whole world, more beautiful than Exos, the Villa Julia, his wife and children? Where could life be easier, with the sun to ripen his lemons; the little stream, which never dried up, to water his vegetables; the vine shading the terrace, where in autumn the ripe grapes hung down so one did not even have to stretch to reach them?

What could have drawn a man away from all this?

The rim of the sun touched the sea. It would be quite dark soon. She turned back, trailing her feet in the water. All this thought about her father had been a barrier, put up to keep Rory McDermot out of her mind.

Now she let him in. *If the young are the only ones brave enough to face naked truth, let me face it.*

I love Rory McDermot. It is because he is going that

the island lacks excitement. Because he won't be there, that Athens seems just a dreary bore. Because he won't see them, that new dresses are not worth bothering with.

"I love him."

She said the words out loud, as softly as the splash of golden sea around her ankles. *I sent him away, with unkind words in his ears. He could have lived in the house; I could have seen him every day; made his bed, done his washing, served his food. He might have loved me. We might have been married and lived in the house, and he could have had his dream after all, and....*

The sun went down. Where all had been light, now there was not even twilight, only a gray land and a gray sea, which in a minute would be quite dark.

What a fool—what an utter fool I have been!

Forgetting her sandals, she raced home. Georgi was lighting lanterns on the terrace, and the good, familiar smell of *moussaka* came from the kitchen.

RORY SCRAMBLED DOWN the steep path, which led to the village. He was somewhat downcast by the quick turn of events at the villa, but he felt in his bones that all was not lost. So he whistled a cheerful jig as he went. He'd be back. The mother was for him. The boy was influenced by his sister, and she was a lass of determination and character. A good hot temper besides, he reflected. Plenty of spirit.

Well, well, we shall see, he thought. He'd had plenty of experience taming fine young horses full of spirit and fight, and he learned patience the hard way. There came a moment to leave the young creature alone, to walk away, to wait. And nine times out of ten, if a man had the patience, its own curiosity about the strange power that it had felt for the first time would bring it back. He saw them now, the shining red horses on the green

grass, bright in the soft Irish sunlight—delicately stepping, fine nostrils flaring, curiosity and the hidden desire
to be mastered bringing them pace by pace toward the
man they feared, yet longed for.

He had almost reached level ground when Marcus
stepped from behind a stand of elephant grass and
stood in the way, glowering.

"Kalispera," said Rory, with deceptive gentleness. A
sixth sense warned him that the young man meant trouble. Something in the way he hunched those powerful
shoulders, or a leery look in the eyes perhaps. The Irishman stood his ground, muscles tensed for action. He
hated trouble and would go out of his way to avoid it.
Yet not too far out. Not far enough to inconvenience
himself.

"Time you left Exos, Irishman," Marcus said bluntly.
"I suggest you take tomorrow's boat if you want to keep
out of trouble."

Rory nodded agreeably. "That's the second invitation
I've had today to leave the island. I really think I might.
Only—" he smiled apologetically—"it's one of the de-
fects in the Irish character that when asked politely to
do a thing, we want to know why. Why do *you* want me
to leave? You might as well tell me. I'm a reasonable
man ... within reason."

"Sofia is my girl and always has been. Keep off her,
that's all. She's so taken up with you, she can't see sense.
I mean to marry her, understand? So the sooner you're
out of sight the sooner she'll listen to me and we can get
back to Greece and start looking for a restaurant to
buy."

"Does she know that?"

"She won't listen. Too busy washing your shirt, or
cooking your meal, or cleaning your room, or waiting
on you at the table. If she's not dancing with you or taking you out in her father's boat."

Rory stroked his chin thoughtfully. "So? The girl is overdoing it, eh? And you haven't told her you want to take her off to Greece?"

"No, I haven't. What do you mean, 'overdoing it'?"

Rory tapped the angry man on the chest. "I mean, my dear sir, that she wants nothing else in life but to leave the island and see the world. And that she's been using me, with my connivance, I admit, to make you jealous. With a view to making you fall in love with her. It seems she's been successful."

Marcus's jaw dropped. "The little—! The deceiving little monkey! I came home for the special purpose of marrying her, if she'd grown into a woman capable of helping me with the restaurant and giving me good sons. A man can't marry a weakling, you know. If she'd only given me a chance ..."

"Your fault," Rory reminded him. He could breathe easier now. There would be no need to fight Marcus. He could have licked the boy, he thought—just. He had the advantage of being lighter on his feet, more experienced, and maybe a shade tougher. But he disliked fighting, being bone lazy. "You gave Evie those flowers, which properly upset the applecart."

Marcus frowned. "Apples? There were no apples. That was Evie's fault for looking so—different. She's beautiful, that girl."

"So I've noticed."

"She has a dowry, too. She told me. But not strong enough for me, *kyrie*. It's plump little Sofia I want. That girl is as strong as a horse, and—" he grinned suddenly, "—I like them plump."

The two men walked toward the village. "What you must do now," Rory counseled, "is to show your hand. Stand no nonsense from the girl. She will come running if you so much as crook your little finger."

"I'll do it. And you'll leave the island?"

Rory halted. "We—ell, there's a difficulty, Marcus. It's another defect in the Irish character, I'm afraid. When asked to do a thing twice, we think there must be some good reason for *not* doing it. So we don't. It makes life difficult for us, but there it is. I'm sorry about that, but I simply can't go now."

"We could make you—the Exos men. Without a word said or a blow struck, we could make you leave tomorrow."

"You could, boy, you could. But it would do you no good with the lady, and you know it. Look, I have a better plan. I think I owe you something. So far, I've played the game on Sofia's side. Now it's time to play on yours. It's rather f-funny, don't you think...."

Suddenly Rory began to laugh, seeing the absurdity of the situation. He bent double with laughter and tears filled his eyes. Marcus watched amazed, but the laughter proved infectious. Slowly, he chuckled. In a moment both men were helpless. Rory punched Marcus feebly, struggling to control his voice.

"You've got to come out on t-top, see? The big hero. So tonight..." he paused to mop his eyes with a grubby handkerchief, "I'll eat outside. If Sofia is on duty...."

"She will be, if you're there. Don't fear for that!"

"I'll make a fuss of her. Invite her to join me for a bottle of wine. She'll play along if you're watching."

Marcus looked doubtful. "Are you sure it will work? What do I do?"

"You march up and tell me to clear off. Throw out your chest, flex your muscles, and look dangerous. You can do it?"

"Sure I can. And you?"

"I go. I don't argue, but pay my bill and leave. Then you sit down in my place—and bob's your uncle."

"My uncle? What has he to do with it?"

"I mean, you're all right. The girl wants no one but

you, Marcus. She's a charmer, I admit. As attractive and merry a little creature as a man could wish to meet, and I can't think why I've never so much as kissed her. But she's yours, man, if you can talk your way out of that business of giving the flowers to the wrong girl. All right?"

Marcus obviously liked the idea. A slow grin spread over his face. "She's been playing a trick on me, eh? Now you and I—" he thumped Rory's arm with a hard clenched fist "will pay her back in her own coin, eh? A trick. Yes, that's good, *kyrie*." He laughed again. "Now we'll separate. It would not do to walk into the village together like old friends."

AFTER SUPPER Georgi drew Evie on one side and whispered, "Where did he go? He said he wanted to talk to *me*, man to man. You had no right to send him away."

"You yourself told him to go."

"That was before. Men should talk over these things. I would have gone with him, but you interrupted and said I had to go with you up the mountain. There's too much women's talk going on. Tomorrow I'm going down to see the Kyrios McDermot, whatever you say."

"You mean you've changed your mind about England?"

"No, I won't go. But I'm not big enough yet to run everything myself, and you and mama are only women. I bet that man has some good ideas, if everybody stopped shouting and listened to him. There's no harm in talking to him, is there?"

"N-no, I suppose not. But listen, Georgi. We need our father now, and I'm going to find him. Tomorrow I'm going to Kyrenia and I'll find a lawyer to act for us. And down there on the beach I had another idea. I think I know how to fix everything."

"What idea? Will it work?"

Evie crushed her doubts. It had to work. "Don't be too hopeful. But it might. Someone—some woman—has to run this house for him, if he buys it. He's not married. He hasn't any sweetheart, at least I don't think he has, and I'm sure I should have known by the way he spoke."

"How soon will you know whether it works or not?"

The girl swallowed nervously. "Tonight. It must be tonight, because I think he'll leave Exos tomorrow."

"Why worry, then? If he's leaving, we needn't bother."

Evie drew him closer to her. How slight he was still, the bone and muscle of man not yet developed. Yet already he thought like a man, not a child. He had begun to shake off the rule of women, like a true islander. Mama's reign was over, though she didn't suspect it yet.

"Little king," Evie whispered, "We're not out of danger. Mama has her heart in this business and if it isn't Rory McDermot it might be someone much worse. So let me try my plan tonight."

"All right. And if it doesn't work, I'll talk to him tomorrow before the boat leaves."

She shook her head violently. "No, no. No. This is all or nothing. One throw of the dice. If we lose, we lose. If he doesn't agree to my suggestion, he'll never come back, and you must never ask him. Promise."

"Tell me what it is, your plan?"

"No, that I can never tell anyone. Only him." She laid her finger on the boy's lips. "Not a word to mama, Georgi. I'll say I'm going down to talk to Sofia about the dress materials."

AT THE EDGE of the village the enormity of what she had come to do brought Evie to a halt. She leaned against a datepalm in the darkness, listening to the voices, the chink of bottles and glasses. Her hands were damp, her mouth dry with nervousness. Her heart beat fast and she found it hard to breathe.

She must go back to Georgi and tell him she had failed, had not even had the courage to put her idea into practice. Why hadn't she realized back there on the beach that it was impossible? It had seemed such a simple business transaction when she first thought of it. Now—she swallowed, her throat stiff.

Peering round the thick trunk of the tree, she saw Rory at a table which bore the remains of an evening meal. She watched him, seeing no one else, though most of the tables were occupied. Then Sofia came, wearing her best Sunday dress for work and skimming through the crowd to Rory's table.

The expression on her friend's face spoke volumes. *She wants Rory,* Evie whispered to herself. *Not Marcus. That's how she used to look when she talked about Marcus, but now it's Rory. That's why she risked the beating. She really has changed. Poor Marcus!*

Poor Sofia! For Rory would never choose her. I know that much about him now.

Sofia set down a fresh bottle and a second glass on Rory's table. Then, half rising, the man put his arm around her waist and drew her down. Heads close, they laughed together, and Rory's hand went to the bottle to fill both glasses.

Faces close together across the table, the pair touched glasses and drank, in a gesture as intimate as a kiss.

Evie turned away with a choking sob. She ran till she was out of breath, then flung herself down on the stony path and pressed her face into her hands.

To have sent Rory away so unkindly was bad enough. But then she had had the secret hope—almost the certainty—that he would come back. At the time she had not known it consciously, but now the knowledge

stabbed her cruelly. She had been so sure, so ridiculously sure.

But to know that the man she loved was sitting there
laughing with Sofia, the pair of them making pictures in
each other's eyes over a glass of wine—that was unendurable.

CHAPTER FIVE

SOFIA WAS ELATED. After a bad beginning things were going her way. Yesterday her father had thrashed her for wasting her time with a penniless holidayer, and although she had yelled and made a fuss, in a way she could not blame him. A girl must keep her eye on the main chance, and her main chance of getting away from Exos was as the wife of Marcus, who had money enough to buy a restaurant of his own.

True, it would be hard work, almost slavery. But at least one would be working for one's own home, husband, and children, not for some fat boss and his lazy, fat wife. One would see life, meet new people every day, count the money every night.

It had been a bad error of judgment to overdo her attentions to the Irishman in her efforts to make Marcus jealous. She had frightened him off altogether. For two days he had not spoken to her, but gone fishing with her brothers or up the mountain by himself. She had nearly lost him for a poverty-stricken tourist. Her father had been wise to take strong measures.

And now everything was fine. The Kyrios McDermot had money. He intended to buy the big villa. Evie's mother had sent word to the go-between and the priest to begin talks about the price. That was an open secret already. Sofia's father had practically apologized for beating her, and her mother was already talking of having a daughter queening it up there on the hillside. *For why*, they asked themselves, *should a stranger buy a house on such a small, unimportant island, if not because he intended to marry a local girl and settle down among his in-laws?*

Now she would see the world at her ease, as a tourist herself. She would have a camera and sunglasses, and laze on hotel beaches in a bikini, as the wife of a well-to-do European.

So she touched glasses with Rory, their faces close together, and his eyes smiled into hers over the wine. She still felt the pressure of his hand, where for a moment his arm had slipped around her waist. She sighed happily.

"You, man," said Marcus heavily, "get out. This is my girl."

Rory looked up at the big man standing over him. To Sofia's disappointment he looked frightened; but then who wouldn't? That Marcus was such a coarse brute.

"I'm sorry, mate," Rory said easily. "We were only sharing a glass of wine. Sit down and have a drink."

Marcus sat down. "I'll finish the bottle. But you'll clear off, mister. I won't have strangers making up to my girl."

"The idea!" Sofia tossed her head. "I'm not your girl. I've better fish to fry than a cheap *taverna* proprietor who hasn't even got a *taverna*. You're just as rough mannered as you were before you went away. Go away, and leave me to talk with my friends."

Rory protested, "But Marcus is your friend. You told me—"

She shrugged her plump, creamy shoulders. "That was a long time ago. I knew no better. He dazzled me with his fancy clothes and tight shoes, and the money he was flashing. But I'm a serious girl, Rory, and I can see here's nothing behind the colored suit and the pocket book. Nothing for me." She gave Marcus a contemptuous look. "Please go away. I'm busy."

The men exchanged a dismayed glance.

"Trick?" Marcus raised his well-marked eyebrows. "Who's playing tricks, Mr. McDermot? You had me fooled. Well, if you're going to marry her, that's your good luck. But if you're not—" His big teak-colored hand folded into a fist. "You'd better be, that's all."

Rory blenched. "It's no trick, Marcus. I've no wish to marry Sofia. She's your girl."

Sofia looked from one to the other, bewildered. "What are you two talking about? Are you playing a trick on me, both of you? If so, it's not k-kind." Tears flowed down her rosy face. The cherry-colored, kissable mouth drooped.

"Don't cry," Rory said gently. He felt himself in a trap, either accidental or perhaps, arranged by these two against himself. His mind worked quickly, but for the moment he saw no opening. He couldn't possibly marry Sofia.

"Sofia, please stop. Marcus and I were playing a little trick on you, that's all. He loves you, he wants you to marry him. He was pretending to scare me, and I was going to run away with my tail between my legs, to make him look a hero for you. Forgive us."

"I'll forgive you. I won't forgive him. He's nothing but a great lout. All he wants a woman for is work and bed. I wouldn't marry him if he were the last man on Exos! I want to marry you, and live in the Villa Julia and do nothing but embroidery."

Sofia's tear-drenched eyes widened as the words poured out of her. Now she had given it all away, but perhaps no harm would be done. There came a moment when a man had to be told straight.

Marcus swore. "So that's how it is? You lied to me, Irishman. You've talked to her about marriage. You must have done."

Rory said desperately, "Oh, for goodness' sake, Sofia, stop sniveling and listen. What's this about the villa?"

"You're going to buy it, everybody knows that. We all thought you hadn't a *mil* and now it turns out you're rich."

Rory stood up and kicked his chair away. "Marcus, come to the harbor with me. I think I can explain. She's given me a clue."

"Too late for explaining. You'll marry her or there are two fists of mine that will make you do it, besides a dozen more pairs like them. Talking of houses to a woman, and then pretending it was all a game! I'm not so easily fooled as you think."

"Yesterday, I swear, she was crazy for you, Marcus. Sofia, for pity's sake tell him that's true. But today there was some talk of my buying the villa, and the Kyria Julia sent Georgi to the priest and a relative called Stephanos with a letter asking them to represent her in any dealings with me. It came to nothing. The family decided not to sell after all. But I suppose the news traveled all over the island before sundown."

Marcus scratched his head. "It would. You think Sofia switched her affections to you because she thought you had money?"

"And perhaps would give her an easier life. Is that it, Sofia? You might as well tell the truth, because I don't intend to marry you in any case, fists or no fists. I know you love Marcus. I know you'd hate my kind of life and the kind of man I am. Marcus is your own kind, girl. Do have a bit of sense."

She wiped her eyes and nose upon her apron. Rory grunted and handed her his handkerchief which had already had a hard day and was none too clean.

"You're all unkind to me! I'm going off with the boat tomorrow. I'm a good waitress and I can get a job in Cyprus now the holiday season is on. I won't have anything to do with either of you. You're cruel!"

She spat on the ground, tossed her head, and flounced

off, pushing her way through the crowd, which had followed the quarrel with intense interest.

"Women!" groaned Marcus. "Now where do we
stand?"

"Keep after her," Rory advised. "She's a girl worth
having. As for me, I'd better leave as soon as possible. I
meant to stay a while in case . . . ." He shot a glance in
the direction of the Villa Julia, whose lights could be
seen high on the dark hillside. "But I'm not safe here,
boy. When can I leave?"

Inquiries among the men sitting around revealed a
small motor boat leaving about six in the morning. "I'll
go with that, if they'll have me," Rory decided. "Wait
for the big caïque at nine o'clock I dare not. Poor little
Sofia is a woman scorned just now, and if I'm not careful she'll have the island knives out for me."

"And you were the man who understood women!"
Marcus mocked not unkindly.

EVIE SPENT A RESTLESS NIGHT. A vision of Rory and
Sofia flashed across her mind and kept her wakeful.
Heads close together, lips smiling over shared wine.
Sofia, so vibrant, so alive, and able to use her attractions
to advantage. Evie had for some time been conscious
that the girl she had grown up with was already fully occupied with the business of selecting and capturing the
husband she wanted. Sofia seemed never to have known
an in-between time, when she had stood with reluctant
feet on the edge of growing up, looking forward fearfully to the anxieties and bewilderment of being a young
woman aware of herself, aware of young males. Lucky
Sofia, to have such confidence in herself!

*Sofia, if she had devised a plan for saving her home,
would have carried it out with an air. I,* Evie remembered
wretchedly, *felt sick with fear and ran away.*

Perhaps Sofia had thought of a plan to get herself off Exos and out into the world? As Rory's wife! True, there was Marcus. But Sofia was shrewd enough to see that her future with Marcus would mean hard work and many children. Rory would be gentle with his wife, not demanding too much.

What if Rory married Sofia and brought her here, as mistress of the Villa Julia? Disturbed by the awful thought, Evie crept out of bed and to the veranda, where a cool air off the sea blew her thin cotton nightdress around her. The moon hung like a ripe peach in the sky, making a silver path across the still sea.

She closed her eyes tightly as if she could shut out the picture of Rory with Sofia. They still floated there, blobs of color printed on her eyelids. Her attention sharpened suddenly, and she drew in a quick breath.

Had Marcus really been there, standing huge and still behind Rory, full of menace as he stared down at the Irishman's back? Or was Marcus only part of her dreams?

Didn't Rory McDermot know that, whatever the custom in his own country, in the Greek islands it was dangerous to play around with another man's girl? He must be warned.

With this thought uppermost in her mind, in the morning she hurried down to the village long before the caïque was due to leave. She must find Rory and warn him. After their tumultuous parting of yesterday, their meeting might cause slight embarrassment on both sides, but that did not matter. There were men on the island capable of slipping a knife between the stranger's ribs. Not Marcus himself, perhaps, though he might use fists. The younger men were more traveled and better educated. But the older men, especially the grandfathers, still had ideas of an older and rougher justice.

The men were working in the fields, the harbor empty

of boats except for the Kyrenia caïque now being loaded. The wooden chairs of the *taverna* were stacked
neatly outside, and Sofia herself was on hands and
knees scrubbing the floor.

"Good morning, Sofia. How are your bruises?"

The girls wrung out her floorcloth. "What bruises?
Where are you going all dressed up so early? If you've
come to see Rory McDermot, you have wasted your
breath. He's gone, left in a fishing boat before dawn."

Relief flooded Evie's mind, till she thought of asking
cautiously whose boat. An accident at sea would be
convenient.

"Marcus and his father. They're taking him to Kyrenia. It seems he was in a hurry and couldn't wait for the
caique. He won't be back. He took his backpack and
everything from his room—not that he possessed
much."

Sofia was in a bad temper, that was obvious. Evie
wasn't surprised. Scrubbing the *taverna* couldn't be
pleasant, and if Rory had gone for good, after last
night's tender little episode at the cafe table, Sofia must
be feeling hurt and angry.

"What happened last night?" Evie asked gently. "Did
Rory quarrel with anyone?"

Sofia slapped her dirty cloth into the bucket. "No, he
did *not*. He and Marcus were as thick as thieves. I've
finished with both of them, and I told them so. I gave
them the length of my tongue, I can tell you. If either of
them shows his face in this *taverna* again, I'll—I'll—oh,
go away !"

Evie sat down on a dry piece of floor. This required
investigation, and she understood very well that Sofia
wanted to talk about it and was only letting off steam
when she said "go away". "What did they do? Something terrible?"

"They were laughing at me, behind my back. I had a

secret with Rory, and he told Marcus. And they tried to play a trick on me which didn't work, because I . . . I...."

Indignation gave way to a choking sob. The big dark eyes filled with tears, and Sofia looked at Evie with an expression of anguish.

"I love Marcus, Evie. Truly I do. But I hate scrubbing floors and cooking, and if I marry him I'll never see anything anymore but a kitchen stove and a tub of baby things to wash. What's the good of being pretty, and having nice clothes, and being the lightest dancer on the island, if it all leads to the washtub and the scrubbing brush? Isn't there anything else for us?"

"There's love."

Sofia looked at her scornfully. "Be your age, Evie! Love's a trap. We've no choice, really; only between scrubbing one's own floor and someone else's."

Evie knew a piercing sense of desolation. "But there must be more than that, Sofia. If I loved a man, I'd want to be with him forever. I wouldn't care how hard life was, or mind working. Just so long as we were together."

If I loved a man! I do. I love Rory and he's gone forever. I'll never see him again. He won't come back, and it's partly my fault.

"You've grown up without a man in the house," Sofia reminded her. "You've had only yourselves to please up there. No man coming in wanting food at all hours, with his tempers and tantrums and lazing about playing cards, or drinking while his wife works herself to death. Men!" She threw the brush across the floor. "I'd go into a convent, only...."

"Only what?"

Sofia shrugged. "Well, I suppose one might miss something. And it wouldn't be much fun. You didn't tell me where you are going? Not Kyrenia?"

Evie nodded. "On family business. And to buy some new dress materials. And I'd like my red shoes back, if you please."

"I'll get them. Wait a minute."

"What's it all for?" Sofia had asked of love. What indeed? Evie wondered, fingering the handmade lace collar on her clean black dress, the scarlet apron rich with embroidery, the white stockings she had washed last night and put on with pride this morning. Why bother to dress up? Much better to stick to old clothes, which wouldn't spoil, and race about barefoot on the hottest days.

"Good morning, Evie." The priest paused in his shuffle down the waterfront. "Going in the caïque? You look too smart for Exos so early. And deep in thought, eh? Dreaming of sweethearts to come?"

"Wishing time could stand still."

"Dear child! When we wish that, it's already too late. You want to stand still *yesterday*, don't you?"

"Yes, I do. Or better still, the day before yesterday."

"You see? Too late already. I can't help you. Even the most powerful saints can't turn the clock back for us. I'm afraid we have to move forward into our own future all the time. Everything comes, if we wait long enough. And everything passes, even today's grief, which seems so interminable. Well, have a good day, child. If you've time, call in and say a prayer with our dear St. Poly. He'll be glad to see someone from home, I daresay."

"I intended to. I have a favor to ask him."

"The saints, and God himself, would be lonely indeed if mankind wasn't always in need of a favor or two. Tell him the island needs him."

Sofia came back with the shoes. The caïque took on passengers and put out of the harbor. Evie settled down for a three-hour voyage, and composed her mind to deciding what exactly she would say to the lawyer.

KYRENIA WAS FULL OF TOURISTS. Like a walking flower-garden of color, they wandered around the old harbor, climbed the great steps to the castle, which had seen so many conquerors and conquered. Under colored café umbrellas they drank tea and studied their history books, or crowded round the water-ski boats. Evie walked up and down several times, carefully studying the dresses. Bright, bold colors looked best under the sun. Pastel colors appeared faded against the vivid sea and sky. She studied the blond girls of her own age with particular interest, even following one group as far as the foot of the castle steps to observe the details; but then she realized her time was flying and she must find the lawyer's office before it closed for the long lunch period.

The lawyer, who was younger and less dusty than she'd expected, listened attentively. He wouldn't guarantee results, but he would try through English agents. Perhaps it would be best to advertise in the English national newspapers. Would that be in order?

"Whatever you think best," Evie told him. "How long will it take?"

"To put the advertisements in, only a week perhaps. But don't expect too much. After so many years, it will be difficult. Perhaps impossible."

"I understand that," Evie assured him. "But at least we shall have tried."

Leaving him, she decided to visit St. Polystemon next, leaving her shopping till the late afternoon so that she could take her parcels directly to the boat. She put the red shoes carefully into her shabby shoulder bag, donned her old sandals and began the long trudge uphill toward the tiny monastery, which had the honor of sheltering the saint's skull. She could eat her fruit lunch by the roadside and with luck she would be offered a lift.

Her luck held. An old man stopped his donkey cart

and courteously offered her his hospitality. She shared
her lunch with him and told him about St. Polystemon
and Exos. When they parted, he kissed her ceremoni-
ously on both cheeks and gave her his blessing. Ten
minutes' scrambling up a steep path brought her to the
old buildings and she was thankful to rest in the shady
cloisters to recover her breath.

All was silent. A cat slept in the sun. The heat
brought out the scent of herbs growing in red pots on
top of a wall. Four tall cypresses stood like dark motionless sentries, and not even a leaf quivered in the still
air.

The interior of the chapel was dark after the sunlight.
Only the gold paint of the icons and the high, gilded
candleholders gleamed dimly. Evie sat on a narrow
wooden seat till her eyes adjusted to the gloom.

She found St. Polystemons' skull in a blackened case
in the darkest corner. Disappointed, for she had always
been told it was in a silver box, she peered closely and
found a hole in the case through which a tiny circle of
bone shone, polished by generations of hopeful fingers.
Closing her eyes, she concentrated her whole mind
upon a fervent prayer to the young saint.

*Please, oh, please bring Rory McDermot back! I want
him so much.*

She opened her eyes, knowing she had wasted her
effort after all. She had meant to ask for her father to be
found. Now she could see much better, and observed
that the case really was silver after all, but it had not
been polished for many years. Now if the monks had a
woman about the place, to do the cleaning and such,
poor St. Poly would not be so neglected. Well, it was
something to tell them at home, and perhaps stop them
asking what she had prayed for.

It isn't, the old priest had told her often enough, that
the saints really do interfere with our lives down here;

but praying so hard, and meaning it, helps us to know what it is we *really* want. Which isn't always just what we think we want.

She smiled ruefully. Well, at least St. Poly might be glad to know he wasn't forgotten in Exos, poor young man. How sad it must be to lose bright life at twenty years old for the sake of an ideal! She stooped and dropped a kiss on the polished ivory bone, and whispered the priest's message.

Then she went outside into the sun, blinking like a little owl. St. Polystemon had done his work well, for there, coming under the archway, his pack on his back, was Rory.

They stared at each other, unbelieving. Then she ran towards him and was snatched up into his arms. He hugged her tightly.

"Evie! Darling girl, what on earth are you doing so far from home? Of all people...."

"I'm visiting St. Poly, of course. Do you think I'd come this far and not pay my respects? But—oh, Rory, I thought you'd gone forever! How come you are here? Did you know about me?"

"No. I just walked up by the footpath. After my stay in Exos, it seemed the right thing to do—as you said, to pay my respects."

There was, after all, no awkwardness. Only a bubbling delight at being with him again, a delight he obviously shared.

"Show me your saint, then we'll walk down the hill together and have tea at the hotel on the beach. A civilized tea, which Cyprus understands, thank goodness. There's a lovely path all the way down and we shall have a fine thirst at the end of it."

"I have shopping to do, and the caïque leaves before dark. Are you coming back to Exos? Sofia says you took all your things away."

Not till they were on the downhill path did he tell her why he had left the island so early. "I ran away. Somehow the news of my trying to buy the villa got out. And Marcus and I burned our fingers trying to be too clever with Sofia. She suddenly decided she wanted to marry me instead of him, and when she understood that wasn't the idea, she was angry with both of us. What could I do but run? With me out of the way, she may forgive poor Marcus in time. I'm afraid it was all my doing."

"When I saw you last night, you were making silly eyes at her over a wineglass. And Marcus—" she stopped suddenly. "Then he *was* there, behind you! Don't you know how dangerous it is to play around with another man's girl? He could have killed you. I remembered in the night that he was there, and I was so afraid for you, Rory. I had to go down to warn you early this morning, but you'd gone."

"That was darned nice of you, Evie. I thought you'd finished with me forever, and I was sorry about that. Much as I wanted the villa, it suddenly seemed to me that I didn't want to quarrel with you over it, so I decided to give up the idea of buying it. Does that solve your problem?"

They had arrived at a flat little clearing and sat down by mutual consent, as from it there was a splendid view down into the inner courts of the castle where once crusaders had walked, and where now colored dots of sightseers moved like insects. Beyond the huge bastion of gray stone the sea shimmered like silk, and waterskiers carved long arcs of white upon the blue. The bank on which they sat was covered in creamy rockroses, which smelled delicious.

"Not exactly," Evie admitted. "Mama won't give up the idea of selling, and if it is not you, it might be someone much worse."

"Thank you."

"Well, there could be worse than you. If you married Sofia and made her mistress of the house, that would be the worst thing of all."

"My dear child, I have no intention of marrying Sofia and never have had. Whatever made you think so?"

"She's so pretty. I'm not in the least like her."

"No, you're not in the least like Sofia."

"I'm not pretty?"

"No, you're not pretty."

"Sofia attracts all the men, without even trying. I can't do that."

"No, you can't."

"Anybody could be in love with Sofia."

He twisted to face her and took both her narrow, tanned hands in his. "Listen, dear Evie. You are not pretty like Sofia because you are beautiful. You have lovely bones and an elegant walk like a queen's, and this beauty you will keep. When Sofia is a fat momma wadding about her work, you will be beautiful still. When you are an old, old lady, you will be as fine and delicate as handmade lace."

"Rory—"

"Sofia is young enough to attract all men. She attracts me, in her way. But you, my sweet, will draw one man to you, and pierce him to the bone with love. And he will love you the whole of his lone life, and beyond the grave itself. You have the power, mavourneen, which one woman in a million possesses. Do you understand?"

She shook her head. "Not entirely. You bewilder me, Rory."

He cupped her face between his hands, "Some day—soon—you'll know what I mean. Meantime, don't compare yourself with Sofia. She's pretty, she's vividly alive, she could win any man's body. Yes, mine too, if she tried, and I were not obsessed with another woman. But you, my sweet, will win a man's soul and keep it."

She did not answer because there were no words. She stared into her hands and felt the warm air moving round her, and inhaled the scent of the rock roses, and heard a bee. She thought, *When I am very old, I shall remember this minute of my life.*

After a bit, she remembered something he had said. "Obsessed with another woman? You mean—there's someone you want to marry?"

He smiled and shook his head. "Wanted. She married another man. I can't get her out of my head. Not yet. It's too soon."

"She pierced you to the bone?"

"It wasn't like that. We grew up together. We were like twins, happier together than anyone else. We thought each other's thoughts. I never dreamed either of us could think of marrying anyone else. There was no one I was more content to be with."

"And she with you?"

"I thought so."

She said carefully, "It seems to me you were good, close friends. Isn't love something different again? You could quarrel every day with someone, and yet be in love."

He stabbed at the dry soil with a broken-off stick. "It could be. Do you know, we never had any need to talk, Clodagh and I."

"Maybe you had nothing to say to each other."

He gave her an odd look. "I'd have walked off and left you on your lee lone if you'd dared say that six months ago. Silent companionship, we used to call it. And I daresay it was, most of the time. Lately I've wondered if we'd exhausted all we had to talk about. A lifetime of it might have proved lonely, to say the least."

"One day you'll wake up and find yourself free of her. I feel it in my bones. Then you'll want another girl."

"I shall never be quite free of Clodagh. She's part of

me, like the sea breaking on the Irish cliffs, and the bare white rocks, and cream-colored Connemara ponies, and the scent of my country." He laughed suddenly. "You couldn't imagine how it smells, Evie. Rotting seaweed in the fields, and the smoke of burning turf from the house fires. And there are the finest horses and dogs in the world there. Times, the sea is as blue as the Mediterranean, but there are tides, and long white combers rolling in on the Atlantic beaches...."

"You love it, Rory? Why do you want a house here?"

"Because any house I had on the cliffs there would be Clodagh's house, don't you see? A white house on a cliff at the edge of the sea, that's what I always dreamed of. I can have it here, and the warmth of the sun beside, and the scent of lemons and lillies, balsam and basil, figs and wine."

He lay flat on his back, his hands under his head, and stared unblinking at the sky. "All over the world, girl, there are men like me; the lonely sort, whose dream is out of reach and can't be replaced by any everyday sort of girl. Men who, for a month, or a year, or forever, want to be alone and not bothered by anyone. We are usually poor, mavourneen, because we have no incentive to keep on the roundabout of money, or to run in the rat race. Our links with life are broken and for a time we want to form no new ones."

Evie stroked his forehead gently, aching with love.

"So when my old da died and left me all he had, which, God rest him, wasn't all that much, I dreamed up a house where such men might stay for a time in their aimless wandering. A healing place, with no ties to it. Where a man could come and go as he pleased, live on what he possessed in a simple sort of way, enjoy the sun and warmth, find a sort of medicine in the earth. Am I talking nonsense?"

"It sounds sensible to me. You think the Villa Julia

might be such a place? There is space, and we grow things. The rooms are big and look out on the sea. But, Rory, think. It would never do. You mean a sort of hotel, don't you? There is only one bathroom, and the water has to be carried."

"Then we should carry it, or wash in the stream. Or go unwashed, if we fancied. But we'd be no hippies, Evie. I don't mean that sort."

"Sheets and tablecloths to be washed. You're not at all practical, my dear man. How would you cook meals for a lot of hungry men in my kitchen?"

"I wouldn't. There's an oven out in the yard, isn't there? They say bread and meat baked in those outdoor ovens taste wonderful. My guests would be content with that, and with honey, and dates, and grapes."

She laughed softly. "And pull faces over our goats milk? And goat cheese is strong."

"All the better. But ... " He sat up and collected his backpack, "that's a dream from which I woke up pretty smartish yesterday. It wouldn't have worked, perhaps."

"Monasteries work. Look at our brothers. I don't see why it shouldn't, except, of course, that it might be difficult to find the right people."

"I don't think so. There's a grapevine among such men. I know, I'm one of them."

"Would you admit women?"

"Why not, if they had the need of such a retreat?"

"And everybody would be free to go back into the world as soon as they were ready to face it? It's a wonderful idea, Rory. Our house and our island working a cure on human hearts. I'd like that. Couldn't we do it without selling you the house? If you planned it all, and mama and I helped with the housekeeping part of it?" Her voice lifted with enthusiasm as the future took shape in her mind. "Mama and I could live in the village and come up every day, so you'd have our rooms for your guests. And we could keep the land for Georgi, and—"

He interrupted sharply. "Forget it. It can't be done that way. Your mother wants the money—needs it. Your way, she'd get nothing for the house, for I wasn't thinking of making a profit, but only enough to pay my way and keep the place in repair. You wouldn't even get any wages, for my idea is that we look after ourselves, doing the cleaning and cooking, growing our own food, doing our own fishing. You see, the place would have to be mine. No woman would go along with my simple ideas. You all want to dress things up, and none of you believes that a lonely man prefers to look after himself. You'd want clean tablecloths instead of scrubbed boards, and regular meal times, and before long you'd be laundering our shirts. I know women! They interfere."

"Mama might. She'd fuss and worry. But I'd never interfere, only help."

"And be hurt if I told you to clear off when I didn't want any help!"

The words came harshly, and almost at once he stood up and hitched his pack on his shoulders. "It wouldn't work, Evie. That's not the way I dreamed it. I can't have my idea cluttered up with a lot of women fussing around. Come on, if you want that tea and to do your shopping. I'll put you on the evening boat, but I'm not coming back to Exos. I'll find my house somewhere else"

Tears stung her eyes, but she blinked them back, too proud to let him see he had hurt her. She sprang to her feet.

"Come on, then, I'll race you down the hill." She sped away, her feet light on the steep track. The path was more fitted for goats than human beings, and, more accustomed than he to such walking, she came to the road and waited for him.

This was the last time, then. After today Rory would be gone out of her life. The thought was anguish and she closed her eyes, trying to fix these final moments in her memory forever. The heat beating on her face, the smell of crushed herbs, the sound of his feet on the stones. She made herself open her eyes to look up to see him, tall and lean, silhouetted against the brilliant sky. The shape of his head, the shape of his ears, the easy way his muscles moved, the shabby blue shirt and strong brown arms. *When he has gone,* she thought, *I might just as well stop breathing.*

Rory, clattering down the steep track, was smitten with remorse at the hard way he'd refused her offer of help. Why, in the name of the saints, couldn't he have said at least a thank you? She'd understood what he was about, and women so rarely did. He believed her when she said she wouldn't interfere. She was nobody's fool, that girl; yet she had a kind of simple humility, a refreshing lack of complication, which he had known sometimes in the older generation of Irish women. It came, perhaps, from living hand in glove with saints and close to the earth and sea. In her beauty there was the same serenity he remembered in the face of his grandmother. Dammit, why did he have to hurt her?

When he stood beside her, he took her hand lightly in his. "Forgive my abominable manners," he said quietly. "That was a kind thought of yours, and if anyone could make it work, you could."

She turned her head away, afraid he would read too much in her face. "It doesn't matter. You were right. Mama needs the money, and I do understand that the house would have to be your own so you could have everything your way. Forget about it."

"Look at me, Evie."

Reluctantly she obeyed, lifting her face to his. His eyes were intent and grave, so close that she could see her reflection in his pupil.

"I hurt you, when you only meant to help. That was inexcusable of me. Believe me, it means a lot to me that you understand me. No one else has in quite the same way. I shall not forget you, Evie, not ever, wherever I go. Maybe I'm a fool to go at all, but I'd be no good to you. My dream is in me, and I can't settle until I find it. But I'll always know there was one girl who understood how it is with me."

She nodded seriously. "I think I do. I think my father was the same. He had to go, you see. The island could not hold him because there was other music in his ears. So he left my mother and I don't think he'll ever come back. If there's a bit of him in me, that's the bit which understands you."

He leaned nearer, and kissed her softly on the lips—a kiss as light as a butterfly's touch, the first she had ever known from a young man, and like no other kiss she had ever experienced. Her pulses raced, the quick response of her body startled her, and she gave a soft cry almost of pain. Before she could move, he pulled her into his arms and kissed her again more closely, his mouth hard on hers.

Terrified, not of him but of her own body, she struggled to be free. He released her suddenly, sensing her terror and remembering the feel of a small, wild creature in his hands.

She stared at him wide-eyed. "What have you done to me? What have you done?"

He drew a deep breath through his nostrils. He could have kicked himself for being so stupid! He might have known the girl had never been kissed before, and was not for casual kissing like any ordinary girl. He had intruded most damnably into the secret places of her being, and should have had the sense to hold back. He had meant the kiss only in the way of friendship and as a token of remembrance; why did he have to follow it

up with the second one, which young Sofia, that hibis-
cus flower open to the sun, would have accepted with a
laugh and returned with delight?

"Nothing at all," he said gently, as he would reassure
a frightened animal. "Just a kiss in friendship, Evie. A
thank you for understanding me. Don't think any more
about it."

She would. And he would, too. "What have you done
to me?" she had asked. *What have I done to myself?* he
wondered. *Why, suddenly, do I feel we belong together,
the way I felt with Clodagh?*

He tucked her arm in his and marched her down the
road. "I promised you tea, my girl, and we're going to
the best hotel I can find, by way of a goodbye party. We
shall gorge ourselves with honey and almond cakes, and
chocolate ice creams, if there's such a thing to be had."

She did not answer, did not look at him. But she accepted his arm in hers, and marched heel-and-toe with
him on the dusty road. *Give her time,* he thought. *A little
time to recover herself and no harm will be done. Only the
first kiss has gone, never to return; and that she needed, to
save for the lad who will marry her.*

That thought had twisted like a knife. What rough
male would handle this soft-mouthed, delicate-stepping
thoroughbred, break the gentle, proud spirit to bridle
and rein? He had suffered much, thinking of fine Clodagh in the hands of the Englishman from Somerset,
though Clodagh herself seemed happy enough. Was he
to suffer again, remembering the silvery girl he had left
on Exos, and forever wondering who? And how?

They came to the hotel. Evie stared at the flower-
hung entrance, the swinging doors of plate glass, the
tourists strolling in and out.

"I can't go in there, Rory. I'm not dressed for a place
like this. Only my black dress and apron—it isn't
fitting."

"Nonsense! You're more beautiful than any of these globe-trotting old dears. They'll envy you your hair, your face, and your mouth. They'll tell all their friends at home about the lovely island girl in her embroidered apron and lace cap, and feel they've been privileged to look at you. You're your father's daughter, my lass, and twice as good as anyone here. Come on."

She hung back. "Wait a minute I've clean stockings and my red shoes in the bag. Let me put them on."

She spent a long time in the cloakroom, enjoying the row of pink washbasins, the shining faucets which gave hot water, the scented soap. There was a towel, snowy-white but too short to use. When she pulled it in exasperation, it startled her by coming out of its white box, seemingly endless, and refusing to be rolled back. Washed and tidied, and in her red shoes, she stared at herself in the long looking glass, which reflected her image over and over again, and touched her mouth wonderingly.

Why, oh, why did he kiss me? It makes it so much harder to forget that I love him.

My father's daughter? She looked more closely at herself. Am I like him? What sort of man was he, my father? I don't really remember him; only what my mother tells me about him, and that isn't the same.

She remembered she had not told Rory about her visit to the lawyer. Well, that was not his affair. He would hardly be interested, as he was leaving Exos and had given up the idea of buying the villa. It was not polite to thrust one's own domestic affairs before other people who could not possibly be interested.

Leaving the luxurious cloakroom with a certain reluctance, she held her head high and walked out to meet Rory, not noticing the admiring glances cast in her direction by the discreet parties of hotel guests gathering in the vast, cool, marble-floored lounge for an English-style afternoon tea.

Rory noticed—and smiled to himself. How easily this girl could adapt to a more civilized background than the island afforded! With the right man to guide her gently along the right lines, she could fit into a new life with natural grace and easy charm. She had the looks, the education, the unaffected manner of a great lady. Surely fate did not intend her to become a village drudge, blowsy and shrewish as so many peasant women became after a few years? If the father came back, he might be the sort of man who could give his daughter a chance.

A white-coated waiter brought tea. Evie poured, her fine hands delicate among the china and silver. There was a subdued murmur of English voices, a tinkle of water in a marble fountain. Beyond the wide windows, a flash of brilliant turquoise was the swimming pool, edged by flowering plants and palms.

Evie sighed. "It's very *rich*, isn't it? I mean, everything must cost such a lot. I'd like to live here for a week. It would take me all that long just to try everything and see how it worked. Pink tablecloths, too. Oh, look, there's a glass case of embroidery. Is it all right to go and have a look? "

"That's why it's there."

She examined the display carefully, and came back to him simmering with anger. "That big cloth is mama's work. It is priced at one hundred pounds. That's sinful! Mama gets no more than twenty, yet it is the best piece of work there. I don't say that because it is my mama's but because it really is."

"Then you've learned something today. Your mama must ask more for her work."

She was disturbed by the discovery. "A hundred pounds! How can people pay so much? How much will this tea cost you?"

Seeing she was serious he told her, adding, "Don't worry! I can afford it."

She shook her head crossly. "We are spending on one meal enough to keep an island family for half a month. Yet there's not much food. It's all the—" she gestured vaguely"—all the pretty surroundings. Big comfortable chairs, and soft rugs, and flowers everywhere . . . and music. How much will you tip the waiter?"

"Ten percent."

She worked it out, and nodded with satisfaction. "Yes, I see now why all the boys want to leave Exos to be waiters. Is there also ten percent for a waitress? Perhaps I could be one, when Sofia leaves. We could go together, and earn a lot. Then I could help mama."

"No," he said sharply. "No, Evie. It is no life for you. For Sofia it's all right. Not you."

"Why not me? I'm very strong, in spite of being so skinny."

"Your father would not like it. I mean—well, I wouldn't like it."

She bubbled with soft laughter. "But, Rory, you are not my father."

"Sometimes I feel old enough to be. But I'm glad I'm not."

Her eyes twinkled mischievously at him. "If you were, you'd beat me, eh?"

"Certainly I would."

It seemed the right moment to tell Rory of her visit to the lawyer, and the advertisements that were to be inserted in English newspapers, but just then a bevy of girls of her own age trooped in, laughing and chattering, and it was necessary to examine their dresses carefully.

"Which one is for me," she wondered. "I can't go about in an old peasant gown anymore."

"The blue," he answered without hesitation. "The style is simple enough, but I doubt if you'd buy one here in Kyrenia. The girls are American." He pulled out a pencil and sketched a dress on the back of a menu card.

"Mama can make it. She's clever with sewing. Draw some more, Rory. Please. And will you help me choose some material? You know about what looks elegant, don't you?"

He laughed. "Since when did our tomboy wish to look elegant? Are you growing up, *macushla*?"

"I have to. So I might as well do it properly. Will you come? Had you planned to do anything else? Where are you going after today?"

"I've no plans, except that it would be fun to spend the rest of the day with you. Now we've stopped quarreling about the house, we get on pretty well, don't you think?"

"I'm glad you think so. Rory, I'm happy *now*. At this moment in my life. If all the rest of it were to be unhappy, I'd have this minute to remember, wouldn't I? So I intend to enjoy it to the very end. Ought we to go now? The shops will be open again. It's quite late."

The shops were opening after the long midday break. Holidayers were out again, now that the afternoon was somewhat cooler. "You must visit the castle," she told him helpfully, "but not till tomorrow because it takes ages and is tiring. Will this shop do? The prices seem reasonable."

He dismissed the shop as too cheap and walked her through the town till he found one to his liking. "In here, and I'll choose."

Meekly, she trotted in after him, but gasped with dismay at the price of the dress-lengths he indicated. "No one in Exos pays that much."

"But you will. You're a special case. Remember, Evie, you must always buy things of quality, because you are a quality person yourself. Look, this is your color. It will match your eyes."

The soft folds of fine cotton fell through her fingers. "It is the color of the sea. It will look beautiful, Rory."

"And this one."

She looked doubtfully at the bold, dark design. "Are you sure? Not the pink?"

"Definitely not the pink. Trust me. I know about colors. Your friend Sofia would buy this and look ghastly in it. You will look superb. And while you are here, if you can afford it, buy yourself some good shoes."

"I have good shoes. The red ones."

He shook his head, smiling.

Her eyes widened. "They look ghastly?"

"Terrible. I prefer your sandals any day."

She flashed him a grin. "So do I. But nobody else on Exos has red shoes and I thought maybe I was a bit peculiar not liking them. I made myself like them, and in the end I did. Is it all right to wear sandals again now?"

"Please do."

To the amusement of the shop assistant, Evie at once whipped off the red shoes, which were making her feet ache, and wriggled her toes ecstatically. Then she put on the old sandals with relief, and considered the question of paying for the materials Rory had chosen. "Mama said I'd need three dresses, one for Sundays and church, one for everyday, and one of going out in the evenings. But I can only manage two at these prices. Perhaps...." her glance strayed towards the pile of cheap stuff on the bargain counter.

"Don't compromise. Take two and wear your old black for every day. And let me buy you the shoes as a thank you present."

"Thank you for what? Sending you to the copper mines on a donkey?"

"For today. For you to remember today."

She looked up at him seriously. "I shan't forget today, Rory, never fear. I'll tell mama I bought shoes instead of the third dress. She'd never approve of a man buying me presents to wear. Only a husband does that." Her color deepened suddenly. "Whenever we get together, I tell lies. Is it dreadful of me to lie to mama? I could manage without the shoes."

"Just this once," he assured her, "I'll overlook it. I am, thank God, not your father."

The shopping done, they strolled to the waterfront. The island men were loading the caïque, but there was plenty of time, Rory pointed out, for a glass of ouzo before it sailed. He found a pleasant *taverna* with basket chairs and tables on the street, and ordered.

They sat in silence, staring at the red marker buoys floating in the harbor.

Rory thought about Clodagh. Today had been a day very like one spent with Clodagh; a happy, untroubled day, warm with the closeness of a person who understood one's inner thoughts and with whom there was no need to pretend. He tried to fix his mind on the Irish girl, but her image was elusive. *Am I forgetting her,* he thought with alarm. *I cannot forget her. She is part of me; without her, I am incomplete. I can't forget Clodagh.*

Yet it seemed to him his childhood sweetheart was drifting into a faint formlessness, like the vanishing of a smoke ring. And here, beside him, was Evie, warm and living; a creature of earth and air and fire, with whom a man might fall in love so easily, and stay in love forever.

His throat burned drily. *By the saints,* he thought suddenly shaken—*it's not Sofia I'm running away from, at all. It's her—Evie. Because I'm so darned nearly in love with her that I'm jealous for Clodagh.*

He remembered the way Evie had looked up at him so seriously, and said in her soft musical voice, "I shan't forget today, Rory, never fear." He mopped his forehead with his handkerchief and a faint groan escaped him.

Evie was clasping her hands, shaking with nerves now that the moment had come. Yesterday she had shirked it and was ashamed of her cowardice. Now time was running out. In fifteen minutes the caïque would leave, taking her back to Exos, leaving Rory here on the harbor wall. So little time in which to keep her promise to her young brother. "I'll do everything in my power," she had sworn, and Georgi trusted her. True, she had put the matter of tracing their father in hand, but the lawyer had held out little hope.

She cleared her throat, swallowed, and turned to him, her eyes big with the enormity of what she was about to say.

"Rory, there is a solution. A way you could buy the house from mama, and yet not take it away from us entirely. I mean, you'd be master of the house because it would be yours, and yet..." she paused, licking dry lips. She could not go on.

His dark brows lifted. "By magic, *macushla*? The house to be mine and yet yours? How?"

She went on hurriedly, "I'd help, I really would. And so would Georgi. He's useful on the land, even at his age, and mama would be quite happy to live in her own little house, and—"

He laid a strong hand on her arm. "Steady, girl. Take a deep breath and tell me slowly. What are you driving at?"

She looked him full in the face, meeting his questioning gaze without fear now. "There's only one way to do it, Rory. I thought—perhaps—do you think you could marry me?"

CHAPTER SIX

RORY SAT STUNNED IN SILENCE, staring at the toes of his dusty shoes on the blue-gray cobblestones of the Kyrenia waterfront. Words rose in his throat and died.

He had enough peasant blood in him from his Irish ancestors to understand that such an arrangement had merits and would be accepted by Kyria Julia and her advisors without surprise. It would solve many problems. It meant, simply that the daughter's children inherited and not the son's. The family was indivisible, so the land would not be divided. From a practical point of view, Evie's astonishing proposal was a good one.

He was more than half in love with her, and Clodagh had gone out of his life forever. Evie would be a good, obedient wife, run his home excellently, take care of his creature comforts, and make no unreasonable demands on him. From his angle, it was a good bargain, since there would never be a great love in his life again, and on the whole a man is more comfortable married than not.

"It wouldn't be fair to you," he said at last, in a croaking voice. "I'm eight years older than you, Evie. Eight bruising years, which have taken some of the youth out of me. You need someone young and untiring, with laughter in his mouth, and not afraid of the future." He put an arm round her shoulder. "Believe me, dear, *dear* Evie, you have paid me the great compliment of my life, which I shall never forget, even when I'm so old that I've forgotten everything else. But it wouldn't do, dear heart. You must see more of the world, more of men and women, You've had no chance yet to know people of your own sort."

"I know you. I don't want to meet a lot of people, and if I did, I'd still like you best and want to marry you."

"Marriage lasts a long time. Have you the least idea what it means?"

Flushing, she turned away. "I'm not an ignorant child. My mother has trained me well. I'd make a good wife, I think. But please forget I asked. If I don't please you in that way, there's no more to be said. I only thought that since you can't marry *her*, it wouldn't make all that difference who you married. I could be useful to you, and it would settle the problems about the house. Only I see it won't do. You're still too much in love with her, aren't you?"

Evie wished she were a million miles away. She had made her supreme effort and failed. Now she wanted only to hide her humiliation from him, and the minutes before the caïque was due to sail stretched out like a whole day.

She had not told him she loved him. That she would never do, until he loved her. A business proposition was a sensible enough thing to make; a declaration of love was something different, and must wait for its proper time. And that time, she knew in her bones, would never come now.

"You please me enormously, Evie. It's just that I couldn't bring myself to take advantage of your inexperience. I've practically no money. I earn a modest amount by writing, but I'll never be comfortably off, and my wife would have to scrape by on very little. That's not for you. You are a jewel worthy of a splendid setting—clothes, luxury, travel, all the things a beautiful woman should have by right. Such a chance may come your way soon and I won't let you tie yourself up to a vagabond while you're still in your teens. It wouldn't be right."

She nodded sadly. "I must go. The men are ready to sail. We must say goodbye now, Rory. But if you change your mind, I shan't change mine. I don't say things lightly and I really meant it. Come to the island any time, if you think my solution would work. You may, when you've had time to think it over. Goodbye now."

He lifted her hand and touched it with his lips. "Bless you, princess. Think kindly of me if you can, and forgive me. I'll never forget the honor you've done me—never." His face was bleak, the high cheekbones showing pale against the dark-tanned skin. There was a lump in his throat that needed swallowing.

He watched the blue and orange-painted caïque out of the harbor, and stayed there, staring out to sea, till the swift Mediterranean night came down like a curtain of violet silk over the end of the day and the stars shone silver.

"Rory McDermot," he told himself at long last, "you are the fool of all the world. There goes a girl in a million, and you have shamed her in her own sight. A decent man would kick you from here to the top of the Troodos Mountains."

He sighed, shouldered his pack again and set off to walk. The top of the Troodos Mountains was as good a place as any, and to get there on his two feet would give him plenty of time for thinking.

WHEN THE BOAT WAS CLEAR of the harbor, Evie's second cousin Andreas, who was one of the vessel's joint owners, came and sat beside her.

"Wasn't that the man who is going to buy your mother's house? They say he's enormously wealthy and will bring tourists by the hundred to Exos."

"He's not and he won't. The deal is off. That man

hasn't the money to buy our house, and who wants tourists? They spoil a place."

"The men don't say so. We want tourists. They bring money with them, and why should Exos be left out when there's prosperity flying around? We heard he was going to build a big hotel up there with a swimming pool. We were considering buying a new boat. This old hulk won't serve the island much longer, and a boat this size costs real money. Your mother wanted to sell, right enough. She sent to the priest and Uncle Stephanos to act as go-betweens. So why is it off, now? Is it your doing? If so, you won't be popular on Exos. We all want change. You'd better get him back, if you're the one who sent him away."

She was nearly dropping with fatigue and lost in unhappiness, but when the sense of what Andreas was saying penetrated, she was furiously angry.

"So? We sell our home, our land, for the sake of everybody else on the island? You're all going to get rich, are you, when we are homeless and Georgi has lost his heritage forever? Why don't you sell your own houses, your own lemon groves? Sell the boat—why not? Because it's your livelihood? But you'd be happy to see my mother sell ours. The land is rightly my brother's. Tell that to your friends when you're drinking ouzo tonight."

"All right, don't bite my head off. I'm only telling you what everybody is saying. News travels fast, as you well know. There isn't a family on the island but is looking forward to money flowing in."

"Pass this news round, then. There isn't to be a hotel. There never was. Swimming pool, tourists, the lot. It's all grown out of your highly spiced imaginations and too much ouzo. He wanted the house for himself and a few friends with as little money as himself, that's all."

She turned away and hunched up into a shawl she had brought for the journey. The sea breeze was cool now the sun had gone.

Andreas massaged his head. "It was all a rumor?" He laughed suddenly and slapped his knee. "That's Exos for you! A man has only to scratch his land with a broken stick and his neighbors are harvesting next year's grapefruit for him."

To Evie's relief, he lost interest and left her. Or maybe he went to break the news to his partners that the old boat would have to serve a few more years. She rested her head against a wooden block, hearing the creaking of the ancient timbers and the hiss of the sea, the hard smack of the sail in the wind. She closed her eyes, and let quiet tears ooze out under the lids. How tired she was, how exhausted.

She had yet to explain to her mother that the Kyrios McDermot had gone and would not be back. And Sofia would drill a confused story into her ears about Marcus and Rory. The instalments of that might go on for weeks, unless Marcus shut her mouth by marrying her.

It had been a wonderful day. There would be no more like it.

EVIE TOOK UP THE THREADS of her everyday life again. A stranger had come and gone, that was all. That he had taken her heart with him, that she lived now with a painful emptiness where that heart used to be, hardly seemed to matter. There were the goats, the lemons to be harvested in due course, the dates to be netted, water to be dragged to the vegetable plot.

Her mother wept and scolded at the loss of a buyer. "It is your fault, child. You were so rude to him, so unkind. How shall I face my husband, your father, now? His son an uncouth islander, uneducated?"

"Georgi is neither uneducated nor uncouth. He's well-mannered and thoughtful, and willing to work to keep his mother and sister. You ought to be thankful for him, mama, and appreciate him as he is. You are look-ing for the golden apples of the Hesperides instead of enjoying the plain good fruit that grows in our own soil."

"How dare you speak to your mother so? You are getting beyond control. I shall have to ask your uncle to thrash you, if you are so impudent."

"Do that, and I shan't be here to receive the beating. I'm not a child to be rebuked, mama. I can lead my own life and earn a living on the mainland, remember."

When her anger cooled she felt sorry for having made her mother cry. A daughter shouldn't do that. A mother suffers enough for her children without their being un-grateful and rude besides. She apologized.

"I forgive you, Evie. You are right. I treat you as a baby still, when you are a woman. Look, I've finished the first dress, the blue one. See if you like it."

"It will do," Evie said indifferently. What use were new clothes now? Then, seeing the tears spring again to Julia's eyes, she tried the dress on and exclaimed with pleasure over the clever way her mother had reproduced the garment Rory had sketched, and the fine stitching.

"I'm lucky to have such a mother," she said with real warmth, and hugged Julia till she protested that she could not breathe.

The girl spent more and more time up at the ruined temple among her childhood friends, the splendid head-less statues of the gods. All she wanted was solitude, where she could live over and over again the moments with Rory. She held long conversations with him, but as she had to provide both sides of the talk, they were never satisfying.

Common sense told her to lose herself in work or study. Only occupation would give her a chance of for-getting the man who had taken her heart.

During the hot summer nights Rory haunted her

sleep. His thin brown face, the smiling blue eyes, the mouth that could be so grave, yet could twist into a mocking half smile. In her dreams that warm mouth kissed her many times. Many times she woke from such a dream to shed bitter tears.

There came no word at all from the lawyer, and as the weeks of summer passed the hope of hearing from him slowly died.

Marcus and Sofia were to be married. Sofia toiled up the hill in the heat to beg the loan of Julia's bridal crown.

"Everybody says it was the most beautiful they ever remember, *kyria*. And—the flushed, excited bride-to-be glanced at Evie—"It isn't as if you'll be wanting it for a long time. Who is there for poor Evie to marry...."

"But you said you didn't want to marry Marcus," Evie reminded her when they were going down to the village, the precious bridal crown carefully wrapped in a white cloth. "You said there'd be nothing but babies and scrubbing, and that marriage was a trap."

Sofia gave her a patronizing look. "How little you know, Evie! Wait till a man asks you to marry him, then you'll understand. It's a pity you didn't try for that Irishman who was here. He wasn't much, and poor as a priest, but at least he was a man and would have given you children. I never did believe that ridiculous story that he meant to buy your house. He hadn't two *mils* in his pocket."

"Then why should I marry him?" Evie said sharply. But even to hear his name was sweet and she led Sofia to talk about Rory.

"Please thank the Kyria Julia for the loan," said Sofia's mother. "I remember her as a bride, girls. She was so lovely and we all envied her. But there—it never does to marry a foreigner. They get homesick for their own country, though by all accounts England is covered with fog all the year round, and it rains every day. Why a man should want to live there—!" She shook her head, as if the absurdity of foreigners was too much for her. "But you're half a foreigner yourself, Evie. Don't you ever want to visit your father's country?"

"Never. This is my country. My mother is Exos-Greek and so am I."

"Your brother isn't," the woman said slyly. "He's an Englishman, or he will be soon. He looks more English every year. And you, Evie, if you take my advice, will put a bit of soft flesh on those bones of yours, or you'll never get a man. They like something to cuddle, don't they, Sofia? I do believe you are thinner than ever these days."

"And paler," Sofia added, not quite unkindly. "You'd look lovely in your new dress if you had more color. Not that I'd have chosen that strong pattern and dark shade for you, yet it suits you wonderfully. It would look better on me, though. Can I try it on?"

"You're too fat," Evie rapped. She and Sofia had always shared clothes, but the thought of the other girl in the dress Rory chose did not please her.

Marcus had spent his savings on putting down a deposit for a small cafe in Nicosia. There was an apartment over it, and Sofia was already putting on the airs of a city dweller.

"We could have bought a bigger place in Kyrenia or Famagusta," she told Evie as the two girls sat stitching the trousseau garments under the shade of a pepper tree. "But Marcus says it is best to be in a fashionable place where the money is. He's ambitious, you see. When we have made a success of a small cafe, he will move to something larger."

"More floors to scrub?" Evie said with a smile. "Oh, I'm so glad for you, Sofia. I'm sure you'll be happy and make lots of money. You do love him, don't you?"

"Naturally I do. But it is also important to have a good living and a home. I am lucky to be getting that, and to like the man, too. When we have a bigger place, or maybe if we do well in the small cafe, you could come and spend the busy season with us if you like. You could earn your keep as a waitress, and we could have a good time together, eh?"

"I'd like that. Would Marcus agree...."

"I'll make him. It was my mother's idea. She said when I'm pregnant next year I shall need extra help and I must insist on having it. Men give way to a wife when she's having the first baby, so it's a good idea to get it into their stupid minds that a woman needs help and rest at such times. Afterwards, they take such an idea for granted. But if you let the first time go by without making demands, forever after they say, "Well, you managed the first all right.""

Evie tried to imagine herself married to Rory, and pricked her finger till the blood made a stain on the seam she was stitching. Her idea of marriage seemed so different from Sofia's. But then Marcus was so different from Rory McDermot.

"Do you think all husbands are the same?" she asked, spitting on the linen and rubbing it with her finger. She bent low over the task so Sofia could not read her face.

"All married women say they are. So they must be. My mother says...."

MARCUS ARRIVED in a new bright blue suit the day before the wedding. With him came Rory McDermot.

"Would you believe it," Marcus roared to all and sundry on the quayside, "we met in Nicosia, and when I told him it was my wedding day today, he said he must come and kiss the bride. Nothing would please him but to come."

Rory hugged Sofia and handed over the wedding present he had brought, a pair of tall carved candlesticks in olivewood. "I wish you every happiness, the pair of you. Now, where am I to sleep?"

"Under a tree. Every spare bed in the village is taken up with all the friends and family. Why not walk up to the Villa Julia and ask them to give you a bed there? They did offer, in case we hadn't room down here for everybody who came over from the mainland ."

He shook his head. "I'd rather not trouble the Kyria Julia. Under a tree will suit me fine."

In the past weeks he had tramped Cyprus, and slept out more than once. He had walked to the top of the Troodos Mountains, seen the beach where the goddess Aphrodite rose newly-created from the foam; he had climbed to the smallest, most remote monastery of them all, perched like a kite upon the summit of Stavrovouni, and knelt in wonder before the silver shrine which held a piece of the True Cross. There he had remembered an argument he had had with his old parish priest as a boy.

"True, my son, there are enough reputed pieces of the True Cross to make a forest, if all were brought together. But sure, if God could make a dinner for five thousand hungry pilgrims out of five little fish and a couple of loaves warm from a good mother's oven, couldn't He make a small forest out of one Cross? Where's your faith, boy? Do I ask you to believe in a God who is no cleverer than a stupid lad out of an Irish bog, now?"

He had been unhappy. At first, because he had disappointed a nice girl. But as day followed day, the knowledge grew in him that he loved Evie and not Clodagh. Her lovely oval face haunted his dreams, and the days held no magic because she was not with him.

"*One man,*" he had prophesied, "*you will pierce to the bone and he will love you forever.*"

When he remembered those words, he stopped in his

tracks and beat his fists upon the green silver bark of a fig tree. "And I am that man!" he cried aloud, startling a goat that had been staring at him with yellow slit eyes. "I love her. Goat, do you hear me now? I am in love with Evie, in thrall till my life's end. And begod, I could have been her husband this minute if I were not such a fool!"

The solitary walking, the quiet monasteries, the watching ruins full of a millennium's wisdom, convinced him that the first decision was the right one. Not for him, but for the girl herself. How could he let her tie herself down to a wandering man like himself, when she had seen no others? None of the sort she ought to marry.

He had fought a devil's battle within himself. As day followed day, he wanted her more urgently. The temptation to take a boat to Exos, hurry up the hill, and beg her to marry him, grew stronger the more he fought it. But the more he loved her, pictured her as he remembered her, half saint and half wild dryad, a creature of trees and water, the more reluctant he felt to hurry her into marriage and responsibilities. Not yet, not yet, he had told himself over and over again. She is not ready; the tree is still in bud. Yet in tortured nights he pictured her hurried into marriage by her mother and uncles, into the hands of a man less able than he to understand her fine delicate quality.

Tired as he was when he flung himself onto whatever bed the night provided, he could not sleep dreamlessly till dawn. But now it was not the running waters of Ireland that sang through his head, the light figure of Clodagh, which eluded him like a small, lovely ghost slipping through the trees, or hurrying before him along the mountain tracks of home.

It was Evie, running light-footed through the lemon trees. Evie, dancing in her blue dress on the quayside, her face pale in the moonlight. Evie, gravely inquiring about the price of tea at a luxury hotel, or sitting beside him on a green bank above Kyrenia among the scent of rock roses.

Evie saying, "I thought—perhaps—do you think you could marry me?"

It's this damned climate, he told himself angrily. *All these flowers, the scent of lemons, the warmth of the air, the sea shimmering like diamonds, the—the softness of everything. It gets under a man's skin. It is not love!*

It was a long time before he admitted to himself that he was head over heels, deep as the ocean, high as the clouds, in love with Evie. For mile after mile of his solitary, angry walking, he argued with himself, putting forward all the reasons why he couldn't be.

But at last, in the midst of the crowds thronging the Turkish bazaar in Nicosia, he admitted the impossible. Why then, he did not know. Perhaps it was the rolls of gaily colored cottons for sale, fluttering in the warm wind, or the bright woven baskets, the piles of pink sugared almonds on the stalls.

He bought cheese and fruit for his frugal supper, and his hand shook as he paid for them. Strolling through the covered food market, he fought the desire to make straight for Kyrenia and catch the morning caïque for Exos.

Be reasonable, he pleaded with himself. *All the arguments for not marrying her remain the same.*

Now all the sensible arguments turned against him, and in favor of an immediate departure for the Villa Julia. What if that mother of hers, with any eye to the cash she coveted, persuaded the girl to marry some rich, fat islander coming home to retire? She'd do it, the little fool!

Coming again into the sunlight at the entrance to the covered market, he stopped dead. Something brought

Evie to his mind sharply, with an impact like a cutting edge. What was it?

Slowly he turned around, looking for some clue. Was it a girl, or a man from Exos? Someone very like Sofia, perhaps?

Then he laughed, startling a sleepy stallholder. Of course—where else but in the fruit market? It was the scent of lemons.

He took his problem into the high, cool mosque at the end of the road. There, barefooted on the rich carpets that were the gifts of the faithful, he sat cross-legged and considered his problem.

So I hurry back and beg her to marry me? She's a girl of spirit, and proud besides, and I hurt her more than somewhat, back there in Kyrenia. Would a lass like that look twice at such a miserable wretch as I, who didn't know enough to catch his luck on the wing when it went by? If she spoke to me at all, which is unlikely, she'd give me the sharp point of her tongue which is all I'd deserve.

But suppose..., just suppose for one moment..., that she forgave you, boyo, and married you? How then? Wouldn't it mean the loss of the fine dream you've been dreaming? The final severance of the thread that binds you to Clodagh and all she stands for? To marry Evie would mean settling for good on the island of Exos, living in the Villa Julia and....

He slapped one hand into the other. "Rory McDermot," he said aloud in the vast silence of the mosque, "you are worse than a fool. Isn't that what started the whole thing? That you wanted to do just that—settle on Exos and live in the Villa Julia? "

"Not with a wife," he protested faintly. "I hadn't included wife and children in the picture, nor a mother-in-law. Nor becoming second cousin by marriage to the whole population!"

He collected his pack, slung it over his shoulder, and

marched purposefully back to the Greek side of the barrier. If there was enough money in his account at the bank—and there should be, if that American magazine had paid promptly for the three pieces they had bought—he planned to book a flight to the States. He had always had a fancy to take a look at Arizona.

The money was not there. No matter, he knew how to wait, and there was much to see in Nicosia. The temple of the dancing dervishes, now. That sounded interesting. Tomorrow....

Three days later, coming out of the bank with money in his pocket, he met Marcus.

The Greek seized his hand, planted a garlicky kiss on each of his cheeks, and hurried him off to look at the cafe he had bought.

"You must come to the wedding, *kyrios*. Sofia will be angry with me if I do not take you."

"Sofia will tear my ears off! I'd never get away alive!"

"Nonsense, nonsense! She's a sensible girl. She never really believed you had all that money, and once I'd started to buy the cafe—" he shrugged and kissed his bunched fingers"—she was mine."

"Always was, Marcus. And...Evie?"

"Too thin, don't you think? Thinner than ever. That girl is unhappy, Rory. I think she'll leave Exos pretty soon."

Rory's heart turned over painfully. Why was he wasting time here, talking idly, when Evie might be leaving the island tomorrow and he would never find her?

Marcus went on, "I mean, she's not content where she is. She's half a northerner, you know. Always on the move, they are. Always wanting to get something done, if it's only moving from here to there as fast as their legs can carry them. Can't rest and watch the world go by. Same as yourself, sir. Now you're a man on the go."

"My dear Marcus, you slander me! I want nothing

more than to take root on a cliff overlooking the sea, and vegetate. All right, I'll be glad to come to the wedding, if you'll have me."

AND SO ON THE NIGHT before Sofia's wedding, he left the bridegroom's rowdy party early and took his sleeping bag up onto the headland, from whence he could look down on the lights of the Villa Julia.

She is sleeping down there, he told himself; and then grinned at finding himself out in such a youthful sentiment. "Be your age, boyo," he said aloud, and immediately fell to picturing Evie asleep, soft mouthed and relaxed, her hand under her cheek, the long, straight hair spread like a net over the pillow.

When the last light went out in the villa, he inserted himself into the narrow sleeping bag and lay awake planning his campaign. He would not go straight to her and expect to begin where they left off. That would be boorish, and taking advantage of the fact that she had proposed to him in a desperate effort to save her home.

It mustn't be like that. If she came to him, it must be in love and because she wanted him and no other. If he could win her that way, well and good. But there must be no question of her saying yes merely to keep the villa in the family. *Softly now, old Rory my lad. She's high-spirited and timid both. This will need patience, and guile besides.*

EVIE WAS NOT ASLEEP. She lay awake thinking about Sofia, wondering how a girl felt on her wedding eve, and what she thought about. Wondering if such a night would ever come to her now. Her body, like a traitor, longed for Rory, remembering with sharp sweetness his kiss, his touch, his voice. She knew with every nerve that if his hand touched her out of ten thousand, she would recognize his touch. Her skin remembered him. There were times when tears forced themselves from under her closed eyelids because of the emptiness he had left in her heart.

But in spite of the moonlight flooding the room, the soft murmurs of the night, the feel of happiness in the air because of tomorrow's wedding, Evie turned away from thoughts of Rory with bitter memories of their last minutes together. Remembering his gentle refusal of her proposal for marriage, she burned with anguished embarrassment. Why, oh, why had she done such a stupid thing? Now he would never, never come back to Exos.

THE VILLAGE WAS ASTIR before sunrise. There was much to be done before the dew was off the ground. The outdoor ovens were swept out, and fresh wood piled inside them to smoulder redly until the metal lining was hot enough to cook the whole lambs and kids for the evening's feast. When the wood was consumed to ash, the men would sweep it out, pack in the joints, fit the heavy iron doors, and seal them with a small boulder. Meanwhile there was the charcoal fire to light under the water-driven communal spit, the long metal spears to be loaded with chickens and lobsters to be cooked later in the charcoal's heat. It was a delicate art, understood best—so they insisted—by the old men of the village, to judge the exact distance between fire and meat, the precise drip of water from the aged brass taps, which would turn the many spits at the right speed. Not too fast or the meat wouldn't brown; not too slow, or it would burn.

Sofia lay in bed listening to the chatter and bustle. A fierce argument blew up beneath her window and died away. She sighed contentedly. This was her day. She was the bride. Tomorrow and all the tomorrows she would have to get up as early as the others; earlier, when she was working with Marcus in their cafe. But to-day she could stretch luxuriously, smile at herself in her looking glass, and think about her wedding dress, the short white veil, the little bridal crown set with pearls.

She had no illusions about marriage. Being a wife didn't make life easier or more rosy for a woman, but at least she would be her own mistress and under no one's thumb but her husband's. And, playing the cards right that wasn't too bad. A clever woman, well schooled by a clever mother, could manage a man without his knowing it. She smiled to herself, stretched and yawned. As long as youth and beauty lasted, she could manage Marcus. After that–she grimaced and shrugged—after that, she would be mama, with a family firmly under her thumb.

JULIA AND EVIE were already busy in their kitchen, baking little biscuits sweet with grapefruit-blossom honey. They had had a brisk difference of opinion over what they should wear, but that was settled now. Evie would wear her new sea-blue dress, made by Julia in the style sketched by Rory. Julia would wear the old traditional dress she had lent her daughter for the dance on the quay. That her waist was still slim enough was a matter of pride with her, and for once she meant to show off among her friends. Not one of them, Julia was convinced, could still wear the dress she had been married in.

"It should be you," Julia grumbled. "We shall have to find a husband for you, Evie, though how, I don't know. Luckily you have your dowry, which should get you a good man. Where am I to look, in God's name? When your father answers the advertisement...."

Evie said patiently, "Mama, he won't. It's too long

ago, nearly three months. I'm sorry I even agreed to the lawyer putting advertisements in. It has only roused hopes in you, my poor lamb. Darling, we must really make ourselves believe he's dead."

"That I will never do, till I have proof. He will come, or send. Then I shall be able to do something about a marriage for you. Why should Sofia be a bride and not you? Do you want me shamed before all my friends and family, eh?"

Evie felt choked with exasperation. There were times when she felt like shaking her mother hard, to knock the obstinacy out of her. Why couldn't she listen to common sense? After all these years, it was absurd to suppose a man would arrive home one day in time for supper as if nothing had happened.

"Finish the biscuits," she said crossly. "I have to go outside a minute." Another second in the kitchen, listening to that eternally hopeful story about George Marsden's return, would be the very last straw.

She found Georgi patiently trotting back and forth from the thin trickle of the stream to the vegetable garden, watering the precious plants before the sun got too high. All the island was arid now, the bare earth showing tan and yellow.

"They've begun!" the boy shouted, pointing down to the village like a white toy below. "Look at the smoke! They'll be making the most enormous kebabs on the spit. How soon can I go down?"

"Finish the work first," she said automatically, and was appalled to hear her voice sounding exactly like her mother's. *I am growing like her,* she thought in a panic. *I do nothing but work, and think about nothing but Rory coming back, even though I know in my bones he never will. In no time at all, I'll be old.*

She snatched the yellow plastic bucket from her young brother. "Put on your wedding suit and go now.

I'll finish your jobs. Hurry or you'll miss some of the fun." She laughed and hugged him tightly. "Oh, I'm sorry, Georgi. I don't play with you any more, eh? But I will, I promise. Being unhappy is silly when you can't do anything to change things. Run along. We're all going to have a wonderful day."

The boy raced into the house to change. Evie took the bucket to the stream. From today on, she would stop thinking about the past and look forward into a future that did not include Rory McDermot. She had longed to believe that he would follow her to Exos. The fact that he had not done so was proof that he did not, could not, love her, and even the bait of possessing the Villa Julia was not enough to persuade him to marry her.

Detestable man! She crouched down beside the stream, noticing with concern that the water would not last much longer. *I ought to hate him. Perhaps I do? They say love turns to hate, and when a man is so stupid as to go on loving a woman who wouldn't have him—well, why shouldn't I hate him?*

Temper rose and choked her. She threw the yellow bucket away from her violently, so it bounced on the glinting stones. *Damn him, damn him, I'd like to hit him!* She clenched her fists and beat them on her knees, letting wave after wave of bottled-up rage sweep through her, exhausting her anger till at last she bent over the limpid water and buried her face in her hands. She had not cried before, but the hurt and frustration of the last months eased themselves now in a wild torrent of tears and shuddering.

Quiet at last, she splashed cold water over her face, then went to catch and saddle her mother's donkey before changing to go down to the wedding.

They went straight to the bride's house, disregarding the excitement on the quay where the caïque from Kyrenia was disembarking a crowd of guests in their best clothes and laden with gifts.

Sofia was dressed except for the crown, which her mother was now pinning on her hair. "Here's Kyria Julia," someone cried. "Let her do it. After all, it's hers. She should know the proper way to fix it."

Sofia grinned at Evie and mouthed, "You next!" as the two mothers fussed gently over the arranging of the crown and veil. There was no time for talk between the girls, but Sofia gave Evie a quick hug and whispered, "It's your lucky day. I'm the bride and I know who's lucky and who isn't. Something wonderful is going to happen for you today, Evie."

"That's good. You wouldn't care to say what? I bet you don't know. You've said the same to every single girl on the island already."

Sofia's grin became more tormenting than before. "Oh, no, I haven't. There's a surprise for you. Wait and see."

Evie shivered with expectancy and her palms grew damp. "You mean, you really know something? Is—is anybody coming with the caïque?" She could not make her lips form Rory's name.

Sofia shook her head, but carefully because of the crown. "No, nothing like that. But I have at least twenty male cousins expected, and that probably means forty will arrive. Surely that's enough to choose from, even for a faddy creature like you?"

The hope died. All Sofia meant was that out of all her relatives at the wedding, her friend might make a match with one. But Sofia couldn't possibly know that if Evie Marsden didn't marry Rory McDermot, who wasn't coming, she would never marry anyone.

"Sofia, stop teasing. You've got love on the brain, and why shouldn't you, on your wedding morning? Listen, isn't that the bridegroom's party arriving? It's time to go. Oh, Sofia, be very happy!"

Sudden tears brimmed the bride's eyes. "Evie! I don't

want it all to happen. I'll be so lonely in Nicosia, away from everybody. ''

Evie carefully wiped the trembling tears so they did not fall. "You're *not to cry!* If you do, you'll look terrible. You'll have Marcus all to yourself, and your own home, and you'll be able to see the shops and all the rich tourists. Smile! That's better. Off you go!"

It was after the solemn part of the morning, when the bride's and bridegroom's friends and family began to mingle, that Evie came face to face with Rory.

She lifted her eyes to the tall figure who stood in her path, and there he was. Her heart beat painfully, and she felt the color drain from her face.

"Rory!" she whispered. "What are you . . . what are you doing here?"

"The same as you. Attending a friend's wedding. Surprised to see me?"

She saw that he was thinner and browner. He wore a new and more shapely suit and a good shirt, which surprised her, for somehow she had never pictured him in anything but the shabby jacket and faded shirts in which she had seen him so often.

"You look very smart," she said stupidly. So often, she had dreamed of this first meeting, but in dreams there are no words to be said.

He smiled. "So do you. The dress, I take it, is the result of our shopping?"

"Yes. But I am still wearing the red shoes which you disliked so much." She forced herself to remain calm, to keep her voice cool and controlled.

"I'm afraid you found me abominably rude about them."

"It doesn't matter. All that is a long time ago. I've forgotten what you actually said, and it wasn't of the slightest importance."

"Some of it was," he said deeply. "I've been kicking

myself ever since for not jumping on that caïque and coming back with you that day."

She shrugged. "There has been a caïque in from Kyrenia every day except Sunday. If you had wanted to come, there was nothing to stop you."

Her coldness frightened him. There was not a spark of expression in her icy voice, no light in the eyes, which looked at him as if he did not really exist. His heart sank. He had a long way to go, and it might be too late even to begin.

"I didn't come before," he said carefully, "because I wanted to be sure there was nothing left over from the past. I wanted the years ahead to be free of ... of memories. I wanted to get things straight in my mind."

She clasped her hands so he should not see them trembling. "And now you are satisfied with your own state of mind?"

"Far from it. But I should be a good deal happier than I have been, if I thought we could start our friendship all over again on a better footing."

"It's three months," she told him flatly. "There are other things in my life now. I don't think our friendship, even on a new footing, could have any real future."

The sight of him had robbed her of coherent thought. All she remembered was her anger of two hours ago, the long sobbing by the brook, the lost sleep, the fury of frustration, which had swept her from time to time in the last three months. She would not go through all that again. If she had to live her life without him, she could not begin too soon the painful process of erasing him from her heart.

"Can't we even try, Evie?" His voice was harsh. He had not expected so much enmity. She had changed. Where was the warmth, the spontaneity which to him was Evie? Now he looked at her more closely, he saw that she was paler, her eyes were dark smudged, the delicate bone structure in her face thrown into relief by her thinness. "We were doing so well that afternoon up by the monastery, when we visited St. Polystemon."

She turned away slightly. "That afternoon contains much that I prefer to forget, *kyrie*. You must understand ... I was driven to desperation by the need to save the villa and the land for my brother. There was nothing more to it than that. I hope you didn't read anything ... anything into my foolishness that I didn't mean?"

"I understood that. I have never flatttered myself that I ... meant anything to you in a personal way. Only that you needed to keep the house in the family. That's why ... I mean, I could hardly let you sacrifice yourself. I can take it you have now made other and more satisfactory arrangements?" There was a faint tinge of bitter humor in his voice. He had never allowed himself to think for a moment that she felt any more than friendliness toward him, but he had left himself room for hope. It hurt more than somewhat to have it spelled out so clearly in that icy little tone.

"I have seen a lawyer about our affairs. I hope to hear something from England very soon."

"I see. Then may I wish you every success in your endeavors?"

The crowd, which had swept them together, now swept them apart, as a stentorian voice invited them all to sit down and eat. The main meal, still cooking in the adobe ovens, would be served after dark, but now there was fish, hot and succulent, baked in vine leaves, and enough sweet red wine to float a fishing boat. Evie had promised to help serve the guests and hurried away to her duties.

So Rory was Sofia's "surprise"? He must have arrived on the island last night, since he had not come with the morning's boat. If he had loved her, he would surely have come up at once to the villa to find her. That he had not done so seemed proof that she meant little to him. Only a casual friend, to be set down or picked up as the mood took him.

The meeting had been disastrous, but at least one good had come out of it. She had been able to make him understand quite clearly that her proposal of marriage had been entirely a matter of business and that his help was now not needed. After what she had said today, he would never even suspect that she loved him.

The day wore on. After midday, when the heat was intense and the trees cast no shade, the older folk withdrew to sleep off the wine and strong coffee laced with brandy, in which they had been indulging for hours. The girls, among them Evie, washed the glasses and re-laid the tables ready for the real business of eating and drinking later. The children went swimming, so many excited small brown frogs in the clear water. The bride and bridegroom disappeared.

So the waterfront was deserted when a neat white launch put in from Kyrenia carrying two passengers. Only Rory, half asleep on a tilted chair under a date palm, saw them land.

Tourists, he thought, noting the camera, the smart cream blazer of the man, the white dress and lobster-red arms of the woman. *Too bad! Nobody free to take them a trip round the island; nobody even awake at the taverna to produce the tea an English lady would be demanding*—he glanced at his watch—*about half an hour from now.*

He watched them from under the brim of his hat, not because he cared what they did, but because there was nothing else to watch. They walked the length of the waterfront and back, talking seriously and looking at the houses more closely than the normal run of tourists.

Bemused as he was with too much food and drink, it took Rory some time to reach the conclusion that they

were looking for someone, or something. He brought
the front legs of his chair to the ground with a thump.
By St. Patrick, what a dolt he was! They had probably
come to the wedding and were bewildered to find not a
living soul about.

He strolled towards them and raised his battered
straw. "Can I help you? Everybody else is asleep, I believe. Have you come to the wedding?"

The woman's face lit up. A pleasant, thirtyish kind of
face, interested in everything. Not the man's wife. His
elder sister, maybe. "Is there a wedding? Oh, how
lovely! I do hope we can see some of it. We rather
hoped to stay on the island overnight. Is there a hotel?"

"Not one I'd recommend for you, ma'am. Only the
taverna, and every bed in that is occupied three deep.
Myself, I slept under a tree last night, but there are apt
to be snakes. It might do for the gentleman, but not for
you."

She glanced at her companion, dismayed. "Oh, Peter,
what a shame! We shall have to go back to Kyrenia tonight."

The man grinned and nodded toward the *taverna*.
"I'd prefer it, if that's the only hotel. The fact is—" he
turned to Rory"—you may be able to help us. We're
here on business, and I'm not sure how many people
here speak English."

"All of them. Same like Cyprus. Some better and
some worse, but anyone you'd be likely to do business
with will be all right. Only with the wedding and all, it's
not a business day. You and your boatmen will be welcome to stay for supper, that I do know. But not to talk
shop. Everyone will be too busy eating, drinking, singing, and dancing to bother. If you stay, you'll see something out of the ordinary tourist run, and I assure you
you'll be made welcome. Everybody is, and there's
enough food for two regiments on foot and a brigade of
guards besides."

The woman pleaded, "Do let's, Peter. We've got the launch for the whole day and the boatmen won't mind if it's a wedding. Go and ask them, there's a dear. After all, it is a holiday first and foremost. The business is only incidental. We can do that by letter if we have to."

The boy smiled. Fresh, young, good-looking, English. Comfortably off, Rory noted. "All right, Anna. Half a tick, I'll talk to them. Oh, by the way, sir, my name's Peter Brown. My sister, Anna Brown."

Rory clicked heels, bowed, and introduced himself. "I could probably rustle up a pot of tea if you'd care to sit under the palms a while, Miss Brown. It may take time. Will you take lemon with it? Unless you really like goat's milk, of course. Some people do."

Anna shuddered and said she would take lemon.

As there was no one in the kitchen of the *taverna* and heavy snoring came from the room above, Rory made the tea himself and carried it out on a tray. "I've brought three glasses, in the hope that I may join you."

"Please do," said Peter cheerfully. "you've been most awfully kind. My sister was dying for a cuppa. So was I, as a matter of fact. Oh, and lemon. Good. You're Irish, aren't you? Do you live here?"

"Not exactly."

Anna indicated the tea tray with a gesture. "But a privileged visitor, I'm sure. Do you know many people on Exos? My brother and I are looking for an English family, a widow and two children. I wonder if you've met a Mrs. George Marsden here?"

Rory opened his mouth to deny any knowledge of an English widow before he recognized Evie's mother under the description. "I've met her," he admitted cautiously.

A shiver of fear crisped his nerves, like a breath of icy wind ruffling the warm calm sea. This well-dressed pair, so English, so entirely foreign to the palm-edged island, seemed to him to threaten the untroubled existence of his delicate, silvery Evie. He felt them as the outriders of the materialistic, ugly age he hated. As they sipped the hot tea from tiny tulip-shaped glasses, he heard with his mind's ears the roaring technology of which the island hardly dreamed. Here was danger for Evie, from which all his love might not be able to protect her.

"Kyria Julia Marsden is not English," he told them. "She is Exos-Greek. Her son and daughter probably resemble their father, both being fair. The boy has blue eyes, but Evie's are ..." he paused, remembering Evie's serious eyes resting on him with a questioning look. "Gray, I think, except when they are blue. They change, like water under the sky. Are you by any chance related?"

The woman answered. "Our family firm act as Mr. George Marsden's lawyers. My brother and I were due for a holiday anyway, and when we discovered his widow lived here, we decided to fly out and visit her, rather than write. I've always wanted to see Cyprus and the advertisement gave us a splendid excuse."

"Advertisement?"

"A clerk in the office always watches the agony column in the national dailies, Mr—er—"

"McDermot. You mean someone advertised for news of George?"

"Exactly. Of course *we* advertised at the time he was drowned, six years ago. But no one replied at the time, so we were pleased when...."

She went on explaining, but Rory was not listening. His world, his new golden world, in which he loved and won Evie, and lived with her in a white house on the edge of a sea cliff, had shattered into a thousand pieces.

Lawyers don't fly across Europe to visit the widow of a poor man, holiday or no. These two had come on business and their business was concerned with wills and estates. George Marsden was dead; and there was cash in the kitty. Maybe a good deal of it.

What could a poor devil of an impecunious Irishman do now but shoulder his bag and away? Having refused the girl when she had no more fortune than he, how could he now turn up on her doorstep as an eager suitor?

He cut through Anna's talk. "If I'm right, that advertisement must have been inserted months ago, when Evie went to Kyrenia. What kept you?"

"Legal affairs move slowly. It wasn't that we neglected the Marsden business, only that our office is like most, chronically overworked and understaffed. We needed to gather a fair amount of information from the Kyrenia lawyer and from our own records. All the material is six years old, remember."

Rory rubbed his ear. "I wasn't complaining, only thinking it would have been a sight more convenient to me, if you'd stayed away a few days longer. There's nobody at home at the Villa Julia today, but if you sit here you'll meet the whole family before long. Anyone will point them out. Me, I'm leaving. There'll be no man sober enough to take a fishing boat out tonight, but maybe I might beg a lift of you, when you're ready to leave?"

CHAPTER SEVEN

As HE TURNED THE CORNER of the *taverna*, intending to fetch his bag, he ran into Evie and a stout, perspiring youth in an elegant suit too tight for him.

"Hello," Evie greeted Rory with a detectable note of relief in her voice. "This is Theo. He's teaching me Italian. We're going to hang up extra lanterns on the waterfront."

"You're not," Rory told her firmly. He took her share of the lanterns and piled them into Theo's arms with a dazzling smile. "*Arrivederci*, Theo, my boy. I must have a long, serious talk with Miss Marsden."

"Poor Theo!" Evie sighed. "He meant well, but his admiration was a bit hard to bear. I want a long, serious talk with you, too, Mr. McDermot, to say I'm sorry I was so bad-tempered about the red shoes. You were right, of course. Why can't we ever meet without quarreling? It's mostly me. I'll never be a plaster saint, will I?"

"You won't, God be thanked. Do you think I'd like you as much if you were? Now listen, this is important. I've news for you."

"What sort of news? What's Georgi been up to?" Her eyes widened with fear. "You said serious? He's not in trouble, is he? Or mama?"

"I haven't seen either of them since the ceremony. This concerns you. Let's go into the church. It's the only cool place where we can be sure of being alone for a while."

Sobered by his tone, she let him lead her into the tiny dark church, empty now, and quiet. "What is it, Rory?"

"As soon as a boat leaves the island, I must be on my way. This must be our own private goodbye. I ... I have business elsewhere."

"No," she said in a choking whisper. "Please, no. Rory, I can't bear it if you go away again. All this summer I ...." Pressing her lips tightly together, she twisted her head away from him. He felt her trembling.

Now was the moment he could have taken her in his arms, found her mouth with his, kissed her into warm awareness of love. If only that darned lawyer had kept away till tomorrow! His arms went out towards her, and only a searing effort of will held him back. What sort of man coaxed a woman to love him five minutes after he'd heard she had money opening to her? And before she herself knew?

His granda, that wise old fool, had warned him once that there was a lot of marriage spent out of bed, and a lot of years to face. And if the day ever came when Evie was his wife, he wanted to face those years with his self-respect intact. She must never be able to throw at him the accusation that she had not had a chance to see the world and spend her money, get what she wanted or thought she wanted from the great oyster now coming before her.

Nor—come to that—did he ever want to know himself a rich woman's lap dog, and end up being despised by her and everybody else.

"There will be more summers and other interests in your life, Evie my dear. The world is a wonderful place, and when you've seen it, you may come home and choose this one spot for your own. Or again, you may not."

"I've noticed nobody seems to like this famous world of yours very much. Everybody who comes here comes to get away from it. All I want is Exos ... and the ... people ... I love."

He sighed and stroked her hair, feeling the silk of it under his hand. "You are so young, mavourneen. And so lovely. And so damned ignorant. Promise me you won't marry any man till you've had an opportunity of meeting more than the islanders and a stray tourist or two?"

"I promise you I won't marry any man till I can marry the man I truly love. Why are we talking like this? And why are you going away so soon? You won't get a boat off the island tonight and tomorrow everybody will be sleeping off the effects."

She was quivering with his nearness, and hard put to prevent herself from flinging her arms around him and begging him not to go. She could keep the promise she had made very easily. She would marry no one but Rory. Why didn't he understand that? She had told him she loved him, as strongly as she dared. Did he want it spelled out? Oh, if he had loved her just the smallest bit, he would have understood what she meant.

She could say no more. For the moment she was unable to speak and had no intention of letting herself be hurt more than he had hurt her already. Not to be twice rejected.

Close together, in silence, they stood a long minute in the dim church. The gold gleamed on the icons. The pale painted face of St. Polystemon hung like a narrow moon in the dusk.

Evie felt crushed, lost, forlorn. The secret hope of Rory's return had buoyed her up over the worst moments of his absence. Now the break would be final. He had come back, and was going away again. The lovely moment when he had stroked her hair so tenderly was no more than compassion, such as he might have felt for a lost kitten.

"Come along now." He broke the hush at last. "Time for your news. And it is not I who must tell it."

At the door he held her in front of him, touching her bare arms, feeling the warmth of her body close to his. The scent of her hair was in his nostrils.

"There's a new boat in the harbour," she marveled. "Someone late for the wedding?"

"Someone to see *you*. And that's the boat I'll be going out in, when it leaves. Look under the palm trees at the end table. Do you see that charming young man in the fine suit, and his sister with him?"

"Tourists? She's thin like me, and that's an elegant dress she's wearing. Looks expensive."

"So do her handbag, shoes, and plain gold jewelry. You like it?"

She shivered, suddenly afraid. "Who are they? Why am I to look at them?"

"Dear girl, you've guessed for some time that your father is dead?"

She had known it in her heart, yet the certainty touched her like an icy hand. She moistened dry lips. "Yes, I guessed."

"Those two are lawyers. They will tell your mother there is money to come from his estate—probably enough for all her needs and yours. Enough for Georgi."

She covered her face with her hands. "I don't want it. Our lives will be changed. Money will hurt us. I can see it as evil. Please, Rory, tell me how to send them away."

His grip firmed on her quivering shoulders. "You can't do that. Your mother must be told. This is your future. Stick your chin up and go out to meet it."

"Alone?"

"Not for long. Those two are kind and friendly; they've taken the trouble to come all the way from England to talk to you in person. That's better than a formal letter. On your way." He gave her a gentle push.

"I feel sick. Am I tidy?"

He studied her gravely. "Wait a minute." Taking a comb from his pocket, he straightened her hair. "That's better." He stooped and kissed her lightly on the lips. "It's been grand knowing you, princess. Now it's good-bye to the beggarman and hop up with you onto your throne."

"Rory—please. Come with me."

"Away with you," he said.

RORY WAITED, watching the slight figure cover the distance between the church door and the table under the palms. Straight and tall she walked, her head high. *Walking into her future like a queen*, he thought, *and God go with her.*

Some day, one day, she may come back. She may look at the world and find it wanting, and come back home looking for the beggarman who loves her. I'll be there, princess, when and if you want me, he vowed silently.

Then he cursed himself for a sentimental Irishman who believed in fairies, swung on his heel, and marched away up to the far end of the harbor, to wait quietly till the boat went. *Ach, you're going soft, boyo*, he told himself. *Did you ever hear such a load of old codswallop as you've been dreaming this last twenty-four hours? Be off with you; find somewhere the wind blows cold and hard, and great waves smash on great rocks all day and all night. Get stuck into some real work for a change.*

"KALIMERA! My name is Evie Marsden. You were looking for me?"

Her arrival brought Peter Brown to his feet. He stood six feet tall, was as slim as a willow, and his fair hair was bleached by the sun. A golden youth, like the gods of mythology, a young Apollo. In her delight at something so unexpected and so perfect, Evie forgot her fears and smiled at him, a smile of pure pleasure.

Anna introduced them both and asked her to sit down. "It must have been you who had the advertisement put in? We're grateful to you, Miss Marsden. You see, if your father's estate—money, that is—was not claimed in fifteen years, it might have been forfeited to the government. And I do hate paying money to governments unnecessarily."

"When did he die?"

"Six years ago," Peter answered the question. "He sold a house and some land left to him by an aunt and bought a good yacht. We were told he intended sailing her out to the Mediterranean, so presumably he was coming home."

"Tell my mother that. She'll be glad to know. What happened then?"

"A sudden squall in the Channel. The lifeboats had a number of calls that night, up and down the south coast. Mr. Marsden's yacht and another were in collision and both were lost. The other sailor was rescued, with his wife and son. Your father was probably knocked unconscious by the mast, and his body swept away."

"And never found?"

"Oh, yes," Anna said gently, "they found him. He was buried at Plymouth. The aunt must have been his only surviving relative, for we discovered no one else at all, although we advertised as we always do in such cases. There was insurance on his life and on the boat."

"Why did he stay away so long?"

"Men get homesick. Who knows, maybe he wanted to establish himself in England again and send for you all, or fetch you? Selling the house suggests he'd given up that idea, if idea it was. That must be his secret now. We don't know why he left here in the first place. A wife and children, and such a beautiful place to live? It seems unbelievable. Yet one can't be a lawyer long without finding out that men do some unaccountable things for ridiculously small reasons."

"One needn't be a lawyer to find that out, Miss Brown. I know it. May I ask a favor, please?"

Peter said heartily, "Ask away." His eyes had never left Evie, and she was uncomfortably aware of his eager gaze. It was not unlike Theo's.

"Need you tell my mother till tomorrow? It is a wedding today and a bereavement would spoil everything. Out of respect for the dead...."

"But George Marsden hasn't been on the island for almost ten years, isn't that so?"

"My mother is bereaved and my brother and I fatherless. Do you think no one will care or notice, Mr. Brown?"

"I'm sorry. It seemed such a long time ago. People have long memories here, it seems."

"Do they forget so quickly where you live? Don't they care for the griefs of their neighbours? I don't think I care much for your England."

"You must see it," Anna put in quickly, covering her brother's confusion. "It's your father's country and he would have liked you to know something of it. Your brother too. He's an Englishman, after all. Why don't you pay us a visit and see London? My mother loves visitors and was so interested in the reason for our coming here. Oh—Peter! I've just remembered, we can't stay overnight, there's nowhere to sleep. I'm afraid we'll have to hire the boat another day. Will it be too expensive?"

"Come in the caïque," Evie suggested. "That's not nearly so expensive as hiring a launch all to yourself. But why must you go back? We have rooms empty at the Villa Julia, and it would be inhospitable not to offer you beds. My mother won't question it. With so many visitors on the island, she'd be surprised if we didn't have the house full."

Brother and sister exchanged glances. "I'd love to," said Anna, "if that is no trouble."

Peter reminded her that they had promised the Irishman a lift back to Cyprus.

"Tomorrow will do for him" Evie told them firmly. "Anyway, if your boatmen come to the wedding feast—and they will—they won't be taking a boat to sea this night. Excuse me, I'll go and arrange it with mama now. And you will keep your promise? Not a word till tomorrow?"

Peter lifted her hand and touched it with his lips. "We promise, both of us. One more night can't hurt. If there's dancing, will you dance with me?"

"Peter—" his sister warned, "perhaps Miss Marsden does not want to dance. She knows, if her mother doesn't."

"To be honest, Miss Brown, I hardly remember father. Tonight I shall remember I have come into a fortune, eh? And think about the things I can buy with my money. There will be dancing and I shall dance. Tomorrow will be the time for mourning."

"Very sensible, my dear. Won't you call me Anna? and say Peter? This is not a lawyer's office, we're on holiday and tired of formality. What will you buy?"

"If you'll say Evie, I will tell you. I shall buy St. Polystemon's skull. It's time he came back home, poor boy. I shall buy—no, wait. I have to think. I must go now. Have a look round the village. The church is good, so our visitors tell us. You'll have some luggage in the boat?" I'll send someone to carry it up. Theo will do it and Georgi will help. Georgi is my brother and as soon as I can find him . . . ."

She hurried away, knowing exactly what she must do.

"That girl's excited," Anna remarked as she strolled with Peter toward the whitewashed church. "Did you see the realization of money hit her suddenly, almost in mid-sentence? Funny how it does that to people. I hope it won't go to her head."

"She's a knockout, Anna, an absolute knockout. Can you imagine what she'll be like in good clothes and with that hair properly done? Got her beautiful head screwed on the right way, too. She saw at once that if the news broke tonight, it would dish the party. We mustn't let her waste her cash on buying up old Thingummyjig's head, though. Wasn't that the one we saw yesterday at the monastery? Cures barrenness in women?"

"That was St. Somebody's belt, love. Don't you go turning the child's head. She's young, beautiful, rich, and a novelty. But novelties don't always transplant. She may be a bit of a freak in London. She had bare feet."

"And gorgeous legs," Peter reminded her dreamily. "Mother will enjoy dressing her. I say, I've just had a dreadful thought. The mama may want to come, too. Well, that'll be your responsibility. You invited them."

"We owe it to them. Part of this holiday goes on a perfectly legitimate expense account, remember. Don't be so solemn, little brother. Ten days in London doing the sights and they'll be on the plane to Nicosia laden with new clothes and presents for all the island cousins-once-removed, and we shall neatly remove George Marsden from our files for ever."

"Famous last words! I may want to marry that girl."

"Idiot!" said his sister fondly as they entered the church, blinking.

EVIE FOUND THEO FIXING LANTERNS, scooped Georgi out of the water, and explained what had to be done. Georgi sulked, but the chance of going aboard the smart launch was too good to be missed, so he pulled his shirt over his head and trotted off beside Theo.

Now, before the people started drifting back to the center of things, she had to find Rory and tell him the rest of the story about her father. She stood still, concentrating, trying to read herself into his mind. He had said goodbye to her, so he did not mean to see her again. If he came to the party, he would stay with the men. At this moment, those men who were awake would be clustered around the communal spit watching the long kebab spears turning, or bringing up the wine from cool cellars.

Not there.

Already the tables were filling up. Laughing, chattering, teasing, giggling, in their different ways the people of Exos gathered for the wedding feast. It was too late. Rory would drift back with the men, take a seat among them, apart from the women as was the custom. Unless and until a man left his chair and joined the crowd, no woman could approach him. Such a thing simply was not done. So bold a creature would lower herself, make her man a laughing stock, a henpecked weakling. And Rory knew it.

There were other unwritten laws to be obeyed. The law of hospitality, for instance. The Browns must be presented to the bride and groom, and to their hostess.

Anna had provided herself with a wedding present, a carved wooden donkey with panniers, bought that morning in Kyrenia.

"That was for mother," Peter protested. His sister told him to shut up and search his overnight bag for a gift for the groom. Shaving lotion or something.

Julia was graciousness itself. "I wonder if you happen to know my husband?" Evie heard her saying. "I'm expecting him home any time, but just now I believe he is in England."

Evie grabbed Peter. "Dance with me. I'll send someone to rescue your sister. Hi, Andreas . . . the English lady needs a partner."

Andreas scratched his good-natured head. "But will she mind dancing with me? She doesn't know me."

"Dance!" shouted Evie imperiously as the music swept her by in an ever-growing circle. When she saw Anna safely dancing, she changed places with Sofia, who was not so much married that she could not appreciate the novelty of partnering a good-looking foreigner and pushing him through the movements of the dance.

Evie stole away. She knew, now, where Rory would be.

She saw nobody as she walked through the lemon grove, which was sheltered by high hedges of thick elephant grass. Nobody under the fig tree, nobody on the path past the Villa Julia and up to the headland. Everybody for miles around was dancing or drinking, working up an appetite for the feast. Even here, high up on the mountain, the faint smell of lamb baked with herbs made itself felt.

Out at last on to the headland, where the wind off the sea blew her thin dress close to her body. Balancing along the flat stone and marble slabs which had once been a temple floor.

He was there in the ruined temple, sitting with his back to one of her headless statues. His hands were clasped around his knees. He was staring up at the darkening sky, at the first star of the evening. There was a glint of tears on his face.

"Rory!" She spoke softly, but he heard. He leapt to his feet as he saw her coming, and opened his arms to receive her.

"Oh, Rory, Rory! I've been such a fool! Why didn't I tell you months ago that I love you? Do you hear, my darling? I love you."

She saw the wild joy on his face. Then his mouth sought hers. They were pressed close, body to body, oblivious of everything but the warmth and young firmness of flesh and bone, of racing blood and quivering nerves. As they kissed hungrily again and again, he rocked her in his arms.

At last he said, "I'd no idea it was like this with you, beloved. I've loved you for months. I fought it, for your sake. I ought to be fighting it now, but you caught me in a weak moment...."

"You were crying."

"That's the hell of it. I was. I'd lost you through my own stupid fault. I let the image of Clodagh come between us, not understanding that it was only an image, a memory in the mirror. When you...when you asked me to marry you, all those weeks ago, did you love me then?"

"Of course. Would I want to marry a man I didn't love?"

"But you said...."

She covered his mouth with her hand. "To save my pride, Rory. Only to save my pride. But when pride is beaten down, love gets a chance. Earlier today even, I wouldn't say the words that were fighting to get out. But when at last I understood that you were going away again, and this time it would be forever, I had to tell you even if it meant being rejected again. Rory, marry me quickly, please. I need you."

He took her wrists and made her sit down in the temple. "Hey, hey, not so fast, little one. What is all this about. I thought you'd inherited a fortune from your dad."

She stopped his mouth with a kiss, murmuring, "Tomorrow, Rory. The English promised not to talk business till tomorrow." She ran her hands up the back of his head, her fingers in his hair. Gently, his hands caressed her shoulders.

Hardly aware that they moved, they lay down on the carpet of scented, herby grass, and clung to each other murmuring small wordless endearments. The world below them forgotten, they were one with each other, with the stars hung like diamonds in the violet sky; with the ancient pagan gods, which stood around them headless but beautiful of body. Time passed unnoticed.

At last she stirred in his arms. Feeling her move, he turned on his side and drew her closer. The night was far advanced and a faint wind rustled the leaves of the wild carob tree, which had pushed itself through the stones of the temple. It was cooler, and the shared warmth of their bodies was welcome now.

His voice was drowsy. "Time to go, *macushla*! You will be missed, down there."

She smiled at him. "On a wedding night, no one will be missed. All the old ones will be drunk by now."

He chuckled. "What? Even your mother?" He felt her hand and kissed each of its fingertips in turn.

"Mama is *never* drunk! But she will have taken a great deal of wine, and brandy, and ouzo, and eaten far too greedily. So she will not be noticing much, you may be sure. And in the morning she will stay in bed with a headache, like everybody else. Exos weddings are like that. We can stay together till dawn."

"Woman . . ." he said softly, "you have driven me mad with longing these past three months, and you must not tempt me any more. I'm a man, not a stone god. Either go home or sit up and talk."

"Talk then. We've so much to talk about. All our lives." Her voice was suddenly fierce. "I want so much of you, my darling. I have so much love to give you. I shall demand so much. We shan't be content with small measures, you and I. I want you to make great demands on me. I want to give till it hurts. We shall fight, Rory."

"Like the devil. At the moment I possess all I ever dreamed of. I hold in my arms a perfect woman, sharing my love and ready to share my life whatever that life may be. Not submissive, but sharing as a partner. I shall have a lioness for a mate. At this moment I want nothing more than to lie here with you like this on the crushed grass. But I shall make demands too. Some of them may hurt."

She flung out an arm, as if in surrender. "Hurt me, then. If I know how to fight, my love will teach me how to be a loser."

He kissed her, and his tones moved toward passion. "Evie...Oh, my Evie!"

DAWN WAS BREAKING when Rory woke. Full consciousness came slowly. He felt supremely happy, relaxed in mind and body. His mind wandered unchecked through scenes of the past where he had also been happy. Irish skies, white clouds piled high, the mountains purple in Irish mist, the silver lakes, the fuchsia hedges crimson and violet. Great Atlantic waves crashing in a flurry of white and emerald over the white rocks.

The sun rose and its light came like a sword across the Mediterranean, across the sunbaked earth, the lemon groves, the fig trees, till he was fully awake and knew he held the world in his arms, a woman who loved him, whose lips would seek his gladly. She was still asleep. He cradled her tenderly, touched her hair with his lips.

It was the sight of an eagle, circling high above, that scattered his dreams. He was not in Ireland, but in Exos, and the girl in his arms should have been safely home in her bed hours ago. Island morals were strict, the little priest no fool; and for all her optimistic belief that no one would notice if a young girl went missing all night, he knew different. There was fat to be pulled out of the fire.

He shook her. "Evie! Wake up! It's morning. Look, the sun's up."

She turned over, opened her eyes and smiled lazily. "Rory! Good morning. I love you."

"And I love you, which is why I want you safely home and in bed before you're missed, if it's not too late already."

"No one will miss me."

"That's not the point. You are in my hands and I'm no foolish boy. I do have a sense of responsibility, child. I intend to take care of you for the rest of our lives, and it would be absurd to start by ruining your reputation."

Her eyes teased him. "Especially when you haven't?"

"No thanks to you," he grunted. "I told you last night I loved you, and my sort of love means taking care of you. Being responsible for you, and for my own behavior. Come on upsy-daisy. You're going home now—and fast. Can you get in without waking anybody?"

"Easily. It's too late to go to bed. Are you hungry?"

He thought about it. "Starving."

"I'll change into my working dress and get breakfast. Then I'll milk the goats and do the outside work. If everybody gets coffee the minute they begin to stir, they'll be so glad to see it, they won't ask questions."

"I hope not," he said grimly. "I don't fancy a shotgun wedding with your uncles and cousins holding the guns."

"Daggers, darling. We are a primitive people when we're roused. You worry too much. Race you down to the beach for a swim!"

THEY BREAKFASTED ON BOILED EGGS and Evie filled the big coffeepot twice. "Being in love is hungry work. What do the English eat, do you think?"

"Whatever's going, so long as there's plenty of it. Today's the day they talk business. I'm worried."

"What about?"

"I figure they'd not send two lawyers from England just for peanuts. There may be a good deal of money involved. Most of it for your mother, but certainly some for you. You may be a rich girl, Evie."

"So? Money's all right, if it doesn't make a person selfish. There are heaps of things I could do with it. I've thought of some already."

"You have? God save us, the girl's ahead of me. I'm a poor man. How can I have such a rich wife?"

She stared, astonished. "Why not? What difference does it make?"

"It could make a difference to me. For one thing, what are people going to think and say? Within a few hours of learning you're rich, I persuade you to marry me."

Evie laughed. "Persuade? Who did the persuading? We love each other, don't we?"

"I haven't set foot on the island for three months. I arrive on the same day as the fortune. It looks too neat altogether."

"But you came for the wedding. It had nothing to do with the English."

"Who'll believe that? In time, even you might begin to wonder."

"Take that back! It's a foul thing to say to me."

"All right, I take it back. But I've seen the power of money and the queer things it can do in families, to people who begin by loving each other and end by hating. I'm afraid of the stuff."

She came to his side of the table, sat by him, and slid her arm round his shoulders. "Trust me, Rory. It can't be all evil. We can use it for good. All sort of plans are buzzing in my head. We can sort them out tidily together, after we're married. It's going to be so simple."

"Is it, dear heart? You don't see problems?"

"There can be no problems if we love enough. Listen

to what I've been thinking. Mama will want to move to her little house, and there'll be enough to put on a new roof and add a bathroom of sorts. My father had ours put in, and we're used to it even though the bathwater has to be carried in in buckets. Georgi will go to school if we can persuade him to. If not, he'll live with mama or with us, as he chooses. If I know Georgi, it'll be both. You and I will live here, and have our guesthouse for lonely people, just as you planned it."

"As I planned it? I didn't plan a wife, but I'm prepared to modify the original idea." He dropped a kiss on her ear. "Go on. Mama and I are furnished with our dreams. What about yours?"

"I get mine. To be your wife, that's all I need. I can manage the housework when the guests come, honestly I can. I'm stronger than I look. We can make extra bedrooms, three or four, by carving up the present rooms which are so big. So we'll be able to have a lot more guests than you at first thought."

"I don't know that—"

"We'd have to pipe a proper water supply in, and make another lavatory, European-style with a pedestal and a flush. And then I plan to get a girl or two in from the village to scrub floors and such, and install electric lights everywhere, and buy a big washing machine to do the sheets and tablecloths. You'll see. It will all be splendid."

"Stop it!" He pushed her aside and leapt to his feet.

Stunned by his furious tone, she gaped at him without comprehension.

"So this is your plan for using your money? I warned you. Don't say I didn't warn you. You mean to buy yourself a husband, buy his dream for a toy, and alter it to suit yourself? I'm to be a tame cat around the house. It won't do, Evie. Forget it all, including the washing machine and the tablecloths. I'm having none of it."

"B-but it's what you wanted."

"It is not. I planned something unique, unspoiled, simple and plain. A sort of monastic life, close to natural things and everyone independent and fending for himself. No woman's fuss, like tablecloths. Plain scrubbed boards, and freedom to eat when and where one chose. What you're planning is nothing more than the average small hotel, or a guesthouse. If you think I'll be content with that—"

"All right, all right, have it the way you wanted. I was only trying to help. I was only loving you. Was I wrong to want you to have what you wanted?"

He pressed his hands to his forehead. "No, no. You meant well, darling. I'm an ungrateful hound, but don't you see—I can't change? All right, I ought to be grateful. But I can't spend the rest of my life being grateful to you, especially for something I never really wanted. It had to be something I did myself. *My* thing, *my* idea."

"It can't be ours?" she asked piteously. She looked childlike in her misery and his heart smote him for his own unkindness. He ought to surrender, to apologize, to kiss the smile back to her drooping mouth.

He could not. This was important. If he surrendered now, he would be surrendering for the rest of his life, and their marriage would never hold up.

"Ours, yes. Perhaps it could. But you are trying to make it yours, to force your ideas on me. It can't be like this. This is what I was afraid of. It's why I meant to clear off and leave you to sort it out by yourself for a while. Maybe neither of us is mature enough yet, but I'm telling you, sweetheart, this money will come between us one way or another."

"It won't. I won't let it. You meant I am the one who isn't mature—yes, you did. Well, I can be mature, too. I'm not so eager for money that I will give up the one thing I truly want in order to have it. I won't take a penny of my father's estate. Mama and Georgi can have my share."

She stood there, feet planted firmly, her proud head flung back, the gray eyes challenging. His heart twisted for the pride he had in her. But he shook his head reluctantly.

"It sounds great, *macushla*. It would be great ... for a time. For months, even for a few years. But there'd come a time, don't you see, when you'd look at me and wonder. You'd remember what you gave up, to be the maid-of-all-work, chief cook, and bottle-washer, to a bunch of no-good, self-pitying, inadequate fellows hiding away from the rough and tumble. Times, you'd hate the house, the work, the men. They won't be grateful chaps, or easy to live with. Few of them will have charm, or even good manners. You'll be slaving away in the heat for embittered, sour types, wondering what I see in them and why we can't get rid of those who don't pay their way. For some won't. Some will batten on us."

"All right, I choose that. I've sense enough to know marriage isn't all honey."

"But you'll remember the washing machine and the maids from the village. You'll think of the clothes you might have had; the luxury hotel where you could have been sunbathing, waited on hand and foot. You'll remember you've seen nothing of other countries, never seen the inside of a big transcontinental aircraft or a luxury liner. These things will rankle, as the years go by. Do you think I don't know?"

"But what difference does money make? I didn't have all these things yesterday and never felt the need of them. I don't know."

"Money. That's the difference. You could have them now. You'd be telling yourself how much you'd given up for me. After a bit, you'd be telling me."

She uttered a long, shuddering sigh. "It's hopeless, isn't it? If I have the money, you don't want me. If I don't have the money, you still don't want me. I'm beginning to think you never wanted me. That last night was just an interlude for you, and now you're making a big excuse to get out of it."

"An interlude?' Is that what you think? Did it mean nothing to you, then?"

"It meant everything. But to you . . . " She began to cry, and although she fought against them, the tears rolled down her face uncontrollably. She snatched a bright orange towel from the terrace rail and blotted her cheeks with it. It smelled of sand and sea and, remembering their morning swim, she choked with unbearable grief.

"Is it my fault? Am I to blame because there's this damned money come out of the blue? Why are you punishing me for it?"

He stood with his back to her, hands thrust in pockets, staring blindly out over the cliff and the sea. He could see no way out of the situation except by his own surrender. With her father's money, their marriage would be beset by perils. If she gave it up to her mother and Georgi, the moment would come, inevitably, when she would reproach herself, and perhaps him.

"Damn the English lawyers! Why couldn't they have come before, or stayed away altogether? It isn't your fault, Evie. I'm not blaming you, I'm blaming fate."

"Why not blame yourself? It is you who are making all the trouble, Rory. *Your* scruples, *your* desires, *your* imaginings. Your pride. You hate it, because you're not the one. But if we truly loved, you wouldn't care. You'd laugh and say what did it matter? You won't sink your pride, that's the whole trouble."

"Oh, for God's sake, don't let's quarrel! It can't be helped, it can't be altered, so we might as well talk sensibly about it. If last night hadn't happened, if I'd not returned to Exos for the wedding, what would you have done now?"

"I don't know exactly. Anna and Peter have invited me to go to London, to stay with their mother. And there's Georgi. Peter will know what to do, and of course mama will take more notice of Georgi's own ideas, now she's not afraid father will come home and be cross with her for not educating him. If he still refuses an English education, he could go to Nicosia for a time, I suppose. He ought to see the world, and make a place for himself. It's more important for a boy than for a girl."

"You'd like to accept the invitation to England?"

"I'd like to go. If we were married, we could go together."

He was silent. She watched him as he stood with his back to her, not speaking. Thinking. While she waited, she wiped her face with the towel, smoothed her hair with her fingers, found a pair of sandals and slid her feet into them. Time was passing. Before long, the English couple might be getting up, asking for breakfast, asking for her mother. There wasn't much time to settle matters between Rory and herself.

She had an empty feeling, as if detached from all her previous life and everything she understood. Life not only stood still. It was floating away from her, leaving her completely alone, isolated; no firm ground under her feet, and nothing to cling to.

The worst thing was that she had brought all this trouble on herself. It was she who had insisted on trying to find her father. If she had not interfered, tried to be so clever and managing, none of them would be in this impasse.

It was too late to turn back the clock now; impossible to stop it ticking forward into a future she did not want.

Rory strode towards her, took her hands in a powerful grip. "Listen to me. There is one way out of all this, if you are brave enough. You said, up in the temple, you wanted me to make demands on you, to ask hard things of you."

"Because I love you. Yes."

"I'm going to ask something you'll hate me for, something which will take all the courage you have. I want you to go to England with the Browns. Meet other people, other men. Taste a life away from the island. Find out what it means to have real money of your own. Can you do it?"

"For how long?"

"A year."

She cried out with the pain of that. "If you loved me, you couldn't ask it of me."

"It's because I love you that I can. Evie, understand me. I desire you, I want you with my whole body. But I also love you, and want you with my whole heart. And I can only take you the honest way, by giving you a real chance to choose me because you've seen no one and nothing you want more."

"Who will look after mama?"

"I will."

"You'll stay here?"

"The Kyria Julia will have her own ideas. But if you think she needs someone, I will stay on the island a year."

"I'll go. Because I love you and because I don't understand you. You've asked me and I shall do it, even if it kills me. Only please leave me now, because I haven't any more courage left and I can't say goodbye to you."

She listened till the sound of his footsteps died away on the hard baked ground. When she turned back toward the house, she came face to face with Peter.

He wore swimming trunks and sandals. The golden tan went as far as his waist. "Is there a way down to the sea? I'd like a swim before breakfast after all that drinking last night. What a party! Did you enjoy it, too?"

So there had been no fuss about her absence. "Very much. I hope your sister isn't too tired. I'll show you the track to the beach. It's steep, I'll come with you if you like."

His face lit up. "That would be splendid. Will you swim with me?"

Her throat was dry. She gave an odd, cracked laugh. "Why not, Peter? Why not?"

CHAPTER EIGHT

As THE PLANE TAXIED preparatory to take-off from Nicosia airport, Georgi gripped Evie's hand tightly. He
had been wildly excited throughout the journey from
Exos to Nicosia. So many new things to see and the
prospect of travelling in an aircraft at the end of it all.
He had kissed his mother goodbye easily, and raced
down to the caïque as if he had been going for a morning's fishing. But now realization had struck him silent,
and more than a little scared.

It would be a long, unimaginable time before he saw
mama again; before he milked the goats, fed the hens,
played with his friends, or swam in a warm sea. He did
not care for what he had heard of England, and though
he liked his new friend Peter Brown, who had taught
him a few things he hadn't known about football, he
was suspicious of an English school and the English
boy, Peter's nephew, who was to be his friend. Friends
weren't made like that, to order and because it suited
grown-ups. Boys made their own, and it could be this
Andrew wouldn't be a friend at all. As for Andrew's
school....

He tugged Evie's hand. "Are we off the ground now?"

A first flight is never without its anxieties. Evie hadn't
looked. Now she peered out of the thick oval window
and reported that the ground was far below. "That was
easy, wasn't it? We never even noticed."

"Do I *have* to go to Andrew's school?"

"Only for a month. You're going to be a sort of visitor
and sit with Andrew in his class. The headmaster says

you needn't do any of the work you can't manage. It's kind of friendly, that's all. He wants you to tell the children about Exos and our life there."

"That's so ordinary. They won't want to know."

"It won't be ordinary to them. You can tell them about the lemons and dates, and how you want to start growing grapefruit. Peter took a lot of pictures with his movie camera and the other children will look at them. Then you can explain what's happening on the film. Peter says it's a very up-to-date school with lots of good ideas, and if you like it, you can stay a year, with me."

"I shan't like it." Georgi made the mental reservation that even if he did like the school, he wouldn't admit it. Otherwise he would have to stay there for ever; or a year, which was much the same thing.

Evie didn't say, "Of course you'll like it!" as everybody else had told him till he was sick of hearing the words. Evie understood that it was a long way from home, and terrifyingly strange; and that the plans other people made weren't always as nice as promised.

"Parts of it you'll hate, I expect," she said comfortingly, "and parts of it I'll hate, too. But everybody says it's what father would have wanted for us, and we mustn't miss the opportunity. No one will guess you're really a businessman with crops to sell, but keep your eyes open for what Britain buys and gather as many ideas as you can."

"I'll do that. I'm the grower, now my father is dead. The land is mine, so I have to think about business. Will any of the other boys have a business of their own?"

"Not one. I'm sure of that. But don't boast about it. Just pretend to be a little boy from Exos, and keep the rest to yourself, eh?"

The idea pleased him. He looked out the window for a while, then decided flying was boring and settled down to a pile of comics Evie had bought him at Nicosia airport. Comics were new to him.

Evie had a new paperback to read, but the troubles of the characters loomed less large than her own for the moment. By this time, Rory would have moved into the Villa Julia, as he had promised. He would take care of mama, do the outside work, harvest the lemons with the help and advice of Julia's friends and relations.

Nothing had been neglected. With incredible speed, it seemed to Evie, all arrangements had been made for the trip to England. Mama had borne up splendidly, under the double blow of her husband's death and the temporary loss of both her children. She had been busy, practical, and happy about their going up to the very last minute, with a new self-confidence which came, Evie suspected, from having money in the bank, security in her own home, and freedom from the unseen presence of a husband whose wishes must be respected and obeyed even when they were not known. She was a woman set free.

But last night Evie had heard her sobbing in her bedroom and crept in to comfort her.

"I'll stay if you want me, mama. Everything can be canceled, even now."

"No, no, you must go. Your father would have wished it. And if Georgi wishes to stay on after his month, he must stay. I won't stand in your way, either of you. Only be sure he gets enough to eat, and keeps warm in that terrible climate. You, too. You're a good girl, Evie, and I trust you to look after yourself and the boy, but be careful. There are a lot of no-good people in the world. I'm not happy about that languages school paying you all that money. It seems too much."

"Peter says it's all right. They want someone to teach modern Greek, and that's the proper salary. I can't spend a whole year doing nothing, and after two or three weeks I must find somewhere to live. I can't stay too long with the Browns, kind as they are. Anna says she'll find me a room in a nice hostel for women. Don't worry about me."

They had clung together for a while, knowing that after all the practical details had been attended to in a reassuring way, there still remained separation.

GEORGI WAS SICK toward the end of the journey, bored and fretful. Once over the English coast, dark clouds piled up about them like vast castles and cloud palaces, hiding the ground. It was raining when they landed.

Anna was there, bustling and cheerful. "The first thing we must do is go shopping; you'll both need warm clothes, and we'd better buy Georgi's as like Andrew's as possible, then he won't look conspicuous. I've borrowed raincoats for you both till you can get your own."

Mrs. Brown welcomed them with a leaping fire, a big pleasant room filled with chrysanthemums, a hot meal. "Andrew's mum, my daughter Kathy, will be in later. We thought it better the boys shouldn't meet today, when Georgi is tired and perhaps a bit homesick. My dear Evie, I'm so glad to see you. Peter has talked incessantly of you, and I'm glad to repay your mother's hospitality. It was kind of her to keep Anna and Peter for the rest of their holiday. They loved every minute of it."

"We enjoyed them," Evie said shyly.

It was true, in a way. Since the wedding day, Evie had existed on two levels, a strange sort of nonlife through which she had walked like a ghost. On the surface, she listened politely to Peter and Anna, showed them the island, swam with them, arranged a fishing trip. Without demur, she allowed arrangements to be made for her visit to England, and herself suggested an extension in which she could find some sort of job and fend for herself for a year.

In an odd sort of way, she even enjoyed the whole

thing. Peter was a new experience; courteous, with an engaging shyness behind an air of competence and authority, he showed a frank interest in her which was flattering, without being in the least alarming. She treated him as if he were another brother, and he seemed content with the role. Sometimes the three of them made expeditions together, but there were times when Anna pleaded letters to write or preferred to lie on the balcony and rest or read.

"You young things get along and exhaust yourselves," she would say. "I haven't your energy."

So Peter was shown all the sights of the island, except for the ruined temple on the headland. Evie could not bring herself to take him there.

But while she went through the motions of a normal life, beneath the surface emotion tore her apart. She lived every hour wrapped in the joy of Rory's love, feeling it around her like a cloak of glory, isolated from the real, solid world like a sleepwalker. There were hours when he was so vividly in her mind that she did not even miss him in the flesh.

There were hours of anguish. Hours when the dream failed her, and she was torn with the hurt of separation. Times when she raged with helpless anger against him, hating him for his cruelty, utterly unable to understand his reasons for sending her away. Why, why had the gods given them love, if they were to throw the gift away? Wouldn't the great gods be angry, and snatch back the gift in their own way?

Once, she went alone in the dark to the temple, but shivered with fear as she moved among the high statues who seemed to loom over her with angry, invisible faces. She had meant to sleep the night with her old friends, but their anger terrified her, and she ran all the way home, arriving breathless, and had to make the excuse that she had been chasing a straying goat.

AFTER THE WEEKEND Mr. Brown took her down to his
office and explained to her gently all the ins and outs of
her father's estate. "It is not a great fortune, Evie. But if
you are reasonably careful, it will give you a modest income for a long time to come. The money has been invested and over the years it has gathered interest. Your
mother is provided for, and she has, wisely I think,
asked us to administer Georgi's share till he comes of
age. So this is all yours. Would you like us to take care
of it and send you a quarterly amount, perhaps? Or do
you want it all out in a lump sum?"

"I don't know yet. It—it seems a great deal to me. But
I don't want it. I wish it had all been for Georgi and
mama. It frightens me. Money has power to change
one's life. I don't want my life changing as it has been
changed recently."

He gave her a gentle, half-pitying smile. "My poor
Evie! I'm not surprised you find it bewildering. Take
heart, you'll get used to it. Meantime, I congratulate
you on your good sense in taking a job. Capital soon
thins out if one tries to live on it."

"My—my friends thought I should stay in England a
year for the experience. It wasn't my idea. I'd rather be
at home. But as I'm staying, I must work. It will help
make the time pass. It was kind of you to find me the
sort of work I can do."

"Not at all. It's what I'm here for, in a way. We have
a client who runs this language school and I telephoned
him. I've an idea for Georgi, too. There's a children's
television program that might be interested in him and
those films Peter took."

"He'd love that. He's taken to television in a big way.
On Exos we don't have it at all. But then there's always
so much to do there. Life in England must be terribly
boring for you all. No wonder you need such amusement all the time."

He coughed and buried his face in his handkerchief. "That's a new angle on London life. Well now, if you can't make up your mind about a lump sum; I suggest we leave the money where it is for the moment. But there must be shopping you want to do immediately—clothes and such. You know, I'm really enjoying this. It's not often a lawyer's office gets a breath of fresh air blown through it. Our work is mostly dusty and dull, sometimes sordid. Once in a blue moon, if that, something delightful happens and a dusty old file comes to life. Now—" he made a move to suggest an end to the interview, "are you sure there isn't anything else I can do for my favorite client at the moment?"

"There is something."

Mr. Brown, who had half risen, sat down again, with a quick glance at the clock. "And that is ...?"

"I want you to buy St. Polystemon's skull. I don't mind how much it costs. I want it for Exos. I've written down the name of the monastery, but I don't know how to go about buying the skull."

"I can't say I've ever bought one before. It might come expensive. Are you sure that's what you want?"

She pressed her hands together earnestly. "Mr. Brown, it's what I want more than anything. St. Poly ought to come home. Will you tell them that? He must come home. He can't work miracles where he is."

"You think he'll do so on Exos?"

"Of course. He'll be at home. We all know him, you see, so we shall trust him and believe in him. It's in the mind miracles happen, Mr. Brown. Didn't you know that?"

He was silent a moment. "Yes, I suppose I did. I suppose I've seen miracles happen in the mind. Yet that sort we don't seem to regard as miracles at all."

Evie opened her eyes wide. "What other kind are there?"

ANNA TOOK HER SHOPPING. At first Evie was shocked by the price tags, but soon became enchanted by the gay little garments she found in young boutiques and lost her excessive caution. The first time she dressed from head to foot in her new things and went to a hair stylist suggested by Anna's young secretary, Peter was stunned.

"We must go out to celebrate. Mother, isn't she marvelous! Didn't I tell you?"

"Yes, dear, you did, many times. And I agree with you. Off you go. Georgi and I are going to watch television."

Peter chose carefully and Evie enjoyed her evening. Unhappiness, however deep, cannot last forever, especially when new impressions crowd one upon another. As the English autumn became an English winter with biting winds and driving rain such as she had never dreamed of, Evie gradually began to forget the sharp bite of separation.

Not that she forgot Rory. He was her first thought on waking, her last thought as she fell asleep. But in the hours between, there were moments when she was happy, interested, and ready for fresh experiences and new friends.

Georgi moved into a room prepared for him next to Andrew's, a bus ride from the Browns. The boys accepted each other philosophically and Georgi, so Andrew reported, wasn't too bad at school, though he had never played football with a proper team and hated standing around in thin shorts and jersey on winter Saturdays.

Evie's room at the ladies' hostel was a narrow slit, one-third of a big bedroom sliced up with wooden partitions. As the latest comer, she had the slice without a window and often it felt like a trap. But after a long tiresome day with difficult, tongue-tied students at the school, there were times when she was thankful to be enclosed by her own, albeit thin, walls, and to close her own door on the outside world.

She wrote every week to her mother, knowing her news would be passed on, for the most part, to Rory. She touched the paper tenderly, pressing it to her cheek, holding the envelope in her hands, as if by doing so, she could touch Rory's hands.

She saw to it that Georgi wrote too. By an unspoken agreement, neither mentioned the unpleasant moments.

If Evie wrote too much about Peter Brown, it was because he was always there. With him, she visited a theater for the first time, an orchestral concert, an art gallery, the British Museum, where she walked a long time through the Greek rooms.

"Why do you have these things here?" she wondered. "Why don't you return what you stole?"

"You always see things as black and white," Peter demurred. "It isn't like that. The English saw the beauty of these things and saved them from neglect or destruction. We...."

Just as the English winter was becoming unbearable, it suddenly blossomed into Christmas. The shops, the street lights, the absurd gaiety of it all imposed on the dark and cold, enchanted Evie. She bought extravagant presents for the Browns, for her hostel friends and fellow tutors at the language school.

The Browns invited brother and sister to spend Christmas with them. Evie accepted gladly, but Georgi was reluctant.

"You said a month, and it will be the end of term soon. That's a lot more than a month and I want to go home. I want mama, and I'm sick and tired of this bloody cold."

"That's not a good word to use."

"Andrew uses it all the time at school. So do the other boys. Why can't I go home, Evie?"

"Don't you want to be on television? It's your favorite program and you'll be able to talk to the people you like. It's what you've done at Andrew's school, telling the children what's going on in the film."

"All right, then. But after that, I want to go home. It's a lot more than a month."

She hugged him. "I promise you'll go home after the program. We all keep on finding reasons why you shouldn't go, don't we? The school concert, the TV thing, Christmas. We think of ourselves and our convenience, and treat you like a parcel. You'll be home for the new year, that's a promise."

When the language school closed for the Christmas break, Evie went to the television studios with Georgi. He recorded well and the producer was pleased. "That boy's a natural," he assured Evie. "We'll use him again. Don't let him go back to Exos yet. We need him."

In the bus going home, Georgi grumbled miserably in spite of Evie's assurances that he would go home, come what may, as soon as possible after Christmas. "Cheer up, small one. The Browns won't want such an unhappy guest for Christmas. Three more days and you'll be hanging your stocking up and there'll be lots of presents."

Three days to Christmas. Evie was buoyed up by the hope that Rory would surely write. In the absence of any word from him since she arrived in England, doubt had crept into her love. Surely if he truly loved her he would have sent a letter, even a message in her mother's letters? Had his love been merely pretence after all, his insistence on a year's separation an excuse to get rid of her conveniently?

She had stopped watching for the postman long ago. The sick disappointment every day was too much to bear. But with Christmas so near, there was a chance, and in spite of herself she had begun the daily vigil again. There were still three more days in which to keep hope alive.

Meantime, there was Peter, always kind, cheerful, amusing. She enjoyed being with him, and day by day they discovered much in common as he opened new doors for her, taught her not only to enjoy but to understand classical music, encouraged her to read with discrimination, to love the theatre.

"I'll miss you, Peter, when I go home," she said one day when they emerged from a bright, warm art gallery into the dark slush of a December afternoon. "You stretch my mind."

"Then why go home? England could be your home, my sweet. I know the climate can be grim, but it's a good place to live. You haven't even seen the country yet, or the coast. Come spring, I plan to show you the Cotswolds, Sussex, Gloucestershire. As yet you've no idea what we can do."

More than once since that day, she had repeated the words to herself, remembering the tone of his voice, the way he had hugged her arm close to his side as they crossed the busy road. Being with Peter had a warmth, a reassurance, a feeling of security. And even an English winter had its compensations.

THE MORNING AFTER the studio visit, Evie found Georgi hot and crimson faced. He could barely croak a word and his bed was rumpled as if he had tossed all night. Panic-stricken, she ran for Mrs. Brown.

"He's very ill. Ought I send for mama? What shall I do?"

Mrs. Brown laid an experienced hand on Georgi's forehead. Her heart sank. Christmas on top of them and now a sick child to nurse. The infection would run right through the household, as like as not. But she turned a cheerful face to the frightened girl.

"It's only flu, dear. Not to worry. In three days he'll be fine."

"*Only*? Georgi has never been ill in his life, and you say *only*? It's my fault. I should have let him go home when he begged to. Oh, how I hate England and its horrible climate!"

Her hostess snapped, "Nonsense, dear. Everybody gets a touch of flu from time to time. I assure you it's nothing to panic over. A rest in bed, plenty of nice cool lemon drinks—"

"He needs a doctor. Now, at once."

"Doctors are very busy with serious illnesses, Evie. We don't trouble them with flu if we can possibly help it. I'll keep an eye on him, and if he needs a doctor I'll telephone for Dr. Evans immediately. Haven't you an appointment for your hair? It's the dinner-dance tonight."

"How can I go, with Georgi so ill? I shan't leave him for a moment. My place is here. Mama wouldn't leave him, and neither shall I."

"Not *go*? Evie, do you realize how much those tickets cost Peter and how long ago he had to book? He will be bitterly disappointed if you let him down. You have that expensive new dress you bought for the occasion, and I'm perfectly capable of looking after one small boy with flu, busy as I am. I don't want to hear any more nonsense about not going. You're dramatizing the whole situation."

Mrs. Brown was exhausted after the long uphill struggle of preparing a family Christmas. She had invited the young Marsdens because Peter had insisted, and because she couldn't see the two strangers spending Christmas far from home and with only Evie's slit of a bedroom as a base. Kathy might have taken Georgi, but she had no spare bed for his sister, and it seemed unkind to separate the pair. Now her kindly impulse looked like backfiring on her—the boy sick and infectious, the girl in a ridiculously unnecessary panic.

"Why you should treat Peter so unkindly," she snapped, "after all his kindness to you, I can't imagine. You're an ungrateful girl."

Evie's eyes filled with tears. "I don't mean to be, but everything is strange to me. I've never seen illness like this. My brother is homesick besides, and . . . and so am I."

"You'd better go home, then, both of you. You've never liked it here much, have you?"

"Sometimes I've been happy, but . . . oh, Mrs. Brown, I'm so unhappy now. I'd give the world to be back in Exos, but I *have* to stay."

"For goodness' sake! Why is it so important?"

"I'm supposed to meet new people, to find out about being rich and all that. Rory said I was ignorant, and in a lot of ways I see I am. It isn't particularly pleasant, being in a place one doesn't want to be, and where one isn't especially welcome. But I promised. Only I can't help wishing I'd never advertised about my father, and that I hadn't any money at all. It was so much happier before."

"The money bothers you?"

Evie gave a sad, defeated sigh which wrung Mrs. Brown's motherly heart. "I hate it."

"Evie, I'm sorry. I'm being horrid to you, but only because I'm tired, and there's still so much to do. Christmas is a bit of a nightmare to a housewife, whatever it is to the others. My bones ache, my feet are killing me, and I'm pretty sure most of the family are going down with flu. It can run through a house, once it starts. But I do beg your pardon for snapping. Didn't my husband or Peter tell you you're not all that rich? I mean, did they ever use the word *rich*, or is that your own idea? I'd say you had a useful little nest egg, but you must realize some people spend the whole of your fortune on—well, on one diamond necklace in Bond Street."

Evie's eyes opened wide. "All I've got?"

"And more. Go and look at Bond Street. It would teach you something about what rich means. You'd find something better to spend your money on than wasting it on old skulls."

"I haven't bought the skull yet. The monks are thinking it over."

"Look, Evie, I didn't mean to mention this to you, but I think I ought to. Have you considered how you feel toward Peter?"

"What do you mean?"

"Quite plainly, do you love him?"

"I'm in love with someone else. But he—he was the one who sent me away, and he never writes, so ...."

"You're beginning to wonder whether he loves you?"

"I can't help wondering. I hate myself for doubting him, but sometimes it gets quite unendurable. I've told myself he'll write for Christmas."

"And if he doesn't?"

"I think I shall die."

"No, you won't," Mrs. Brown said briskly. "No one ever died of love. Do you know your Shakespeare? Men have died ... and worms have eaten them, but not for love. Snap out of it, dear. Here's Peter head over heels in love with you, and if I'm not much mistaken, intending to propose to you this Christmas. Think about Peter. He's a good, loving, thoroughly nice boy, thoughtful and considerate to a degree. He'd make any girl a marvelous husband, though I do say it. Good men don't come two a penny, child."

"I suppose not. But there's Rory. I love him."

"I don't doubt it. But remind yourself it takes two to make a marriage. He doesn't sound a good proposition to me. Now, are you going out with Peter tonight, like a sensible, grateful girl?"

"What if he proposes to me? I won't know what to say."

"Then don't let him. Be a clever girl and keep him off the subject. Don't you know that in these cases the woman always sets the pace, without letting it show, of course? Men like to think they're guiding the horse, but it's the woman who is holding the reins. Use your wits, child. And be kind to my Peter. He's too nice to be hurt."

Helping with the house, wrapping parcels, running up and downstairs to a fretful Georgi, Evie thought about Peter.

Wasn't it better to have a kind, affectionate husband than a man who could be as cruel as Rory had been to her? Peter's wife would not be bullied, neglected, ignored. There would be no mad quarrels, no hard words. His wife would be a queen in her own home.

A kind man. That was what the island girls prayed for. Wasn't she a fool to go on all this time yearning after Rory McDermot, whose heart was really Clodagh's though he didn't admit it anymore?

She dressed for the dinner. The new dress, deep green like seaweed, was a long way from anything she had worn on the island, or was ever likely to wear as Rory's wife.

"You look a dream," Mr. Brown declared when he came in. "If I were thirty years younger I'd give that son of mine a run for his money. Oh, by the way, your monks have decided. They'll sell the skull, provided it goes to Exos, and under proper escort with all due reverence. That means they won't wrap him up and send him by post. He'll have to be fetched. I suppose your priest would organize that?"

"The whole island would go to meet St. Poly. Was there any other mail from Cyprus?"

"Were you expecting some?"

"It's Christmas, Mr. Brown. I can't help hoping for news. Have you time to answer a question?"

"If it's not a long one—I'm due at choir practice soon. We're doing a new anthem for Christmas Day."

"Could I spend all my money on one thing? Say, a diamond necklace from Bond Street?"

"Easily. I hope you don't want to?"

"No. At least, I might, but I'd never dare wear it. Do you think the money I have would spoil a marriage? If the wife had it, I mean."

"You mean your own marriage, don't you? My dear little girl, that is entirely up to you. You'd have to see to it that it didn't."

"Thank you," she said meekly.

PETER WAS ENCHANTED. "Do you know, you've paid me more attention tonight than ever before. You always seem so other-worldly, Evie, as if more than half your thoughts were elsewhere. But tonight you are all mine. I hope that means you ... you think a little bit more about me than you've done up to now."

"I think you're kind and sweet, Peter. And terribly good-looking. I have the handsomest escort in the room."

His hand closed over hers. "And I the loveliest girl. The day I first saw you, I told Anna you were a knock-out. You've certainly knocked me out, Evie. If I—if I plan a certain Christmas present for you, would you come with me to a jewelers tomorrow to choose it?"

"You shouldn't be buying a girl jewelry."

"You're not just any girl. Will you?"

"If Georgi is better. I'm worried about him. I've never seen anybody so ill. I can't remember seeing anybody ill at all in that way. Couldn't we wait till he's better?"

"If that suits you, dear. After all, it's only flu. He'll be up and about by Boxing Day at the latest. I can wait, but not too long."

She felt a corner had been turned in safety. If, tomorrow, there was no letter; if no word came from Rory, of love, or even a simple greeting, she would know he was trying to put her out of his life. One couldn't hope for ever. She would give him, give herself, one more day, one more chance.

THE PARCEL CAME LATE on Christmas Eve. It contained a small icon of St. Polystemon. Evie recognized it at once for the work of one of the monastery brothers. She had seen him so often, painting in the small courtyard, lovingly producing these miniature icons for sale; doing his part to earn the money to keep a roof over the monastery and provide the meager meals he and his brothers ate, year in, year out.

Hands shaking, she riffled through the wrappings looking for a letter. There was only one word—*Rory*.

It was enough. She understood how he had watched the icon slowly grow day by day. How he packed it, holding it in his hands, smoothing the boy's face, touching the edges because that was where her own hands would hold it.

She kissed the painted lips. "Thank you, dear sweet St. Poly. It's going to be all right now. We're all going home. All three of us."

She raced upstairs to tell Georgi. The boy was much better, sitting up in bed reading a comic. "Honey, listen. We're going home!"

"Both of us? You're coming, too? Oh, Evie, I'm so glad. Can Andrew come for the summer holidays? I sort of promised."

"Anyone you say. You're the master, remember. You'll be twelve, and that's almost a man. From now on, Georgi, nobody is going to bully us into doing what we don't want. *Nobody*!"

"I don't have to be an English boy anymore? Actually I'd *much* rather have a grapefruit plantation."

"Have it. Oh, Georgi, I'm so frighteningly happy. I think I shall burst!"

PETER SAW the difference in her. Ordered by his mother to trim the tree, he steered Evie into the drawing room with him and said at once, "It's no good, is it? You've heard from him—Rory. Anna warned me he loved you, but we weren't sure whether you were in love with him. I—well, if anything goes wrong for you, I'll be here, just waiting."

"Peter, you're so *terribly* nice. I almost wish it could have been you, but Rory pierced me to the bone. I didn't know what he meant, when he first said that. It hurts so much to be truly in love, Peter. I don't think you've felt it yet. I didn't pierce you to the bone, did I?"

He bent over the fairylights, knowing the truth must show in his face.

SHE FACED PETER'S FATHER. "I've decided. I need all the money in a lump sum, please."

He studied her gravely. "Are you quite sure, Evie? You're doing the right thing? It seems such an extraordinary decision, but you're entitled to do as you please with your share of your father's money. You realize it will leave you penniless when you've carried out all your plans?"

She agreed happily. "That's what I want, thank you. This is the way I have to do it. And thank you, Mr. Brown. You've been so understanding and kind, all of you. My father was nothing to you but a name on some papers and you've all taken such a personal interest in Georgi and me."

"I wish it could have been even more personal, Evie. I wish you could have been my daughter. I'm not blind and I know my boy. Anna warned us the Irishman loved you, but it's human nature to hope, I suppose."

"Anna knew? But how? I never told her."

"He knew the color of your eyes, she said. And that they could change from blue to gray under the sky. Only a man who loves a woman knows a detail like that."

"You're not angry with me? Have I seemed ungrateful?"

He laughed and gave her a fatherly hug. "No, love. The young go where they have to go, and where their stars lead them. Don't think we don't understand. We've all been young ourselves, believe it or not. That Irishman of yours must be a remarkable man! I wish I'd met him."

She hugged him tightly. "I wish you'd been my father. I never saw the use of one till now, except to make decisions and give orders. Would he have minded what I'm doing?"

"No. He sold all he possessed in his own country to buy a yacht and go home to Exos. And what are you doing, but going home? You're his daughter, all right. Good luck, small one."

St. Polystemon went home in state.

The Exos caïque, newly painted, flower-hung, met him at Kyrenia. On board were the monastery brothers, the village priest, and more islanders than the boat would safely hold. There was Julia, tearful and happy, hugging an excited Georgi.

Evie, carrying the silver casket newly polished, searched the boat with her eyes for Rory McDermot.

He had not come.

Why wasn't he there with the others? Was he so angry that she had come home without waiting the year he had decreed? Had he already forgotten the island girl and gone off on a new adventure?

It was impossible to ask someone about Rory, with the crowd chattering away fifty to the dozen and her mother unable to speak for tears; and Sofia and Marcus at the harbor to see the boat off and full of their news.

Sofia was already expecting her first baby and bloomed with happiness. "I hope you've found yourself a rich Englishman, Evie." The dark eyes flicked over the crisp white pant suit from Harrods. "All the tourists are wearing those in Nicosia. It makes you look more English than ever. You won't want to stay on the island now. This is just a visit, I suppose?"

"I want to stay forever. Sofia, tell me quickly. Have you seen Rory?"

"He was in Nicosia before Christmas. He stays with us when he comes. He said your letters were full of that Peter, and what a wonderful time he was giving you in London. Lucky you! Operas, and dancing, and dinners in great hotels. We're all too small for you now, I guess."

"The opera once. And only once in a really grand sort of hotel. And—oh, Sofia, you can't imagine how lovely it is to be home again. If only . . . ." Evie cast another longing glance along the quay, hoping to see the one person she wanted.

All the way home to the island, she pressed the saint's casket close to her stomach and prayed hard. *Please, please, St. Poly.*

Luckily the Mediterranean stayed calm and smooth for the saint's crossing, or the old, overburdened boat would surely have capsized.

As the caïque entered the harbor, the cracked bell of the church rang out. Evie searched the waiting, cheering crowd on the quayside.

He was there. Evie's heart soared with joy. She turned to the priest and thrust the relic into his hands. "You take him ashore. It should be your privilege, Father. You've wanted him all your life."

Rory clasped her in his arms. "Welcome home, stranger. You both look uncommonly English! And you look uncommonly beautiful."

"Are you angry, Rory? I had to come. Georgi has been so ill, but they just laughed. They think that terrible flu is nothing at all. I couldn't make them understand the boy has never been ill in his life before. I was terrified! I *had* to bring him home myself."

A procession had formed, to escort the saint to his new home in the church. Rory nodded toward it. "You brought more than Georgi home! You've certainly set the whole island by the ears. I hope these old monks didn't charge you too much for the privilege."

There was a touch of aloofness in him, a distance between them, a reserve in his eyes, his voice.

It will wear off, she reassured herself. *We've been separated, grown an extra skin to hide our feelings. Soon we'll be together again and as we were. I feel stiff and shy myself. It will pass.*

Not until after the service of thanksgiving, until after the long-drawn-out feast, did she find herself alone with him again.

"We must talk," he said abruptly. "Let's go up to the headland. What I need to say can't be said in a crowd, and the talk will clear my head. I'm half drunk with ouzo, like everybody else."

"Why not?" she smiled up at him. "You're an islander now."

His face closed, as if the words had chilled him. Fear struck her. She felt a mist of tears before her eyes. Somewhere, in the months that lay between them, she had lost him.

In silence they climbed to the headland. At the top, she stretched out her arms and drew in a deep breath. "It's good to taste such sweet air. London air isn't for me, Rory. It tastes nasty. So does their water. Ugh! You can't begin to imagine how homesick I've been, for all this."

"I can begin. I know about homesickness. But I thought you were happy there. In your mother's letters—"

"I'd have written to you, but you never wrote to me, and I though you'd rather I didn't. I wrote long letters telling you how I felt, but they never got posted, Rory. Why didn't you write? I'm not blaming you, just asking."

"I wanted to give you a chance. To let my image fade in your mind, so that if you came back to me, I'd know you came because you had me in your bones, your heart, and your mind."

"I had and I have."

"Your letters were full of Peter."

"Why not? He was kind to me. So were they all, Rory. If any man could have made me forget you, it might have been Peter. He offered me all he had, but he didn't have the thing I wanted. I tried not to hurt him, but in the end the only kind thing was to leave him. It wasn't fair to him to stay."

"You're not going back?"

"Not ever. I'm sorry if I've disappointed you, and I can see I have. You're angry with me. Not terribly angry, just grieved perhaps. But you're not the same, Rory." She reached out and touched him. "What is it? You seem...different. Has something changed for you? Have you stopped loving me?"

He gripped her hand till it hurt. "Never. Never that, my heart. But you are a different girl now. You've known what it is to have another man in love with you,

you've seen something beyond your island, you've money behind you. What can I give you? The only thing I had, I've—lost."

"Lost? What have you lost, if you still love me? That's all I want."

"No, it is not."

"What do you mean?"

He turned to face her at last, and now she saw the marks of strain on his face. He was like a man who had gone through some private hell of his own. "For a long time, Evie, I have lived for myself in a world I created for myself. A selfish world, where I hugged my misery and enjoyed it after my fashion. You broke into that world, bringing me warmth and joy, bringing me to life again. The blood ran in my veins again, I could feel the sun and the wind. You healed the sick places in my mind."

"I'm glad." The words were barely a whisper. She was deadly afraid. At the end of what he said, there had to be a "but!"

"No one," he said harshly, staring out to sea, "ought to be allowed to love the way you love, Evie. Giving all of youself, without a glimmer of protection. God knows I tried to protect you, save you from your own generosity by forcing you to see a bit of the world and taste other fruits before you made a final, irrevocable choice. Because with you, it would be irrevocable."

"It *is* irrevocable."

He gripped his hand into a fist, till the knuckles showed white. "It must not be, Evie. There's something between us now. It's my fault and it can't be cured."

"It's the money," she said flatly. "You still can't accept that. Well, that's over, Rory. Finished. I spent it."

The shock showed in his face. "You did what? You couldn't have!"

"You told me I had to learn about being rich. All

right, so I learned. Firstly, that what on the island I
thought was wealth wasn't really very much at all. Just a
nice nest egg, which would last all my life if I was careful and didn't demand too much. Also, that my share
was mine alone. Georgi and mama have theirs. I could
do what I liked with my own."

"So—you spent it? The saint wasn't all that expensive, was he?"

"There were other things. A new caïque for my uncles
and cousins. The money is with the boatbuilder, but
they're to say what they want. I haven't told them yet.
And presents for everybody—a sewing machine for
mama, a London baby carriage for Sofia. All those will
come by sea."

"The lawyer allowed this?"

"He couldn't stop me. I'm of age. I didn't properly
understand that till he explained. Of course he argued.
But I made him understand in the end, and he was
sweet about it. He did all the business about the caïque,
and St. Poly, and—one other thing." She reached for
the small shoulder bag she had brought with her to the
headland. "A rich girl needs a handbag, Rory. But I
shan't need it much longer. Look. In a way of speaking,
this is your present. A wedding present, if you still want
a girl without a *mil* to her name."

He groaned, "Don't go on. Listen to me, Evie.
There's something—"

"You listen to me first. Then it will be your turn. Because now I've started, I have to finish telling you everything. Mr. Brown, who is wise and kind, told me it
would be up to me whether my money came between us
or not. And as you couldn't bear it either way, whether I
had it or whether I hadn't—I had to find a way of having it and not having it, all at the same time."

"Did he also tell you how to do that?"

"Oh, no. He wasn't wise enough." She nodded towards the temple behind them. "They did. The Old Ones. There's wisdom in them, Rory. They've been there thousands of years. Look here."

She opened a long black case from her handbag. In it, on a velvet bed, sparkled a diamond necklace.

His jaw dropped. "Good heavens, girl! If those are real, they must have cost thousands."

"They did. All I had left. I put all my eggs in one basket."

He reached out and took the bauble in his hand. On his tanned skin, it shone like raindrops. "But why? You'll never be able to wear it. You might lose it. It might be stolen."

"I don't intend to wear it. Nobody but you will ever know I have it. Don't you see, it's our nest egg? If ever we need money desperately, we have it. If we don't need it, it lies hidden. And if ever the idea of money makes trouble between us, I have my remedy. Quick and easy. Look now."

She snatched it from him and held it at arm's length over the cliff. "The island people have always made sacrifices over this rock, to the Old Ones. I have only to open my hand and—it's gone, forever. Now do you understand?"

He drew a long, quivering breath. "Put it away, child. You've shaken my nerve. I never heard anything so ridiculous in my life, but I've got to admit you thought it out well. Did you also tell your famous Mr. Brown about the headland?"

"Yes. He tore his hair. He said I was mad, and that he couldn't think of any better solution himself. So if it's only the money that stands between us, there's no need for us to wait any longer, is there?"

He was silent.

"There is more?" she said softly, when he had been silent too long.

"There is more. You mustn't doubt that I love you, heart of corn. I shall love you to my life's end. But there are other things you love, and I can't ask you to sacrifice those things. No, not the money. That's totally unimportant between us."

"What, then?"

"The island. Your home, your mother and brother."

"The island? Rory, you're talking in riddles. You're frightening me. What *is* this? You don't want to marry me after all, is that it?"

"How can I make you understand, my darling, that I have discovered something about myself which is going to make all the difference to the way you think about me?"

Her heart died. "You love Clodagh still?"

"Not that. But in these past months, I've found out I can't live here. Not forever. This sea is not my sea. I need the wild roar of a great storm, the crash of water on the rocks. I need the wind blowing off the Atlantic, the smell of gorse and turf. I need the great horses I meant to breed, and my home must be there, in Ireland. A man must go back to his roots in the latter end."

"But you still love me?"

"With my life's blood."

She slid her hand over his clenched fist. "Then what does it matter where we live? Maybe a man must live where his roots are, but a woman must live where her man is. I understand you, Rory. I think I understood my father. He went home, to England. I don't think he'd ever have stayed here long. If you want to go home, and if you want to take me with you—I'm ready."

He groaned and snatched her into his arms. "If I want you! Oh, Evie, you don't know how much! How every day has seemed like a year! How my blood has thirsted for you!"

Her hands cupped his face. "Foolish, foolish Rory! Of course I know. Why do you think I came back so soon?"

After a long time, she drew away from him. "Are there mountains in Ireland? High cliffs, and white houses overlooking the sea?"

"Surely."

"Then I'm safe. I shall take my necklace with me as an insurance. If ever it comes between us, it can go just as easily over some Irish cliff." She stretched her arm as far as she could reach over the water and the diamonds flashed again in the sun.

He grabbed her. "Drop the damned thing, if you care to. Let it go. But you are my dearest possession, and if the old gods took you over that cliff, I'd follow; for my life wouldn't be worth a flea's hide without you." He began to laugh. "Darling girl, you take things so literally! I believe you'd really do it."

"If it were the only way of making you understand I love you, Irishman."

"I'm convinced. Now it's my turn to do the asking. Princess, will you marry a beggarly Irishman and live with him in the singing hills of Connemara? Because he loves you beyond loving, and will be your liege man of life and limb till death do us part."

She smiled, and gave him her hand, and he kissed her fingers one by one.

COUNTRY OF THE VINE

Country of the Vine
Mary Wibberley

CRAIG

It seemed ideal, so Charlotte applied for the position as companion to a young French girl. Perhaps the change would ease the unhappiness of losing her parents and erase the bittersweet memories of a holiday spent in Paris.

Marie was a delightful child. Everything went well until Charlotte met Marie's beloved uncle. The face of Jared de Marais had haunted Charlotte for two years since she'd met him in Paris. Now, instead of the gentle stranger of her dreams she found him hostile and unwelcoming.

"Why have you come?" he demanded.

In time Charlotte armed herself against him; she must not let him know how she felt. But she could not hide from herself the fact that Jared would always deeply disturb her!

CHAPTER ONE

THE ADVERTISEMENT wasn't exactly encouraging. It didn't give the impression—or even try to—that this would be the job of anyone's dreams. It was, if anything, couched in discouraging terms. Charlotte Lawson looked at her aunt. "Oh, dear," she said. "You thought *this* would be interesting?"

Aunt Emily smiled. "Well, it is different."

"It's that all right," Charlotte agreed.

They were sitting in the comfortable living room at Emily Lawson's house on the outskirts of Pickerton. Charlotte held the newspaper on her lap, folded to show the advertisement that her aunt had carefully marked, and she looked again at it as she spoke, then read it slowly aloud.

"Responsible young woman to take care of French girl for period of several months. Able to travel. Only those with impeccable references and good knowledge of French need apply. Handwritten letters only to Box No. A177." She shook her head. "Impeccable references. Aunt Emily, how would I even get one reference? I've never had a job—"

"My dear, you've lived on a farm all your life, and you worked jolly hard for your parents—God rest their souls—and you're a lot brighter than most of these flighty secretaries...."

"I don't think these people—" Charlotte touched the newsprint lightly "—would give a jot about the fact that I can milk cows and round up sheep and fill in forms, somehow."

Her aunt laughed, her blue eyes shrewd in her lined pleasant face. "You can but try, can't you? The vicar, and the doctor, and your old headmaster would be only too delighted to give you these impeccable references—come to that, I could give you one! A magistrate is supposed to be a worthy citizen...."

"Oh, Aunt Emily! You are sweet. But that would be cheating! And anyway, what makes you think I'd be interested in the job?"

"My dear," her aunt said slowly, "we never know what's round the corner for us. Now I may be an old fogy, but I do occasionally get flashes of something ... call it insight if you like or even woman's intuition, but when I read that ad, I knew."

"Knew what?" Despite everything, Charlotte was intrigued.

"Knew it was for you."

Charlotte gave her aunt a disbelieving smile, which slowly faded as she saw the seriousness of the other's face. On impulse she went over to hug the older woman. "Oh, aunt," she said. "You've been so wonderful these past few months since—" she faltered "—since the accident. I'll write to the box number. Then we'll see."

"All right," her aunt agreed. "And don't think I want to get rid of you. Nothing could be further from the truth. But you're twenty-one now, and it's time you struck out for yourself. It'll do you good. Why, the last time you went anywhere was that holiday with me to Paris—" She stopped abruptly, aware of the expression of pain that crossed her niece's features, then went on hurriedly, too hurriedly: "I'm sorry, love! What a fool I am...."

"No." Charlotte shook her head, and now she smiled. "It's nothing. Really. I'll go and make us a cup of tea before I write that letter. We need one." She went swiftly out to the kitchen. She wasn't aware of the way

Aunt Emily looked at her as she went out—of the deep concern on the older woman's face.

Charlotte filled the kettle. Her hands were very steady. Everything was under control. Two years ago, that holiday in Paris; and sudden memories still had the power to hurt her. But not during the day. Only at night when darkness came, and with it remembrance. Remembrance of a man she had met for such a brief time. Met and fallen in love with, and in doing so changed from a girl to a woman.

Life was lonely on the farm, and there had been ample time to think about the handsome drifter who had captured her heart in the brief space of a few utterly wonderful days. Three months previously her mother and father had been killed when their car had been struck on a level crossing as they drove to York from their farm on the Yorkshire moors. And since that dreadful day Charlotte had lived with Aunt Emily, only sister of her father, and there had been so many other things to think about that thoughts of Jared had been pushed to the back of her mind. Now a casual remark had brought him startlingly back, and she was frightened. Was he to haunt her again as he had done for so long?

She didn't know. She made the tea and took it in, and she was already mentally composing a letter in answer to that so cool advertisement.

SHE DREAMED OF JARED again that night. The bedside clock showed three-thirty when Charlotte woke, her heart beating fast, and sat up to switch on the light. The clock ticked away quietly, and she looked around the quiet room, reassuring herself that she was really here and not . . . . She took a deep breath. Useless to fight it any longer. The image of him was as strong as if he were actually there in the room with her. Yet she was alone. The window was wide open, an owl hooted distantly, and a faint breeze stirred the leaves on the old beech outside the house. From somewhere deep in the house came the sonorous ticks of the grandfather clock, but apart from that everything slept. And Jared was no-where near. He could be thousands of miles away, cer-tainly not thinking of a shy English girl who had made a fool of herself....

Charlotte lay back. Let the thoughts come; they could hurt, and they did, but there was a certain pleas-ure to them, too, seeing again his face, hearing his voice....

It had begun at dinner one evening in the small quiet hotel. Aunt Emily and Charlotte shared a table with a young American couple, brother and sister, Jack and Cathie. Toward the end of the meal, Cathie looked across at Charlotte. "Hey, Charlotte, we're going to a party tonight—why don't we take you?" Charlotte had been about to refuse, but Aunt Emily had replied:

"Why not, child? Don't think you have to stay here with me all the time. I could do with a quiet evening after all that walking today."

Charlotte, inwardly panicking, had looked desper-ately at her aunt and been met with a bland smile. How could you say "I've never been to parties—I don't know what you do?"

"There y'are," Jack said, amused. A lanky twenty-five-year-old, he looked as if nothing would ever bother him. Both he and his sister were pleasant and easygoing, clearly suitable companions in Aunt Emily's eyes.

"I've nothing to wear," she said, which was true. Nothing for evening, anyway. Cathie laughed.

"No problem, honey. It's very casual. Go as you are. That dress is cute."

An hour later Charlotte found herself in a taxi with

the young Americans, speeding through the Bois de Boulogne at a ridiculous speed. Paris at night was a glittering city. She was nineteen, and she should have been looking forward to going out, but she wasn't. She was scared.

The crumbling mansion was ablaze with light and they were swept into a warm welcoming crowd of people instantly. It was like nothing that had ever happened before, the noise, the color, the sheer variety of what seemed like hundreds of men and women of all types. Young and old, and some dressed like hippies, others in evening dress, yet more dressed casually. One woman, easily in her forties, was dressed in blue jeans and dark sweater. And around her neck was a diamond collar that if real, was worth thousands. And it *looked* real....

Jack and Cathie looked after Charlotte at first, but soon, inevitably, were drawn into a circle of young Americans, and somehow she got left out. She stood in a quiet corner watching, deafened by the music from a gigantic stereo, clutching a glass of wine as if her life depended on it, praying for the hours to pass swiftly. She didn't even know *where* she was....

"You're too beautiful to be alone. Where's your escort? Is he bigger than me?" The voice was deep and held laughter. Charlotte looked up and in that moment of time her life changed.

The man stood in front of her, and he was big, and deeply tanned, and smiling. She shook her head gently. She had seen films occasionally, and she knew that everyone talked in witty fashion at parties, and that she should reply with something clever—but she couldn't have done that, not for anything.

"I'm alone," she said. "I came with an American couple, but they seem to have vanished."

He overwhelmed her. Why should anyone like *him* stop to talk to her? She had never seen such an attractive man in her life. Over six feet tall, broad shouldered, his face dark and hawklike with fascinating tawny eyes under thick level brows, a nose that might have been broken at some time, a wide well-shaped mouth, good teeth—because he was laughing she could see his teeth were white and strong—and he said, "Then it's my lucky day, isn't it? Come on, let's grab a drink and talk, then we'll dance." He was taking charge in a quite unsubtle way, and Charlotte, to her surprise, found that it was a delightful sensation.

Within minutes they were sitting on the uncarpeted stairs, each holding full glasses, and with a loaded plate of ham and olives and onions in front of them. The noise was no less intense, but somehow they were apart from it now, and the man, so close beside Charlotte that she felt his hard muscular body against hers, said, "I'm Jared. Who are you?"

"Charlotte. How . . . how did you know I was English?" she asked shyly.

He laughed. "How did I know? I just *did*."

"Oh."

"Come on, eat up. This ham is delicious. Then tell me all about yourself." He must be teasing. She looked down at her lap. If only she could indulge in small talk, the light badinage she had heard amid the noise swirling around her in the room before. That was what this man wanted—not to hear her life story. In a minute he would go away and she probably wouldn't see him again. So there was no point in keeping him here against his will.

She turned slightly sideways to look at him and was aware of the faint but disturbing tang of some spicy after-shave lotion. He wore a deep blue shirt, unbuttoned nearly to his waist. It was a hot night .

"Look," she said. "It's very kind of you to rescue me from the corner, but I'm sure you've got friends here—"

"Trying to get rid of me? Hmm, I see." He gave her a mock-serious glance from those startlingly golden sherry eyes. "That's nice. I haven't even made a pass at you yet."

She had to smile. There was something irresistible about his expression. "That's better," he said. "Do you know how beautiful you are when you smile?" She knew she was going pink. She could do nothing about it. No man had ever before spoken to her as he did. It was exciting in a way. She felt breathless.

He stood up and held out his hand. "Come on," he said. "Let's go for a walk in the gardens. We can't talk here."

"The ham—" she began, protesting faintly, but already his hand was over hers and he was pulling her along, gently down the stairs, stepping over the plate carefully, leaving their empty glasses beside it.

"Damn the ham," he answered. "Let's talk. We can get some more when we come back if that's gone...."

Charlotte turned restlessly in bed. She could remember quite clearly, even now after the space of two years, her feelings at the time as Jared had led her out of a doorway and into the dark garden. She should have been nervous—he was a complete stranger—but she hadn't been. Instinct had told her to trust him. Instinct had been right. The memories flooded back, and she couldn't have stopped them if she had wanted.

"Mind the path, there are stones. You don't want to trip," and as he said it he put his arm around her. The house was left behind them; its lights flooded out but didn't reach their part of the path, and the racket of the overloud music was muted by the distance so that it became almost pleasant.

"Where are we going?" she asked.

"To look at the ducks, of course." He seemed faintly surprised. "Why else would I bring you out?"

And suddenly, quite suddenly, Charlotte realized that she was enjoying herself. One evening of her holiday, an unwilling partygoer, and she would never see him again after tonight; but it didn't matter, because he was a most fascinating man, and she was in a darkened garden with him, and she trusted him completely.

She laughed. "Of course," she said. "The ducks! *That's* why I came to this party—just to see them."

"We should have brought the food out. They'd enjoy the ham, though I'm not so sure about the onions. Do ducks like onions?" He spoke as if deeply interested.

"I don't know. I must try ours with a few when I get back home. Perhaps fried ones, you never know."

"You have ducks?" He seemed impressed, and somehow, the next minute, Charlotte was telling him about the farm. Now there was no constraint, no forcing it; he was genuinely interested, she could tell.

They stood by the dark expanse of lake, still and cool, with weeping willows trailing their leaves in the water, and only the occasional rustling of feathers to betray the sleeping birds. She shivered because it was colder there by the edge, and Jared said, "Do you want to go back?"

"No, not yet." She looked up at him. His face was shadowy, a gray blur, and he was much taller than she. From nearby came the sound of whispered voices and muffled laughter: they were not alone, it seemed.

"Good. I like it here. It's peaceful. Very peaceful. And we won't be disturbed if I—" He didn't finish the sentence. He bent his head and kissed her.

Charlotte had never been kissed before. She had imagined it happening, of course, and had wondered what it must be like to have a man kiss you. But she hadn't known the reality. It was simply beautiful; there were no other words to describe the experience. Strong and tender, his arms were around her as if they would never let her go, and she responded instinctively to his mouth.

And even when the kiss was over, the magic continued. It continued for three days, during which time Charlotte knew that she had fallen deeply in love with the dark mystery man who had come into her life so unexpectedly.

She put her hand to her mouth. It had all ended so suddenly. Ended with ten red roses and a brief note delivered to her hotel when she had been waiting for him to phone on the last day of her holiday. But she had sworn never to think of that anymore. She had decided to put it all out of her mind and remember only the happiness. Easier said than done....

Aunt Emily had been a brick. Charlotte had looked back at the airport as their plane left Paris. Her eyes ached with unshed tears, her throat was dry. It was all over. She didn't even know his surname, or where he came from, or how old he was. She knew only his first name: Jared. And knew only the bittersweet memories of kisses freely given.

She slept little during the rest of the night, and when morning came she posted a letter to the box number in the newspaper.

THE ENVELOPE was heavy, the paper more like parchment than notepaper. Charlotte looked at the spidery writing with its Gallic flavor. The writer had apparently scorned to use her stamped addressed envelope.

"Well, go on, open it," her aunt said impatiently. "Let's see what they say."

Charlotte smiled. "I haven't drunk my tea yet." Then, seeing her aunt's expression, "Oh, all right." She read aloud:

Dear Miss Lawson, will you please arrange to attend
an interview at the Royal Station Hotel in York on
Tuesday next, at 2:00 P.M. Ask for Madame Grenier.

It was signed "Heloise Grenier." There was no address at the top of the page, merely the date. Charlotte
passed the letter over to Aunt Emily, who read it slowly
again, as if to find subtler shades of meaning that her
niece might have missed.

"Hmm," she commented. "Like the ad, brief and to
the point. Tuesday—that's tomorrow. Now, what will
you wear?"

Despite herself, Charlotte experienced a prickle of excitement. "I'm frightened," she admitted. "Isn't that
strange?"

"Hardly," her aunt said, "seeing that you've never
been interviewed before. But I wouldn't worry. I told
you—I've got a *feeling* about this. Now, let's see, we'll
go to York in the morning and have lunch, then you go
off to your interview and I'll meet you in the hotel
lounge afterward. We don't know how long it'll take, so
I'll order myself coffee and read a book—"

"About five minutes, I would imagine," Charlotte answered. "I'll bet she's a real dragon."

"Rubbish!" Her aunt looked severely at her. "She'll
probably be quite charming. I wonder how many others
are being interviewed?" she added thoughtfully. Her
eyes went up and down Charlotte's slender figure,
stopped at her niece's face, and then she nodded.
"Hmm, yes."

"Hmm, yes, what?" Charlotte was intrigued.

"I think a touch of makeup wouldn't come amiss—"
Then as Charlotte was about to protest, she added
quickly, "Just a *touch*, love; I know you don't like the
stuff, but I've always fancied myself as a makeup artist,
and you look so young—"

"I am young!" Charlotte laughingly replied. "You'll be telling me next you want to do something with my hair."

"Yes, well, I was about to come to that, too. Now it's lovely as it is, all short and blond and wavy, but if we could just put in a couple of curlers—"

"No," Charlotte said, but faintly, for there was that look on Aunt Emily's face, and it was the kind of look she wore when she was about to get her own way. She sighed. What did it matter? Aunt Emily was so good, it would do no harm to indulge her little whims for once. "All right, you win," she said. "I give in."

Her aunt smiled. "Good," she said. "Now I'll just pop out to the drugstore in the village. I won't be long...."

CHARLOTTE SAT PATIENTLY at her dressing table. Tuesday morning, 10:00 A.M., an hour's drive to York ahead of them, and it was all planned. Her aunt had taken over with great efficiency; Charlotte looked in the mirror and then closed her eyes obediently at Emily's command. She hid a smile. The older woman was really enjoying herself. It was almost worth it.

"There, that's it. Just a touch of blue eye shadow. Too much is vulgar during the day, but you have such lovely deep-set eyes, it's a shame not to enhance them a little."

Charlotte kept her eyes closed. It might be interesting to see what transformation, if any, had been wrought when her aunt had finished. Aunt Emily had come back the previous day loaded up with bottles and jars from the local drugstore. There was even a bottle of perfume in the collection. Charlotte hadn't even looked at it yet. She had never used perfume in her life.

"There, you can look now. How's that?" Her aunt stepped back to admire her handiwork, and Charlotte opened her eyes. For just a split second she didn't recognize herself. Then she laughed.

"Is that *me*? What have you done?"

"Something you should have learned long ago: I've given nature a little helping hand." Charlotte had good bones, high cheekbones, an oval face, and a gently rounded chin; her golden hair, newly washed and curled, softly framed her face. A touch of pencil to skill-fully darken her well-arched eyebrows, pink lipstick on her full mouth, eyes glowing darkly blue. She didn't re-alize that she was beautiful, she only knew that she felt good, and turned around to thank her aunt and tell her so.

Aunt Emily saw the beauty there, the soft gentle radi-ance that could so easily remain hidden, and she was well satisfied with her work.

"Right," she said briskly, "let's get ready. Mind how you put that dress on, don't disturb your hair or make-up. Want any help?"

"No, thanks, I'll manage," Charlotte assured her. "I'll not take a minute."

And then, within half an hour, they were on their way to York. It was a gloriously sunny day and Aunt Emily sang as she drove along, which was always a good sign, for she usually tended to get slightly impatient with other road users.

Charlotte smiled at her. "You're very good to bring me," she said. "I could have got the bus; I know Tues-day's a busy day for you."

"Huh, it's only the guild this afternoon. They can manage without me for one week. Can't have you arriv-ing all dusty from that bus. No, I'm enjoying myself, dear, don't you worry."

They ate lunch at a restaurant near the hotel, and lin-gered over coffee so that at a quarter to two Aunt Emily said, "We'll go now; I'll get settled in the lounge, and you can make a good impression by being precisely one minute early."

"Yes, aunt," said Charlotte obediently, but with a trace of impish humor in her voice. "I don't know about being a makeup artist, you should have been a stage manager, you seem to be managing my interview very well up to now."

"I'm glad you think so," her aunt agreed graciously. "I do my best."

She had a moment of panic as she approached the receptionist. What if they should look at her blankly and say they had never heard of Madame Grenier?

She ran her tongue over dry lips and asked the fateful question. And the next minute she was being whisked up in an elevator, accompanied by an affable man who guided her to a door, knocked, waited a moment, listening, then said, "You can go in, miss."

A woman sat facing the door. She was elderly, but it was difficult to see her face, for the window was behind her, leaving her in shadow. Her voice was cool.

"Miss Lawson? Good afternoon. Please sit down."

"Good afternoon." As Charlotte sat down in an easy chair, her nervousness dropped from her like a cloak. It was strange to feel like that. Perhaps something in the woman's autocratic manner did it—the way she sat, straight backed and intimidating in the chair. She intended putting Charlotte at a disadvantage. She could not know that Charlotte had only come to please her aunt, not because she was desperate to get the job. It made a subtle difference, and suddenly Charlotte was no longer afraid. She tilted her chin, and met the other's glance with her own direct gaze, and waited for her to speak.

The older woman gave a slight nod, a mere inclination of the head. It was almost as if she acknowledged Charlotte's thoughts. "Now, miss," she began. "Tell me about yourself."

There was so little to tell, and no use at all in pretending anything. Charlotte didn't want to try. She told the older woman of her life on the farm, of her parents' accident, and that she was now living with her aunt in a village on the Yorkshire moors. The woman listened in silence. Charlotte finished: "I have never been employed by anyone, as I always worked on the farm, so I have no job qualifications at all. I can only offer you references from my doctor, vicar, and old headmaster."

"And why did you apply for this position?" The voice was cool, giving nothing away. Was this how prospective employers behaved? Something told her that this woman was a law unto herself. No use telling half-truths, pretending it was something she really wanted.

"My aunt read your advertisement. It was she who told me to write to you. She thought it would be a good position." She had probably finished her chance now. For some reason she didn't care. And it was therefore almost a shock when the old lady smiled.

"I like your honesty," she answered. "Yes, I like that. One other young lady that I interviewed this morning told me that she had always wanted to care for a child—what a stupid response! It didn't fool me." And then, almost in the same breath, she added, "*Vous semblez très jeune, mademoiselle. Quelle âge avez-vous?*"

It was calculated to confuse. Charlotte had a good knowledge of French and had been waiting subconsciously for something of the kind. Without hesitation she answered, "*J'ai vingt-et-un ans, madame.*" And she smiled.

"*Bien!*" She switched again to English. "Your accent is good enough. Tell me, Miss Lawson, when would you be able to begin your duties?"

For a moment Charlotte looked blankly at the older woman. Then she found her voice. "But you have others to interview?" It was all too sudden.

"No. I have seen three young women today. I made

yours the last appointment because I liked your handwriting—I find that a very interesting guide to character. I have told the others that I will let them know. I do not need to tell you, for I have decided. How soon can you begin?"

Charlotte swallowed. "As soon as you like."

"I wish you to meet my granddaughter as soon as possible. Say tomorrow? I will send a car to your house for you at ten in the morning. And if everything is satisfactory, I would like you to begin next Sunday."

Charlotte sensed that the interview was over. Just like that. It was as if the woman had lost interest in her. She stood up. "Thank you, Madame Grenier," she said. "I'll be ready at ten in the morning. *Au revoir.*"

"*Au revoir*, Miss Lawson."

She went out in a daze. Aunt Emily would never believe it—or would she? Charlotte went down to tell her.

CHAPTER TWO

THE CAR, a sleek black Daimler, arrived at five to ten the following morning. Aunt Emily was looking out of the living room window and called Charlotte to her. "It's got a chauffeur," she hissed, as if the man might hear her, "and I'll swear there's someone in the back!"

Charlotte dared a quick peep. "Oh! It looks like Madame Grenier," she said. "What shall we do?"

"Ask her in for a coffee, of course," retorted Aunt Emily, "what else?" and went to the door. Charlotte waited. She was making a big mistake, she knew that now. She should never have listened to her aunt in the first place....

"It won't take a moment, *madame*." Aunt Emily was coming in, ushering the old woman in front of her, and now, for the first time, Charlotte was able to see her new—her *first*— employer. She was probably seventy, hawk-nosed, her white hair swept severely back from her face into a bun at her neck. She wore a fur coat, although the day was warm, and a long black skirt. Eccentric but extremely dignified, she swept in, her eyes missing nothing, Charlotte would have sworn, noting every item of the too old furniture her aunt so loved.

"It is extremely kind of you, Miss Lawson," said Madame Grenier. "Good morning—" this to Charlotte, who only resisted curtsying by sheer willpower. She had that effect on you.

"Good morning, *madame*. I'll make the coffee, Aunt Emily." And Charlotte escaped to the kitchen before her aunt could reply. Not that she seemed inclined to;

she was sitting down, asking the older woman to do the same, already talking. She could hear the voices faintly as she prepared coffee in the percolator, and bit her lip. Knowing her aunt as she did, she could imagine that the Frenchwoman would be getting a subtle grilling. Emily Lawson hadn't been a magistrate nearly thirty years for nothing. The gentle exterior hid a formidable personality. She would undoubtedly be assuring herself of the suitability of the position for her niece. Charlotte put her hand to her mouth to stifle sudden laughter. What would Madame Grenier make of *that*? She was soon to find out.

As they drove along the country lanes a half hour or so later, the Frenchwoman said to Charlotte, "Your aunt is very concerned for your welfare, is she not?"

"Yes." She wondered what was coming next.

"That is good. I like that. So many people nowadays do not care." She took a sharp sideways glance at Charlotte sitting beside her in the back of the roomy vehicle. "That is partly why I came with Yves this morning. Your references to your aunt yesterday intrigued me. I have assured her of your welfare, and I am sure she is satisfied."

"Yes, I'm sure she is," Charlotte murmured, and managed a smile. So everything had gone off all right. They were traveling swiftly, but the driver seemed to know the road well, and Charlotte, who had never been in such a luxurious car, began to relax. She wondered what the child would be like. She didn't know her age or her name, and she was certain that this meeting would be to see if they both got on together.

"Do you know where we are going?" asked Madame Grenier.

"No. To the hotel in York?"

"No. I merely took a room yesterday for the interviews. We are staying at a house a few miles outside York, Redvale Manor."

Charlotte couldn't hide her surprise. One of Yorkshire's statelier mansions, Redvale Manor was a house
of great beauty and charm. She had seen photographs
of it, but never the actual place. And now she was going
there for a day, or at least for a few hours. It began to
seem as if Aunt Emily's intuition had been right on tar-
get. They swept up a wide tree-lined driveway that
curved gradually around, hiding the house effectively
from the road and the gaze of passing cars. It was even
more beautiful in reality than in a photograph. Charlotte took a deep breath. This was more than she had
bargained for. Madame Grenier had made a bad mistake choosing her for this position. She looked down at
the plain blue dress, the same that she had worn for her
interview on the previous day. It was her best one—her
only one, come to that. Living on a farm that had been
remote enough to discourage casual visitors, Charlotte
had always dressed in trousers and sweaters, and never
been interested in clothes. But she might have to buy
some, she realized that now. She sighed inwardly.
Money wasn't the problem. It was a question of choice.
She had no idea of fashion at all. Yet this formidable
Frenchwoman would hardly be expected to understand
that.

And then they were stopping in front of the gracious
red brick house, lit by the sun so that it glowed and the
windows sparkled, and in an upstairs room a curtain
moved slightly, then was still. Someone was watching
them get out of the car. Charlotte wondered if it was the
girl.

The driver held the door and she looked at him. She
had expected a middle-aged man, but he was young,
probably in his late twenties, and good-looking in a
dark gypsyish fashion. He looked at Charlotte in a way
that made her go warm. Madame Grenier swept up the
steps, calling in French, "Leave the car there, Yves."

"*Oui, madame*," he answered. But his eyes were still on Charlotte, and suddenly he smiled. She smiled back, then turned away and followed the old woman up to the house. So that was Yves, the chauffeur, and Charlotte didn't know what to make of him at all. He was quite unlike Jared. With that thought came a pang, a slight ache of the heart, and she took a deep breath and tried to dismiss it. She must try to forget Jared now. Only that was going to be difficult, as she found out a short while later when she sat in a beautiful drawing room drinking coffee with Madame Grenier.

A maid had brought in a trolley and been told to leave it, as they would look after themselves. They were alone, and Charlotte sensed that she was in a way on trial. There had been no mention of the girl she was to look after. The conversation was general, the older woman telling Charlotte that she had been staying at Redvale Manor for two months and was soon to return to France. Charlotte had poured out their coffee at her new employer's request, and then Madame Grenier said, "You have a passport, Miss Lawson?"

"Yes. I had a holiday in France with my aunt two years ago."

"Ah! Good. Then you will be prepared to return there with my granddaughter?"

She should have known. Perhaps, subconsciously, she had already done so when she had read the words "able to travel" in the advertisement. Even so, the words sent a slight shock through her. She managed to hide it.

"To France? Of . . . course." There was only the merest thread of hesitation as she replied. *Not to Paris, please not to Paris*, she prayed inwardly.

The old woman smiled. "You are perhaps curious to know whereabouts in France you will be going?"

"Why, yes, of course." And Charlotte smiled. Autocratic and regal her employer might be, yet there was something about her that told Charlotte that she could be warmhearted and kind.

"We have a vineyard in central France. My grandchild, Marie, is heiress to half of it when she is of age, and it is a beautiful place. We will be leaving in two weeks. You and Marie will travel by car and boat. I will fly, as I am a poor traveler—the quicker the better for me." The dignified face relaxed slightly at Charlotte's expression. "Ah yes, you are wondering something?"

Charlotte shook her head. There were several questions that presented themselves, but it certainly wasn't her place to ask. The main one: Why didn't they all fly? The second: Would Yves be driving them?

They were answered almost immediately. "No, *mademoiselle*, you are merely being polite. But you must ask yourself why do we not travel together? *Eh bien*, it is simple. Marie's parents—my son and his wife—were killed in a plane crash one year ago. She is not permitted to fly anywhere *at all*, whereas I am old and can please myself. Yves is very reliable. I trust him implicitly. He will look after you both well. His knowledge of English is limited, but he and Marie get on well and I am sure you will find that you do, too. The present owner of the vineyard is my nephew, Monsieur de Marais. When Marie is grown up, he and she will share it."

Charlotte nodded. "I see, *madame*."

"Your duties, after we are there, will be to be companion to Marie—and of course to help her with her English. She is a clever child, but rather delicate, as you will see."

"Will I meet her today, *madame*?"

"Of course. Soon I will send for her. But first I wished us to have our little talk. We will have lunch later, and then perhaps a walk around the gardens. And then Yves will take you home to your aunt."

Madame Grenier leaned back in her chair and closed

her eyes, as if tired. Charlotte waited silently. Her mind was a turmoil of mixed emotions. Companion to an heiress! She imagined Aunt Emily's face at that little bit of information and smiled slightly to herself. Her aunt would probably nod and say something like, "I'm not a bit surprised!"

"Good!" The old woman's voice startled Charlotte out of her daydream.

"I'm sorry?" She was puzzled.

"You have that quality of silence that I admire—by that I mean that you do not feel it necessary to talk all the time. I feel we may get on well with each other, *mademoiselle*."

Charlotte smiled gently. "I have been used to being alone most of my life, *madame*. I am not used to doing a lot of talking."

"Marie is a lonely child, Miss Lawson. Perhaps you will understand her. She can be moody. Maybe, if she had a brother or sister . . . ." There came an eloquent shrug. "*Hélas*, that is not possible now. But you will be good for her, I am sure." She pointed to the fireplace. "Be so good as to press that bell, *mademoiselle*."

Charlotte obeyed, and a minute later the maid came in.

"Brown, please bring Marie in to us."

"Yes, ma'am." The maid gave Charlotte a long look and went out.

There was a waiting silence for a few moments, then the door opened again and a child walked in. Her eyes met Charlotte's and Charlotte was startled to see in them a certain lost look. The girl was nine or ten, tall and thin with long dark hair down her back. The eyes that met Charlotte's were a clear light blue. She was dressed in a short summer dress of white, with a grass smear on the lap, and on her feet were white sandals.

"*Tiens*, Marie, could you not have changed your dress?"

"*Mais, grand-mère, j'étais—*"

"English, Marie. Please speak English in front of Miss Lawson."

"I was playing, grandmother." She said it slowly as if the language were very strange to her, and the old woman looked at Charlotte and clicked her tongue.

"Never mind, child. Come here and be introduced."

The handshake was formal. The girl had good manners. She gave Charlotte a smile, and a sudden warmth lit her rather plain features. "I am pleased to meet you, Miss Lawson," she said haltingly.

"And I am pleased to meet you, Marie," Charlotte answered.

"Good. Now go and change your dress. Then come back for lunch."

"Yes, grandmother." With a last quick look at Charlotte the girl ran out. Madame Grenier sighed.

"She will need training, that one, before she is a young lady. She prefers animals to humans, I am quite sure. No doubt she has been feeding the rabbits, not playing at all."

Charlotte laughed, unaware of the older woman's eyes on her. "Then I'm sure we'll get on well."

"I hope you do, I really hope you do." The small sigh that followed the words was a mere whisper, but Charlotte wondered at it.

They ate lunch in a large, long dining room, just the three of them, and it was delicious, from the smoked salmon to the dessert of fresh strawberries and thick cream. Afterward Madame Grenier looked at the fob watch she wore on her black dress and frowned.

"Oh dear, I intended to show you around the gardens now, but I really must make some phone calls. Marie, will you show Miss Lawson around for me?"

"Yes, grandmother." The girl looked at Charlotte. "You wish to go now, miss?"

"If that's all right, I'd like to very much." She wondered if the old woman really had phone calls to make, or if this was a way to let them get to know one another. It seemed quite possible. And suddenly, she didn't know why, it was important to Charlotte that she and the girl who was to be her charge should get on well. She didn't understand it herself. She just knew that this position was assuming greater importance with every minute that passed.

Perhaps it had been the look in the girl's eyes. A look that Charlotte had understood only too well.

They went out of the front door, down the steps, and Charlotte looked around at her surroundings for a moment in silence. "Marie," she said. "Madame Grenier tells me there are rabbits here. Will you show them to me?"

"You like rabbits?" She sounded surprised, making Charlotte laugh.

"I have lived on a farm all my life. I like all animals—but if I had a favorite, I suppose I would have to say dogs."

"Ah—*les chiens*! *Pardon*, miss! I forget sometimes."

"That is all right, Marie. You speak English very well."

The girl pulled a little face. "*Grand-mère* insists that I do. I prefer to speak French, of course."

"Of course. And I would like to practice my French sometimes, too." Charlotte grinned impishly at her young companion. "Perhaps, just *occasionally*, we can speak a little French?"

Marie laughed. "Occasionally, yes. Come, I will show to you the rabbits."

They were behind the house, in a large wire-enclosed run, half a dozen or so, pink eyes watchful as the two girls approached. Then, as if recognizing Marie, two ran forward to the wire netting, and she knelt down and touched their noses, then looked up at Charlotte, her eyes shining.

"They know me, miss."

"I can see that," Charlotte agreed smilingly. "But you won't be able to take them back with you when you return to France."

"Ah no, but there I have my two dogs waiting for me to return." The girl stood up. "And perhaps it is better that the rabbits stay here. My two dogs would eat them." She looked at the rabbits, then turned away. "Come, we will walk around now. Then we will return to grandmother and tell her that we get on well enough, for I feel that is why she has sent us off together."

Charlotte looked at her. There was no doubt about the girl's intelligence. The words were said quite calmly and logically.

"Do you go to school, Marie?" she asked.

The girl shook her head. "No. I have a tutor." She pulled a face. "She is very strict."

"But it is important that you learn your lessons."

"Perhaps. But it has been nice here. No—" she hesitated "—I do not know the English word—*devoir*?"

"Homework?" Charlotte suggested.

"Yes, homework, that is it. I can read my books instead."

"Ah, you like reading, too? So do I. We'll have to compare notes."

"*Comment*? What does 'compare notes' mean, please?"

"Oh, talk about books, I mean—see if we have read the same ones."

"Yes, I see." Marie nodded wisely. "I like the adventure stories, and travel tales—things like that."

"Hmm." Charlotte was going over her collection mentally. "Would you like me to bring a few from home when I come here? It might be fun to try to read in English. And in return, I'll promise to read some of yours in French—that will be like homework for *me*."

Marie suddenly started to laugh and took hold of Charlotte's hand in an impulsive gesture. "I think I will like you!" she announced. "Of course, please let me see some of your books. Oh, what a pity you are not my tutor instead of Mademoiselle Lucy."

The gardens were extensive, well tended and beautiful, and nearly an hour had passed when at last they returned to the house to find Madame Grenier waiting for them.

They drank coffee in the drawing room and talked, and when Marie went out to bring some books to show Charlotte, her grandmother said, "I am pleased with your visit today, Miss Lawson. My granddaughter's happiness is important to me. And I can see that you have a certain empathy with each other."

"We've discovered that we have one or two common interests, *madame*."

"Yes, I am sure. Well, soon it will be time for you to go. And I will send the car for you on Sunday, after lunch—will that be suitable?"

"Yes, of course."

"Perhaps your aunt would like to come here with you and see you settled in." A faint trace of a smile accompanied the word.

"She would love to, I'm sure, *madame*."

"Good. That is arranged, then. On Sunday you will commence your duties."

IT WAS RATHER A SAD MOMENT when the time came for Aunt Emily to leave on Sunday evening. Charlotte went out to the car with her and they stood talking for a few minutes. Yves was nowhere to be seen, and they were alone. Aunt Emily squeezed Charlotte's hand. "Madame Grenier can be formidable," she whispered, "but she's a very charming woman inside."

"I know," answered Charlotte. "You were right about that ad—I think."

Aunt Emily laughed. "There you are!" she said. "Told you so." She looked around her, to the twilight that was turning everything to silver gray shadow. The bright lights shone out from the house, bathing them in warm gold. "You'll phone me when you can, of course—let me know how everything's going?"

"Of course—" Charlotte hugged her "—and thank you for everything." Yves appeared silently from the back of the house. He was an impressive figure in smart dark uniform, and the light caught his face as he came up and said in French, "Is *madame* ready to leave?"

"I think so, Yves, thank you." He no longer made her feel uneasy, as he had done, unaccountably, on that first occasion. He seemed harmless enough, and his manners were good. Charlotte kissed her aunt warmly. "Bye-bye, love. See you soon."

She watched them go, the taillights dwindling down the driveway to vanish with a final wink and blink into the darkness of the trees. Then with a little sigh she went back into the house. This was it, the beginning of a new life. She couldn't help wondering if she was going to be happy.

YVES DROVE THEM TO YORK the following week, on Wednesday, and Charlotte helped Marie choose some coats and shoes and dresses to add to her already extensive wardrobe. She was aware that it was a compliment on Madame Grenier's part to trust her with such a task, and she was determined not to let her down. Marie had strong ideas of her own regarding clothes, as Charlotte soon discovered, and her intentions were not quite as easy to keep as she had thought.

"No, Marie, honestly, those shoes don't suit you," Charlotte assured the girl as she tried on a pair of brightly striped, clumsy-looking clogs and looked admiringly at herself in a mirror. Charlotte's heart sank. She could imagine the old woman's expression if they returned with *those*!

A ten-year-old French girl, already with strong views on fashion! And that thought inspired Charlotte. In her calmest voice—almost casual—she said, "As a matter of fact, they make your legs look rather plump, whereas these—" and she picked up a pair of smart red ones "—make you seem like a teenager."

There was a pause—a doubtful pause—then Marie said, "Hmm, perhaps I will try those red ones on again, Charlotte. Pass them to me, will you, please." Nothing showed on Charlotte's face. Inwardly she breathed a sigh of relief. She was learning. It would perhaps take time, but she was beginning to find out the best way to treat this young French girl who had a mind of her own hidden under that gentle exterior.

Yves took them to Scarborough on Saturday. She and Marie wandered along the front thoroughly enjoying themselves, eating ice creams and marzipan candy from a shop on the promenade, playing the fruit machines, laughing whether they won or lost. Yves accompanied them, because he said Madame Grenier had told him to. Charlotte wondered whether this was in fact so, and while she and Marie were playing a game of football in one of the amusement arcades, she said, "Does Yves always come with you when you go out?" He had been with them on Wednesday, but that was understandable as there was a lot of shopping to carry. Marie shrugged.

"Oh, yes. Grandmama thinks someone may try to kidnap me or something." It was said in matter-of-fact tones, and for a moment Charlotte thought she was joking—then saw her face and knew she wasn't. It jolted

her. She looked around to where Yves waited, feeding
pennies into a one-armed bandit. He might not have
been with them at all.

"Oh, Charlotte, your face! I have shocked you,
perhaps?"

"No, of course not." Charlotte smiled warmly at her.
She was begining to realize something of the little girl's
isolation. Perhaps there was no fun in being an heiress
after all. She had a sudden remembrance of something
Madame Grenier had told her about the vineyard.

"Is your uncle married?" she asked. "He might have
young children...."

"Uncle Zhar? Oh no!" Marie laughed in great amusement. "He is a spinster."

Charlotte joined the laughter. "You mean a
bachelor!"

"Yes, a bachelor. Aren't I silly? A spinster is a lady,
isn't it?"

"Yes. He lives at the vineyard, does he?"

Marie sighed. "Yes. Only since . . . since a year ago."
Charlotte bit her lip, wishing she had not asked. She had
only done so to change the subject from talk of kidnap-
ping, but she had no wish to distress the girl. She went
on hurriedly, "It will be nice to see him again, I'm sure."

"Oh, yes. We get on well enough, he and I. But—"
and here she shrugged "—he does not really want to run
a vineyard. He prefers to travel around. He has many
girl friends." She rolled her eyes and grinned mischievously.

"Oh, I see." Time to change the subject. "We'd better
move on, I think those boys want to use this machine,
Marie. Come, let's go along the beach for a while."

"All right." Marie was always agreeable. They went
out of the arcade into bright sunshine, and Yves followed them.

"You would like Uncle Zhar, I think," confided Ma-

rie as they walked along the dry golden sand; Charlotte
had imagined that he had been forgotten. "He is very
dark and tall and handsome." And she sighed. "I am
sorry he is my uncle, I would like to marry him when I
grow up."

"Never mind, I'm sure you'll meet someone equally
nice," Charlotte said, straight-faced.

"Perhaps. But he makes me laugh—oh, he is *funny*!
You'll see—he will make you laugh, too. And he is
strong! He can pick me up and throw me to the
ceiling...." Charlotte was only half listening to this eul-
ogy. Understandable for a child with few playmates—if
any at all—to idolize a relative. She let the girl ramble
on happily as they walked along the beach, Yves casually near, but not too near, so that whatever they said
was private. This Uncle Zhar—what a strange
name—sounded more of a playboy than anything else.
Marie seemed convinced that Charlotte would like him.
She herself was not so sure.

A small incident as they returned to the car served to
accentuate the differences in Marie's life from that of a
normal child. Two youths were playing with a ball on
the beach and one sent it flying toward Charlotte so that
she had to duck to avoid it. It landed at her feet and one
of the youths—about nineteen—dashed up laughing
and called, "Want a game?"

"No, thanks—" she began, and he grabbed her arm.

"Don't be snooty—" That was all he said, because
Yves was there, and knocked his arm away. The youth
looked at him sharply, about to say something, then saw
Yves's face. The chauffeur's eyes were very cold. The
youth pulled a face, muttered, "Keep your hair on,"
grabbed the ball, and swaggered away.

Charlotte felt suddenly angry. She said to Marie,
"Walk on, please, I want to talk to Yves." Then she
turned to him and said quietly in French, "You had no

need to do that. I can look after myself. He was only a
boy."

Yves looked at her. No expression showed on his
face. "I have my instructions," he said calmly.

"Yes, to look after Marie. Not me."

"You, too, *mademoiselle*." And he smiled slowly.
"You are with her, therefore I look after you, as well."

Marie was standing nearby, watching them. Charlotte
decided not to pursue the matter. She didn't want an argument in front of the girl, and it wasn't important anyway. It had been only a slight incident, better forgotten.

She shrugged. "Very well. But remember, I'm not a
child."

"I am well aware of that, *mademoiselle*." The look he
gave her said more than his words. Charlotte turned
away to go to the girl. Outwardly calm, inwardly she
was shaking. There was something about Yves that disturbed her, but she didn't know what it was.

A WEEK LATER they left Yorkshire and began the journey that was to take them to France. Charlotte turned
around and took a last look at the gracious old house
before it was hidden in the trees. Madame Grenier had
left earlier that morning, to catch a plane. She would be
at the vineyard before them.

Marie sat beside Charlotte in the back of the car.
Yves drove, and his manner was correct and formal.
Since the incident on the beach at Scarborough, Charlotte had seen little of him and had begun to think that
it had all been her imagination. She hoped so.

They were driving to London, stopping overnight
there, and going by car ferry the following day. There
would be one night in Paris—not in a hotel, but in the
family apartment near the Champs-Elysées—and then
they would go on to the vineyard the following morning. Charlotte sat back in her comfortable seat.

Everything was arranged, all planned to a nicety, working smoothly. Nothing like this had ever happened before. She had worked hard all her life for very little reward, save the satisfaction of helping her parents. And all that had ended so tragically a short while before. And now there was nothing. Nothing to show for those quiet busy years on a farm, save enough money to last a while. She looked out of the window. It was up to her to make this job a success. It was only temporary, perhaps for a few months, maybe a year, and when it was over she would return to England. But for that time she would have the opportunity to live a life with very wealthy people, to taste something completely different from anything she had ever known. It would all be experience. She looked at Marie, who sat quietly beside her. She would do her best for the girl, she knew that.

At first Marie chattered incessantly about everything, and Charlotte listened and answered the child's questions. They got on well, had done so from the beginning, but Charlotte couldn't help wondering if the situation might change when they were in France. One thing—she would soon know.

Then Marie dozed, and Yves spoke for the first time since getting in the car. He drove swiftly but very well, not aggressively, as so many drivers of large cars did, but with consideration for other road users. Although they passed everything within sight on the highway, Charlotte didn't feel the slightest bit uneasy. She was completely relaxed.

"You will please tell me when you wish to stop for lunch," he said.

"Yes, of course." Marie stirred slightly beside her and murmured something in her sleep.

"Good." After that there was silence again and Charlotte was left to her own thoughts. She wondered, as she had found herself doing frequently, what Uncle Zhar would be like. She imagined he would be in his thirties. Tall, short, fat or thin? From Marie had come the impression of a tall handsome prince of a man. Charlotte hid a smile. The reality might be completely different. A child's impression of a beloved relative could occasionally color a picture, and she knew that Marie's imagination was vivid, from other things she had said.

The girl woke soon afterward, stretched and yawned, and said, "I am hungry, Charlotte."

"You are? Then we'll stop." She told Yves and he nodded.

"Very well, miss."

She thought he would wait until they reached a highway restaurant, but he went off at the following turnoff, drove a few miles down a country lane, and stopped.

Charlotte looked blankly at him as he turned around. He gave a slight smile, as if sensing her faint alarm. "Madame Grenier has packed a picnic basket for our lunch," he told her. "It is in the trunk. Excuse me."

Silently, efficiently, he unpacked the basket beside the car. They were on a remote country road, and no cars passed. Distantly the highway throbbed with life, and from a nearby field several cows watched them with complete disdain.

He folded down trays from the back of the front seats, and produced plates. Charlotte thought, *I should have known*! There was chicken, and ham, salad and fruit, and two Thermos jugs of coffee; paper plates and napkins, and plastic cups that looked like china. After they had eaten the two girls went for a short walk, leaving Yves by the car. A distant farmhouse reminded Charlotte, with a pang, of her own home, and she turned away quickly. "Come on, Marie, we'll go back now," she said.

"Yves looks after us well, doesn't he?"

Charlotte smiled. "Indeed he does. Do you know where we are staying tonight?"

The girl shrugged. "With friends, I think. Yves has it all written down. *Grand-mère* is very careful. She gives him all the instructions, and he always does everything right."

"I'm sure he does." So they were staying with friends of Madame Grenier in London. Yves would find the place without any trouble, she felt quite sure of that. There was something rather intimidating about such efficiency. Charlotte wondered if the vineyard was run equally well. *And that*, she thought as they returned to the car, *is something else I shall soon find out*. And despite herself, a strange little prickle of excitement ran up her spine.

CHAPTER THREE

CHARLOTTE FOUGHT AGAINST THEM, but the thoughts and images of Jared were too powerful to resist, and she stood at the window of the luxurious apartment and let the pictures come. Marie was in bed, fast asleep; Yves was in the kitchen talking to the housekeeper and her husband; and Charlotte was in her bedroom. In the bathroom she shared with Marie a scented bath awaited her; she was clad only in her dark blue dressing gown, and in a minute she would slide into the pink foaming water and wash all the travel stains away. But now was a quiet moment, a precious few minutes of peace after many miles of travel, and Charlotte stood there in the shadowy room and looked down to the glittering lights of Paris, and remembered.

The traffic along the Champs-Elysées was a muted roar, a rich blur of yellow light, dazzling to the eyes. Paris hummed with life as it always did at night, and she wondered if Jared was out there in the crowd, sitting perhaps at a table in a restaurant, with some woman....

"Stop it!" she told herself. It didn't matter anymore. It was all over, had never really begun, and this return visit to Paris might be all she needed to cure her once and for all. Perhaps....

"Oh, Jared," she whispered, putting her forehead to the cool glass. Useless to try to forget the man who had changed her life so suddenly and wonderfully two years ago. She would never forget him. With a quick shrug she turned away from the window. A bath would do her good. Tomorrow they would reach the vineyard, and then there would be no time to think wistfully of a man who couldn't even say goodbye, who had run away....

BREAKFAST WAS EATEN with Marie sitting impishly crosslegged at the foot of her bed. Charlotte spread apricot jam over the meltingly flaky croissant and grinned at her young charge. "You want some?" she asked.

"Please," Marie nodded. "They are delicious. I have had four already."

"You'll get fat," Charlotte told her severely.

"Ah, not me," Marie shook her head. "Uncle Zhar tells me I will grow up as slender as a gazelle."

"Hmm, perhaps he's not seen you eating, like I have."

Marie laughed, full of amusement. "He has taken me for meals sometimes," she answered. "Just the two of us, and occasionally with friends of his. I like that."

"I suppose," Charlotte said, very casually, "Uncle Zhar will be there when we arrive at the vineyard today?"

Marie shrugged, too busily engaged in keeping apricot jam off her chin to notice anything in Charlotte's tone. "He is lovely, my uncle, but he is a strange one, too. He goes off sometimes. But I think," she added thoughtfully, "I *think* he may be there. I have a little present for him."

"Ah, then I'm sure he will be," Charlotte said, smiling. "Is it a secret, or can you tell me?"

"I will show you." The girl slid off the bed and ran across to her own adjoining bedroom. A tie? A book?

"There." A box was being opened carefully and Charlotte peeped in to see a pair of silver cuff links nestling on a bed of deep velvet. She smiled.

"Why, Marie, I'm sure he'll love those," she said, and saw the pink spread in the girl's cheeks.

"You think so? Good. It is so difficult to choose pres-

ents for a man," she added with grown-up wisdom.
"For ladies you can buy perfume and makeup and lots
of nice things, but for a man," she sighed, "it is very
hard."

"I know." Charlotte answered with a smile. She
looked at her watch. "It's nearly nine. I think we'd better get dressed and ready, don't you? Yves will be waiting for us."

"All right." Marie obediently took her box back. "I'll
put this away and have a wash—or do you wish to wash
first?"

"No, after you." Charlotte put her breakfast tray on
the table and slid under silk sheets again. She had not
slept well, and a few more minutes would be very
welcome....

"Charlotte, come, you have fallen to sleep." Marie
was tapping her arm and she jerked awake guiltily.

The girl was dressed, her hair brushed dark and
shiny, her dress clean and neat.

"Oh, Marie! Heavens—all right, I'll not be a minute."
She scrambled out of bed and flew into the bathroom.

PARIS WAS LEFT behind them, and the road they traveled now was long and straight and wide, lined with tall
trees. Marie wasn't tired, although they had been driving for four hours. She sat up, looking eagerly around at
the countryside surrounding them.

"Here is my home," she said proudly. "The most
beautiful country in the world—at least I think so," and
she looked swiftly at Charlotte sitting beside her, who
laughed.

"Of course, it is right that you should think so, Marie," she answered. "Just as I love England, and especially my own county, Yorkshire. And I'll tell you a little secret. I'm looking forward very much to seeing your
home, too."

"You will like it, I know." The girl nodded wisely. "And my dogs—and the cats. Oh, I have so much to show you."

Charlotte sat back and at that moment Yves spoke. "You wish to stop for a drink?" he asked. "There is a good café in a few kilometers."

Charlotte looked at Marie, who nodded. "Yes, please, Yves," she answered. It would be a good opportunity to freshen up, nearing the end of their journey.

They sipped ice-cold *sirops* in the garden of the café, just a few yards from the busy main road. Cars of all nationalities were parked at the front, and brightly-dressed tourists walked around the garden buying souvenirs from the packed stall behind where they sat. The sun shone down from a cloudless sky, and for no reason Charlotte thought suddenly of Jared, and it was like a pain. Where was he now? Because this was the country where she had met him, the only place she had known him, and yet he had been a wanderer, and he could be anywhere in the world. Anywhere....

"I'm sorry, Marie, what did you say?"

"That man looks like Uncle Zhar," and Marie pointed. Several men were buying gifts at the stall, but Charlotte saw immediately which one Marie had indicated. Of medium height, he was dark and pleasant-looking, and a little boy held his hand tightly. There were other men there, of course, but it was quite obvious that Marie meant the one Charlotte saw, for she could just imagine Uncle Zhar like that.

"Well, you'll soon see him again, won't you?" she said, and turned away, back to the table. There had been a tall dark figure to one side of the stall, and she would be imagining she was seeing Jared if she wasn't careful; she must stop *that* at once. The sooner she could put him completely out of her mind, the better.

They ate a light lunch at the café after all, because

there were several more hours' traveling to be done, and Yves had assured them that the proprietor was famous for his *omelettes aux fines herbes*. And rightly so. The meal was just enough to satisfy them without filling them, and they set off again refreshed and fed.

The heat grew more intense as they went south. It was so strong that at times the road ahead shimmered and danced in a kind of mirage. Villages were passed in a blur of gray stone buildings, and colorful dresses, and bright cars, and dogs that darted out as though asking to be run over, and pigeons that flew in front of them as they went more slowly through cobbled streets.

They bought some fruit at another roadside café. Sitting in the car after drinking iced lemonade, they peeled oranges and bit deep into luscious peaches. Yves was courteous and attentive, never a word out of place; Marie chattered to him in French, and Charlotte sat there and let it all wash over her. The memory of the man she had glimpsed at their previous stop came back to her, but she determinedly put the image out of her mind lest it disturb her too much. She was going to forget Jared. And the sooner she did so, the better.

Yves phoned to Madame Grenier before they left, to let her know when they would be arriving. So it would not be long now. A small excitement was building up inside Charlotte, and Marie had a rosy flush to her cheeks that told her own anticipation. Only Yves remained calm, which was just as well, Charlotte reflected, as he was driving.

The road was eaten up smoothly beneath the wheels and the golden day gradually turned to blue dusk. They passed through yet another village and Marie leaned and touched Charlotte's arm.

"We are almost home," she said. "We are nearly there."

Charlotte looked down at her and smiled. "And you are tired," she told her.

"Huh, a little, that is all."

The stars were out in a deep velvet sky, and the air was fresh and cold. Charlotte waited. There was a long high wall that seemed to go for miles at the side of the road, then Yves was slowing the car and she saw high wrought iron gates swinging slowly open as he turned to go through them. So this was it!

The driveway was long and straight and seemingly endless. Then they turned to the right again; the trees that had hidden the house from view were left behind them, and Charlotte saw her new home for the very first time. Only it wasn't a house. It was a castle, a magnificent high-towering white château. Nobody had told her that.

The car rolled to a stop and Yves came around to open the door for them. Both girls got out and Marie ran toward the steps to where a familiar figure waited. Charlotte remained where she was, stunned at the sheer beauty of the building that rose before her like something out of a fairy tale, ablaze with light from the tall elegant windows and wide doorway.

"Welcome to La Grande Baronnie," said Madame Grenier as she walked slowly down the steps. "It is perhaps a surprise to you, *mademoiselle*?"

"A great surprise, *madame*," agreed Charlotte, going forward to greet her and shake hands. "It is a beautiful castle. I didn't realize—"

"No? You will see it better by morning, of course. Come in. You have had a good journey?"

"Very good, thank you." They were going up the gray stone steps and into a wide hall that shimmered with light and color. Charlotte blinked, too dazzled to take it in yet, and very tired.

"Come, I have some supper prepared, and then I think it will be time for Marie to go to bed." Her grandmother ruffled the child's hair fondly.

"But Uncle Zhar—where is he?" Marie asked.

"Ah, *ma petite*, he will be here tomorrow. You will see him in the morning."

The girl's face fell; although she tried to hide it, she was clearly disappointed.

"He says he is sorry not to be here to greet you, but he had to go to Lyons on urgent business."

They sat down in a room that had a curved ceiling. The walls were completely white and covered with tapestries. In the window alcoves, also curved, were murals of brightly colored battle scenes. Everything about the room was rich, too much for Charlotte's tired eyes to take in—and yet there had been something strange the moment she had entered, something in the atmosphere of the place. It was almost as if she had been there before, as if she, too, had come home. It was a most odd sensation, and one that she put down to travel tiredness, but it returned to haunt her later as she lay at last in a soft, comfortable bed in her new bedroom.

The images were bright in her mind, and she lay on her back and let them all wash over her in a multicolored kaleidoscope that was almost disturbing in its vividness. And yet out of all the dazzling confusion there came again the sensation she had known when she had first entered the magnificent salon with its curving ceiling. She shivered, for the feeling was almost an eerie one. She had never been here before in her life—and yet there it had been, an instant atmosphere that had reached out to enfold her and touch her with a kind of warmth. It was as if she had known all her life that she was one day to come here. In the last few drowsy minutes before she fell into a deep sleep, the words of a poem came into her mind: "I have been here before, but when or how I cannot tell. . . ." She wondered if she would remember who had written those lines. And then she slept.

NOBODY CAME TO WAKE Charlotte in the morning. When she opened her eyes it was to find sunshine streaming in through the two high narrow windows, and a faint breeze stirring the deep gold curtains. She sat up slowly, stretching, and remembered where she was. A clock ticked busily away on the mantelpiece and it said, unbelievably, ten o'clock.

There was no sound. She might have been alone in the world, yet there was nothing worrying in that thought. Charlotte got out of bed and went into the adjoining bathroom, one that she was to share with Marie. She opened the door at the other side and saw the child still fast asleep in a four-poster bed similar to her own. She smiled and softly closed the communicating door. No doubt Madame Grenier had peeped in on her granddaughter and decided to let them both sleep off the effects of their long journey.

She washed and dressed in a simple white dress, one of four that she and Aunt Emily had chosen and bought after the interview in York. And that reminded her that she must write or phone as soon as possible to let her aunt know of their safe arrival. Charlotte brushed her short wavy hair, applied a dash of lipstick and, picking up her handbag, went quietly to her bedroom door and opened it.

There was a faint scent of lavender in the corridor outside. Her feet made no sound on the thick red carpet as she walked quickly downstairs. In the hall, sunlight streamed in through the windows and wide-open front door. Her employer appeared as if by magic from the doorway of the beautiful salon, and said:

"Good morning, Charlotte. I may call you Charlotte, I trust?" She acknowledged Charlotte's smiling nod with her own slightly more austere movement of the head. "*Bien!* And did you sleep well?"

"Very well, thank you, *madame*. I had a look at Marie, but she was still fast asleep."

"Ah yes, I am leaving her until she wakes up. Traveling is very tiring, is it not? Come, I will show you where you will breakfast, and afterward you must feel free to wander around and find your bearings."

Charlotte followed the older woman into another larger room across the hall. The magnificence of it took her breath away. With a high, wood-paneled ceiling, and crests and shields pictured in triangles at intervals, it was an imposing room, far grander than the one of the previous night—and yet without that other's warmth.

The long table shone with loving polishing, and french windows were flung wide open, at least six of them all down one side of the room, all with rich gold curtaining, all admitting the strong sunlight.

"This, as you can see, is the dining room." Madame Grenier allowed herself a little smile at the obvious wonder on Charlotte's face. "I see, too, that you appreciate beauty."

"The whole castle is quite beyond anything I imagined," Charlotte answered truthfully.

"I can understand that it might have that effect on anyone when they first arrive, yes," the older woman agreed. "But you must not let yourself be—what is the word—overawed by it. It is a home as well as a beautiful building. I want you to be happy here."

"Thank you." The table had two places set at the near end, and the older woman indicated that Charlotte should sit at one. She seated herself after pressing a bell by the fireplace. "I will have a coffee with you, I think. And then I will show you around the castle."

The maid who brought in the tray was clearly curious. A pretty dark-haired girl in her late teens, she gave Charlotte several sidelong glances and a quick shy smile as she set out the plate of flaky croissants in front of her.

"*Et café pour moi aussi*, Mado," said Madame Grenier as the girl turned to leave.

"*Très bien, madame,*" answered the girl with a quick bob in the old woman's direction.

Madame Grenier drank her coffee while Charlotte ate her breakfast, and told her briefly about the castle, its age, and some of the history of the family. At the close of the meal the old woman said, "My nephew may return home today. He will probably phone first."

That reminded Charlotte of her own intention, and she asked if she could phone very briefly to tell her aunt that all was well.

"Of course. I will take you to the telephone afterward. But I have already informed your aunt of your safe arrival last night when you and Marie went up to bed."

"That's very thoughtful of you, *madame.*" Charlotte hid her surprise as best she could, but Madame Grenier smiled.

"Do not be so startled, Charlotte. It was natural for her to be worried. *Eh bien,* I have reassured her. But I'm sure she will be even more pleased to hear your voice."

"I shall only make it a brief call. I'll write and tell her all about it this evening."

"And have you any other friends you must write to?"

Charlotte shook her head, cheeks faintly pink. "Not really. I never had time to make many while I was on the farm. I kept in touch with one or two school friends for a while, of course, but...." She shrugged.

The older woman's face softened slightly. "That is why I feel you will understand Marie better than most. Her life is of necessity rather lonely, but—" she raised her hand in a Gallic gesture of dismissal "—that is life, is it not?"

"I feel as if I do understand Marie, *madame,*" Charlotte answered quietly. "And I think we will get on well while I am here."

"I am quite sure you will. Well, if we are finished, shall we go?"

The château was large, as was obvious from the outside, and the rooms had all been decorated and furnished with great care so as to retain the flavor of the past that was so redolent. The old woman took her time, clearly deriving great pleasure from showing Charlotte around the beautiful building.

There was a library full not only of books, but with cases of exquisite china ornaments and statuettes, a grand piano in the corner, several musical instruments carefully placed, obviously very old, and one very new looking guitar hanging on the white plaster-washed wall over the fireplace. Charlotte looked from it to her employer, who smiled.

"Ah yes, my nephew's. Marie is also learning it. You must get her to play for you. She does very well."

"I would like that. And your nephew, Monsieur de Marais—does he play well?"

"I don't know," was the rather surprising answer. It was accompanied by a faint dismissive shrug. "My nephew entertains his friends, of course, but I generally find an excuse to go to bed early on those evenings." There was nothing in the words, but a small question was put unwillingly into Charlotte's mind. If there was tension, however slight, in the relationship between Madame Grenier and her nephew, it could make things difficult for Marie. And Charlotte might be able to help there, however slightly. She was already feeling protective toward her new charge. She was also wondering just what this mysterious nephew would be like. The mental picture of Uncle Zhar—a strange name—was clear but could be highly inaccurate. Yet every little thing she heard about him added to the portrait. Maybe he and his aunt were the best of friends. Maybe she was just jumping to conclusions. Maybe . . . .

She phoned Aunt Emily very briefly and promised to write that evening. Marie was up and dressed by this time, and they had a light lunch, after which both girls went to see around the estate. Marie was clearly looking forward to showing Charlotte her home—and her animals.

The vines stretched forever—or so it seemed to Charlotte's bemused eyes. Neat rows and rows and rows of rich dark grapes ripening in the blazing sunlight, and in the distance, faint blue hills. So beautiful, yet so completely unlike anything Charlotte had seen before.

Two Labradors appeared from nowhere and bounded up barking excitedly to greet them—Marie with love, Charlotte with slight reservations until Marie introduced her as a friend. They were huge golden dogs, well groomed and cared for, and they followed obediently as the two walked on away from the castle. Charlotte looked back and drew in her breath at the sheer beauty and majesty of it as she gazed at the white turrets, dazzling in the sun; the clock set in one tower; the long high windows, many open, others tightly shut. She had seen most of the castle that morning after breakfast, yet it was impossible to take in its sheer grandeur or atmosphere in such a brief look around. There would be other times, with Marie, to do so.

Behind the castle, to the right of it, were many long low outbuildings. Charlotte pointed to them and asked Marie what they were for.

"Oh, I will show you. Come." It was a relief to get out of the sun, for in the middle of the afternoon, and with not a single cloud in the sky to hide it for even a moment, the heat was intense.

It took her eyes several seconds to adjust to the gloom of that first shadowy building, and Charlotte hesitated by the door, blinking. Rows and rows of barrels stood silently like sentinels, seeming to stretch as endlessly as the vines themselves did outside.

Marie laughed and pulled Charlotte's arm. "Come, this is dull," she said, "come and see the horses."

The stables were farther along. High hedges blocked their view of the château; it was very English, approaching those familiar doors, open at the top, to see horses' heads looking out, curious to know who the visitors were.

"Why, Marie, you never mentioned horses," said Charlotte. "Do you ride?"

The girl pulled a face. "Only when Uncle Zhar is here—unless . . . ." She took a deep breath and her eyes widened. "Can you . . . do you . . . ?"

"Of course! Do you think your grandmother would let me take you out?"

Marie jumped up and hugged Charlotte before she could finish the sentence. Her eyes lit up with sheer happiness as she called out, "I will go and ask her *now*. Oh, Charlotte—" And then she was gone, running swiftly before Charlotte could stop her or tell her to wait. The dogs ran after her barking excitedly because something was happening, even if they didn't know what it was.

Charlotte turned back to the first velvet-eyed horse and put out her hand. "Hello, boy," she said.

She walked to the second door and spoke to a bright-eyed animal that shied away and snorted. The third door was wide open, both sections of it, and as she neared it a man came out and then turned toward her as if realizing suddenly that he was not alone.

A big man, dressed in jeans and denim top, and with espadrilles on his feet. Charlotte jerked to a standstill, her head going back in stunned disbelief. The memories of Jared were still painful, but she didn't think she was so bad that she was now going to start seeing him everywhere.

Her hand went to her mouth to hide the pain. And then he spoke, and his voice was flat, harsh, equally disbelieving.

"What are you doing here?" he said.

CHAPTER FOUR

FOR A MOMENT Charlotte didn't speak. She couldn't. She felt, terrifyingly, as if she were going to faint, but it passed and she found her voice.

"Jared," she said. "It is you."

He came nearer. His face was precisely as she remembered from so many painful dreams. Yet gone was the tenderness, the love with which he had once looked at her. Those tawny gold eyes were hard now, like a stranger's.

"Why are you here?" he repeated. "Who sent you?"

Swift flaring anger replaced her astonishment. She looked up at him, eyes lit with a quick rare temper. If he thought she had come chasing after him, he would soon discover just how mistaken he was.

"I work here," she said quickly, "No one *sent* me. And what are *you* doing here? Don't tell me you work here, too—" She caught her breath. It was like one of those dreams that suddenly turn into nightmares. That she should be talking to him like this was bad enough—almost unimaginable—but even worse was his own attitude as he stood there before her, tall, powerful, seemingly angry. Angry? Jared? She had never known him like this in those few blissful days in Paris.

And then he laughed. There was no real humor in it, none at all.

"Ah, come on," he said. "Don't give me that. You've—" He stopped because there was a scurry of flying footsteps, and Marie's excited shout:

"Uncle Zhar! *Grand-mère m'a dit—*"

Uncle Zhar. Zhar—Jared. Waves of horrified realization swept over Charlotte in that stunned instant of time. A girl's pet nickname for her uncle, and she had not even for a moment connected the two names.

Marie flung herself in Jared's arms, to be swept upward, and Charlotte heard him say in French, "So you're back are you, little one? And what have you been doing, hey?"

It gave her time to recover slightly. She fought desperately to hide the trembling shock she still felt. There would be time to think when she was alone. The important thing now was not to let him—not to let this hostile *stranger*—see just what effect he had had on her.

Marie turned, her face alight with happiness. "This is Charlotte," she said, speaking in English as if remembering. "She has come from England to look after me. Charlotte, this is my Uncle Zhar."

Charlotte nodded, smiled, but didn't offer her hand. "I'm pleased to meet you," she said. She met his eyes now. She could manage that. "Marie has told me a lot about you."

Something touched his face, a fleeting expression, then it was gone.

"I'm delighted to meet you—Charlotte," he said. "I trust Marie is showing you around?"

"Oh, yes," Marie answered before Charlotte could do so. "*Grand-mère* says I may go riding with her tomorrow—I forgot you would be home, though." She wrinkled her nose thoughtfully. "Perhaps we can all go together? Yes?" She looked up at her uncle anxiously.

Jared laughed. "We'll see." His eyes met Charlotte's. There was a warning in them, a warning to her not to say anything. She lifted her chin. She had no intention of doing so. Let him speak. She would hear what he had to say. For there was something seriously amiss here, and she wanted to know what it was.

But the time to discover what was not going to be now. Jared turned away toward the open stable door. "Come, Prince," he said. A magnificent bay stallion emerged, throwing his head back in anticipation, ready saddled.

"*Au revoir*, ladies," Jared said, with only a faint tinge of what could have been mockery in his voice.

"But, uncle—"

"Later, Marie. I will see you later." The big man mounted the horse, and the picture they made caused Charlotte's heart to quicken. Two truly magnificent looking animals—she had never pictured Jared riding, but he looked so right. He looked down on them, and the hostility she had seen was now veiled. Then he nodded, and they trotted away toward the driveway, and when the echoing hooves had vanished there was nothing.

Perhaps it had all been a bad dream, thought Charlotte. She still shook inwardly with shock, but Marie noticed nothing of this.

"My grandmother told me that Uncle Zhar had returned," she said excitedly, "when I went to ask her about riding. How nice that you should meet. I am so pleased. Do you not think he is lovely?"

"He seems very...pleasant." Charlotte hesitated only slightly, for how did you begin to tell anyone what had just happened, who he *really* was? You didn't.

"Yes. Come, we will return to the house. There are drinks waiting for us—it is such a hot afternoon. I am surprised Uncle Zhar should want to go out riding in this heat. But then—" she gave a graceful, almost womanly shrug "—men are funny, are they not?"

Funny isn't the word I'd use, thought Charlotte. *Not about him.* Her head began to ache and she wanted to be alone, just to think about the situation, but she was going to have to act as if everything were normal. She didn't realize how difficult that would be—nor how shrewd Madame Grenier was.

As they entered the long cool room in which Charlotte had received such a distinct impression of *déjà vu*—of having been there before—the previous night, the older woman looked up and frowned slightly.

"Why, Charlotte, you are quite pale," she said. "Come and sit down. Marie should not have kept you out so long in the heat."

Before Charlotte could answer, Marie spoke. "We met Uncle Zhar," she said, smiling. "He is going out riding."

"Ah yes, he returned after lunch." The old woman nodded, and her keen dark eyes were on Charlotte, who sat down gratefully on an elegant brocade-covered settee. Marie passed her a long cool drink and she sipped at the icy fruit syrup, wondering if there was anything in her face to give her away.

"So, you have met Jared—" she, too, pronounced it in a similar way to her granddaughter, more like Zhard "—at last. He insisted on going out on Prince straightaway." She smiled slightly. "I sometimes think he is more fond of horses than of humans." Then, as if regretting an indiscretion, "But that is life, is it not? Who knows, perhaps he is right?" But her eyes were suddenly darker—almost cold.

There was nothing Charlotte could say, and she had no desire to talk about the man who had come into her life so abruptly—so shockingly—again. "This drink is delicious, *madame*," she remarked. "And I enjoyed seeing around the vineyards. I didn't image they would be so enormous."

"Ah no?" She shrugged. "They have been in the family for generations. I was born here. I moved away when I married but returned on the death of my brother, Gilles, when the vineyard passed into the hands of my son, Paul, and Gilles's son, Jared."

"I see." Charlotte had no desire to hear family secrets, but it seemed that Madame Grenier was disposed to talk, and there seemed no harm in one small question anyway. "Then Marie and J—Monsieur de Marais are second cousins?"

"Yes. But as he is so much older she has always known him as uncle."

"Of course." Charlotte smiled. There was another question, but how dared she ask it? Perhaps Madame Grenier was a mind reader, for the next moment she said:

"Did you not find it strange that my nephew spoke such good English?"

"I...I...had wondered, yes." *But then, two years ago, I had thought him to be an American—certainly not a Frenchman*, Charlotte added silently.

"His mother is American. She took him all over the world when he was younger, instead of settling him to his heritage—" She stopped abruptly because Marie was listening intently. "*Tiens*, child, you have Mademoiselle Lucy here for lessons tomorrow. Go and prepare your books."

"But you said I could go out with Charlotte riding, *grand-mère*." Obediently the girl left the room, and Madame Grenier sighed. "Ah, you will get no peace now. I should have warned you, Charlotte. Marie is obsessed with horses, as well."

Charlotte laughed, partly with relief at the change of subject. "That's fine by me, *madame*," she answered. "I love horses, too. It was a surprise to see them here, and they are beautiful animals. It will be a pleasure to ride. Are we allowed to go anywhere?"

"Well—" the old lady frowned thoughtfully "—my nephew will be the best one to advise you on that subject. There is good riding country hereabouts, and one is perfectly safe. You will have a talk with him this evening."

It all came back to Charlotte in a sudden wash of panic—the memory of Jared's face when he had greeted her outside the stables. He not only didn't want to talk to her, she felt sure, he didn't want her there. But why? What reason could there be for the startling hostility? She possessed the quality of patience. She would wait. After all, she reflected, she had no choice anyway.

There was something she wanted to know, and as it seemed quite reasonable to ask, she said, "*Madame*, where shall I eat? With Marie?"

The old woman seemed mildly surprised. "Why, Marie eats with Jared and me. As you will, too." She hesitated. "There will be occasions, naturally, when we entertain guests—you understand—when Marie has her evening meal in the nursery adjoining her room. Then, of course...." She paused.

"Of course, *madame*," She tried to hide the dismay. To have to eat with *him*! Perhaps he would put a stop to it, she thought. For he was the man in charge, no doubt about that. She bit her lip. It would be humiliating, but in one way it would be a relief. For the thought of having to make polite conversation with him while she tried to eat was an impossible one. She would just wait and see.

BUT JARED WAS NOT THERE at dinner that evening. For the hour beforehand Charlotte wrote to Aunt Emily in her room, and it was difficult to make the letter light-hearted, hard not to blurt out the truth on paper. Instead she described the château, the extensive vineyards, the horses—and not a word of Jared. For how did you tell anyone what had happened? Her aunt had met him briefly on that Parisian holiday, and liked him. But he had never been mentioned since. And her aunt was so delighted that the position she had chosen, had

had a "feeling" about, had turned out so very right that Charlotte would not even have known how to begin.

She finished the letter with a sigh of relief. The next one would be easier to write, she felt sure as she sealed the envelope and addressed it. Putting it on the dresser in her bedroom, she picked up her handbag and went downstairs, filled with trepidation.

A deep gong sounded as she reached the hall, and she crossed to the large dining room to see Madame Grenier and Marie already seated waiting.

"Good. Sit down, Charlotte." There were only the three places set at the end of the long dining table. "My nephew has had to go out again, so we will begin." She nodded, presumably to some servant waiting by the door, for Charlotte heard quick footsteps moving away.

She made a mental note, as each course was served, to write to Aunt Emily with all details. She would appreciate that, with her interest in food and wine. And although it was delicious, right down to the fresh peaches that served in place of any other dessert, Charlotte had little appetite and had to force herself to eat.

Marie went to bed after the meal, and Charlotte and her employer went into what she now privately thought of as her room—the main lounge of the castle. Seated there, Madame Grenier said, "Now that your day is over, Charlotte, I will tell you that your evenings are free to do as you wish. There is, alas, not much entertainment for you outside the château. The nearby village is small, with only one cinema—a place I do not recommend. But we have television, and you are free to watch that. Also the library—take what books you wish to read. At weekends Yves will take you and Marie out in the car for rides, perhaps for picnics."

"Thank you, *madame*," Charlotte smiled, aware of the older woman's concern. "I'll be quite happy with books in the evenings. I'm not used to going out at night any-

way. And of course I'll enjoy watching television sometimes. Do you ever watch?"

"Ah, sometimes. I am an old woman. Bed at ten
o'clock for me, I'm afraid."

Charlotte nodded. "Not only you. I had to get up
early on the farm, so I'm usually in bed by then. If I
may take a book up tonight ...?" She hesitated.

"*Mais naturellement*! Go now if you wish. I will sit
here until you return. I find this room very restful."

Suddenly it seemed the most natural thing in the
world to tell the old woman about her own feelings on
first entering it. She didn't know why, but as she stood
up to go out to the library, Charlotte said, "I had the
strangest sensation when I came in here for the first
time. It was as if I had been here before ...." She stopped, biting her lip, wondering if her words sounded
foolish to the other's ears.

There was an odd expression on the old woman's
face. She nodded, her eyes dark as she looked up at
Charlotte. "Yes, yes. I was not mistaken—I saw something on your face when you came in. I was watching.
How strange, Charlotte, that you should feel that. How
very strange." There was something in her words that
made Charlotte stop, and the old woman went on:
"Like all old buildings—and this is very old, as I'm sure
you can imagine—there is an atmosphere that has come
down through the years. I don't mean ghosts, or anything like that, but a certain *esprit*—a spirit to the place.
And this room has always been a happy one for me."
She stopped and shook her head gently, sighing.

"It is where I first met my dear late husband." Charlotte could not be sure, but it seemed as if tears might
gleam in those dark eyes. She would not have interrupted the old woman for the world. "And where he
proposed to me. Yes, it holds many memories for
me—but how strange that you, too, should feel this
when you entered it. You must be very sensitive."

Charlotte smiled. "I don't know. I just felt I had to tell you, though."

"Yes, yes. I am pleased that you did. These things happen. Who knows why? We do not understand everything—and it is as well that we do not. Ah, well, away with you, child, to find your book. Then return to me here."

"Yes, *madame*." And Charlotte went quietly out to the library. The powerful lights in the chandeliers flooded the room with gold when she pressed the switch by the door. She stood for a moment to get her bearings before moving toward the first rows of books. The choice was overwhelming. There were books in both English and French. New ones, old ones, thick and thin ones; the shelves were crammed with richness enough for the greediest bookworm. She moved along the shelves, pausing, taking one out for a moment, constantly amazed at the variety of literature thereon. Charlotte had vaguely imagined that the library would be old-fashioned, the books heavy in both weight and content, but she was wrong. The whole series of James Bond thrillers sat next to another set, in English, on Hollywood movies through the years. There were books on vine growing, diseases in vineyards—these in French; the complete *Encyclopaedia Britannica*; short stories by Somerset Maugham next to those of Guy de Maupassant.

Charlotte took a deep breath and eventually picked a volume of poems and a detective novel by Margery Allingham. She switched off the lights before leaving the room, and went back to join her employer.

SHE TRIED TO READ, to shut out the disturbing thoughts of Jared, but it was in vain. Putting the novel to one side, she gave herself up to the memories of what had happened only hours previously, lying back on her pillow looking at a shaft of moonlight as it slanted across the ceiling. Cool gray yellow, the light was restful but she did not see it. She saw a man's face instead, a hostile, unwelcoming face. Jared. There had been, she knew now, the faint idea at the back of her mind that one day she would meet him again. Impossible to deny even to herself, but she could never have imagined such a setting for their meeting.

Charlotte closed her eyes. How much better it would have been had Aunt Emily not seen that advertisement in the paper. No—Charlotte frowned. Not true. For she had a genuine affection for Marie, and the desire to help this lonely child; and she knew the affection was returned. Together they would speak English, go riding, share the discoveries to be made in books, and Charlotte would justify her employment by Madame Grenier. She would learn to harden her heart against Jared so that it would not matter—*he* would not matter.

She turned her head restlessly on the pillow. It was easy to tell it to herself. Simple to decide, but maybe not so easily done. But there was one thing she was determined, which she had a right to know, and that was to hear why, from Jared himself, he was so hostile. And then she would try to put him out of the place he had so long unknowingly occupied in her heart. She suddenly felt very tired. With the making of the decision, the restlessness left her. Charlotte closed her eyes. A few minutes later she was asleep.

A noise woke her up hours later and she sat up wondering if at first it was Marie—then realized that the sound was a car door closing. She ran barefoot to the window and looked out. The moon had vanished behind a cloud, everything was dark and shadowy, but there was no mistaking the figure walking away from the long, sleek sports car standing outside. So Jared had come home.

Charlotte crept back to bed and picked up the clock from her little table. The luminous dial told her that it was four-thirty. She wondered where Jared had been. But there was no one to tell her. It took her longer to get to sleep that second time.

MARIE WAS OCCUPIED with her lessons, Madame Grenier had gone out with Yves in the Daimler, and Charlotte went into the library because she had nothing to do for an hour until Marie was finished. She imagined that Jared would still be in bed. Already she had begun the painful process of hardening her heart against him. She bent to a bottom shelf where she had seen some promising-looking books the previous night, and turned as there came a faint sound from the doorway, and Jared walked in.

Charlotte stood up slowly, her heart threatening to burst with the shock. She tried to keep her face calm, and she looked at him.

"Charlotte," he said, and came over to her. She waited silently. Let him speak.

"I thought I would find you here," he said.

"Did you? Why?" It was an effort to speak calmly, but she managed it because something told her it was important to do so.

He looked down at her. Impossible to tell what was in his eyes this morning. He looked tired, but then, she thought, he would be with only a few hours' sleep.

"It's the most interesting room in the house, that's why."

"Is it? I came because I like books, and Marie is having her lessons." Then she turned to face him fully. One hand on a library shelf kept her steady. "Why were you so rude to me yesterday?" There, it was said. She felt almost light-headed.

"Don't you *know?*" he said. He was like a stranger speaking.

"I wouldn't ask if I did," she answered, surprised at how much easier it became with each minute that passed.

He looked at her for a moment. How tall, how strong he looked—and yet how different from that carefree man of two years ago. Then he spoke, and the new hardness of his eyes was matched by his voice. "You're either a very good actress or a natural liar," he said. The words were like blows, and she flinched, unable to help herself, then fought for calm.

"Do you think I knew you were here?" she gasped. "How dare you speak to me like that!"

"I'll speak to you how I like," he answered swiftly. "This is my house."

"And I'm only an employee here—yes, I see." She couldn't hide the anger in her eyes now, they blazed with it. "If I had known you were the 'Uncle Zhar' Marie spoke about, I wouldn't have come, I promise you that. You made your feelings quite clear two years ago when you sent me those roses with a letter. Do you think I would have come chasing after you or something? My God, but you're conceited!" She turned away, nearly blinded by temper and tears, but managed to say as she moved, "I'll get out of *your* library."

He caught her arm as she passed him. "Just a moment," he said. She didn't want him to see the scalding tears. She had to get out. With a strong effort she knocked his hand away.

"Don't *touch* me," she said loudly. "You may be the boss here, and I a mere employee, but that doesn't mean you can touch me—ever!"

She swung past him, ran out of the room and swiftly up the stairs to the safety of her bedroom. With trembling hands she bolted the door and went over to the bed.

Sitting there, recovering from the shock of what had just happened, Charlotte tried to remember what had been said. It wasn't easy at first. She rubbed the place on her arm where his hand had tried to hold her. It burned like fire. What had he called her—either a good actress or a natural liar? So he imagined she had come chasing after him. It was like some nightmare that could only get worse, for whatever she said, he would not believe her. She put her hand to her cheeks, feeling the wetness where tears had been. She would have given anything for him not to have seen them.

It was nearly lunchtime, and before she went down to it she would wash and put some makeup on. It was important for her to look her best. At least she would feel more confident then, and how she needed it! She went to the washbasin by the window and rinsed her face and hands in cool water. Then she sat by the dressing table, and praying that she could remember exactly what Aunt Emily had done, she began to apply makeup very carefully. The concentration needed had the effect of soothing her somewhat. And as she worked, gently applying a touch of eye shadow and smoothing it in, she made an effort to see the situation from Jared's point of view. He had had a light holiday flirtation with a naive English girl—that was certainly all it had been for him, she knew that now, and the sooner she accepted the fact, the better it would be.

And then out of the blue, this same stupid English girl had appeared at his home—and denied all knowledge of him. Charlotte closed her eyes for a moment. Of course he didn't believe her. Looking at it logically, as she was now attempting to do, it was hardly to be wondered that his reaction had been the one it had. Yet how could she explain to him? She couldn't. All the talking in the world would not convince him that she hadn't somehow found out who he was, where he lived, and jumped at the chance of a job that would enable her to see him again.

Then she looked at her reflection in the mirror. That was it! Surely Madame Grenier would be able to sort it out in just a few words. The advertisement had been a box number, the interview in an anonymous hotel room where she couldn't possibly have . . . . And then Charlotte stopped, putting down the lipstick she had only just picked up. It was no good. The old woman would wonder at the reason for the explanations; and if she knew that her nephew and Charlotte had met previously, would she not herself begin to ask questions? Charlotte could not bear that. She might be asked to leave, and that was unthinkable now. Marie was learning to trust and accept her as a friend; she was the important one, not Jared. Charlotte picked up the lipstick again and, steadying her hand, began to apply it. Dreadful as the situation was, she had no choice but to accept it. It might even, she thought, be a good thing. Seeing the man as he really was, and not how her memory had colored him for two long years, would help her to get over him at last. It was almost as though he were two people: the happy-go-lucky wanderer she had known and fallen in love with, and this grim-faced man with his hard eyes and cruel accusations. Only when she reconciled the two would she be cured. And the sooner she managed to do that, the better for her. Her face looked back at her from the mirror. She saw a new calmness, almost an acceptance, in her eyes. She wasn't aware of the soft shining beauty of her features—only others could see that. Walking slowly, she went to the door and unlocked it, took a deep breath and went down to face Jared at lunch.

CHAPTER FIVE

IT WAS AS IF fate was determined to throw them together. How odd it was, Charlotte reflected after lunch, as she went outside to meet Jared and Marie at the stables. She had stayed behind because Madame Grenier had asked her to do so. It was to impress on Charlotte the fact that she was not to let Marie out of her sight when they were on their ride, and she had assured the older woman that she would be careful on that score.

Stepping out into the heat, she thought back over the lunch, when yet another side of the puzzle that was Jared had been shown. He had been the perfect host, treating her with a cool courtesy that could not have been faulted. And now he was going to choose a horse for her, and one for his niece, because his aunt had asked him to do so. How cleverly he had hidden the resentment he must have felt, for his tone, when he had answered Madame Grenier, had been quite pleasant.

She walked toward the stables and heard the voices of the two standing there talking, Jared and Marie. There was a third man—Yves. Charlotte had scarcely seen him since their arrival, although she had met most of the other staff, and some of the vineyard workers. Jared turned around at her approach.

"Yves is going with you today," he said. "Until you can find your way around."

"I see." Charlotte smiled at Yves. "Hello," she greeted him.

He bowed very slightly. "*Bonjour, mademoiselle.*" His eyes met and held hers for an instant, and Charlotte was aware that Jared noticed.

"Marie has her own horse, and you may ride Prince today." Jared's eyes were very cool as they glanced at Charlotte. "He is a good beast. You are experienced?"

She smiled. "I've ridden horses since I was five," she said. "I've lived on a farm all my life, Monsieur de Marais. I'm sure I'll be able to handle Prince." There was no flicker of reaction at her formal use of his name, but he turned away and opened the stable door without another word. Charlotte felt strange, as if she were an onlooker watching a scene being enacted in a play. Marie was too excited to notice anything, but Yves looked at Charlotte and gave a slight smile. Dark gypsy eyes held a certain awareness and she caught her breath. Better if he guessed nothing was amiss. She turned to Marie, who like herself had changed into slacks and shirt. The girl's cheeks glowed, and her eyes were alight with anticipation as she returned Charlotte's grin.

"I will take you somewhere very nice," she said.

"Good. I'm looking forward to this ride," Charlotte answered. Three horses were ready, beautiful, well-groomed animals with glossy coats and alert eyes. One, the smallest, clearly Marie's, whinnied softly and the girl went to him and patted his nose. "Patience, my little Pierre," she said. "Patience."

Jared lifted her up onto the horse's back. As he did so, Charlotte took Prince's bridle and, talking softly, led him to the mounting block outside the stable door. Even if he had the intention of helping her in the same way as he had his niece, she had no intention of letting him. She slid her right leg over and seated herself comfortably, and heard Jared's voice. "One moment. I will adjust the stirrups."

She waited, reins in hand, and he bent to alter the straps, and said, "Is that better?"

She tested them. "Yes, thank you, *monsieur*." Cool voice. It was becoming easier than she had expected.

She held tightly to the reins, wondering why she should have the sudden almost uncontrollable urge to strike the man. Something perhaps showed in her eyes as she looked down at him, for he glanced up sharply, his own eyes narrowing as he moved away.

Yves sat comfortably on his own mount, and Jared gave a nod. "All well?"

Marie waved to him. "Of course. *Au revoir*, Uncle Zhar."

"*Au revoir*, Marie. Be good." He returned her salute, and Charlotte looked straight ahead of her, keeping behind Yves the leader, not looking back at all as they set off down the magnificent driveway that led to the road. She began to relax once she knew Jared was out of sight. She would not spoil her pleasure by thinking about him. There was an hour's good riding ahead of them at least, it was months since she had been in the saddle, and this was a new, beautiful countryside for her to see.

Yves said something to Marie, and she answered. He nodded, then put his horse ahead again, leaving the two girls to ride side by side. "He asked where we wanted to go, and I told him," Marie said.

Charlotte laughed. "I see. And where is that?"

"It is a surprise."

"Oh. That's nice."

It really was too hot to talk, and the horses were content to move at a steady trot along the wide, flat driveway. It was the first time that Charlotte had been outside the estate since her arrival, which had been in the dark, so that was new to her. She looked at her surroundings with interested eyes as they went along the road, lined with tall leafy trees that provided some shade from the fierce sun.

Traffic passed, and in the distance she could see the village, but before they reached it they struck off across a field, careful to skirt the edges, for more vines grew there. Charlotte wondered if this, too, was de Marais property, but did not ask. It did not seem important. Nothing did, save the pleasure of riding a beautiful horse that responded to her every touch, an animal with whom she felt instinctively akin. Then they were climbing, quite gradually, and distant mountains beckoned, cool and unapproachable.

"I have a flask of wine," said Yves, "if anyone is thirsty." She should have known! *If I have any more*, she thought, *I'll fall asleep.* One glass with lunch had been sufficient, and she had only drunk that to steady her nerves in the silent battle with her employer's nephew.

"Not for me, thanks. Not yet, anyway," she added. It was cooler in the wood they now entered, and thin shafts of sunlight were all that pierced the green shade. Perhaps this was Marie's destination. She waited for the girl to call a halt, but she didn't. They left the wood behind, and she looked back, downward, and caught her breath at the dizzying splendor of the view. The castle dominated the landscape, a white pearl amid the rich green of vines and trees. Distant figures moved, as small as ants, and doubtless as busy. And the air shimmered with heat. It was so achingly beautiful that it brought a lump to Charlotte's throat.

The earth was dry underfoot, the horses slowed their pace, and Marie said, "We are nearly there. Soon—over this hill—you will see why we have come."

Charlotte waited. It could hardly be more interesting than that which they had left behind. The animals picked their way delicately over rock-strewn ground, and no one spoke, so that the only sound was of hoofs on stone.

They reached the summit of the hill, and there before them was a village, cobblestoned everywhere, with houses and shops, and a fountain in the center of the one street. Trees were shivering their leaves faintly in a slight breeze. They both looked at Charlotte, and she knew why they were watching her, quite suddenly, as she realized what was wrong.

The fountain was silent; no water filled its basin. Nothing moved, save the trees; no person walked that cobbled street, no pigeons flew above it. The town was deserted.

"It's . . . empty," she said at last when she had found her voice.

"It's my ghost village," said Marie. "No one lives here anymore. Is it not a strange place?"

"Very strange," agreed Charlotte, and dismounted, followed by Yves, who helped Marie from her horse. He tethered the animals in the shade and returned to them, smiling at Charlotte.

"We'll show Charlotte around," Marie said to him in French. It was an odd sensation to peep in at open front doors, to see the occasional chair, or bed, threadbare pieces of carpet—and not a soul, not even an animal. An open shutter creaked slightly, and Marie jumped, then laughed.

"I thought it was a ghost!" she exclaimed.

"Why is the village deserted?" Charlotte asked.

"It has been empty for ages. All the wells dried up one year, and the vines died, and people moved away. Those that stayed had to rely on a water cart to bring them fresh water once a week," Yves answered, speaking in French. He shrugged. "Soon there were only a few old people left, and gradually, as time passed, they too died, until one day there was just one old woman, Madame le Brun. Her son came and took her away to live with him, and so the village died."

"But it's like something out of a weird film," said Charlotte. "I'm seeing it, but I can't believe it."

"It happens," he said. "That is life. There is nothing here now."

They sat in the shade of a huge oak tree and he produced the flask of wine from his hip pocket and unscrewed the metal cap, which also served as cup.

Both girls drank enough to quench their thirst and he finished the flask off and put it back. Whether it was the wine or the heat, Charlotte didn't know, but she experienced a feeling almost of light-headedness. She looked around at the deserted village street, and the cracked fountain, its basin now full of dead leaves, and sensed the uncanny stillness of the air, as if time itself stood still here. Then it was time to leave and they stood up, brushing the dust from their clothes, and walked slowly back to where the horses were tethered. Something gleamed in a gutter and Charlotte bent to pick it up. A metal button with an anchor on it, perhaps from a boy's sailor suit or a woman's dress. Maybe it had lain there for years. She put the button in her trouser pocket, not knowing why, except that in some way she wanted a souvenir of their visit to a silent, ghost village.

It grew warmer as they went down the hill again. The light-headedness had passed, yet there still clung to her a sense of unreality. Almost a feeling that if she were to rush back, the place would have vanished. She chided herself. What an absurd thought! But it was almost a relief to see again the château, and the vines stretching away into the distance, and nearer, cars whizzing along the main road. Here was the real world—and Jared.

Charlotte took a deep breath. She had managed to forget him for a while. Perhaps he would have gone out. She hoped so.

YVES SAID SOMETHING to make her laugh just as they were rounding the outbuildings toward the stables. Marie was well ahead and could not hear, but his remark was a trivial one, only mildly amusing—in fact she forgot it immediately. Some comment about the effect of too much sun and wine, and she threw back her head and laughed, as a relief from a certain tension. Jared was there, watching them, and he saw.

He went over to Marie, who put out her arms to be lifted down. "You enjoyed your ride, little one?" he asked her. And although he smiled at his niece there was a hardness about his face—and instinctively Charlotte knew that he had been displeased at her laughter. A stab of satisfaction touched her. Good. She must laugh more often with Yves. Though why Jared should have such a reaction she did not know. She dismounted, as did Yves himself, who said:

"Shall I attend to the horses, *monsieur?*"

"No, Yves, you may go. My aunt wants you."

"*Merci, monsieur.*" He turned to Charlotte and Marie. "*A votre service, mesdemoiselles.*" He saluted and turned away again to go toward the château. So that was the reason Jared had been waiting for them, thought Charlotte—because his aunt wanted Yves. Or was it?

She began to lead Prince into his stable, and Jared asked, "Where are you going?"

"Why, to rub Prince down," she answered.

"Perhaps you didn't hear me tell Yves that I would attend to them—" he began.

But Marie interrupted him, "Oh, no, Uncle Zhar, let us help, please. We would like that, wouldn't we, Charlotte?" Charlotte waited and looked at Jared—and smiled slightly. Not easy, but she did it because for some odd reason, just at that moment, she felt supremely confident. It was a pleasant sensation, after the doubts and uncertainties of the past couple of days, and she intended to make the most of it.

"As you wish. Come, let us get these animals out of the heat first," and he led Yves's mount into the stable, followed by the girls. It was light and airy and clean inside, with a faint scent of hay, and Charlotte looked around her in approval. A comment of Madame Grenier's, that Jared cared more for animals than humans, might well be true, she thought. Perhaps *that* was why he had been so hostile to her. She repressed a giggle at the thought. So engrossed was she in unsaddling Prince that she was hardly aware of Jared addressing her until he repeated the question. "How did you find Prince?"

"He's a beautiful animal," she told him with truth. "I enjoyed riding him very much."

"We went to the old village," Marie said, "and Charlotte was very surprised."

"Ah yes?" her uncle replied. "But you must never go there alone, you know that."

"I can go with Charlotte," she answered. "*Grand-mère* says I can."

"I prefer you not to." There was a flat certainty about his tone, and Marie looked sharply at him.

"Why not?" It was the first time that Charlotte had heard her question anything an adult told her. *Good for you*, she thought.

"Because, I say so, that is why."

"Oh! You are not fair!" And Marie rushed out of the stable. Charlotte busied herself rubbing down Prince, her face straight. If he expected her to comment on the little scene, he was going to be disappointed.

He waited until Marie's running footsteps had died away, then looked across at Charlotte. Immediately tension filled the air, now that they were alone, and she knew that he was aware of it, too.

"Well?" he said.

She paused in her task and met that hard gaze. "Well what?"

"Have you nothing to say?"

"No. I haven't. It's no business of mine how you deal with your niece. Don't worry, *Monsieur de Marais*—" she accented the words heavily "—I don't take sides."

"Good. But I had a reason for being so bossy—as I'm sure you must think I was."

"Did you? And do you expect me to ask what it was? I'm not going to."

"I'll tell you anyway. There are occasionally tramps and Gypsies who go to the village to camp. Do I need to explain further?"

She hesitated. "We saw nobody this afternoon."

"Perhaps not. You were with Yves anyway. He's well able to take care of you."

"You talk as if we wouldn't be safe."

"No. And so, I'm telling *you* now, you don't go to the village with Marie again, unless Yves or I am with you."

She raised her eyebrows in astonishment. "*You*?"

"I often go out riding with Marie, why are you so surprised?"

"Forgive me," she laughed. "Did I look surprised? But then it's hardly to be wondered at. I mean, I don't imagine you'd want *me* with you when you take Marie out—or not after your enthusiastic reception the other day." She was being reckless and stupid, she knew that, but she couldn't hold the words back.

She saw quick anger—as quickly controlled as he said, "As you are employed to be companion to Marie—that *is* your job, isn't it? I would naturally expect you to accompany us, and so would my aunt."

"Yes, of course," she agreed with a nod. "That is what Madame Grenier would expect."

She turned away, because there was a tightness about his face and she was almost frightened. She didn't want to see it. The fragile bubble of her newfound self-confidence was ready to burst. He must not know.

There were dragging footsteps outside, a pause, then Marie entered. Her eyes went straight to Jared, who looked sharply at her but said nothing.

"I . . . I'm sorry Uncle Zhar," she said. Charlotte felt a

rush of protectiveness to the little girl. If he spoke harshly to her now, she would have to walk out, she knew. Or she would say something she would surely regret.

Then he smiled. She was watching him as he did so, and her heart gave a quick painful flip. Just like those other smiles, when . . . .

"That's all right, Marie." He rumpled her hair and the child flung her arms around him. "There were reasons little one, as I told Charlotte. Sometimes strangers go there to stay for a few days. It is not safe for women alone."

"Then you will take us, perhaps?"

"I'll see. Don't try to bully me."

"Pooh! As if I could—as if anyone could bully you."

"You do your best. Now, attend to Pierre, and then we will go in for a drink of something."

"Yes, uncle." The child obediently bent to her task, and they worked in silence until the horses were comfortable.

It was strange going into her favorite room with him, seeing him sit at ease on the long settee, while Marie sat beside him. Charlotte hesitated by the door, wondering if she should leave, and he said, "Please sit down, Charlotte."

She did so on a settee opposite theirs. He was watching her and she began to feel uncomfortable. Was he doing it deliberately?

"Tell me, Marie," he said, "how did your lessons go today?"

She pulled a face. "All right. I would rather have Charlotte teach me, though," and she looked impishly across at Charlotte, who smiled.

"I'm not a teacher, Marie," she said gently. "Although if you do your lessons as well as you speak English, you have nothing to worry about."

"I think Marie is rather lazy," said Jared, but he grinned at his niece as he spoke. "She needs a firm hand." Then he looked directly at Charlotte, and there was a challenge in his eyes. It was as if he were daring her to speak up. She had no intention of rising to the bait. So she smiled, and said nothing. Let him do all the talking. How different he was from that gentle stranger she had known so long ago, how very different. She would soon be cured of the hopeless love that had filled her for two years if he carried on as he was doing. And then she might thank him. Perhaps an anonymous gift of ten red roses—the thought was almost appealing. Something must have shown in her eyes, for she saw a muscle tighten in his cheek, an almost imperceptible sign of stress.

"Would you be able to be firm with her?" he asked pleasantly.

"I think so. Marie and I understand one another, don't we?" she asked the child.

"Oh yes. We both love animals—and books." Marie turned to Jared as she said it.

"Ah, I see! And that is important. Go and tell Mado to bring us something to drink. Milk for you, I think. Charlotte? Coffee—or do you prefer something cool?"

"Coffee would be perfect, thank you," she answered.

"Coffee for two, and milk for you. Away you go."

The moment that Marie left the room, Charlotte went to the window and looked out. She couldn't sit still opposite him for a second longer. The vines stretched endlessly away, and nearby an old man in blue vest and denims was busily spraying a plant, pipe firmly planted in his mouth, engrossed in his task.

"Tell me," he said, "do you have an evening dress with you?" The question was so completely unexpected that she turned quickly.

"What?"

"I said do you have a long dress with you?"

"Why?" She didn't care if she sounded rude. What business was it of his?

"Because this evening I am having a few friends for dinner."

"I see. Then Marie and I will be eating in the nursery, I take it."

"No. You will come down for it."

"But Madame Grenier told me that when there were guests, Marie and I would eat alone."

"Not tonight. We will all dine together."

There was a moment's pause, then Charlotte said softly, "I'm afraid not. I haven't brought anything with me. I don't even possess a long dress."

She could smile now with relief. The very thought of eating with him and his friends could not be borne.

He looked at his watch. "There's time. We'll go and buy one." Panic filled her in a blind rush. She moved toward him. He was doing this for some obscure reason of his own, and she was alarmed.

"No," she said, "I can't. I don't know anything about prices here, and I have only a little money until my first week is—"

He shrugged and stood up. "Yes. That's no problem. We'll go after our drink. Marie will come with us and help you choose one."

She looked at him, then, helplessly, feeling small and powerless in the face of his utter hardness, "Why?" she asked. "Why?"

"Because I've invited you, that's why."

"No." She shook her head. "You have some reason . . . but I don't see—" and Marie came in, followed by the young maid, Mado, carrying a silver tray with coffee pot and cups and saucers.

"Good, then that's decided," Jared said very pleasantly. "Drink up, Marie. We're all going out to Mâcon; Charlotte is going to buy a dress for herself, and you will help her choose it. How do you like that idea, hey?"

The girl's eyes lit up. "Oh yes! And do I get a little—" she stopped and bit her lip, still mischievous, waiting.

He laughed. "A present? Hmm, we'll see. It all depends on how well you behave."

The coffee was scalding hot and went down like fire. He lit a cigarette and sat back and sipped his coffee. Why, oh, why? The question hammered in Charlotte's brain, but he was not going to tell her. She concentrated on her drink, looking at the pattern in the exquisite china saucer, counting the tiny gold roses that covered the brim.

"Drink up. We haven't much time," he said, and she looked up.

"I'll go and wash first." If she took long enough, the shops would be shut. He could hardly come and drag her out of her room. She went out, more confident now, ran upstairs and into her bedroom. Safely there, she took off slacks and shirt and washed quickly, immediately feeling cooler and better. She found a simple blue dress in the wardrobe and put it on. Then, very deliberately, she went and lay down on the bed. It was just a matter of waiting....

There was a sharp rap on the door. She waited a second, then called: "Marie?"

"No. Are you ready?" Jared's voice.

"No, I'm not." She sat up and hugged her knees. Let him wait.

"How long wlll you be?"

"Hours and hours," she said, too softly for him to hear. She heard the handle turn and stood up quickly, nervously. He wouldn't come in, would he? She wouldn't put anything past him.

"Wait a moment," she said, and crossed to open the door.

"So you are ready." He looked down at her.

"Yes."

"Then come on. Time is short. Do you think I'm stupid?"

"Do you want an answer?" She turned her back on him and picked up her bag from a chair, and he stood by the door waiting. She looked up at him then. "All right," she said, "Monsieur de Marais, I'm ready."

The car was by the front door, and Marie was sitting in the back. It was a long, sleek sports car—the one she had seen him get out of in the early hours of that morning. Dark rich blue, it looked capable of great speed, a powerful monster. *Just like it's owner*, she thought as she slid in.

He went at a sedate speed down the driveway, along the road, through the village, and then with a quiet roar opened out. Nothing passed them. Trees and houses blurred dizzily past, and Marie from the back called: "Lovely, lovely! Faster, Uncle Zhar!"

"This is fast enough for you," he called. Then to Charlotte: "Is it fast enough for you?"

"Not as long as you know what you're doing," she answered, determined not to show any fear.

"Oh, I know what I'm doing all right." There was something more to the words than their simple meaning, she knew, and her lips tightened. Soon she would hate him. Soon, if he carried on the way he was. Perhaps that was his object.

Then, all too soon, they were on the outskirts of a large town, and he slowed, and turned down quieter streets, then stopped. They were outside a shop with just a few dresses in the window. Charlotte was no expert on clothes, but she needed no one to tell her that these were expensive. She looked at him in faint alarm.

"Not here," she said. "I can't possibly—.'

"Yes, here." He was out, coming around to her side, opening the door, and it was no use her sitting there because Marie was already clambering over from the back, pushing her, saying:

"Come on, Charlotte. Oh, isn't this *lovely?*"

Feeling as if she were about to go to her execution, Charlotte stepped out onto the baking hot pavement and looked into the shop. She was terrified. And Jared gave her a cool glance and said quietly, "In we go, then."

CHAPTER SIX

OH, CHARLOTTE, you look absolutely *beautiful*! Truly. Come and show Uncle Zhar."

Marie tugged her arm, and Charlotte said, "Wait a moment. I just want to see." It was odd how quickly her nervousness had left her after they had entered the shop. It might have been something to do with the obvious delight with which Jared was greeted by the proprietress, a tall statuesque woman dressed in black. Or it might have been his own manner, which changed completely once they were inside. Gone the veiled barbs; he behaved in a way that despite herself made her feel less tense. Subtly in charge in an instant, he had spoken quietly to the woman, telling her that Charlotte needed something simple, that everything that could be in any way suitable was to be brought out for inspection.

The woman ushered Charlotte into a large changing room and measured her swiftly and efficiently. There was nothing intimidating in her manner. Clearly Monsieur de Marais was an honored client, and anyone who came in with him got five-star treatment, Charlotte reflected as dress after dress was brought out for her to see, carried by one of the three young assistants, all, it seemed, only too anxious to please.

And then she saw a dress, and pointed to it. "May I try that one on, *madame*?"

"But naturally. And this as well, *mademoiselle*?" pointing to a deep blue velvet that Charlotte had lingered over, and which had been put to one side. Marie watched wide-eyed as Charlotte tried on first the blue velvet, and then the one she had just seen.

Now she stood in front of the mirror in the changing room and looked at herself, and Marie was urging her to show Jared. It was simple, a long flowing skirt in deepest black, thin belt at the waist and a spectacular blouse top in dazzling white guipure lace. The lace was softly ruffled at the neck, the sleeves were wide and full, tapering at the wrists to button neatly and demurely. Charlotte didn't need anyone to tell her that she looked good in it, for she *felt* good. But it might be very dear. She had a feeling that it would be expensive.

She allowed herself to be dragged out by Marie, followed by the owner, clasping her hands and exlaiming that never had she seen such a perfect fit.

Jared stood up and looked at them. Then slowly his his eyes surveyed Charlotte from top to toe. He nodded.

"Very nice, *madame*."

"There is a blue velvet—" the woman began, and Charlotte cut in:

"Yes, if you would prefer me to get that...."

"Will you try that on again and show me?"

She turned and went back into the changing room, followed by Marie. She heard their voices as she drew the curtains. Good. They would be discussing prices. If he thought them both all right, he would naturally pick the less costly. She would have to pay back monthly, out of her salary, for she intended sending Aunt Emily as much as she could spare. Feverishly changing as she thought, passing the first one to Marie, she slipped on the dark blue velvet again. It was sleeveless, with thin satin straps supporting the straight bodice that swept out in spectacular fashion into a long skirt. She liked it as much as the first.

"Oh, Charlotte, you look beautiful in *that* one, too," Marie sighed. "Is it not difficult to choose?"

"Yes—" Charlotte smiled "—it is."

She walked into the shop again and Jared turned

slowly and gave her a long keen look. "Which do you like best?" he said.

Charlotte shook her head, soft hair tumbling around her cheeks. "I like them both," she said. "Either will do. Whichever you—"

He nodded to the woman, who smiled. "You can get changed now," he told Charlotte. "Then we'll go for shoes."

"Oh, no," she protested. "I've got some quite decent ones." The proprietress had vanished toward the back of the shop, and they were alone, for Marie had drifted back to the changing room.

"I insist," he said calmly. "Go and change, please."

Without answering, she went. There was no point in arguing with him, she knew. There was a certain look on his face and it brooked no disagreement.

She didn't even know which dress he had bought, because it was packed into a huge box in the changing room after she had dressed and gone into the shop again to wait with Marie. She wasn't sure if she cared.

He threw the box on the back seat and locked the door again. "Come on, we'll walk to the shoe shop," he said. "It's only around the corner."

Marie skipped along, holding his hand, and when they passed a sweet shop he told her to wait and went in, leaving both girls outside. He came out with a big heart-shaped box, which he handed to his niece.

"Your present, you little minx," he said. "And no eating before meals."

"Oh, thank you, Uncle Zhar, you are a *darling*!"

"Mmm, you women are all the same. Come on."

Charlotte was beginning to feel confused. If anyone had once told her she would soon be hurrying through the streets of a French town with a man who was extremely hostile to her, but who had just insisted on buying her a dress for a dinner and was now taking her to a shoe shop, she would have said they were mad. But it was happening. In a way it was almost as dreamlike as the village earlier on. Perhaps she *was* dreaming, she thought.

The slippers he chose were real enough. Fragile sandals, a bare couple of strips of silver attached to the sole, they fitted her perfectly, and she nodded.

"Yes, please, I'd like these."

"And the bag to match," he told the shop assistant.

"But—" Charlotte protested feebly, and looked at Marie clutching her box of candy. What was the use? Marie laughed.

"It's no good talking to Uncle Zhar," she said. "He doesn't listen."

A minute later they were on their way back to the car.

SHE OPENED THE BOX when she was in her room. She was not alone. Marie had come up with her. Tissue paper hid the dress.

"I wonder which one it is?" said Charlotte, and smiled at Marie. "Guess."

Marie looked at her in surprise. "Don't you *know*?" she said. "They are both in there."

"What?" Charlotte gasped and tore the tissue paper to one side with trembling fingers. "Oh, no!" She sat down on the bed in dismay. "Oh, *no*!"

"What is the matter?" Marie's face held genuine puzzlement.

"I can't afford—" Her lip trembled momentarily, and she put her hand to her mouth to hide it.

"Oh, poor Charlotte. It is all right. Uncle Zhar has treated you."

"Oh, no, he hasn't!" She stood up. "Where is he, Marie?"

"In his room. But why—"

"Stay there. I'm just going to have a word with him." She was frightened that if she hesitated, the resolution would be lost.

She knew his room, for Madame Grenier had indicated it on her visit around the château. She knocked on his door and waited, a cold anger growing inside her.

"*Entrez.*" Perhaps he expected one of the servants. She didn't care. He was shaving at a washbasin, naked to the waist, his torso brown and muscular.

She faltered, then as he looked across at her said, "Why did you get both dresses?"

"Because they both suited you, why else?" His tone was casual, almost amused.

"I can't afford *two*. I don't even know how much one cost; I think you did it on purpose. . . . " He was striding toward her, wiping lather from his face with a towel. He passed her and slammed the door shut.

"You're not paying for them," he said. "I am."

"Oh, no, you're not." she breathed. "I won't take anything from you."

"Then they cost one franc each, how does that suit you?"

She fought for calm. "Don't . . . don't be ridiculous. I know they were very expensive. I'm not a fool."

"Then consider them as part of a uniform if you like. It's important to keep up appearances, and as I require your presence—to accompany Marie—at certain dinners, it's only fair that you're suitably dressed for the occasion." He rinsed his face at the bowl and dried it. "All right? Is that all? I want to get changed."

"If I'd known, I would have refused to come with you," she said.

"Would you? Yes, I think you would. How refreshing to meet someone who's not out for all she can get. Quite a change. Now, I shall have to ask you to leave, I'm afraid, much as I'm enjoying this conversation—" he wasn't even trying to veil the sarcasm "—as I need to change, and I'm sure you don't want to stay." And he touched her arm very lightly as though to usher her to the door.

Charlotte stood her ground. "You're contemptible!" she breathed. "You're behaving like some lord of the manor who thinks—"

"Why, yes, that's *exactly* what I am." His eyes glinted hard amber at her, and his face was lean and cruel as he stood there before her. "Didn't you know? My word is law around here. How do you like that?"

"I loathe you," she whispered.

"Well, that will do for a start," he shot back, and took her arm. Without thinking Charlotte instinctively lashed out at him. She caught him a stinging blow on his face.

"Don't ever touch me again," she said trembling. "I told you once before, I don't care *who* you are, you'll keep your hands off me!"

He put his hand to his cheek. "And if you ever do that again," he said softly, "you'll regret it." He took his hand away.

"Oh, will I?" she said. Her hand trembled with the urge to strike him, but the anger was deep in his eyes, smoldering dark anger that could erupt at any second.

"Yes, you will." He stood there very still, waiting for her to move. Unbearable tension filled the room, vibrating around them with almost the quality of sound. As if in a dream, Charlotte turned away, her limbs heavy, like one of those nightmares where you try to run and can't, and something awful, some nameless horror is after you. A sob escaped her throat and she put her hand up to shield her face as if from a blow, and heard him say, "Charlotte...."

Then his hand was on her shoulder pulling her back, and she gasped because she thought he was going to strike her, and he was too strong, she couldn't fight him....

"Charlotte," he said again. She cried out, "Oh, no, no, stop it!" She pushed at his hand on her shoulder, trying to escape, breathless, helpless, in desperate fear.

"I'm not going to—" he began, but her fear rose in her throat, choking her, and she thought she was going to fall.

"Let me go," she said. "You're too strong for me to fight—I can't—" The room spun around and he caught her and held her.

"I'm not going to hit you," he said. "My God, did you think I—"

He was holding her now, and she struggled vainly to escape, like a moth caught in a light's beam, hypnotized, weak. "Yes, I did," she managed to get out. "Why don't you now? You said . . . no one would dare . . . ." Fear gave her the strength to free her hand, to push his chest, and he released her quite suddenly, eyes darker now, mouth a grim line.

"Then go," he said, "go now. You're free. What are you waiting for?"

Wide-eyed, she stared at him for several seconds, then turned and ran to the door. A moment later she was in the corridor, and she shut the door behind her and walked back to her own room on very unsteady legs.

Marie jumped up as she went in. "What's the matter, Charlotte?" she asked.

"Nothing," she answered, shaking her head. "I have a headache, that's all. I'll be better after a wash."

"I will go and get something for you. Do not worry. Lie down on the bed."

"Marie," Charlotte said weakly. "I'm supposed to be looking after you, not you after me—"

"Hush! I will be soon back." Marie swept the box of dresses onto the floor and pointed. "Lie down, please."

Charlotte obeyed. Her head throbbed painfully. She

wished desperately that she could stay there and not go down for dinner, but that was impossible. In a way, Jared was right in what he said. She felt as if she had not the strength to resist him. The thought of trying to defy him by remaining in her room when the gong went was frightening. He would simply come up and make her go down, because for reasons of his own he wanted her to be at that dinner.

She felt very lost and alone, quite suddenly. She was on her own in a foreign land with no one to turn to for help. No one. Marie was perhaps the most understanding person, but she was a child, and more, she loved her uncle, that was obvious. *And so did I*, thought Charlotte softly, *but not anymore. Not anymore.* She closed her eyes and waited for Marie to return.

SHE WAS READY when she heard the gong. Ready, waiting, and nervous. She had seen two cars arrive, and there could have been more, for it was not possible to see along the front of the château, and some of the engines were as soft and purring as cats. She looked at herself for the last time in the mirror. The blue velvet dress looked better than it had in the shop. Silver sandals peeped out, and she held the bag to her side.

"Charlotte, may I come in?" came Marie's excited voice from outside the room.

"Of course." She would feel better going down with her. "Come in."

Marie was dressed in a long floral-sprigged dress, and looked very pretty. "Why, you look lovely," Charlotte told her with a smile.

"*Merci, mademoiselle.*" Marie dropped a curtsy. "And you look *ravissante!*"

"Thank you." She looked around, then remembered something. The bottle of perfume that Aunt Emily had bought was on the dressing table. She went and sprayed some on. "There, I'm ready."

"Mmm," Marie sniffed. "That's *nice*."

"Good. Let's go."

Voices came from the dining room, and Charlotte clutched Marie's hand as they went downstairs. "Oh, Marie," she confessed, "I don't know what to do."

"Pooh!" said Marie. "Just stay with me. I will look after you—and you look far more beautiful than anyone, I can promise you. There will be a lot of silly people who are all very boring. I make up games to myself on these occasions and try to imagine what they would look like in bathing suits!"

And suddenly, there halfway down the stairs, Charlotte began to see the funny side of the situation. "Oh, Marie," she whispered, "what a lovely idea! You know, I'm beginning to feel *much* better," and she went on down with the girl at her side and walked into the crowded room with a smile on her face.

She saw Jared watching her from across the room. Glass in hand, a beautiful blonde at his side, he turned as she came in with Marie, murmured something to the woman by his side, and came toward them. Charlotte took a deep breath. Now was the test. She had to pass it or the evening would be ruined.

"Charlotte, Marie. What will you have to drink?"

"I'll leave it to you, thank you," answered Charlotte calmly.

A fat middle-aged man appeared from nowhere and said to Jared. "Are you going to introduce me, hey?"

Jared bowed and nodded. "Mademoiselle Lawson, may I present Monsieur Reynaud, an old friend of the family?"

Charlotte took the man's hand and found her own being raised to the other's lips.

"*Enchanté, mademoiselle.*" He leered warmly at her,

and Charlotte thought, *Why, I can soon sort him out!* Because the image of him in a bright red swimsuit had suddenly popped into her mind, and it was all she could do not to laugh.

Jared handed her a glass, and Marie one, and she sipped at the sharp aperitif and listened to Monsieur Reynaud, wondering why she had ever been afraid. Of the scene in Jared's bedroom she thought not at all. She would do so later, but not now. She was finding to her surprise that she was actually beginning to enjoy herself.

She thought she knew the reason for Jared's summary invitation later on, as they all sat eating at the long dining table. The clatter of knives and forks, the chink of heavy crystal glasses and the murmur of voices were all around her, and she looked up from the wafer-thin slivers of beef on her plate, together with tiny peas, carrots and potatoes, to see Jared talking to the blonde sitting at his side. She was exquisitely beautiful, a Dresden doll of a woman in a simple black dress that plunged almost to her waist. Her hand rested on his arm for a second, a curiously intimate gesture, and then Charlotte knew. Quite simply, Jared had wanted her to be there to see the woman with whom he was in love.

She felt no pain with the knowledge. There was a strange blankness instead. She was free of him at last. She turned and spoke to Marie, who sat beside her. "What time will this evening finish?" she asked.

"I am sent to bed at eleven . . . usually," the girl answered.

"Then I will go with you when you leave," Charlotte said softly. Let him try to stop her!

Madame Grenier was at the far end of the table, nearly opposite her nephew. Gracious and dignified, she had greeted Charlotte with little surprise, admired her dress and introduced her to some more men and women there. Charlotte wondered what Jared had told his aunt, but it wasn't really important. What was significant, she realized was the fact that she did not feel overwhelmed by the splendid company she was in. She had imagined she would be nervous, but she wasn't. In a way she was almost indifferent.

After the meal, which lasted until past ten o'clock, the women drifted across to the large salon to drink their coffee, leaving the men in the dining room. Madame Grenier came over to Charlotte and Marie as they waited near the door, unsure where to sit.

"Do not forget, Marie, that soon is your bedtime. Do not drink coffee, but have a little wine."

"Yes, *grand-mère*," the girl obediently replied.

"May I be excused when Marie goes up to bed?" Charlotte said.

"Of course. You have enjoyed your dinner?"

"Very much, *madame*, thank you."

"Good. My friends are much impressed with our young English lady." And Madame Grenier allowed herself a little smile.

"Thank you, *madame*." *I wonder*, thought Charlotte, *if you would smile if you knew about the little game Marie taught me*. It had helped, oh, how it had helped!

There were ample chairs for everyone, the staff brought coffee around, and voices filled the room again, feminine voices. Charlotte looked up from her discussion with Marie to see Jared's woman companion watching her. There was no expression on the other's face, just bright eyes watching her with a strangely cold look about them. *You're well matched*, Charlotte thought, *both cold and hard*. She smiled, and the woman looked away and spoke to the elderly bejeweled matron by her side.

"She is pretty, is she not?" Marie whispered.

Charlotte pretenced ignorance. "Who?"

"Why, Uncle Zhar's friend, Margot."

"Oh! The blond lady? Yes, she is very nice looking." Charlotte smiled down at her young companion.

"*I* don't like her, and neither does *grand-mère*," Marie whispered.

"Ssh! You mustn't say such things."

"But it is true. Why should I not say them?"

"Because . . . ." Charlotte struggled to find the most tactful way to explain to this child that it was not wise for her to pass personal opinions of her uncle's friends to someone who was virtually a stranger. "Because things like that are private, and I'm sure Uncle Zhar wouldn't like you to tell me them. And besides, that lady might be hurt if she knew we were talking about her."

"Hah! She could not be hurt, that one! She has more money than she knows what to do with, and she is very selfish—"

It was time to stop her. "Marie, I think it must be nearly bedtime for you—and I'll come up, too. We had better go and say good-night to your grandmother."

"Can we talk for a while if we go up now?"

"Just for a few minutes. All right?"

"All right."

They said their good-nights, and Charlotte was keenly aware that several pairs of eyes were watching them as they left the large room. Her timing could not have been more unfortunate, for Jared was about to enter. He stood to one side to let them pass.

Charlotte looked at him and smiled. "Good night, Monsieur de Marais. Marie, say good-night to your uncle." He was very dark and attractive in his black dinner jacket and pearl gray tie, and he let his eyes rest on Charlotte as his niece bade him good-night and he responded.

"And are you leaving us, too, Charlotte?" he asked coolly.

"Yes, I'm very tired. Thank you for letting me come down to dinner, *monsieur*. I found it very enjoyable. It was *very* kind of you to ask me."

The tone in which she said the words was a study of politeness, but a muscle moved in his jaw, and she thought, *Oh, yes, he got the message*.

"Then good night."

"Good night." She took Marie's hand. "Come, Marie. It's late."

They walked away to the stairs, and Charlotte didn't look back. She wondered why she had ever thought she loved him.

THE NEXT FEW DAYS were spent almost exclusively with Marie. Charlotte saw little of Jared, and although Yves accompanied them on the horses, it was he who saddled them. They went on a long ride out on Sunday down country lanes, stopping in a small village for long cool drinks. On the return journey, when Charlotte and Marie were riding well ahead, Marie leaned over and whispered, "I think Yves likes you a lot."

Charlotte looked quickly at her, to see the mischievous pleasure in the girl's eyes.

"You mustn't say things like that, Marie," she said.

"Why not?" she responded in surprised tones. "It is true. I have seen him look at you."

So had Charlotte, but she wasn't going to admit it to Marie. "Well," she said, "I think he is very pleasant, and a good driver, but I don't—" she hesitated, "—well, I don't like him in any special way. So I'd rather you didn't talk about things like that."

"Oh, you *English*," Marie sighed. "You are so nonromantic!"

Charlotte laughed. "You mean unromantic, I think."

"Yes, that is it. Unromantic. Do you not want a boyfriend?"

"Someday, perhaps. I'm too busy looking after you at the moment." And that effectively ended the conversation. But it stuck in Charlotte's mind—to be dismissed when they returned to the stables, hot and dusty, to be met by Mado, who had clearly been watching for them.

"Mademoiselle Marie," she called. "You are to go in to your *grand-mère*, please."

With a look at Charlotte, Marie slid off her horse's back, helped by Yves, and ran in, followed by the maid.

Yves turned to Charlotte and held out his arms. "And now you, *mademoiselle*," he said. It would have been ill-mannered to refuse his offer, and Charlotte allowed him to help her down, unwittingly slightly tense because of Marie's words, which now returned.

He held her too long when she was down, and she tried to pull away. "Thank you, Yves," she began, feeling hands on her sides, beginning to move around her back.

"I frighten you?" he said curiously, his dark eyes on her face.

"No, of course not, only I...I—" She was silenced as he kissed her very gently, and then he stood back, still holding her, smiling now.

"There—that didn't hurt, did it?"

"Let me go, Yves. You have no right to do that!" She looked around, horrified, and pulled his hands away from her. "What if someone saw?" Her heartbeat was erratic, her breathing quickened. She had no idea where Jared was, even if he were at home, but the thought of him witnessing what had just happened was one she didn't relish.

Then she heard the voice calling her, Mado's voice—"Mademoiselle Charlotte!"—and she was able to escape.

"Coming, Mado." She fled from Yves without looking back, ran quickly away from him as if pursued, and into the house.

Madame Grenier was in the salon with her grand-daughter. Marie looked around as Charlotte came in, then ran to her, "Charlotte, I have to go away—"

"*Tiens*, Marie. I will explain to her." The old woman looked at her.

"Sit down, please, Charlotte. Have a drink of coffee." Then, as Charlotte hesitated, "Yes, yes, I know you have been riding, and must be hot, but this will not take a moment, and then you may both go and wash."

Charlotte took the proffered cup and saucer and sat down, waiting for what was to come.

Madame Grenier looked at them both. "Marie's god-mother, a very dear friend of the family who lives down south, is ill. We are naturally concerned, as you may imagine, and she has expressed the wish to see Marie. I would like you to accompany her for a few days' visit."

So that was it! So great was Charlotte's relief that the coffee cup trembled momentarily. Visions of dismissal because someone had seen Yves kissing her faded away.

"Oh, *madame*, of course. When will we go?"

"In the morning, I think. You will soon be there. Yves will drive you—" and she stopped as Jared walked in.

"No, aunt," he said, "I think not. I will take them."

Madame Grenier looked up sharply, clearly surprised at having her wishes countermanded. "*You*, Jared?" She didn't trouble to hide her astonishment.

"Yes, me." As he looked across the room at Char-lotte, she saw what was in his eyes—and she knew, as certainly as if he said the words, that he had seen the in-cident by the stables. Of course! His room overlooked them! She had not thought to look up. But how did it concern him? She lifted her chin and met his glance.

He looked back to his aunt. "I was going in a few days anyway. I can go sooner, and kill two birds with one stone."

His aunt was not pleased, but she hid it well. "As you wish, of course. Can you be ready in the morning?"

He turned to Charlotte. "Can *you*?"

"Yes. At what time?"

"Nine."

"Yes."

Marie went over to him. "How nice, uncle; can we go in the Lamborghini?"

He laughed. "Of course, and you are to behave yourself."

"I always do when I'm with Chàrlotte," she answered in all innocence, and Charlotte saw the fleeting expression that crossed his face. She could almost have read his thoughts at that moment. Then she realized the full implication of his words.

He was taking them. She stood up and put the empty cup on the table. "May I go and wash now, *madame*?"

"Yes, yes, off you go—both of you." They were dismissed with a wave of the old woman's hand. "Jared, I would like to speak with you a moment."

And I can imagine what you'll be saying, Charlotte thought as she and the girl went out. But she had other things on her mind now.

CHAPTER SEVEN

THERE WAS A STORM during the night, so different from those she had known at home in Yorkshire that she went to the window to see it, because sleep was impossible with the thunder reverberating directly overhead. There was little rain, which made the greeny yellow crackles of lightning even more eerie and frightening. The sky was dense black, lit by those brilliant flashes every minute or so to reveal the outlines of the land in stark silhouette that had a strange beauty of its own. She shivered, holding her arms hugging her sides as she watched. She heard Marie cry out, and quickly went through the adjoining bathroom to the girl's bedroom.

"It's all right, Marie," she said. "I'm here."

"I don't like storms," Marie answered. "I can't sleep."

"We're safe here, love, don't worry." Charlotte sat on the edge of Marie's bed, and the child sat up, long hair tousled, her nightgown gleaming whitely in the shadowy light. "Just lie down and dream about our journey tomorrow—or rather today." She caught a glimpse of Marie's clock face as lightening flashed again. "It's nearly two o'clock. You must try to get to sleep."

"I would if I had a drink."

"Oh! A drink of what?"

"Anything. Milk would do. Warm milk."

Charlotte had never done more than take a quick glance around the huge gleaming kitchen of the castle. She swallowed. Well, now she would have to have a proper look. "All right, love, I'll get you some. Lie still and count slowly to...to a hundred. All right?"

"Yes." The little girl lay back sleepily. One ... two ... oh, Charlotte, do I have to count in English or French?"

Charlotte laughed. "English. That will take you longer." She went quickly back into her own room and put on her dressing gown. Then, creeping very quietly so as not to disturb anyone, she went downstairs, along what seemed miles of corridors, and at last reached the kitchen.

Once there, with the light on, she found milk in the refrigerator and switched the electric stove on. Rows of pans hung on the wall and she picked the smallest and began to warm the milk. A search through several cupboards revealed only exquisite china, no mugs. She bit her lip, feeling quite helpless. If the worst came to the worst, she would have to use one. But what if there were an accident? She started on another row of immaculately neat cupboards, bent down to open a door, and a voice said from the doorway:

"What the *hell* are *you* doing here?"

Slowly she turned and stood up. Jared was angry, that was obvious. He was also wet. His hair gleamed in the light, and the shoulders of his jacket were dark with rain.

"I was—" she began, then turned in horror as the rushing sound of boiling milk reached her ears. "Oh, the milk!" She pulled it away from the heat just in time and switched off the burner . She took a deep breath. "I was getting a drink for Marie. The storm woke her."

He looked at her in silence for several seconds. He seemed to be fighting for calm. "Don't you know that we have servants?" he said at last. "*Nobody* comes down to the kitchen at night. You ring the bell in your bedroom and someone will come."

She felt suddenly stupid. "I didn't know," she managed. "I mean, I didn't know I'd got a bell. And even if I had I wouldn't have dreamed of ringing it at this time of night."

"Then I'm telling you that you must. The bells are switched through to Roberts's room at night. He would come to see what you need."

"There's no point now, is there?" She was getting over the shock of his arrival, and worse, his anger. He couldn't do much worse than he already had, she thought, as she looked at him. "I'd like a mug—if there are any."

He strode over to a cupboard she had not yet reached, pulled open the door and put a mug on the working top beside the stove. "Is there anything else you need?" he asked, voice heavy with sarcasm.

"Thank you, no, I'll manage."

"You don't think I'm leaving you here alone, do you? Hurry up and get it done. I'm tired, and I've a long drive in the morning."

She turned away from him and filled the mug with the hot milk. Carrying the pan to the sink, she was about to wash it out when he said, "For God's sake, leave that. Someone will do it in the morning."

She glared at him. His tone was the last straw. "Leave me alone," she said angrily. "I'll wash it if I want to. I don't take orders from *you*." She switched on the tap and, filling the pan with hot water, picked up a scouring pad from its dish.

"Oh, yes, you damn well do!" He strode over to her and wrenched the pan from her, sending it rattling into the sink. She threw the pad at him and it landed on his jacket lapel and fell to the floor, leaving a soapy blob. Charlotte began to laugh. She couldn't help herself; she couldn't stop, although she was frightened at his anger.

"You little—" he bit off the expletive and grabbed her firmly with both hands on her shoulders. Shocked, suddenly sobered at his violence, she was jerked into silence. Smoldering eyes met hers and she gasped at what she saw, then the gasp died away as his mouth came down on hers in a kiss of earth-shattering, explosive passion.

Lights burst in her head as she fought for her freedom, loathing him, struggling desperately to get away from the warm lips crushing hers into submission. As easy to escape from an enraged tiger; his hold tightened inexorably and his warm breath was on her face, his arms crushing her. She was powerless to move. She didn't try.

At last he freed her. Shaking, gasping, she fell back against the sink and he said, "Now why don't you see if Yves can do better?"

She rubbed the back of her hand across her bruised lips. Jared picked up the mug full of milk and said, "Come on."

She thought she had never hated anyone as much as she hated him. She couldn't speak. Trying to keep her steps steady, she went over to the door and went out. She heard him switch the lights off, close the kitchen door, and then he was following her along the wide passage that led to the hall.

She couldn't even run fast enough to get away from him. It took all her strength to merely walk up the stairs. And Jared was close behind her. At her door he handed her the mug. His face was a blank mask of indifference. "Good night, Charlotte," he said. "Sleep well."

She went in without answering and bolted the door. Marie lay fast asleep, deaf to the still rolling thunder, her arm flung out, hair fanning the pillow. Softly Charlotte tucked her in, carried the milk to her own room, and drank it. She was crying now, and the tears slid down her cheeks as she swallowed the last drops of warm liquid. Then she climbed into bed, exhausted. A few minutes later she was asleep, the tears still damp on her face.

"YOU HAD BETTER take your swimsuit," Marie suggested as she watched Charlotte pack some clothes into a small weekend case.

Charlotte looked at her in dismay. "I didn't bring one," she said. She didn't add that the only one she possessed was a plain school regulation navy blue.

"What a shame! Never mind, we can buy one in Cannes," said the fashion-conscious young woman, then added, "You would look lovely in a bikini."

"Oh, would I? But what makes you think we'll be going swimming?"

Marie raised her eyebrows. "Aunt Marie—I am named after her—has a beautiful swimming pool."

"Of course," Charlotte murmured. "Have you packed?"

"Mado has done mine. I am ready."

"Good. Then shall we go down to breakfast?"

When they had eaten, Madame Grenier appeared and handed Charlotte a bulky envelope. "Will you be kind enough to give this to Madame Dupont? You are ready for your journey?"

"Yes, thank you, *madame*."

"And you will phone me when you arrive?"

"Yes, of course."

"Then everything seems in order. Your cases have been taken down to the car, and Jared is waiting outside." She sighed. "*Et alors*, it will be quiet now without Marie." She led the way through the hall, and the front door was wide open, letting in a golden stream of sunlight. Charlotte blinked as she went out. It was incredible that there had been a storm during the night. Except that the green of the trees was richer and deeper than before, there was no evidence to show that there had been rain. And what of Jared? There was no forgetting what had happened in the kitchen only a few hours before. The memory of her humiliation was burned forever within Charlotte. She hated him now. Even without that final taunt about Yves, she would have loathed him. That had just set the seal on it.

She looked up to see him waiting, standing by the sleek Lamborghini, dressed in fawn slacks and matching open-necked shirt with short sleeves. Sunglasses hid his eyes, but he took them off as they came nearer.

"Good morning," he said, but only Marie answered. Charlotte couldn't.

Madame Grenier kissed her niece, then shook Charlotte's hand. "*Au revoir, mes enfants*," she said. "*Bon voyage.*"

Doors slammed, they all waved, and soon the castle was left behind as they sped down the driveway.

Marie was in the back and Charlotte sat beside Jared. She still had not spoken to him. She could not avoid it forever, she knew, and she had no intention of letting Marie see that anything was wrong, but she could not for the life of her have made small talk with the cool dark man by her side. He turned on the radio, and music filled the fast-moving vehicle.

"Where are we stopping for lunch?" Marie leaned forward and asked him.

"You'll see when we get there. Is that all you think about?" he demanded.

"No. But I like you taking me out for meals. It is always so *interesting*."

"Oh. In what way?"

"The way you make all the waiters rush around. Do you frighten them?"

He laughed. Charlotte would have sworn it was genuine. *Perhaps*, she thought, *he's forgotten about last night*.

"No, but I tip them well, that's all."

"Ah, I see." Marie nodded wisely. Then, as if remembering, she went on, "Oh, and we must stop somewhere to buy Charlotte a bikini."

Charlotte took a deep breath and closed her eyes. *No, no, Marie*, she said inwardly, but it was too late. "Why?" Jared asked, and glanced momentarily at her.

"Because she has no swimsuit with her, and Aunt Marie has a beautiful swimming pool."

"It doesn't matter," said Charlotte faintly. Perhaps he didn't hear her.

"Then we must stop, of course. Avignon will do, I think, after we have eaten."

Charlotte clutched her bag. She had sufficient money to buy a swimsuit, and she was absolutely determined that Jared should not go in any shop with her. Marie, yes, but not him. She sat back in the comfortable seat and tried to relax. It would have been a pleasure to travel in a car like this normally. The windows slid open or shut at the touch of a button, the radio was soft and beautifully toned, the seats luxurious. And the air conditioning ensured that they were not too warm, just pleasantly so.

The road was long and straight, lined with the tall trees so distinctive of French *routes nationales*. They passed heavy trucks loaded with fruit and vegetables, vacationers' cars loaded with luggage, and the occasional cyclist plodding steadily along. The sun blazed down on the car, and on the road ahead so that it shimmered with heat. Charlotte looked back to see Marie lying down with her eyes closed.

"Is she asleep?" Jared asked.

"I think so." That was the first time she had spoken directly to him; it was unavoidable.

"Do you want to stop for anything?"

"No, thank you."

Then there was silence, only the music above the muted roar of the powerful engine filling the car. Charlotte looked out of her side window at the fields and farms flashing past. She still felt the touch of his lips on hers, the crushing, bruising pressure that had left her weak, helpless and angry. *I'm glad I don't love you anymore*, she thought.

"Clothes are dear in this country," he said. She looked at him.

"It was Marie who suggested I needed a bikini," she answered. "Not me. I'm not bothered."

"But if she goes swimming she'll want you with her."

Charlotte shrugged. "Then I'll buy one. Don't worry, Monsieur de Marais, I can afford one." She saw his jaw tighten and looked away again.

"Do you mind if I smoke?"

"Do you normally ask your servants questions like that?" She couldn't help it. She had vowed to herself to ignore him as much as possible, but the temptation, and the inward bitterness, were too strong to resist.

She saw his hands tighten on the wheel, felt his quick anger, but she no longer cared. He jabbed the cigarette lighter button and reached for a cigarette from the packet in his glove compartment.

A few minutes later he drove off the road and down a quieter side lane, surrounded by fields. Charlotte tensed, wondering why. What was going to happen? But she would not ask.

A village lay ahead of them. Before it was a garage, and at the far side of that a large house at the front of which were tables, shaded by gaily colored umbrellas advertising popular apertifs.

He slowed down beside the house, stopped and switched off the engine. Then Charlotte looked at him again.

"We're stopping for a drink," he said.

"I don't—" she began.

"Don't argue," he said. "Just get out. *Please*." The last word was stressed almost grimly.

Silently she obeyed. There had been something in his tone that warned her not to say more.

He walked around to her side. "What if Marie wakes?" she asked. That was all right, a safe question.

"We'll see her, won't we? Sit down at that table nearest the car. What will you drink? Coke? Aperitif? Lemonade?" He looked down at her and she sensed the enormous power within him, the hidden fire ready to flare up.

"Anything. I'll leave it to you." She sat down, brushing a leaf from the chair before she did so.

There was silence from the car. He had slowed and stopped very carefully, and perhaps Marie would not wake at all. Charlotte wasn't sure whether she hoped she would or not. She sensed that Jared hadn't finished with her, and he might as well get it over with now instead of smoldering all the way to Cannes.

He came out carrying two glasses of dark brown liquid that fizzed and bubbled. Two straws bobbed in each glass. He sat down opposite Charlotte.

"Coca-Cola," he said. "Drink up."

"Thank you." Ice cubes chinked in her glass, and the drink was refreshing. She didn't realize how thirsty she had been until she began sipping. The silence began to get unbearable and she stirred uncomfortably. Jared sat there smoking a cigarette and picking up his glass to drink, and he was just looking at her. When she could stand it no longer, she burst out: "Why don't you say it now?"

He lifted one dark eyebrow. "Say what?"

"Whatever's eating you. Marie's asleep. Don't think I don't know how angry you are. You make it quite obvious."

"Do I? That's interesting. And why should I be angry with *you*?"

She took a deep breath. "You were in the kitchen this morning."

"And do you expect me to apologize for what I did?"

"You? Apologize? That's something I couldn't begin to imagine," she answered bitterly. She held the glass tightly. "I don't know why you insisted on bringing us."

"I think you do." His eyes bored into hers now, hard and cool.

She shook her head faintly, overwhelmed. She should never attempt to argue with him. It was impossible to get the better of him verbally, or any other way, for he resorted to brute strength when all else failed, as she had already discovered.

"What, nothing to say?" The voice mocked her.

"No. It's no use, is it? Not with *you*."

"You're learning fast. Want another drink?"

"No."

"Then we'd better go."

She stood up. "I'll go to the ladies' first. Should I wake Marie?"

"No. I'll stop if she wants me to. At the back of the house." She walked away from him without another word.

When she returned he was in the car, waiting. She closed the door and he drove off, back to the main road. Nothing was resolved, she thought unhappily. It was, if anything, worse than ever.

They stopped for lunch at a place called Le Petit Moulin—The Little Mill—a beautiful restaurant set well away from the road and traffic noises. Water tinkled through the slowly turning mill wheel, and they ate their meal by the fast-moving stream surrounded by trees. The place was obviously well known, and popular, and it was plain that Jared had been there before, for the service they received was first-class in every way.

Marie looked around her with delight, pointing out birds to Charlotte, exclaiming at the huge ginger cat that came to rub its back against the legs of their table. She was wide awake and refreshed after her rest. *I wish*

I was, thought Charlotte. She didn't even feel hungry, although it was nearly two o'clock and they had been driving for several hours.

Jared sat opposite Charlotte, looking at her as she searched desperately through the menu for something light. "What will you have to eat?" he asked. His manner, as always when anyone else was with them, was polite and correct.

"I'm not hungry," she answered. "Can I just have a coffee?"

"No," he said. "You need food or you'll feel sick. Have an omelet if you can't manage anything else. This place is famous for its omelets, I assure you."

"All right. Thank you." She handed the menu to him.

He didn't ask Marie what she wanted to eat. He had merely grinned at her when the menus came, and said, "You leave it to me, okay?"

"Okay," she agreed, nodding happily.

He ordered, and Charlotte sipped at a light clear wine as they waited for the food to arrive. There was a leisurely air about the place, an atmosphere of unhurried calm. White-coated waiters carried dishes to the crowded tables, and a bee buzzed around them searching for flowers, pausing to investigate the roses on their table before wandering away. Charlotte looked at the tall slender vase holding the three red roses. Red roses. She looked up, and Jared was watching her. She caught her breath. Just for a moment there had been something in his eyes. Something she could not understand. Perhaps he, too, remembered...

He and Marie ate hors d'oeuvres, brought on a huge tray from which they chose what they wanted, and Charlotte watched them and drank her wine. What a wonderful place to come with someone you loved, she thought. How romantic the setting, especially at night, for fairy lights were strung across from the trees, and the cool evening breeze would then be scented with flowers. And she was here with him instead.

Her omelet came eventually, light, fluffy and absolutely delicious, tasting delicately of herbs, tiny button mushrooms at the side of the plate. Although still not hungry, she ate it all and enjoyed it. Marie and Jared had prawns Provençal with vegetables, and the girl tucked in as if starving.

Jared looked at Charlotte. "Well, was it good?"

"Very good, thank you. You were right."

A cart loaded with desserts followed, and here Charlotte was sorely tempted by flaky, cream-loaded slices of *gâteau*; luscious strawberries encrusted with sugar; melting, mouth-watering éclairs.

Marie had to be restrained from choosing a selection of everything by her uncle, who said sternly, "We are traveling, remember? One portion only, miss." To Charlotte he added, "And what will you have?" very coolly.

It was useless to resist the temptation. The *gâteau* looked too delicious to refuse. She would only spend the rest of the day wondering if it would have been as good as it looked. She told him, and he ordered the same for himself and Marie, who had announced that if Charlotte was having it, then so was she. They drank coffee afterward, and Charlotte found it difficult to keep her eyes open when at last they made their way to the car. In spite of everything, she felt she had to thank Jared. The meal had been superb, no doubt about that, and she told him so.

He accepted her thanks with casual indifference. It made her feel as if she need not have bothered. As they walked to where the car was parked, she looked at him. Tall, broad-shouldered, he strode along with an air of complete self-sufficiency, almost of arrogance. And she saw various women watching him with interested eyes. At her they glanced not at all. It was useless for Charlotte to even try to pretend to herself that she didn't know the reason. She herself had been fascinated by him—once. No more. The cure had been painful, but it had been effective.

IT WAS DARK when they arrived at the villa on the hillside high outside Cannes, and the villa was a blaze of light, like a fairy-tale palace, long and low and colorful. The car's headlights fanned the hidden shadows of the driveway upward to the front door, and Charlotte sat forward to see it better.

"What a beautiful place," she said. "Will Marie's aunt know we're arriving tonight?"

"If I know Aunt Marie, she'll have kept awake especially. The sooner we're in the better."

Marie, behind them, was tired with the traveling, but roused herself to exclaim, "Oh, this will be a beautiful visit! Three of my favorite people, all together." Charlotte didn't know exactly what she meant, but a strange prickle of something ran up her spine, and somehow, Marie's next words came as no surprise. "Charlotte, Aunt Marie, and you, Uncle Zhar."

She closed her eyes. *Oh, no, don't let him say anything...cruel,* she thought.

"That's good. So your behavior should be something special, eh, little one?"

"Oh, yes, of course. I am always good, aren't I, Charlotte?"

Charlotte laughed. "Of course you are."

The door was flung open and a white-jacketed manservant came down the steps to greet them.

"Madame Dupont is awaiting your arrival, *m'sieur,*" he told Jared, who opened the door for Charlotte and Marie.

"We'll go right up to see her, Henri. Right away."

Jared turned to Charlotte. "You will come, too; she's looking forward to meeting you."

"And I have an envelope for her from Madame Grenier." She held it up.

They went into a wide hall whose floor was a vast expanse of polished black and white tiles. White louvered doors led off from both sides, and the hall was dominated by a white statue of the *Winged Victory* in the center. A white marble staircase with delicate gold and black wrought iron balustrades led upward to the left, and Henri led them up to a room at the front, knocked and waited.

"*Entrez*." The voice came instantly in response.

Charlotte waited just inside the door while Jared and Marie went across the pearl gray carpet to the huge bed. Aunt Marie was not remotely what she had expected. Visions of someone similar to Madame Grenier vanished forever as she gazed at the huge resplendent woman lying propped up on a sea of pillows in the bed. Immaculate blond hair was elaborately curled—not one out of place, it seemed—and Aunt Marie's face was split in a huge welcoming smile as she greeted first her goddaughter, then Jared.

"Oh, my dear—and Jared, too. Why this honor?"

"How could I miss my favorite woman?" he rejoined lightly. "I think you've brought us here under false pretenses, you old fraud."

Her laughter boomed out. "Ah, but I'm better for seeing you. These stupid doctors—they know nothing at all, I tell you. They say I must rest, and not eat so much, or—" and then she saw Charlotte. "So! you let your English miss wait by the door while you talk. Shame on you! Come and say hello, my dear."

Charlotte went forward to shake the woman's hand, to smile into a pair of startlingly bright blue eyes that were as guileless as a child's, and as full of fun.

"So you are Charlotte, hey? And they did not tell me you were beautiful. *Now* I know why Jared came with you!" And the hearty laugh came out again, joyously full of life. Charlotte felt herself go warm.

Jared, without a pause, said: "I had to come down anyway. I have to see old Mercier on business—tiresome but necessary—and you never invite me here, so I have to invite myself."

Seen close to, it was clear that Aunt Marie was in her sixties. Wrinkles were concealed by makeup, and the immaculate hair was an elaborate wig, and yet strangely enough there was a beauty about her. Charlotte sensed instinctively that she was a person that everyone loved and trusted.

"Madame Grenier gave me an envelope for you, *madame*," she said, handing the bulky package over into a heavily beringed hand.

"Ah! You will call me Aunt Marie, no? That is better. We are all one family while we are here, eh, Jared?"

"As you say, aunt," Jared agreed, and he was smiling. "But now your family is going to leave you to get some sleep, or your doctor will shoo us away tomorrow, and—"

"All right, don't go on. You always were bossy, even as a chid!" The old woman winked at Charlotte. "Don't let him bully you, my dear!"

Oh, if only you knew, thought Charlotte, but she smiled and shook her head. "No, I won't, ma—Aunt Marie."

"Good! Then off you go. There is food ready for you. Henri will look after you. And in the morning I expect to see my little Marie again, and we will breakfast together."

"Yes, aunt." Marie leaned over to kiss her godmother. "Good night, sleep well."

"And you, too, child. Away you go now. I feel better already."

Supper had been set out for them on a small round table in a room whose picture windows looked out now into pitch-black night, but, Marie assured Charlotte, overlooked the swimming pool.

Henri hovered around them, concerned that everything should be just right, telling Jared that their cases had been taken up to their rooms, that Madame Dupont would undoubtedly start to improve now...

Charlotte's head swam with tiredness, but she drank coffee and ate wafer-thin sandwiches in an effort to keep awake long enough to reach her room.

Jared looked at her and frowned. "Are you all right?" he asked.

"Yes, thanks. I'm just tired, that's all."

"So is Marie. Hey, child, don't go to sleep here." But Marie's eyes were closing and she smiled dreamily and snuggled down into her chair. Jared stood up. "Time to go." He picked his niece up and carried her out of the room, followed by Charlotte, who thanked Henri and wished him good-night as he held the door open for them to go through.

She and Marie had adjoining rooms, each with its own bathroom. Jared put Marie down on her own bed and turned to Charlotte. "Can you manage?" he asked.

"Yes, thanks." She waited for him to go.

"All right. I'll see you in the morning."

"Yes. Good night." He didn't move, merely stood looking down at the inert figure on the bed as if debating something.

Charlotte felt uneasy. Without considering why, she went to the door and opened it. "I *can* manage," she repeated. "And I'm very tired. Thank you for bringing Marie up."

He turned toward her and for a moment she saw a look in his eyes that set her heart pounding in her breast. She couldn't look away, his glance held her, and tension vibrated around them. Then he walked toward her and for a moment she feared that he would touch her. Instinctively she backed away from him, nervous, and he spoke, his voice harsh.

"I'm not going to touch you," he said, "Did you think I was?"

"I wouldn't know," she answered. "I don't know anything about you, do I? Why don't you go?"

Without another word he walked out. She closed the door after him and leaned against it. She was weak and trembling, but she didn't understand why. She hoped that she would see very little of him during the next few days. Hate him she might, but he had the power to disturb her deeply. She went over and began to undress the sleeping child.

CHAPTER EIGHT

RICH, MUDDLED DREAMS filled Charlotte's sleeping hours. A road vanishing under the wheels of a superfast car; an old woman by a swimming pool whose laughter boomed out as she told Charlotte that Jared was madly in love with her, that that was why he had brought her....

She woke up suddenly because a maid was standing by her bedside smiling down shyly at her.

"*Bonjour, mademoiselle*. Your breakfast is here." Charlotte struggled to sit up, only too aware that she wore a thin cotton nightie she had made herself, and that it was woefully unsuitable for the opulent bedroom that was hers.

"Thank you. What time is it?"

"It is nearly nine, *mademoiselle*. Marie is already with Madame Dupont. You are to take your time, she says. Shall I run your bath?"

"Yes, please." Charlotte smiled at the girl. "What is your name?"

"I am Lucia, *mademoiselle*." The girl was Italian, she realized that now. There was the trace of accent in her French and she had dark Latin eyes.

"Thank you, Lucia." Charlotte took the tray from the girl and began buttering a flaky croissant. The coffee in the pot was scalding hot and black, and she added to it from the tiny jug of milk and sipped gratefully.

Lucia vanished silently. *I shall have to write to Aunt Emily*, thought Charlotte. *She'll never believe this place. I'm not sure if I do myself.* She was looking forward to seeing it from the outside in daylight, and the swimming pool she had heard so much about. The thought of that brought back the memory of their stop in Avignon the previous afternoon. Jared had pulled up in a quiet street and turned to Charlotte.

"Off you go," he said. "The shop's down there. Are you going, Marie?"

"Yes. May I, Charlotte?"

"Of course." So he had no intention of coming with her anyway. "I'll be as quick as possible."

"Take your time," he had replied indifferently. "I'll buy an evening paper and read it," and he had got out and strode back to a newspaper seller on a corner.

It hadn't been a bikini after all, because they were ridiculously expensive, but there had been a sleek-fitting black swimsuit that Charlotte knew immediately was the one she wanted. She could afford it, too, and had tried it on, knowing it would fit. It did, perfectly.

They went back to the car and Jared opened the door, putting the newspaper he had been reading to one side. "Get one?" he asked with no trace of interest in his voice. "Good. We'll go." And that had been that.

Today, if Marie wanted a swim, Charlotte would wear the swimsuit for the first time. The important thing, of course, was that the child would be spending a lot of time with her godmother, the reason for their visit in the first place.

So it was a pleasant surprise when at last Charlotte went down, a little unsure of where she should go, to be met by Henri. Perhaps he had been waiting for her. "Mademoiselle Lawson," he said, "Madame Dupont and Marie are by the pool. Follow me, please."

He led her out of the front door, along a gravel path and around to the back of the villa. Green shutters were flung back, all windows open to let in the sun. The grass was a rich green that almost hurt the eyes, and perhaps the lushness was partly due to the sprinklers that set off a constant rainbow sparkle of water at intervals across its vastness. Bushes and shrubs full of flowers provided relief from the greenness of the lawns—reds and pinks, mauves and yellows, a profusion that was too much to take in all at once. Charlotte sighed, and the man heard and turned his head slightly, and he smiled.

"*Mademoiselle* slept well?"

"Oh, yes, thank you. I was just looking at all this," she explained, waving an arm. "It's almost too much to take in."

"Madame Dupont likes beautiful things around her," he said. There was a slight smile on his face as he said it, and she didn't understand it. "Wait until you see the pool. I think you will find that agreeable."

"Hello! Charlotte, I am here!" Marie's voice greeted her as they rounded the back of the house, and Charlotte stopped in wonder—and just looked.

The pool was kidney shaped, filled with sparkling blue water, and Marie was splashing around, her long hair streaming out, a glimpse of a multicolored floral swimsuit as she jumped up and down in excitement. Colored paving stones surrounded the pool, and several comfortable chairs were dotted about, topped by sunshades. In one was Madame Dupont, who waved.

"Come and sit down, Charlotte," she called. "Henri, drinks, please."

"Yes, *madame*." He melted away, and Charlotte skirted the water to sit beside Madame Dupont. A light rug covered the old woman's legs and a huge red umbrella shaded her from the sun's glare.

It was a relief not to see Jared. Charlotte sat down in an adjoining seat and sank back into the cushions.

"Well, and how did you sleep, hey?"

"Very well, thank you." Charlotte smiled.

"That is good. Jared offers his apologies, but has had

to go into Cannes on business. I told him that it is ridiculous to think of work in this weather, but—" she
shrugged "—men! They cannot be told anything."

"No," Charlotte murmured in polite agreement. She
didn't want to talk about Jared. She was to be disappointed.

"Still, he will return soon, I daresay." A look from
those startlingly blue eyes, and Charlotte was unable to
look away. "He is no fool, that Jared." She bit her lip.
The old woman's meaning was obvious—especially remembering her remarks the previous night. Marie was
out of earshot, making her way up the pool in a puppy-
ish breaststroke, clearly proud to be showing off her
swimming prowess. Charlotte felt the need to put Aunt
Marie right on one or two points—but how to begin?

"Er, *madame*—" she began, only to be interrupted by
the other's:

"Aunt Marie, if you please!"

"Aunt Marie, Jared is not, er, he doesn't . . . ." Oh,
where were the words? "I mean, he has a girl friend—"

Laughter boomed out, hearty and unrestrained. "Ah!
He has, has he? Tell me, is it the delectable Margot?"

She knew her! "Yes," said Charlotte, relieved. Surely
there would be no need now for further explanations?

"So? And you have met her? So tell me, what do you
think of her, hey?"

Charlotte shook her head, dismayed. This was getting
worse with every moment that passed. "She seems
very . . . nice," she said at last.

Those blue eyes were too shrewd to be fooled. "She is
nice? Hmm, her parents have a villa near here, and
I have met her more than once. Nice is not a word I
would use, but perhaps you are a kind person—yes, I
think you must be. Tell me, did Jared tell you anything
about me?"

The sudden change of subject startled Charlotte.

"No," she said. "I only know you are Marie's godmother, and one of her favorite people."

"I am? Good! Marie and I have always had good rapport. We are of an age, she and I; I still see things with the eyes of a child. Does that surprise you?"

"No." Charlotte looked at her and smiled. "I felt when I first met you last night that you . . . ." She hesitated, wondering if it were good manners to express personal opinions.

"Yes? Go on." Just like Marie, impatiently.

"Well, that everyone who met you must like you."

"Well, thank you, child. I see you are a young woman of shrewd judgment." But even though she said it half jokingly, Charlotte knew the older woman was pleased.

Drinks came, brought out by another maid carrying a silver tray, with matching silver jug and three tall glasses. A bowl of ice cubes with tongs was set out on a low table, as well, and the maid bobbed a curtsy and departed quietly. Aunt Marie grinned, "I'll let you pour out, Charlotte," she said. "So Jared didn't tell you about me, hmm? So you expected a dear old lady, I suppose?"

"Well . . . ." Charlotte bit her lip. "Yes, I suppose I did."

"And you saw me?" Her laughter echoed around the pool and Marie turned around in surprise, then waved.

"Come on out, little one," Aunt Marie called. "We have a drink for you." She went on, as Marie scrambled out of the pool, "I shall never be an old lady, *dieu merci*. I do not allow age to interfere with my enjoyment of life. I am a widow now, with four daughters, seven grandchildren; they live far away, but often come to visit me—you remind me very much of my second granddaughter, Angeline, a sweet girl—where was I? Oh yes, I have had a full and interesting life, and I wouldn't change a minute of it, and not many people can say *that*." And then, as Marie ran up, shaking herself and scattering drops all around her, she continued, without a change of tone, "I was a dancer in the Folies Bergère when I met and married my dear husband." Charlotte tried to hide her astonishment, but Aunt Marie chuckled. "Yes, I can see your surprise. *Et alors*, I was a very respectable girl, I assure you. My *maman* chaperoned me constantly, and my life was possibly quieter than most. Then Jacques came on the scene, and whisked me away on a honeymoon that lasted a year, then we came and lived here, and here I have been ever since." She stopped and waited as Charlotte handed her, and then Marie, a glass full of sparkling lime cordial.

"Ah, lovely. Now Marie, drink up and then dry yourself or you will take a cold. There are plenty of towels in the changing rooms."

"Yes, aunt." The girl sipped her drink obediently, put it down on the table with the words "I'll finish it when I come back," and ran off to the other side of the pool where there was a row of doors set in the long white building. She vanished through one, and for a few moments there was silence.

"So you see," went on the old woman, "that is my life. And I constantly get lectures from my doctors on taking it easy, and eating less—and all sorts of boring things. Already I am better for seeing you all—they know nothing, these stupid men, but I let them have their say. It is one way for them to earn a living, I suppose! And besides, every so often, if I feel a little lonely, I can send for my dear ones—nobody dares refuse poor old Aunt Marie when she is poorly!" The chuckle grew to a laugh and Charlotte found herself irresistibly joining in.

"Oh," she managed at last, "I think Jared was right. You are a fraud!"

"Yes, I am." Then the old woman's voice changed, became quieter. "And now tell me. What is wrong with you and Jared, hey?"

"Wrong?" Charlotte swallowed. Her hostess had a most disconcerting habit of switching subjects in a matter of seconds. "I don't see—"

"Rubbish! I have never seen him so jumpy before. I wondered, and then I saw you standing by the door and I thought, aha!"

"Oh, no, *madame*—I mean Aunt Marie," Charlotte said hastily. "You are mistaken, I'm sure. Jared doesn't like me at all, and I certainly don't like him—oh, I'm sorry, I shouldn't say that—he's a r-relative of yours—"

"Say what you like! This is just you and me talking, and will not go any further, that I can promise you. And may a nosy woman who should know better ask you *why* you don't like one another, hey? Here you are, a beautiful young woman with a good sense of humor—important, that—and he a *most* attractive specimen of manhood—let's be in no doubt about that, he *is*—and there you are both sending off very disturbing vibrations across the room—oh, yes! I felt them, so no use to pretend."

And Charlotte looked at her, and saw not just plain curiosity but a kindly concerned look in those blue eyes. And she knew that here was someone to whom she could tell the truth. All the pain, the hurt she had had to keep within her for so many days because she was alone in a strange land, came bubbling to the surface, and she said, "When I went to work for Madame Grenier at the château I had no idea that Jared would be there. You see, I had met him two years previously when I was on holiday in Paris with my aunt . . ." And thus she began the story that had begun at that fateful party, and never really finished.

The older woman listened in fascinated silence until they were interrupted by Marie. Madame Dupont asked the child to go into the villa to find her shawl, and she told Charlotte to go on.

At last the tale was done, for there was not really much to it after all, and Charlotte felt surprisingly light with relief when she had finished. Aunt Marie turned to her and spoke softly: "Oh, my dear girl, my dear Charlotte, thank you for telling me." She shook her head. "That man!"

"Please—please don't say anything," begged Charlotte.

"Ah! No. That is definite. Tell me again, when exactly was it that you met him in Paris?"

"The end of June—exactly two years ago, almost to the week." Charlotte said, and realized with a pang that it was precisely to the day—tomorrow would be the second anniversary of their meeting. How strange!

"Yes, I thought so." Aunt Marie nodded sagely, as if something had been confirmed. "I remember the time well."

Charlotte looked at her, puzzled by what was in her tone, but Aunt Marie smiled. "It is my birthday on Friday," she said. "So of course it is a time of year I always remember." But Charlotte was left with the feeling of something else left unsaid. Something important.

"Thank you for taking me into your confidence," the old woman said after a moment. "I appreciate it, and I will respect it, have no fear."

Then Marie ran out from the house, followed by a tall, thin, worried-looking man carrying a black bag.

"Madame Dupont," he began, "I am *most* distressed to see you out here."

"My doctor, or one of them," the older woman whispered loudly to Charlotte, "a real old fusspot, I'm afraid." Then, in a much lower voice: "Ah, doctor, I feel much better today, you see, now that some very *dear* people have come to visit me...."

Charlotte stood up, smiled at the doctor, said, "If you will excuse me..." and walked back into the villa with Marie.

Aunt Marie's ringing tones followed her: "Come back soon, I will get rid of this bossy man in a few minutes...." They fled.

DINNER THAT EVENING began quietly. Jared had returned in the middle of the afternoon and gone swimming with his niece. Madame Dupont had come out again well after lunch, assisted by Charlotte, and sat herself down by the pool to watch them. Charlotte had used the excuse of a headeache to avoid going into the pool with him, although she longed to plunge into the cool blue water. Instead, she sat beside the old woman, who reminisced about old times, old friends, and journeys over the world. It was difficult for Charlotte to avoid watching Jared; he dived and swam like a fish, and took Marie for rides in the water. He was built like an athlete, splendidly muscular, perfectly proportioned, looking like some dark Adonis as he paused at the side of the pool before scything through the water yet again.

Now, sitting with him at dinner, Charlotte looked across at him and wondered what he would think if he knew that she had told Aunt Marie all about their brief romance in Paris. He would, she felt sure, be furious. She no longer cared.

They were waited on by Henri and the dark Italian girl Lucia, and the food was superb, as it had been at lunch.

Conversation was general, and pleasant, and then, toward the end of the meal, Aunt Marie dropped a bombshell. Very casually she said:

"Ah, I have just remembered! I have two tickets for a grand ball in Cannes tomorrow. Very expensive, I might add, and *very* difficult to get hold of—and now that I am not allowed out I cannot go. So, Jared, why don't you take Charlotte?"

Charlotte froze, looked wide-eyed at the old woman, and felt a wave of sheer horror sweep over her. What on earth did she think she was doing?

Jared looked at her, too, but there was nothing on his face to give him away. "*You* were going? With whom?"

"Does it matter now?" the old woman retorted. "And do you think I am too senile to enjoy myself? You sound astonished."

Good for you, thought Charlotte, hiding a smile. Jared might be able to boss everyone else around, but in Aunt Marie he had met his match.

"No, I beg your pardon, aunt. Of course I didn't think that for a moment. But I didn't think you enjoyed the kind of occasions where, to use one of your own expressions, "everyone is decorated like a Christmas tree.""

"Did I ever say that? Hmm, maybe I did. Anyway, you've not answered my question yet. Why don't you and Charlotte go?"

"She may not want to," he replied very evenly. "Do you want to go to a 'grand ball' tomorrow, Charlotte?"

"I've never been to one before," she answered. Now the onus was on her. A refusal would seem ungracious—even though Aunt Marie must surely *know* how she felt, after their talk that morning. "And I've nothing to wear."

"You should have brought your dresses with you," chimed in Marie helpfully.

Charlotte looked to the old woman in appeal. "It's true, Aunt Marie," she said. "I have nothing to wear."

"My dear, there is a wardrobe full of superb gowns upstairs!" was the surprising reply. "You and I will go after dinner and look at them." Was there to be no escape? The subject was dropped then, but when they eventually went upstairs to a large bedroom covered in dust sheets, Charlotte turned to Madame Dupont.

"Oh, please," she said, "tell me why you've asked Jared to take me out tomorrow?"

"Because I would have done so if you *hadn't* told me what you did." The old woman seated herself heavily on the bed. "And it is true, the tickets are very expensive and would only have been wasted—and I *hate* waste—and thirdly, my dear child, quite simply, it could be a good evening out for you. Jared will be a good escort, I can promise you that. He has manners, that one—and he will not risk my displeasure by behaving badly."

Charlotte felt mean. She went over to the old woman and sat beside her. "I'm sorry," she said. "I just thought that perhaps you were trying to—" She stopped.

"Who? *Me*? Trying to push you together, you mean? *Mon dieu*, no, I would not be so cruel, when it is so obvious that you and he are poles apart in every way!" Aunt Marie chuckled. "It is selfish of me really. As I cannot go, I want you to go instead and tell me all about it. That is all."

Charlotte stood up. "I'll look at the dresses if I may," she said, and went to the long wardrobe covering one wall. She didn't see the expression on the other's face.

"There is a collection from years, I must warn you," her voice came as Charlotte slid open the doors. "And some belonging to my daughters and granddaughters, too. So you see, there must be *something*."

Charlotte gasped at the glittering display before her eyes. A long row of every kind of dress hung there, all colors, different lengths, some sparkling with silver or gold threads, others in plain muted shades. Rows and rows of shoes lay neatly at the bottom of the wardrobe.

Charlotte began to laugh. "I don't believe it!" she gasped. "There are even more here than in the shop Jared took me to."

"Take a look, pull them out, and then try on those you like. It will be interesting to see if your taste is similar to Angeline's, will it not?"

There was a tap on the door and Marie peeped in. "May I come and look?" she asked.

The next hour passed quickly—and quite delightfully. It was so different from the shop in Mâcon, when Jared had been waiting and watching. Here she was relaxed and, in a way, at home, with just Marie and her godmother commenting and admiring. Madame Dupont told the story of each dress as Charlotte took it out. That one had been worn by her daughter at a very grand ball in Paris several years ago at which President de Gaulle had been guest of honor. This one was worn by Angeline at a yacht party in Monte Carlo with foreign royalty present, and this one—"Ah!" Aunt Marie sighed as Charlotte lifted out an exquisite red velvet gown in Regency style, rich and yet simple in design, with short puffed sleeves.

"That one," she said, "bring it to me, my dear. That was mine—years ago." She began to laugh at Marie's startled gasp. "Ah yes, my child, I was as slender as Charlotte in those days. You do not believe, hm? Well, I can hardly blame you, but ah, what memories that dress brings back! Do me the honor of trying it on, please, Charlotte."

"Of course," Charlotte responded with a smile. She had to stoop slightly for Marie to fasten three tiny buttons at the back, then she stood up and walked slowly toward Madame Dupont, seeing the memories in the old woman's eyes, the wistful nostalgia of days long past and gone....

"It's simply beautiful, even today. I am astounded!"

"Charlotte, you look much nicer than you do in those others," Marie exclaimed.

It was a perfect fit in every way. It might, Charlotte thought, have been made for her. A faint lavender scent clung to it, and she looked across the room and took a look in the long miror, and caught her breath. For a second she hadn't recognized herself. She saw only a tall slender girl standing there—and then she went closer to the glass, and it was really her. She laughed.

"I wasn't sure if it was me," she said.

"Do you like it?" Madame Dupont asked.

Charlotte turned to her. "It's the most beautiful dress I've ever tried on in my life," she said simply.

"Then it is yours to keep. And you will wear it tomorrow?"

"Of course, with great pleasure—but I can't possibly let you give—"

"Nonsense! Do you think I shall ever wear it again? Nothing would make me happier. *Alors*, that is decided. Now, try on some of those ridiculous sandals and let us see which go best."

CHAPTER NINE

THE POOL WAS PLEASANTLY COOL, and both Marie and Charlotte swam and splashed happily the following morning, watched by Madame Dupont from her usual place on the terrace. As they swam to the side for drinks, she told Charlotte, "I have phoned my hairdresser to come and do your hair before this evening."

Charlotte was too astonished to speak for a moment, then managed, "Thank you, but I was going to wash my hair this afternoon—"

"Yes, and I'm quite sure it would look fine, but allow an old woman to have her own way in some things."

Charlotte laughed as she scrambled out. "I thought you said you would never be old," she said.

"I am whenever I want my own way," Madame Dupont said complacently. "So that is settled. Madame Claire will arrive at six, and then at nine you will depart for the grand ball."

Charlotte took a long sip of her drink and thought about that. She had managed to put all disquieting thoughts about the evening ahead out of her mind, but Madame Dupont now brought it all back. For the old woman's sake she would try to enjoy it, and store up as many memories as she could to tell her the following morning, but Charlotte had to admit that she was not looking forward to having to spend so many hours in Jared's company. How could she, after all that had happened? The scene in the kitchen at the château still rankled. She would never, she thought, forgive him for what he had done, the bitter contempt with which he had kissed her. For that was what it had been, she realized now; he despised her.

She looked up, and the old woman was watching her with a very knowing look in her eyes, almost as if she knew her thoughts.

"Don't worry," she said.

Charlotte smiled, shaking her head. "No, I won't," she answered softly. But it was easier to say than to do. And as the hours passed, she grew more apprehensive.

IT WAS NEARLY NINE—the fateful hour. Charlotte, who had not eaten a bite since lunch at two, felt faintly sick. She wished desperately that she did not have to go, but it was too late for that; her hair was done, the dress was on, and Madame Dupont had spent nearly an hour giving her the most astounding makeup tips and watching them put into practice. She was seated at the dressing table in her room, Marie at one side, Aunt Marie at the other, and the old woman was sitting forward on her chair as Charlotte put the finishing touches to her eye shadow.

"No, *smooth* it in, child, there, just above the eyelid. Ah! That's it." She sat back as if a hard task had just been completed and looked appraisingly at Charlotte. "Hmm, that *is* it. You look superb. You did not think I knew so many tricks, did you?"

Charlotte looked at herself. A cool blond beauty gazed back at her from the mirror, someone whose eyes were dark and sparkling, whose mouth was as richly red as the fabulous dress that she wore.

"I don't believe it's me," she said faintly. "It is, isn't it?"

"It is." Madame Dupont stood. "Come, we will go and show Jared."

He was waiting in the hall. As Charlotte slowly

walked down, he looked up. She saw the sudden shock in his dark eyes, the tension he could not hide immediately, and she was satisfied. It had shown on his face, just for the instant before he managed to conceal it; he was sharply aware of her as a woman. There was a sense of power in the knowledge.

Madame Dupont's voice from the top of the stairs shattered the fragile mood.

"Come and help an old lady down the stairs to see you off," she called.

Jared waited until Charlotte reached the last step, then ran up to where his aunt waited with Marie. They came slowly down, and as Charlotte looked up, Aunt Marie closed one eye in a huge wink. The other two didn't see it, only Charlotte, who smiled in acknowledgment.

They all went to the door where Aunt Marie kissed first Charlotte, then Jared. "Have a lovely evening, *mes enfants*," she said. "And remember, I want a full report in the morning."

"Yes, I promise," Charlotte answered.

"Yes." He patted the pocket of the white evening jacket he wore. He was immaculate, his tan accentuated further by the dazzling whiteness of lacy shirt front, black bow tie at his neck, dark hair brushed back, powerful features with an inscrutable expression. Now, but not before—not for an instant of time when Charlotte had seen what she had seen. And she smiled to herself.

He spoke when they were halfway down the driveway.

"That dress suits you," he said.

"Does it? Thank you. Madame Dupont has given it to me. That's three evening dresses I have now," she answered.

He negotiated the bends in the driveway with care, and once away from the house, darkness rushed in and surrounded them, leaving only the powerful twin beams from the headlights to show them the way. Through the gateway, down the path to the main road into Cannes they went, and he spoke not another word.

It was a beautifully clear night, with a sickle moon high over the Mediterranean. *A night for lovers*, thought Charlotte, *and here we are together, only we hate one another, we're only going to please an old woman.* And she sighed, only a tiny sigh, but he heard it, and said sharply, "What's the matter?"

She had already decided that come what may, she would not get involved in any argument with Jared, so she answered, with bright determination, "Why, nothing, I was just thinking what a lovely night it was."

"And are you looking forward to the evening?"

She might not be going to argue, but she saw no reason to lie. "No," she answered. "But then I don't think you are, are you?"

She saw his shrug in the dark. "I came to please Aunt Marie—as you did. She is a woman who usually manages to get her own way in things—as you may have noticed."

He waited at the edge of the main road for an opportunity to ease into the stream of traffic, and the minute he had done so, Charlotte answered him. "Perhaps she does. But then I imagine everyone would want to please her. She's one of the nicest people I've ever met."

"I wasn't attempting to criticize her, merely stating a fact," he said coolly. "I'm very fond of her myself."

"It's her birthday on Friday," Charlotte said, because there had been a slight something in his voice that threatened to start the argument she was so determined to avoid.

"My God, so it is! When did she tell you?"

"When we were talking about—" and she suddenly remembered exactly what they had been discussing, and went hot and cold as she fumbled for words. "About th-things yesterday." She hoped he didn't notice her stammer of confusion.

If he did, he didn't comment on it, merely said, "I must get her a present."

"Are there any shops near the villa?" she asked.

"No. The nearest are in Cannes itself. Why, do you want to get her something?"

"Perhaps Marie and I can go down and get her a little gift," she answered. "Tomorrow."

"Walk it, you mean? You must be joking."

"I wasn't. I don't know how far it is, do I?" she answered reasonably enough.

'I'll take you both tomorrow afternoon," he said. "I can spare an hour."

She felt her mouth tighten at his tone. Swallowing hard, she said, "Thank you."

"Don't mention it." He jabbed the cigarette lighter button in and lit a black cheroot. "We're nearly there," he told her. "Aren't you nervous?"

Did he expect her to be? Of course he did. He would be delighted if she were. Charlotte took a deep breath. "They're only people, aren't they?" she asked in a mild tone. "Are they so very grand and important that I should be shaking in my shoes?"

"You said yourself that you'd never been anywhere like this before," he answered, avoiding a direct answer. "It must be strange."

"Of course it will be. But no more so than going down to meet guests at dinner in your home—as you insisted I should do, if you remember. For that I must now thank you; I'm sure *that* experience will be a help to me tonight." And she smiled in the darkness of the car. She felt almost light-headed, partly due to hunger, no doubt, but also in a strange way because she was rapidly regaining confidence.

He laughed, not entirely without amusement. "I'll say one thing for you," he remarked. "You're very good at giving your answers."

"I've learned a lot since I came to France," she answered. "One way or another." The last four words were said in a very dry tone, and let him take that how he chose, she thought.

"I'm sure you have. Do you like working for my aunt?"

"Madame Grenier? Yes. I like Marie very much, as well."

"It may be only a temporary position. Marie may be sent to a boarding school when she's a little older—we haven't yet decided."

"Oh, no!" The words were wrenched out of her in a shock of dismay.

He said sharply, "What do you mean?"

She stiffened in her seat. Perhaps he thought . . . . "I know the position is a temporary one," she said quickly. "I knew that when I took it. That wasn't why I was shocked."

"Then what? Because of boarding school?"

"Yes." She knew she would have to speak carefully now. It was not her place to pass comments, she knew, so she said, "I'm sorry. I had no right—"

"Yes. I'm asking you now. I want to hear your opinion."

"Then I'll tell you." She was not aware of him pulling off to the side of the busy main road until the car halted and he put on the hand brake.

"I—why have you stopped?"

"Because I want to hear what you have to say."

"We . . . won't we be late?" she asked.

"No. Now tell me why the mention of boarding school shocked you."

"All right. It's only my own opinion, though. It's this:

Marie has never been used to other children's company, has she?"

"No."

"Then it would be hard for her to adjust to being with others of her own age—a lot of them, all at once, as she would be if she were flung in at the deep end, as it were, in a boarding school. Not only that, but to leave home for the first time at the same moment—she . . . she would be very unhappy."

"She's an intelligent child. She would adjust."

"Would she? How do *you* know? Other children can be cruel, you know. She wouldn't know how to mix—not straightaway. She might adjust, but she might suffer first. I know, I was an only child—perhaps I was luckier than her, for I went to a small village school when I was young. She's always had a tutor." Charlotte had forgotten that she was talking to the man she loathed, that she was on her way out with him; all that was in her mind was the desire to put across to him the importance of her feelings.

There was a brief silence. Then he spoke. "You sound concerned about her welfare."

"Concerned? Of *course* I'm concerned. I—" She stopped. She had nearly forgotten her promise to herself not to argue with him at all. "I . . . I'm very fond of Marie, although I've not known her for long. I can see something of myself in her, even though our circumstances are vastly different, of course." There was no irony in her words. "Basically every child is the same. They need security—and love." She stopped, wondering if she had said too much.

"She has both those, surely?"

"Yes, I'm sure she has—I didn't mean . . . ." She paused. What was the use? How could Jared possibly understand—a man like *him*? "I've told you, it's really nothing to do with me, as a mere employee."

He looked sharply at her and she waited for the blast of anger that would surely come. Strangely enough, she no longer cared.

"Perhaps it has," he said, in a mild tone. "I'll think over what you said." He wasn't angry!

She turned to look at him, utterly astonished, and he gave her a cool smile. "You don't need to say it," he said. "You expected me to be annoyed, didn't you? I'm not. Because what you've just said only confirms something I'd already thought about. I'll try to work something out." And he started the car and looked back to check the following traffic. In doing so he moved nearer to Charlotte, and she stiffened slightly, instinctively. Then they were roaring down the road, and the moment of brief tension passed.

But it left Charlotte in a state of confusion. She had thought him insensitive—he was not, not entirely anyway. She had thought herself immune to his nearness—she was not. She would, she decided, be glad when they arrived at their destination.

SHE HAD BEGUN STORING IMPRESSIONS the moment they arrived. Not only for Aunt Marie and Marie, but for Aunt Emily, as well. The doorman who had ushered her from the car, dressed like something out of a musical set in Ruritania; the discreetly dressed swarthy men who had scrutinized their tickets before deciding they weren't gate-crashers; the opulent ladies' room, lavishly pink-curtained, with mirrors in which you could see yourself from all angles; the people. People who looked as if they spent their lives jetting around the world, who glowed with the kind of tans that took years to acquire, whose clothes where stunningly expensive, who just looked *different* from any she had met before.

And she was nervous, no use to try to hide it. Charlotte was unaware of the glances cast in her direction by others—unaware that in that hothouse setting there was a clear, fresh beauty about her that was equally distinctive, that her very shyness lent her an aura of fragility that could not but appeal to jaded palates.

There were several hundred people in the vast ballroom of the hotel. Next to that the equally large restaurant had been converted so that there was a permanent running buffet attended by dozens of white-gloved waiters and waitresses. The orchestra was loud; it had to be to rise above the hundreds of voices all talking at once. Couples whirled around, men with trays of drinks skillfully avoided collisions as they threaded their way through a jostling, pushing throng; and Jared behaved with impeccable manners toward Charlotte.

She began to relax slightly. She was here at Madame Dupont's behest, and it wasn't turning out as bad as she had feared. In a way she could even begin to enjoy herself, simply by letting it wash over her, by imagining Jared was a polite stranger. They danced, and they spoke only of trivial things; he pointed out one or two celebrities, acknowledged the greetings of acquaintances, and Charlotte wondered why he couldn't always be like that.

And then it changed. He had gone away for a few minutes, asked her to excuse him, and she imagined that it was to talk to someone he had spoken to in passing only minutes before. He left Charlotte sitting on a gilt chair with a plate of smoked salmon by her side, a half-full glass of champagne in her hand. "I'll not be a minute," he said. "You don't mind?"

"No, of course not." She wasn't alone—a couple of heavily jeweled matrons were a few seats along, tucking into caviar while they busily gossiped. Charlotte took a sip of the bubbly liquid and watched the couples whirling past, and a voice said:

"So there you are, all alone—that is terrible!" A tall, very tanned, extremely attractive man sat beside her and, still speaking French, added, "And your glass is nearly empty!" He clicked finger and thumb, and a waiter with a full tray materialized from nowhere and bowed.

"There we are, thanks, Gaston." He took two glasses, handed the bemused Charlotte one, took the other from her and downed it in a gulp, and handed the empty glass to the waiter, who melted away again.

All Charlotte could think of to say was, "Is his name Gaston?"

"Haven't a clue!" her companion confessed. "But mine's Paul. You're English?"

"Yes. Does it show?"

"Considering that you stand out like a rose amid a load of tatty orchids—yes." He had switched from French to very good English. "And personally, if I were your escort, which sad to say I'm not, I wouldn't leave you alone for one second. How about a dance?"

"Oh, I don't think—he'll be back any second. . . ." She looked around desperately. It was all too much like a certain party in Paris, and she didn't want to be reminded of *that*.

"Not him. He's busy talking to a crowd of Greek millionaires—I saw him leave you," Paul said. "He'll not get away for *ages*." He stood up. "Come on. It'll do him good."

Why not? It would be something to tell Aunt Marie. *She* would appreciate it. Charlotte put her glass down. "But the drinks—" she began.

"So?" He shrugged. "They'll be there when—if—we come back," and he held out his arms, and Charlotte, swallowing her last remnants of doubt, went into them.

Suddenly she saw Jared returning, but it was too late because Paul had quite a firm grip and was already

skillfully whirling her into a crowd, ignoring her protests. Jared's eyes met hers across that short, rapidly
growing distance, and she saw the expression she had
most learned to dread—hard cold anger.

"Paul," she said, "my escort's back. I thought you
said—"

"Did I? I must have been mistaken." He looked down
at her and laughed softly. "You look terrified, my sweet.
Now why should a gorgeous girl like you be frightened
of a man like Jared de Marais—"

"You *know* him!" Her eyes widened. "I thought—"

"Who doesn't know him? It'll do him good to wait."

He had said that before, just a few minutes previously. A tiny suspicion grew in Charlotte's mind—a suspicion that Paul was using her for reasons of his own because he didn't like Jared. *Well, neither do I*, she
thought, *but nobody is going to make me the scapegoat for
their own personal quarrels.*

"Why don't you like Jared?" she said abruptly. They
were in the center of the floor where it was noisiest, and
no one could possibly have overheard them.

He laughed and his eyes gleamed. They were a very
pale blue, a not unattractive color, and were darkly
lashed. "Did I say that?"

"No. But it's fairly obvious."

"Smart girl! You know, I like you. You never told me
your name, by the way."

"I don't want to now. I'm going back to Jared—will
you please let me go?"

"I'll take you back if you're so anxious to see him.
Come on." Getting out from the milling bodies was
more difficult than getting in. The world's most expensive perfumes assailed Charlotte's nose as they struggled
through the crowd. She felt sick.

Jared was standing there, and close to he looked even
angrier than before. Angry—yet in a strange way very
controlled.

"Evening, Jared." Paul nodded. "Enjoying yourself?"

"I was."

"Were?" Paul grinned. "Don't tell me I spoiled it for you?"

Jared was slightly taller than the other man, but they were built on the same lines. And Charlotte thought, *they really hate one another*.

"No, you didn't. It's getting a bore now, though. Thank you for looking after Charlotte for me. Your friends are looking for you."

"Charlotte? You wouldn't tell me your name, would you?" He turned and smiled down at her. "Now you've seen Jared, shall we continue our dance?"

Before she could answer, Jared said, "I don't think so."

"I was asking her, not you. Don't be tiresome, old boy, Charlotte can speak for herself."

"But she doesn't know you. I do."

Paul's eyes had turned to flint. "Is that supposed to mean something?"

"You can take it how you like—old boy."

Charlotte had had enough. The whole situation was beyond her, but they were both using her as a means to some curious ends of their own.

She bent to pick up the silver bag that Madame Dupont had lent to her, scooped the cobwebby lace stole from the back of the chair, looked at them both, said very coolly, "Excuse me," and walked away. She skirted the room, dodging couples, sidestepping to avoid waiters, her heart beating fast with fear and anger. Jared might be angry; she was equally so. She didn't know how much a taxi would cost to the villa, and had in any case only brought a few francs with her, but she wasn't spending another moment with either of the men. They could sort out their battles without her assistance.

The Ruritanian doorman moved forward as she went

down the steps. "*Madame* requires a cab?" he inquired expressionlessly.

"Not . . . not yet, thank you." She couldn't walk back to the villa, that was obvious, but she had to get away, if only to think—an impossibility with the hundreds of noisy people around her in the hotel. She moved briskly away from the brightly lit front of the building, then as it grew darker her footsteps faltered. The night air was still warm, but she drew the stole around her shoulders and shivered slightly. Let Jared and Paul fight it out if they wanted to. For her the evening was over. She didn't care. She sat on a low wall, oblivious to the stares of passersby, until a gendarme stopped and spoke quietly.

"Is there anything wrong, *mademoiselle?*"

She looked up, forcing a smile. "No . . . no, thank you, I'm quite all right."

"It is not advisable for *mademoiselle* to be out alone so late."

So late? "What time is it?"

"Nearly twelve-thirty." And as he spoke, she turned and saw Jared walking toward her. She stood quickly, and the policeman looked around in the direction of her glance and frowned.

"Charlotte, what the hell do you mean by running off?" he demanded, and the gendarme grinned broadly.

"*Ah, je m'excuse, mademoiselle!*"

"No, don't go," Charlotte began, but Jared was there, and the dapper gendarme gave him a broad grin, a quick salute that spoke volumes.

Oh, but you don't understand, thought Charlotte bitterly. *It's not a lover's tiff, far from it!* Then Jared was beside her, face shadowed in the darkness of the night.

"Running off?" she retorted, her temper rising swiftly at the sight and angry sound of him. "How *dare* you! Do you imagine you can use me as a . . . a . . . scapegoat in your pathetic little squabbles with your so-called friends?" As she moved away and he grasped her arm, she tried to shake it free.

"Get off me! Or I'll call that gendarme back!"

"No, you won't. Don't ever walk out on me like that again. No one does that." He was still controlled, but less so.

"I just did!" she rejoined. "And don't tell me what I can and can't do."

"Listen," he grated, "this place isn't fit for a girl alone at night, it's as simple as that. I brought you here—you stay with me."

"When you behave yourself I do; when you act like a child I don't!"

"And how were you going to get back home?"

"To the villa? I hadn't decided. Probably by taxi."

"But in the meantime you were sitting out here? Who were you hoping would come along—a fairy prince...or Paul?"

"Well, either would be preferable to *you*!" she shot back.

He laughed. "You reckon? Paul eats little girls like you for breakfast."

"I'm not standing here while you get rid of your temper on me," she said. "You should have had a fistfight with Paul—it's what you were both heading for. What happened—did you back down?" It was intended to sting him and it succeeded.

"I wouldn't waste my time fighting—I'd have sorted him out with one hand tied behind my back."

And Charlotte began to laugh. "Oh, you should see your face! Just like a little boy bragging—ow! Let go of my arm!" She struggled and he released her abruptly.

"We're getting the car. Come on," he said grimly. She rubbed her arm and glared at him.

"Go to hell!"

"I'm going to count to five, and if you don't move I

shall pick you up and *carry* you to the car. One . . . two—"

"You wouldn't dare!" she gasped, but he continued counting.

"Three . . . four—"

"All *right*." She moved away from him and toward the hotel. Because she knew then that he meant what he said.

A couple of notes changed hands, the doorman blew a whistle, and a few minutes later the Lamborghini glided to a halt in front of them, and a well-dressed youth got out, saluted, and handed Jared his keys.

She was helped into the car, and not a muscle had moved in that doorman's face. He could probably write a book about the things he had seen, she thought. Perhaps he had.

Jared roared away from the curb, along streets still full of people, out of Cannes itself and along the main road toward the villa.

He had only done a mile or so when he swung abruptly from the main route and upward on a smaller road. Charlotte looked back in puzzlement.

"This isn't the road home," she said.

Jared ignored her, drove upward, and the track grew narrower and more twisting, and it was all dark now, no more lights to guide them, only the headlamps sweeping through the impenetrable night. Then he pulled off the road, and switched off the engine and the headlamps, and it was pitch-black save for the dashboard gleam.

Charlotte turned to him, suddenly frightened, saw the expression on his face, and took a deep breath.

"I'm not stopping here with you," she breathed, and started to open the door. Silently he learned across and clicked the lock.

"Oh, yes, you are," he said softly.

CHAPTER TEN

She went very still. There was nothing she could do, no way to escape from Jared. Yet strangely there was no fear in her. Perhaps she was past it; she no longer knew. She leaned back in the seat and realized she was utterly exhausted. Silence washed in all around them, broken by a click and the crackle of paper; then the rich aromatic scent of a cheroot filled the car, and she said, "Why have you brought me here?"

"Because it's quiet, and because I don't fancy wandering around Cannes."

"Why haven't you driven us back to the villa?"

"It's too early. We're not expected until two or three at the earliest." His answers didn't make sense. She turned and looked sideways at him.

"I don't understand you."

"Don't you? It's quite simple. We're staying here for another hour at least—and then we'll go."

"You must be joking! Sit here for an hour? What will Aunt Marie think?"

"That we stayed until the end—or nearly—and that we had a pleasant evening."

"Oh, really? She won't when I tell her what happened."

"But you won't, will you? She's been ill—still is—and you're not going to upset her. She wants a full report—and you can give her one, can tell her what she wants to hear, and keep her happy."

"You mean tell lies, don't you? Why don't you say it properly?"

"Because lies aren't necessary. You just omit to tell her about Paul, that's all. There are enough other events to mention, I'm sure. And if all else fails, you can describe the food—she'll like that."

Charlotte was silent. *I'm damned if I'll just tamely do everything you tell me to*, she thought. But she kept it to herself.

"So do you want to listen to the radio, or talk?" he added.

"I certainly don't want to talk to you," she answered.

"No? Then we'll have some music instead." And he switched the car radio on. Charlotte leaned back again and went over the evening's events in her mind. The pictures were still vivid, the impressions too fresh and colorful to even try to sort out. But when morning came she would, she knew that....

She opened her eyes because the car was moving. "I thought you said we were stopping here," she said, feeling very confused.

"I did, and we have—you've been asleep," he answered dryly.

"I don't believe you," she said.

"Look at your watch."

She did. It was past two. "I must have been tired," she admitted.

"No doubt. At least you didn't have to make conversation with me," he said, and did a rapid gear change that sent them speeding even faster along a nearly deserted highway.

Charlotte didn't speak. Because she was remembering her dream now. It came back to her clearly and in great detail, and with it a wave of disturbing emotion. For in that dream Jared had kissed her, not once but several times, and not as it had been in the kitchen, but as it had been two years previously: warmly, affectionately— beautifully. And her heart beat faster with the recollection, because something she had been trying to deny would no longer be denied. She had thought she hated Jared—had imagined that all the feelings for him had been erased by his brutal behavior. But now she knew differently. In spite of everything, she knew beyond a shadow of doubt that she still loved him. She turned slightly to look at him, to see his hard hawklike profile as he drove along the road. *What a fool I am*, she thought. *I should have been cured by now, seeing him with Margot, knowing how he regards me . . . how he despises me—but I'm not.* And the knowledge was painful. Perhaps Aunt Marie knew. Charlotte closed her eyes. *If so, let her be the only one*, she prayed inwardly, *let no one else see, for I couldn't bear it.* She moved restlessly in her seat, and they started up the road to the villa. Jared slowed down slightly and said, "We'll have a drink when we get in."

"Will we? So that you can brief me on what to say and what not to say?" she retorted, her voice made sharper because of her efforts to hide the pain.

She saw his mouth tighten, saw his hands gripping the wheel, and she regretted her reply. Why rouse his anger unnecessarily? It did her no good.

"We've already been over that once. A drink will help you sleep, that's all." His voice was calm.

"Oh. All right."

He laughed. "You're full of surprises. One minute spitting like a kitten, the next as cool as buttermilk."

"Am I?" She bit on her tongue to hold back any more words, and he stopped the car, there, halfway along the driveway, and turned to her.

"Yes, you are. Why the sudden changes?"

"Why the questions?" She felt breathless, because the last thing she wanted was this closeness, this intimacy—not feeling as she did, bruised and vulnerable with the weight of her new knowledge.

"Because I want to know, that's why."

"And supposing I don't w-want to tell you?" she ventured.

"I can't make you, can I?"

"Don't try." Her voice came out as a whisper. Tension was mounting within her. In a moment, if he didn't drive on, she would get out of the car. And he moved, only slightly, but it was enough.

"No! Oh *no*—don't—" She fumbled desperately to open the locked door, heard his startled, half-bitten-back oath, then strong fingers clamped down over hers, and he pulled her hand from the lock.

"What the hell's the matter?" He twisted her around to face him. "God, but I can't make you out at—"

"Let me go!"

"I'm not going to rape you, for heaven's sake—and I'm damned if I'm going haring after you in the dark. You'll break a leg or something, you idiot. Now calm down and we'll get into the house. Don't worry," he added grimly, "I'll be glad to get rid of you." And he started the engine as he spoke so that his words were nearly lost. Nearly, but not quite. Charlotte heard them and closed her eyes. Of course he would. And it was at that moment that she knew she could not go on working for Madame Grenier for much longer. The image of Margot's cool beautiful face floated before her in the light from the headlamps. Margot. It was her he wanted. Yet how could she leave Marie? She couldn't do that, either. Jared . . . Margot . . . Marie—the names repeated themselves endlessly in her tired brain, and Charlotte put her hand to her head to stop it spinning around.

The car stopped, but this time it was at the door. A few lights shone out as if to welcome them home, but the bedrooms were in darkness. Jared closed his door quietly, came around to Charlotte's and opened hers.

"Gently does it," he said. "We mustn't wake the sleeping population," and he put his hand under her arm to help her out. Charlotte didn't try to resist. There was only one person she could confide in, and perhaps in the morning she would do so. Aunt Marie, because she, and only she, would understand.

MARIE WOKE HER at nine from a sound sleep. Charlotte opened her eyes to see the swimsuited girl sitting on the bed.

"Ah, you are awake—good!"

"With you bouncing up and down there's not much chance of rest," Charlotte responded, still sleepy.

"Hah! Aunt Marie said I was not to wake you, so I thought, if I just sat here *quietly....*" Marie grinned impishly. "I will ring for your breakfast now," and she pressed the bell by the bed. Then seating herself, she said, "Now, may I hear everything about your splendid evening? Jared has gone out—he is always dashing off somewhere, that one, but he told me before he went that he is taking us into Cannes this afternoon for a present for Aunt Marie." She hugged her bare sun-browned knees. "Isn't that *lovely?*"

"Lovely," agreed Charlotte, and struggled to sit up. "What else did he tell you?"

"That you had spent a nice evening and met lots of interesting people."

"Hmm, did he?" The more painful memories were returning now, and the knowledge that she still loved him—which had never really gone away—flooded back with an intensity that hurt. "Yes, I suppose we did, though I don't remember all their names." She began to describe the hotel with its grand ballroom, the huge chandeliers that had glittered their golden lights on everyone, the women's dresses, the dazzling jewelry. Words came easily and the child listened, utterly fascinated by the picture Charlotte painted.

In retrospect, she realized, it had been an experience not to be missed, something to remember for years and years—up until the moment when a man called Paul had spoken to her and the evening had gone horribly awry. She must have hesitated, because Marie said impatiently, "Yes? And then?"

"That's all for now. I want my breakfast, and anyway I'll be telling the whole story to your Aunt Marie later on."

"All right." There was a tap on the door and Lucia came in. "May I stay while you eat?" Marie requested.

"Of course."

Later, as they sat out on the terrace, Charlotte repeated her vivid account of the evening. She described the food in minute detail, the impression made on her by the magnificently uniformed doorman, the discreet way their tickets were inspected, the wine, the dancing . . . everything in fact except the one incident that had caused the ball to come to an end for her—and for Jared.

She sensed that Madame Dupont was regarding her oddly once or twice, but it wasn't until Marie had at last scampered away to dive into the water that Charlotte found out why.

"So, you enjoyed your evening, did you?" the old woman asked with an innocent smile.

"Very much, thank you."

"But you do not mention something that I would have thought even more fascinating than what you have already told us."

Charlotte looked at her, puzzled, and Aunt Marie began to chuckle. "Ah, yes—I refer to Paul, of course."

"Paul! But...did J-Jared tell you?"

"Him? Hah, certainly not *him*—no, I had a little phone call earlier this morning from a dear friend who wanted to tell me of the most interesting incident that occurred at the ball, when Jared and Paul had a slight difference of opinion—."

"Oh, dear!"

"Oh, dear, yes! Now come on, child, Marie is safely engaged in practicing her Australian crawl, or something approaching it, and I am all agog, to put it mildly."

Charlotte looked at her and gave a rueful smile. "Jared practically forbade me to tell you. He said that as you'd been ill—" She was interrupted by a disbelieving snort, but went on, "You shouldn't hear—but oh, I'm glad you asked. I need to tell someone, and I couldn't have a better person than you," and she told the old woman exactly what had happened when Jared had left her alone for a few minutes.

When the story was done, Madame Dupont sighed. "Ah, *quelle histoire*! And this Paul, you do not know who he is?"

"Only that he and Jared appear to dislike one another intensely."

"Oh, yes, that is true!" Aunt Marie's laugh rang out loud and clear. "Ah, that I had been there! I will tell you about Paul. A very handsome man, is he not? And before Jared came onto the scene, he was Margot's constant escort. He is also the son of a man who was my dear late husband's greatest rival in business...."

But Charlotte had gone numb at the old woman's first words. So that was why! Humiliation washed over her as she realized now the reason for the bristling enmity between the two of them. Margot! She should have known! She closed her eyes to hide the pain from the other's shrewd gaze, and Aunt Marie said, "But there is something else distressing you. Tell me."

"I don't think I know how to begin," Charlotte admitted.

"You do not? Then you must leave it. I have no wish to force anything out of you, my child."

And Charlotte turned to her and said, "It's just that—I don't think I can go on working for Madame Grenier for much longer. I thought my feelings for Jared were dead, but...but they're not."

"Ah!" A long sigh. "Love can be painful, *n'est-ce pas*? And men can be very blind. You poor girl. What are we to do with him?"

"Nothing. I shall have to sort it out for myself." And she added quickly, "I know you won't say anything—"

"Of course not! You will have to learn to be strong, Charlotte. It is the only way. Easy to say, difficult to do, I know. I, too, have had my heart broken in the past. But one recovers."

"Yes, I know." *But when*? she asked herself. *How long do I have to wait before I'm cured...again*? Not even the wise old woman would be able to answer that one.

"I think I'll have a swim with Marie, if I may." Charlotte stood up and smoothed down her suit over her slender hips.

"Of course, of course. Away you go. Jared tells me that he will be in for lunch today. Please ring for Henri. I will have a little discussion with him about that, I think."

Charlotte did so, then descended the steps into the glistening water. No diving today for her; her hair still felt too good from its careful dressing the previous evening. She intended it to last a while longer. She smiled wryly to herself for this small vanity, and had no idea just how beautiful she looked as she slid into the water. Nor had she any idea of what lay behind Madame Dupont's inscrutable expression as the old woman watched her go.

She and Marie laughed and played ball in the water for a while, and Charlotte could almost feel the sun tanning her as the wet droplets dried on her skin. She caught the ball and turned to Madame Dupont to make some remark about the heat, then caught her breath, because Jared was standing beside the old woman's seat, just watching her.

"Uncle Zhar!" Marie shrieked at the same moment. "Go and get your trunks on and come in!"

"No—" he glanced at his watch "—it's too near lunch now. Perhaps later. And you had better get dressed if you and Charlotte are coming for a ride with me afterward."

"Oh, yes! I forgot! Come on, Charlotte. We will let Uncle Zhar pull us out of the water. He is very strong, you know." And Marie dived under and swam just below the surface to where Jared waited.

Charlotte saw his eyes rest on her arms as he pulled her up from the water, saw his slight frown, and looked in the direction of his glance. There was a large smudgy bruise just below her shoulder.

"Thank you," she said, then to Aunt Marie: "Marie and I will go and get changed."

"Off you go." Bright blue eyes had missed nothing, Charlotte felt sure. But she was equally sure that the old woman would say nothing. She still felt shaken from the brief encounter at the poolside when Jared had pulled her from the water— and just before that when she had looked up to see his eyes on her. The shock had been almost physical.

She chose a simple yellow dress that fitted her perfectly. But it was sleeveless, and she frowned as she looked in the mirror and saw the bruise. How. . . And then she realized. Jared had held her just there in their difference of opinion outside the hotel. Perhaps he, too, had remembered.

Aunt Marie remarked on it at lunch, and Charlotte said easily, "I bumped my arm on a door," and smiled, but her smile didn't reach Jared.

"Hmm, I see. Now, Jared, if you are taking the girls

for a little ride—I wish I could come with you, but there, these doctors think they know best—I will give you a list of a few items I would like you to pick up for me in Cannes. You will do that?"

"With pleasure, Aunt Marie," he answered.

"You are leaving for home on Sunday?" she asked, a little wistfully, it seemed to Charlotte.

"I'm afraid so," he answered with a shrug. "Duty calls. You know how it is. I spoke to Aunt Heloise yesterday on the phone and she seems to think we've all been away long enough. So—" he pulled a face "—there it is."

"But you will come again soon?"

"Of course."

"And you, Charlotte, you will come, too?" The old woman turned to Charlotte, who nodded.

"Of course—if I am asked." *And if I'm still there*, she thought.

"Then that is settled. And if Heloise needs reassurance, I will have to be 'poorly' again, won't I?"

Jared laughed. "You could get away with murder, and you know it, aunt. Anyway, what's to stop you coming up to visit us? I'll even come and fetch you if you want."

"You will? Hmm, now *there's* a thought." The old woman's eyes brightened, and Charlotte thought, *I bet she will, too.* "Of course, I'll have to get a little better first—but it would be something to look forward to."

"Then we will make arrangements now. You *will* be better by the time of the harvesting of the grapes. Think of the parties— think what a time you will have, Aunt Marie. All you have to do is obey the doctors and ... *voilà!*"

"I am tempted." Aunt Marie pushed away a piece of crusty bread that Marie had offered her. "No child, *rien plus de pain*— I will start on that diet this *minute!*" Her hearty laugh shook the wineglasses on the table, and so infectious was it that they all joined in.

THE ROAD WAS LONG and Jared's driving assured as he took them in the Lamborghini to Cannes later that day. He parked behind a hotel where he was obviously well known, for there was a whispered consultation with an attendant and notes changed hands. He caught up with Charlotte as she followed Marie out toward the promenade.

"Did I make that bruise?" he asked quietly.

Charlotte looked at him. "It wasn't anybody else," she said. "But don't apologize—I wouldn't expect it of you."

"Then I won't. It wouldn't do to spoil my image, would it?" he answered easily.

To think that I love you, she thought. *I must be mad.* "Where are we going?"

"It all depends what kind of present you want. Marie seems to be heading for one of those outrageously expensive girls' shops. Hey, Marie, wait!" he called.

The girl halted and turned, eyes alight with happiness. *At least one person is enjoying herself*, Charlotte reflected.

"What are you going to buy for Aunt Marie?" he demanded.

"A vase or a statue or something. Why?"

"I just wondered. I know a shop that might just do...." And he paused deliberately, smiling.

She jumped up and grabbed his hand. "All right. Where? Let's go now."

"Patience, child, patience. There's plenty of time. It's too hot to rush. Now, follow me."

The streets were crowded, the tall buildings elegant and beautiful, shimmering in the sun, and beyond that

the green Mediterranean beckoned them with its
moored yachts bobbing gently in the harbor. In the distance a water-skier cut a white foamy path across the
water, and gulls cried their sad cries, and Charlotte
gazed around her in wonder. This was the paradise of
the very rich, and she was staying here in a villa that
was the ultimate in luxury. It was a situation she could
not have believed possible only weeks before.

And what was it Aunt Emily had said? "I have a feeling that this job is for you." In one way her hunch, her
womanly intuition, had been right; in another, sadly
awry. For who could have foreseen Jared?

Charlotte bit her lip. She would have to tell her soon.

"Mind the traffic." The voice of the man in her
thoughts jerked her back to the present from her mo-
mentary daydream. His hand on her arm was warm and
restraining; she saw the shirt-sleeved, white-gloved gendarme directing the traffic at a busy junction, and they
waited to cross with the colorfully dressed throng. A
hand waved, traffic screeched, feet marched across, and
Marie held tightly to Jared's hand and said:

"I'm thirsty."

"You want a drink now?"

"Yes, please, Uncle Zhar." She had seen the pavement café before they had.

"All right. Charlotte, what will you have?"

"Lemonade—anything cold, please."

They sat at a red metal-topped table shaded by a
huge umbrella emblazoned all around with the word
"Martini." A handsome young waiter brought them
their drinks on tiny saucers, and Marie sighed luxuriously.

"This is *lovely*!" she said. "I do like coming out with
you, Uncle Zhar—and Charlotte, of course," and she
smiled at Charlotte reassuringly. "I mean, it's so *nice* to
be with my favorite people. What a pity Aunt Marie

couldn't come, as well. Do you think she will come and visit us?"

"I'm sure she will," he answered. Charlotte sipped her icy fizzy drink and watched him. In an open-necked blue sports shirt he looked strong and attractive, a deeply tanned man, seemingly unaware of the lingering glances of passing women. "But first she must get better. Then I will come and fetch her, as I promised."

"And can Charlotte and I come, too?" the girl asked. *Oh, please*, thought Charlotte, *please don't go on. You don't know what you're doing.*

"I'd need a bigger car, wouldn't I?" he̅ asked. "There's only room for us—"

"But you could come in the Daimler," she interrupted. "See, *that* is big enough for *lots* of people—"

"Drink up, chatterbox. No wonder you're so thirsty. You never stop talking!"

Marie laughed. "You are funny. You try to sound cross, but I know you're not. I can tell by your face. All those little laughter lines around your eyes disappear when you are angry. But they are still there."

"All right, Sherlock Holmes. Drink up, and if you're so clever *you* can take us to the shop."

"What is it called?"

"Cobwebs."

"Cobwebs. . . . " Clearly the girl was puzzled. "I don't know the word."

"And I thought you knew everything! *Les toiles des araignées* in French, okay? And before you ask, it is called that because it belongs to an English friend of mine, and it's full of antiques and all sorts of interesting things, and it's in the next street—so you can lead the way and find it for us."

"All right." Marie finished her drink and stood up. "I'm ready."

"Are you ready, Charlotte?" he asked politely.

She stood up. "Yes. Thank you for the drink."

"A pleasure." The smile he gave her was for Marie's benefit, not hers, she knew that. A helpless sensation swept over her. A feeling of frustrated anger, and no way to escape it. As long as she stayed working for Madame Grenier she must suffer it whenever he was near. She looked directly at him and met the challenge of his gaze with her own clear blue eyes. *Why should I suffer?*, she thought suddenly. *Why the hell should I? I've had enough from you, taken all I can stand. I'm going to start fighting back now*. And something must have communicated itself to him, for she saw the hardening of his face, and she smiled slowly at him. All in the space of a few seconds it had happened— Marie was a few yards away, fascinated by the antics of a small boy with his parents, oblivious to them—and in those few moments Charlotte had been possessed by a new resolve, perhaps triggered off by Madame Dupont's words: "You will have to learn to be strong, Charlotte."

"Marie isn't watching you," she said quietly. "You don't need to put on the act for *me*."

"What do you mean?" Calm, not aggressive—yet.

She lifted one eyebrow. "I don't have to tell you—for you already know. But you can't bother me anymore—I don't *care*." And she turned away to follow Marie, and left him waiting by the chairs. It was like a warm glow inside her. Somehow she had found the strength. She would not let him hurt her anymore. When they returned to the villa she would tell Aunt Marie so.

CHAPTER ELEVEN

SHE KNEW SHE WAS DIFFERENT now. It was as though she had succeeded in building a wall around her heart. It might ache inside, but he would never know. No one would. And as they walked along baking pavements she remembered the look she had seen on his face, just for an instant, when she had come down the stairs at the villa the previous evening. She had known then the dizzy sense of power possessed by a beautiful woman. Just for a second, but if it could happen once, it could do so again. *It's all in the mind*, she thought in wonder. *If I tell myself that I'm beautiful, I will be; and if I tell myself I'm full of confidence, then that will also be so.* She took a deep breath and held her head high. Would Aunt Marie understand? Somehow Charlotte knew that she would. There would be much to talk about at the villa when they returned.

Marie skipped ahead, reading the signs above the shops, hesitating, frowning, then going on. Then she stopped and pointed. "Look, Uncle Zhar," she called. "We are here!"

"Right!" He held up his hand in acknowledgment. He was walking beside Charlotte, had been since he'd caught up to her after their drink. They hadn't spoken; there was nothing to say. But the air was charged with brittle tension; only now Charlotte, instead of feeling frightened by it, was enjoying it. For he was puzzled—she knew that as surely as if he had told her. *Good*, she thought. "I hope this shop isn't too pricey," she remarked as they neared it, "these sort of places usually are."

"Don't worry, I know James too well."

"How nice for you," she murmured, almost as if to herself, then smiled as he glanced at her quickly.

She paused outside the window, to which Marie had her nose glued. Her heart sank slightly. And hopes of a dusty antique shop crammed with bargains vanished in an instant as she looked inside. Pictures, ornaments, vases and jewelry were there all right, cleverly arranged to tempt the passerby, and not a price ticket to be seen—which was probably just as well, she thought. It was certainly not a place she would venture in alone, for every item in the window had the stamp of quality and luxury about it. Rich dark green velvet was the back-cloth on which everything was placed. Larger pictures at the back; figurines in the center; a few rings scattered, seemingly casually, in the foreground—heavy antique rings that glowed with beauty and color.

Marie pointed to a small figure of a girl holding a basket of fruit. "I like *that*," she announced. "Will you ask your friend how much it is?"

"You have undoubted good taste, my child," he commented, grinning. "That's Capo di Monte and probably costs a fortune. However, we'll go in and see, shall we?" He held out his hand to usher them in.

The interior was cool, and they were surrounded by antique writing desks, chairs, bookcases full of old books, picture-covered walls, a row of grandfather clocks. Charlotte looked around her in quiet wonder. What a splendid place to browse uninterrupted. How Aunt Emily would love it!

"Jared! Come on in. You're a stranger, how are you?" The voice came from the back of the shop, and then a man came forward to shake Jared's hand. Probably in his early forties, he was dark and smiling, stockily built, with a black bushy beard obscuring most of his face. His eyes were friendly enough—and shrewd. He looked at Charlotte and grinned, then at Marie. "And friends, too. Welcome, all of you."

"Charlotte, I'd like you to meet James Walker, an old friend of mine—James, Charlotte Lawson and my niece, Marie. We're staying at my aunt's place for a few more days," he said as they shook hands.

"How is Madame Dupont? I've not seen her for ages."

"Not too bad at present. Why don't you go and visit her sometime? She'd be glad to see you. It's her birthday tomorrow, which is why we're here."

"Ah!" James nodded. "Thought you'd have a good reason for coming. Well, this is the right place, old boy. I'll look after you."

Jared smiled, "Take us for a ride, you mean."

James's face expressed great pain. "You wound me. And in front of ladies! How could you?"

"Because I know you."

"Hmm, you have a point. However, it's bargain day today. Now—" this more briskly "—what have you got your eye on?"

"My niece is interested in this particular item," Jared responded, indicating the small figure previously admired by Marie.

James winced. "Capo di Monte? Clever child!" He grinned at Marie.

He looks like a sea captain, thought Charlotte, *not an antique-shop proprietor. But he seems nice—I wonder what he's doing being a friend of Jared's?*

He lifted the figure out carefully. It was exquisite, a miniature of a girl who looked in a way like Marie herself. The little girl took a deep breath. "How much is it, please? I have my purse."

Jared raised a finger. "Can I just have a quick word in your ear, James—won't take a moment?"

James put the figure carefully down on a rosewood

table. "Look at it, Marie," he said. "But if you pick it
up, do so very gently." He vanished with Jared to the
back of the shop. Charlotte thought she knew why they
had gone. Well, that was fair enough. He had more
money than he knew what to do with, and doubtless
Marie's pocket money was rationed.

They were only away a couple of minutes, and neither face gave anything away when they returned.
James clapped his hands briskly together.

"Where were we?" he asked. "Ah, yes, you wanted to
know the price of that charming piece, didn't you,
mademoiselle?" Then he said it, and Charlotte kept her
smile to herself. A quick mental calculation to translate
francs to pounds, and it was obvious what arrangements
Jared had come to with his friend. He was almost giving
it away.

"Then may I have it? I have enough!" Marie almost
gasped in delight.

"You certainly may. We'll find a box and some packing, shall we?"

Jared spoke. "You aren't looking around, Charlotte."

"No," she smiled. "I don't think—"

"Try, you never know. Hey, James, anything interesting for Aunt Marie?"

The voice came from the back recesses of the shop
where James and Marie were clearly searching for
something, judging by the sound of drawers opening
and closing. "Some odds and ends in a box at your left.
Try it. I know Madame Dupont likes chunky jewelry."

Jared lifted down a heavy old box and opened it.
Charlotte took a deep breath at the sight of the treasures
within—bracelets, rings, necklaces, pendants—everything jumbled up as though poured in willy-nilly.

"That's some new stuff I haven't sorted through yet,"
James's voice called. "It'll want cleaning, too, but I can
do that in a jiffy."

Charlotte knew she wouldn't be able to afford anything, but the temptation to handle such beautiful jewelry was too strong to resist. She lifted out a heavy gold ring with a deep red stone and slipped it on her finger and sighed. "Beautiful!" she whispered. Jared didn't attempt to touch anything. He just stood there, watching, waiting. Only now Charlotte didn't care. She riffled through the rest, carefully untangling a fine silver chain before lifting out the pendant that it held and resting it in the palm of her hand. It was small and quite simple, a stone of blue shading to mauve. She put it out on the table beside the box and dug in again, this time to bring out a chain bracelet fastened with a tiny padlock. No, that was plain and heavy. She didn't even like it. Her eyes were dazzled with the color and sheer variety of it all. And each item told a story, each was old, that was sure.

"Seen anything you fancy?" Jared's voice was almost an intrusion.

She looked up at him. "Nearly all of it—but you don't need to tell me it'll be dear."

"That pendant—why have you left it out?"

She picked it up. "I like the stone; I'd like to ask your friend how much it would be."

"How much is this pendant, James?" Jared called. "It's got a stone that looks like an amethyst."

"A what? Hang on." James bustled out and picked it up. "Hmm, that one—I don't know how that got there—oh, you can have it for a couple of quid. Do you want it, Jared?"

"Charlotte might. Well, Charlotte?"

Two pounds! She looked from it to James, who seemed frankly disinterested, and back again to the pendant.

"I'll have it," she said. And she still didn't realize. Not until later, and then it was too late.

Jared chose a picture that Charlotte had noticed on entering the shop, and liked—a landscape that might have been a Constable but obviously wasn't, but was very pleasant and restful to look at. He didn't even ask the price, just told James he would take it.

"Right. Now you'll come in the back for coffee before you go?"

Jared looked at Charlotte. "Charlotte? Would you like a coffee?"

"Oh, yes, thank you very much," she answered, smiling at James.

It wasn't until she had begun her coffee that she realized she still wore the ring with the red stone. Putting down the cup, she said faintly, "I'm sorry, I put this ring on to try it before—and forgot I had it on."

Marie laughed. "Wouldn't it be funny if you couldn't get it off? Then you'd have to buy it!"

But Charlotte had already taken the ring from her finger and put it on the table beside her. In a way, the room in which they were sitting was an extension of the shop, full of antique furniture and heavy lamps and statues. But it was all arranged in such a way that they sat comfortably, Charlotte and Marie on a purple velvet-upholstered chaise longue, the two men on hard-backed dining chairs. "Shall I put it back in the box?" she volunteered.

"No." James shook his head. "Enjoy your drink. Have another biscuit?"

Marie was the only one who wanted one, and they stayed for a while longer before Jared looked at his watch and remarked that they really ought to go if Aunt Marie wasn't to sent out search parties for them, which amused Marie greatly. Both girls paid for and received their gifts, and Jared stayed behind as they walked out.

He caught up to them as they were halfway down the street. He carried the wrapped picture under one arm.

But that hadn't been the reason for his staying. He had waited for them to go before paying for the picture, and the extra for Marie's statuette, and .... And it was then that Charlotte saw what she should have seen half an hour before when she had asked the price of the pendant. What a fool she had been! What a *stupid* idiot. She stopped walking and looked down at the two small packages she carried, her own and Marie's. Jared paused, looked back, and she glanced up—and the expression on his face told her what she needed to confirm her deep suspicions. But she said nothing. She merely met his look with her own. Her newfound confidence was still too fragile to risk challenging him now. Later, she would. Later, when she had planned what to say, and how to say it.

"Anything the matter?" he asked.

"Nothing ... nothing at all. Should there be? The presents are delightful, aren't they? I'm sure Aunt Marie will be very pleased." And she smiled innocently at him and walked on. That was two evening dresses, and now the difference in price of a pendant. One day soon she would pay him back every penny of the money. Busily planning how to save it up, she walked quickly along. When she left the château, as she eventually would, she would be in his debt for nothing.

THEY WATCHED FILMS that evening at the villa—not on television, but on a large screen fitted up in the lounge. Nothing surprised Charlotte anymore; she wouldn't have been astonished if an usherette had appeared with ice creams in the interval between the cartoons and the main film, but it was Lucia who came in with champagne instead. Madame Dupont was comfortably ensconced on a settee, Charlotte and Marie by her side on another settee, Jared slightly behind them on a chair.

Henri operated the projector, and with the faint blue smoke wreathing around them from Jared's cigar, the atmosphere was almost that of a real cinema.

It was an American Western—these were Aunt Marie's favorites, as she told Charlotte while they sipped their champagne before the start—and it was funny to hear James Garner speaking perfect French even though she knew it was dubbed. She was very aware of Jared behind her, although he didn't speak. She had had no chance to speak to Aunt Marie alone since their return from Cannes, and any conversation had been general. They had called at a shop to collect some flowers that Madame Dupont had ordered before they returned to the villa, and had each bought a birthday card from the shop adjoining it. The only problem Charlotte had had since returning was preventing Marie from blurting out about the presents. And now it was late, and Marie would soon be in bed, and tomorrow they would be giving them anyway.

The film over, the screen rolled away by Henri, Marie looked at Charlotte.

"Shall I go to bed now?" she asked her.

"I think it would be a good idea," Charlotte answered, and winked at the girl, who stood and went over to kiss Aunt Marie.

"Oh, you're going to have a marvelous birthday tomorrow," she whispered as she hugged her.

"Am I?" The old woman chuckled. "Good. Off you go, *ma petite*. Sleep well."

Then Jared stood up. "I'm away myself, Aunt Marie. Shall I help you upstairs before I go?"

"No, Henri will do that. Are you deserting me, too, Charlotte?"

Charlotte shook her head. "Not if you'd like me to stay. I'm not tired."

"Good. We will have a drink, as well. Good night, Jared."

"Good night, Aunt Marie." He bent to kiss her forehead. "Good night, Charlotte," very formally.

She turned and smiled at him. "Good night," very brightly.

Aunt Marie let out her breath in a deep sigh when he had gone. "There are drinks in that corner cupboard, child," she said. "We won't bother Henri. Now, what have you to tell me?"

Charlotte couldn't stop the laughter that bubbled out. "How...how do you know I have anything to tell you?" she asked.

"Ah! I've been watching you! And Jared is one very puzzled man. And you—*you* have a certain air about you that is difficult to describe. So what is it?"

"I think it's something you said, as a matter of fact," Charlotte began after she had poured them both a glass of wine on Madame Dupont's instructions. "We had just finished a drink at a sidewalk café in Cannes, and I looked at him and thought, 'Why the hell should I let *you* upset me?' Something clicked, as I remembered your words about being strong, and I told him that nothing he could do would bother me anymore; then I walked off and left him standing there." She remembered the scene vividly, the expression on his face, and was filled with remorse. "Oh, was I terrible?"

"Terrible? You? No! I would like to have seen that! Perhaps that is the first time anyone has treated him thus. Good for you, Charlotte. I love Jared dearly, as I'm sure you know, but I am well aware that he is arrogant at times—he's a very strong character—and likes his own way, which is only like most men, I suppose. It will do him good. But do you think you can keep it up? You mustn't weaken once you have started."

"I know—oh, Aunt Marie, it is awful to feel like this about anyone, isn't it? And it's awful for me to be talking about him like this—I know that, too. I am an employee of his aunt, and you are their very good friend, and I—"

"And you are a young woman who has been badly treated by him. Do not forget *that*, my child. This in a way has nothing to do with the fact of your employment. You are doing your task well with Marie, I know that. You are a person, and we are all important—remember that. You are doing the right thing—remember that, too. So now I know why he is so mystified—you see, I was aware of the difference in your manner. It suits you!" Seeing Charlotte's expression of concern, she added, "Yes, it does, truly! Don't let *me* down."

"All right, I won't. Oh!" Charlotte sighed. "Wouldn't it be nice if you were at the château—I could come to you when I needed advice."

"You can write to me or phone me if you feel the need to talk. I am always here—and I understand, perhaps as no one else could, my dear. For I know Jared very well, and I feel I am beginning to know you, too—in many ways I am reminded of myself when young every time I look at you." She nodded. "Oh yes, don't look surprised, it is quite true. One is very unsure of oneself when young—ah, to have the knowledge at twenty that one has at forty! But you are learning fast."

"You make me feel better," Charlotte confessed. "Much better—about everything."

"Fine. Drink up your wine. A drop more?"

"No, thanks, or I'll have a hangover in the morning—and I want to be wide awake to enjoy your birthday."

"Then I won't bother, either. I, too, need to be fresh, for I have a feeling I may be woken early by Marie with some little surprise."

"I think you will," Charlotte agreed.

"There will be a few old friends in to dinner—just two or three. Will you wear that dress?"

"Of course, if I may."

"It is yours now, don't forget that. You are to take it with you when you go. I couldn't be more pleased. What use is it hidden away in an old wardrobe? My granddaughters scorn it for the more modern clothes—they do not realize, as you and I do, just how very feminine the older-fashioned dresses can be."

'Thank you very much for it, Aunt Marie."

"And now, I think it is bedtime. Will you ring for Henri?"

IT WAS NOT MARIE who woke Charlotte, but the insistent ringing of the front doorbell at the villa. She heard voices, then the sound of movement, as if something heavy was being carried in. She found out what it had been when, washed and dressed a short time afterward, she went out of her room to go downstairs. The hall was filled with masses of beautiful flowers arranged in tall baskets, dozens and dozens of them. For a moment she stood there just looking, astonished beyond words, and Jared's voice came from behind her: "Good morning."

She turned to him. "Good morning. I was looking at that gorgeous display."

"Yes. Aunt Marie likes flowers. She's living in the right place for them, too. Are you going down to breakfast?"

"Yes." She didn't wait to see if he was, just started walking down, slowly, calmly. It was all too easy now—but would it be the same when they were back at the château? That was something no one could answer. One thing was sure—she would soon find out.

Aunt Marie was already up, walking slowly to greet them as they reached the dining room. Clad in a long white dress with batwing sleeves, she held up her hands in welcome.

"Good morning, my dears. Marie woke me at crack of dawn with the most exquisite present, so I had to get up to make the most of my day!"

Charlotte went forward and kissed the old woman's cheek. "Happy birthday, Aunt Marie," and she handed her the wrapped gift.

"Oh, come, I must sit down and open it." She embraced Jared, who wished her a happy birthday and then added:

"I'll go and get my present. I didn't think you'd be up yet. Excuse me."

"What a lovely pendant! Oh, I shall wear it now. Carefully, Charlotte, mind my hair!" The deep chuckle rose from Madame Dupont's throat as Charlotte slipped the chain over the old woman's head while she sat in a chair in the dining room. "Marie is out picking me some roses from the garden—there, that looks lovely. Thank you, Charlotte—but you shouldn't have spent all that money, you know...."

No, thought Charlotte, *that's the one thing I could hardly tell you, but dear Jared will be paid back, every franc.*

It seemed as if the doorbell never stopped ringing all morning, with cards and gifts galore arriving by messengers and postmen. The sun shone brightly from a cloudless sky as they sat on the terrace by the pool, and the extension phone shrilled constantly by Aunt Marie's side. Charlotte lay and sunbathed while Marie swam with Jared in the pool. There was ample time to think. What would the dinner be like that evening? Would it only be two or three old friends for dinner, as Aunt Marie had assured her? Or would there be a crowd? Mentally she went over all the makeup tips the older woman had taught her before the disastrous evening out on Wednesday. They were all clear in her mind. She resolved to look her very best. In a way it would be an important test, she felt sure, although she didn't know quite why.

"MMM, YES, Charlotte, you can put more eye shadow on, you haven't got quite enough," Marie said, frowning thoughtfully, clearly taking over where Aunt Marie had left off.

"Thank you," Charlotte answered, and carefully shaded more of the silver gray powder above her eyes. She was taking her time, not rushing at all, and actually enjoying it. *I'm getting a conceited hussy*, she thought wryly. *At one time I would have scorned this performance, but it's a challenge now. And in a way, it's all due to Jared—although that's something he'll never know.*

"Is that better?" she asked her critical watcher at last.

"Oh, yes, you look simply beautiful, Charlotte. I hope *I'll* be beautiful when I'm grown up."

"Of course you will!" Charlotte smiled at her warmly. "And now, are we ready?" She eased off the towel she had put around her shoulders while she made up, and moved from the stool. The dress glowed warmly on her, complimenting her golden skin and hair, giving her the appearance of a fairy-tale princess: But she knew only that she felt good, and that would suffice.

Marie had a long dress on, pale blue with small flowers. Charlotte had brushed the child's hair until it shone, and her cheeks glowed rosy red. "You look extremely pretty," she told her. "Let's go down and greet Aunt Marie's friends." Together they left the room.

IT WAS LATE. The dinner was over, the night was so warm that they had all drifted out onto the patio, and Charlotte, standing quietly beside Marie, looked around her treasuring the scene, knowing that this was something she would remember for the rest of her life. The

meal had been superb, but more important, the people,
Aunt Marie's friends, were delightful. The 'one or two'
had turned out to be eight, so that twelve people had sat
down to eat at nine o'clock, and since that time, nearly
three hours previously, the talk had flowed as freely as
the wine. Aunt Marie was the center of it all, no doubt
about that, and enjoying every moment of her own day.
And now she was calling something to Jared, who
stopped talking to a couple near to Charlotte and Marie
and answered his aunt.

"But I insist!" she shouted, and Charlotte began to
listen. There was a general burst of laughter, a rising
murmur of voices, and the man nearest Charlotte, an
elderly doctor, said, "It seems as if Jared has no
choice."

"I didn't hear—" she began, smiling.

And Marie pulled her hand and said loudly, "Aunt
Marie wants Jared to play the guitar!"

"Oh."

The man, Dr. Roche, smiled at them both. "You have
not heard him before?"

"No," Charlotte admitted. She didn't particularly
want to, but she thought it more tactful not to add that.

"Ah, then you will have a pleasant surprise. And if we
are lucky, no doubt Madame Dupont will sing for us."

She really shouldn't feel so amazed, she knew that.
She should have got used to the constant state of bewilderment by now. So many things, in so few weeks....

"Madame Dupont sings?" she asked faintly.

"But yes! You will see."

The lights blazed out from the house onto the terrace,
and moths fluttered around their heads, and the air was
sweet with the scent of flowers, and everyone drifted to
the chairs set beside the pool and sat down.

"Come—" Dr. Roche touched Charlotte's arm. "Sit
down here, and you, too, Marie."

Jared had vanished through the french windows, the murmur of voices began again, and Charlotte and Marie obeyed the doctor, who then sat beside them. Henri moved discreetly among them, distributing more champagne, removing empty glasses, quiet as ever.

Charlotte found herself waiting for Jared to return, and in spite of everything, a small, unwilling excitement grew within her—a sense of anticipation that she didn't quite understand.

And then he was there, and pulling a chair up beside a table so that he could sit on the table and rest one foot on the seat. "Talk among yourselves," he called. "I've got to tune this damned thing." A burst of laughter followed his words, and Charlotte, watching him, thought, *Everyone likes him, you can tell*. It showed before and during dinner; he was amusing and courteous to everyone—including Charlotte. Only once she had found him looking at her before he could glance away, and her breath had caught in her throat, because there was something in that look.... Only for a moment, then it was gone, but she remembered it now and she watched him as with bent head he tuned the instrument. Long fingers caressed the strings, he listened intently, then looked up.

"All right. What's it to be?" he called. "Aunt Marie, it's your party. What shall I play?"

"You know my favorite—'Mes Jeunes Années.'" There was a quiet murmur of approval and Charlotte puzzled over what the song could be, for she didn't recognize the title. Then he began to play, and a shiver of excitement ran up her spine as she recognized the tune—and heard words that she remembered only too well. She had to sit still, had to deliberately force herself from moving away, for the last time she had heard it had been at the fateful party in Paris when she and Jared had met. They had danced to it, and then the words had held a special magic, because it was a magical night. And now he was singing it, and something tore at her heart and made her want to cry out, to tell him to stop....

"Dreams never grow old, they shine through the years. ..." That record at the party had been sung by Les Compagnons de la Chanson, in English, and Jared was singing it in French, but the words were the same and their message was eternal.

His voice was pleasant, and all except his were stilled, with not even a glass chinking. Applause flooded the terrace when he had done, and then Aunt Marie sang another song, and everyone joined in a third, and Charlotte gradually relaxed. He hadn't done it deliberately, because Aunt Marie had requested it, and in any case he would have forgotten. Charlotte hadn't, but she knew he had, for what was one party to him among so many?

But then he sang it again and she wasn't so sure. Because, as he began it, he looked across at Charlotte, and it seemed as if his eyes mocked her. She couldn't stand it anymore. "Excuse me," she whispered to the doctor, who sat with eyes closed, listening, enjoying himself. She passed him and quickly, quietly, walked into the house. No one noticed. They were all too enraptured with the sweet soft sound of the guitar being played.

Charlotte ran up to her room. Tears filled her eyes. Blinking furiously, she dabbed with a handkerchief, careful not to smudge the mascara she had so recently applied, trembling with an inner sadness that was almost overwhelming. She didn't want to go down again, but she would have to, if only to be with Marie, for it was late. But at least not until the song was done, for it was unbearable. She sat on the bed. Through the open window she could hear the faint strains of the music in its closing bars. Then it was over, and they were clapping, and then laughing, and she wondered vaguely why, but she didn't care anymore. She looked ceiling-ward, not really seeing anything, only wondering how soon the pain would disappear completely.

It was time to go now. Before anyone commented on her disappearance. She opened the door, and Jared was coming along the corridor. She shut it again—too quick-ly, and heard his voice, "Charlotte?"

"No," she whispered. "Oh, no, go away," but too qui-etly for him to hear.

Then he was opening the door, coming in, and she looked at him, too shocked to speak. There was a very strange expression on his face.

CHAPTER TWELVE

CHARLOTTE FOUND HER VOICE. "What do you want?" she asked.

"Why did you disappear?" he asked, and his voice had a quality to it that made her go warm. He stood there in front of her, and he had never seemed so tough and powerful as he was now. Charlotte was frightened. Easy to be confident in daylight, easy to talk about it with Aunt Marie, and receive good advice, but her nerves were raw, her whole body still shaking from the effect of hearing a song that had brought back too many memories, far too many....

"Do I ... do I have to explain all my moves to you?" she asked, and prayed for courage, because he was shutting the door, and the handle clicked with a note of finality that made her nervous. It was as if he didn't intend to leave.

"No. But I was watching you. It was the song, wasn't it?"

She looked up at him then, eyes widening. "You knew—you *knew*?"

"Yes, I knew." There was something wrong. His aggression was gone; he stood there in front of her, and the tawny gold eyes held an expression she had thought she would never see again. Her heart beat faster, and then she turned, so that she didn't have to face him, so that he wouldn't see....

"Please go away," she said. "Please leave me alone."

"No," he said. "It's no use, Charlotte." He put his hand out and touched her arm, and his touch was of fire, but she made no attempt to shake him off. She doubted that she had the strength. Instead she stood very still. *Very* still. Tension throbbed in the air they breathed, and the light shimmered on the mirror, casting rainbow-colored darts of light from its surface. She took a deep shuddering breath, and Jared reached out his other hand and pulled her gently around to face him, and for a second he looked down at her. Then with infinite gentleness he bent his head to kiss her.

Charlotte didn't struggle. She no longer knew how to. Her face was upturned, and his lips were warm and tender, and this kiss was like no other she had ever known in her life, and it went on forever and ever....

Jared looked down at her again, and there was such a great agony on his face that she gasped and instinctively put up her hand to touch his cheek.

"Why, Jared, what is it?" she whispered.

He turned his face toward her hand, to rub his mouth against her palm, and in a husky voice answered, "It's no use fighting it any longer, Charlotte. I've tried to hate you, to put you out of my life—but I can't. If Aunt Marie hadn't asked me to play that song, I would have done so anyway. Because I wanted—I *needed* to know something. And I think I do."

"What do you know?" It was unbelievable. She was in his arms, but she wasn't trying to get away because she didn't want to.

"I think I know that . . . you don't hate me, either." She could barely hear the words.

"I tried to—oh, how I tried!" And now she had strength enough to move free, and did so. She could see him more clearly that way. "When you greeted me that first time at . . . at . . . the château—" her voice faltered as the memories came back "—I felt so unhappy, I—"

"Don't, Charlotte. Please don't—" He moved as there came a sound from outside.

Marie's voice was calling; "Charlotte? Uncle Zhar? Where are you?"

With a muttered oath he went to the door and opened it.

"Yes, Marie, what do you want?"

"I want Charlotte to hear me play, too—" so that was the reason for the laughter "—and I thought you'd come to fetch her."

"Yes, yes, I had." He looked around at Charlotte. In his eyes there was a plea. But for her the spell was broken. What madness had possessed her—and him? She didn't know.

"I'll come now," she answered. "I was just coming anyway." There was a lump in her throat.

"Wait, Charlotte—" he began, but she ignored it and passed him, and they went down the stairs. She heard her door close, looked around, and he was following them.

Marie could have been the best player in the world—or the worst. Charlotte didn't know, for she heard nothing, but she clapped when the others did, and it was like being in a dream suspended from all reality, sitting there pretending to listen, and Jared only a few feet away. When Marie's little recital was over Charlotte stood up and walked quietly away, melting into the shadows, unnoticed by anyone. She needed desperately to be alone, to have time to think. Was this just another episode in the difficult series of days through which she was living? But how—why—could a man be so deliberately cruel as to pretend an emotion he didn't feel? She had seen his face, seen the pain in his eyes as he told her certain words that implied . . . . Charlotte paused. She was well into the shadows now, well away from the villa, and surrounded by trees and shrubs. And no one to see. What had his words implied? That he loved her. And because of them she had foolishly opened her mouth and admitted . . . . She put her hand to her face in utter, overwhelming dismay. "Oh, no," she whispered. "Oh, *no*—"

"Why did you run away?"

She whirled around at the sound of his voice. Outlined in the very faint lights that showed from the villa, Jared stood there watching her. There was nowhere to run, because she didn't know the grounds and could see nothing save a distant glow from the house.

"I want to think," she whispered.

He walked toward her and she remained where she was, despite her instinct to flee. "Charlotte," he began, "I want to talk."

"No. There's . . . there's nothing to say—"

"There is. There's a lot—a great deal," and he put his hand out to touch her face, and said in a tone of wonder, "Why are there tears on your cheeks?"

"I don't . . . there's n-nothing to talk about," she stammered.

"Yes, there is. Beginning with why I ran away from you two years ago."

With a wordless cry of pain she turned from him, unable to bear any more, uncaring that the darkness was complete and all enveloping, only knowing that she could not hear any more of those words. And he caught her and held her, and turned her around to face him.

"Please," he said. "Please let me tell you."

She was helpless in his grip. His strength was great; although his grasp was a gentle one, she knew he would not release her.

"You're hurting me," she whispered.

"No, I'm not, I'm being very careful not to. I've hurt you enough; I won't do so anymore—ever."

"Oh, please . . . Jared, it doesn't matter . . . I don't . . . you mustn't—" She didn't know what she was saying, but she didn't want to hear anything.

"It does matter—and I must, Charlotte. I love you—can you hear that? I *love* you."

"Oh, no!" She began to laugh helplessly, tears streaming down her face as the tension finally broke.

Then he kissed her. He kissed her so effectively that the laughter was stilled and became a murmur of protest, which died away almost immediately. And then he didn't need to hold her anymore, because Charlotte reached up to put her arms around his neck as his own arms enfolded her tightly and held her as if he would never let her free.

Two black silhouettes merging into one, and the only witness a wide-awake owl perched in a tree beside them, who suddenly flew away with an ear-piercing shriek. The shadows moved, and Jared whispered in Charlotte's ear, "Don't run away."

"I couldn't if I tried," she whispered back. "You're holding me too tightly."

"Good. Then you've got to listen to me."

"I suppose so." But she wanted to—now.

"I met you in Paris two long years ago, and I've thought of you ever since—oh, I know you won't believe me, but my dear one, it is quite true. I was a wanderer then, a nomad, restless and unsettled, and searching for something—or someone, I knew not what. Then I saw you standing there all alone, a lost little girl, and I knew I'd found what I'd been looking for." He moved his hand to caress the back of her neck, and it was just right. "Listen to me well. I said a little girl—and that is what you were, and still are in many ways. Charlotte, I'm thirty-five—I'm fourteen years older than you." He paused, as if he had just said something so terrible that she would have to respond to it. She did.

"Is that all?" she said.

"All?" he groaned. "No, it's not, but it's enough. Then, I was not prepared to be enmeshed by any woman. I was free, my own man. I'm a very reluctant vine-yard owner, as you may have noticed. My plan was to wait until Marie was old enough to take over and leave her to it. Was—until a week or so ago." He stopped again and buried his face in her neck. "Oh, God, what's the matter with me? The words aren't coming out right at all."

"Yes, they are. I'm listening," she responded simply.

"No one will ever know my thoughts when I came out of the stable and saw you standing there. I didn't know what I felt myself—only that I was shaken beyond all understanding. And I hit out, because my own reaction frightened me. Everything was all tidied up in my mind. You'd been put to the back of it—although you were always there, because I couldn't help it—and I wanted you to go away."

"I know that. Oh, yes, I know that," she whispered, and began to shake.

He held her closely. "Do I frighten you, Charlotte?"

"Not...not anymore. Don't let me go."

"No, I won't. Oh, love, my love, I ache all over for you. Life has been hell for me—but it's no use fighting you anymore. When I played that tune, I knew...." He kissed her, then his face was wet with her tears, and in a husky voice he said, "Tell me something. Does Aunt Marie know? Have you told her anything?"

"Everything," she answered.

"Ah!" He gave a deep sigh, then began, most surprisingly, to laugh. "Ah, yes, *now* I see."

"I don't understand." She was puzzled, but not too much so, because there was that comfortable feeling that everything was going to be all right, and it was the most wonderful sensation in the world.

"Sorry, my love. I'll tell you. Two years ago—after that meeting—I came down here because I needed someone to talk to. Only I found I couldn't tell her anything; but that tune—*our* tune—was stuck in my head, and I found myself playing it on that same guitar constantly until it even drove Aunt Marie mad. So now we both know why she asked me to play tonight, don't we?"

"You mean—you think she *knows*?"

"I think she's known all along. She must be far cleverer than I am."

"Haven't you forgotten something?" The image of Margot's face was disturbingly before Charlotte all of a sudden. "You already have someone."

"Margot?" Even in the darkness she sensed his smile. "That has been fading fast for a while. We both knew it—"

"Then why do you and Paul dislike one another so, if you're not jealous?"

"Paul hates me—I was indifferent to him until I saw you in his arms. Then I was jealous, but it was not because of Margot, it was because of *you*, in the same way that I saw red when Yves kissed you outside the stables. I wanted to kill him there and then—and I'm not a jealous person as a rule. That was when I suspected I was fighting a losing battle—against you, my love."

He gave a deep sigh. "Oh, God, it's good to get it all out in the open at last. Do you know something? I bought you a little present yesterday. You remember the ring you tried on?"

"You didn't—you bought it?"

He laughed. "Don't sound so surprised. You're going to be showered with them from now on. That's just a start—"

"Oh, yes. My present for Aunt Marie, the pendant. You came to an arrangement with James about that, didn't you?"

He gave a gasp of mock dismay. "You're too shrewd for me. What am I going to do with you? There's only one solution that I can see. And you can guess what that is?"

She could, but she wanted to hear it. "No," she answered.

"Come into the light. I want to see your face when I ask you."

"No. I like it here." And she smiled up at him.

"I can see enough," he said softly. "Will you marry me, and live at the château?"

"Yes. The first time I went into that room, it was as if I was going home—it was the oddest feeling, Jared."

"But a true one. It will be your home for as long as you want it to be, my dearest Charlotte. You know, I had planned it that when Marie was old enough I would leave and go round the world; but somehow the idea no longer appeals—I wonder why?"

"I don't know." She reached up to stroke his face. "What about Madame Grenier? I don't think she'll be very pleased with this."

"She'll learn to live with it. We get along well enough—we respect one another, but there's not much affection between us. The main thing binding us together is Marie—we both love her. And you do, too, don't you?"

"Yes."

"It will be all right, you'll see. Aunt Heloise has a high regard for you. I know that already. And as for Aunt Marie . . . ." He paused and began to laugh softly. "Oh, I can't wait to see her face. What a birthday present we have for her, eh, Charlotte? Come now, we'll go and tell her—though I suspect she might well know already."

The guests had departed, Marie had gone to bed. Aunt Marie waited on the terrace for them, and as they walked slowly toward her, hand in hand, she lifted her arms.

"Oh, my dears," she said. "My dear children. Come into the light, I want to see your faces."

They stood before her, and she indicated a bottle of champagne by her side.

"Tell me," she said, her voice softened, "have we a reason for opening this now?"

"Oh, yes, my dear cunning aunt, we have, thanks to you, and a certain tune," and Jared bent to kiss her. "Will you be well enough to go to a wedding in a few weeks' time?"

"Will I?" Her laughter echoed around the pool, a joyous sound. "Let them try to stop me!"

A startled dragonfly skimmed the surface of the water and vanished into the night as the champagne cork popped and the three of them drank their toast. Over the glasses Charlotte and Jared looked at one another, and he raised his and said softly, "Dreams never grow old—and we have many more years of dreaming ahead of us." She didn't need to answer. The love shone in her eyes, and was matched by that in his own.